THE VIGILANTE

ROB SINCLAIR

Boldwⓞd

First published in 2022 as *Vigilante*. This edition published in Great Britain in 2024 by Boldwood Books Ltd.

Copyright © Rob Sinclair, 2022

Cover Design by Head Design Ltd.

Cover Illustration: iStock

Every effort has been made to obtain the necessary permissions with reference to copyright material, both illustrative and quoted. We apologise for any omissions in this respect and will be pleased to make the appropriate acknowledgements in any future edition.

A CIP catalogue record for this book is available from the British Library.

Paperback ISBN 978-1-83603-701-9

Large Print ISBN 978-1-83603-702-6

Hardback ISBN 978-1-83603-700-2

Ebook ISBN 978-1-83603-703-3

Kindle ISBN 978-1-83603-704-0

Audio CD ISBN 978-1-83603-695-1

MP3 CD ISBN 978-1-83603-696-8

Digital audio download ISBN 978-1-83603-699-0

Boldwood Books Ltd
23 Bowerdean Street
London SW6 3TN
www.boldwoodbooks.com

1

An oven. At least, as close to being inside a heated oven, and still being alive, as James Ryker could imagine. Over thirty degrees Celsius outside with a blistering sun in the sky and not a wisp of cloud. Who knew how many more degrees inside the thick-walled metal van whose occupants sizzled. Ryker's blood was surely on the brink of bubbling and boiling. In the dry heat, he wasn't even sweating anymore. Every minuscule droplet of water pushed through his skin simply evaporated into the baking air almost instantaneously.

The van went over a bump in the road. No, the van had gone over hundreds already – wherever they were going, the road was a pile of crap. Ryker hadn't seen the bump coming. How could he? There were no windows here in the back, the only light coming from the plastic panels in the roof. Even if he couldn't see the bump, Ryker certainly felt it, as he had with every other. Every rattle of the van's suspension sent a cascade of vibrations through his bones. That last bump though... Ryker stumbled to his left. Pulled down on his hands to help keep himself from falling.

Not that falling was really possible. Not with his wrists secured

together as they were, two chains reaching up above him, diago-
nally, one to the left, one to the right, the other ends of the chains
fixed to the roof. The other five 'passengers', in their individual box
cells, were similarly secured, and Ryker and each of them had no
choice but to remain standing for the uncomfortable journey. At
least, unless he felt like hanging from his arms like a monkey. He
didn't. But if the heat didn't let up, if there was no relief, then how
long before he simply couldn't stand any longer?

'Hey!'

A shout from across the way. More of a slur. Almost delirium.
Or was that only how Ryker's sloshy brain had processed the
sound?

'*Hui s'gory!*'

Russian. All of the guards hailed from Russia, and all of the
prisoners were either Russian or at least spoke the language. The
shouted insult finally got the attention of one of the guards. Ryker
shuffled closer to the small square of bars in the door in front of
him, which gave a pretty poor glimpse of the rest of the inside of
the prisoner transfer van. Across the way two beady-looking,
bloodshot eyes stared at him from behind the bars of the opposite
cell. Ryker knew the man. Knew of him, at least. Igor. Perhaps not
his real name, perhaps a reference to his hunched appearance.
Igor was big, tall, bald-headed. Standing straight, his eyes would
have been above the bars, yet his face was pressed up against the
hot metal slats. To have reached forward to the bars – face first –
with his hands still secured, he was surely off his feet, somehow
hovering on the chains connected to his wrists, like a gymnast on
the ring exercise. A lot of effort to get the attention of one of the
guards. Particularly given the debilitating heat.

'*Hui s'gory!*' came the shouted insult again. Even louder this
time. It literally translated as 'penis from the mountains'. Ryker
smiled.

A black-clad guard came into view. Big black boots, bulky black clothing. Black helmet, black leather gloves. Weighty utility belt that was crammed full of equipment. He was surprised the guards – four of them in the back – hadn't passed out from heat exhaustion already.

A modified AKS-74U assault rifle, the shortened barrel pointing to the floor, dangled from the guard's shoulder, but his gloved hands were empty as he moved closer, his hands held out at the ready to steady himself from the bumps in the road.

Another one. The biggest yet. Ryker jolted. The eyes of the prisoner opposite went wide as his face squashed and contorted against the bars of his door. The guard stumbled and reached out to place his hand against Igor's cell door to stop himself from falling. Still, his near-trip didn't go unnoticed. The beady-eyed Igor guffawed, then roared in amusement, soon followed by shouts and calls and heckles from the other cells.

The guard whipped his gun up, pushed the barrel against Igor's forehead.

'Step back,' he said in Russian, calmly delivered.

A moment of silence before Igor's face glided back from the bars, neat lines of red down his cheeks from where he'd pushed himself up against the metal.

'We're dying in here!' another prisoner shouted. 'My insides are cooked. Roasted meat. I'll eat myself soon enough if I don't get some water!'

A raucous rally of insults and demands and bravado followed from the other prisoners in response, though Ryker didn't say a word. Even if he felt many of the points were justified. He had no clue how much of the journey was left. How many of the men inside the superheated tin can would still be alive when they eventually made it.

The noise died down. The guard had said nothing more.

Remained facing away from Ryker, the gun now back down at his side.

'There is no water,' the guard said. He turned left and right, as though addressing a large audience in a theatre. 'Even if there was, you wouldn't have it – we would. Another word from any of you...'

He spun around. Locked eyes with Ryker. Whatever threat he'd been about to deliver never came. Instead, he simply stared. Glared, more like. The guard had a young face, but it was lined with anger and swagger. He definitely enjoyed his position of authority. Perhaps too much. But he wasn't the bad guy here, not really.

Eventually, the guard turned and walked back to where he'd come from, toward the front of the van, out of Ryker's sight.

Ryker was left staring across at the cell opposite. Igor hadn't returned his face to the bars, but Ryker still had a good enough view of him. He glared at Ryker, much like the guard had moments before. His bloodshot eyes were squinted, menacing – full of distrust and distaste, though Ryker had no idea why. They'd never set eyes on each other until today, though had shared sightless conversations with each other through the wall of their prison cells plenty of times.

Ryker's momentum shifted as the van pulled to a stop. He listened. The diesel engine chugged away, the van jostled from the vibration.

'*Hui s'gory!*' came the renewed shout from across the way. 'How about that water now!'

No noticeable response.

Igor shouted again. Again. Soon others were shouting too.

The van remained at a stop. With no windows in Ryker's view, he had no clue where they were, or what was around them, but beyond the bulky walls of the van, he heard the deep rumble of machinery nearby. A truck of some sort, pulling close to them.

Was this it?

He'd be ready, even if he remained shackled.

The noise inside ratcheted up a level or two. How many of them knew? The prisoners shouted, banged, stamped. Then Igor did the inexplicable. He rushed forward – or his head did, at least – and his face slammed into the metal bars of his cell door. Ryker winced and reeled back. Igor smashed his face into the bars a second time. Was the guy out of his chains?

Ryker winced again with the third blow. Blood streamed down Igor's face and dripped down off the bars. Igor paused as he glared at Ryker. Then a manic laugh. A crazed cackle, together with an open mouth full of broken and bloodied teeth.

Smash.

He did it again and finally two guards rushed forward.

'What are you doing!' one of them shouted.

Igor's mania didn't stop. He spat blood at the guards, then laughing, coughing, spluttering blood, he shouted out insults and hit his head against the bars, over and over. One of the guards fumbled with keys. The other brought his weapon up, pointed it at the prisoner. The door opened...

BOOM.

The thunderous explosion lifted the van from the ground.

2

The van crashed back down. Ryker and the guards and the battered prisoners all tumbled. Ryker's insides rattled and his brain whirred.

No smoke. No fire. So perhaps not an explosion at all, but an almighty impact? Something big. Something powerful.

Ryker tried to right himself, but the next moment the engine growled and revved and the van shot forward.

CRASH.

Another jolt and Ryker was sent flying the other way, his body twisting around his bound arms, nearly pulling his shoulder out.

He tried to push his weight back to his feet. The van lurched backward. High revs again. They were under attack. No doubt. Wedged in position? He imagined the driver, desperately flooring the gas pedal, the van pushing backward and forward as he attempted to maneuver out of the hold before...

Before what?

Above the prisoners shouting, the guards shouting, the clank and clanging of the van... Gunfire. *Rat-a-tat-tat.* Quick-fire rounds. Close by. Ryker looked out his cell door. Igor... His door was open.

His hands now freed and wrapped around an AKS-74U. The guard the weapon belonged to lay by his feet. Down. Dead. The other guard was reaching for his own rifle.

Igor darted forward, thwacked the butt of the gun against the guard's head before he could do anything. With another jolt of the van, both figures lost their footing and collapsed out of Ryker's sight.

The van moved forward at speed once more. Where to, Ryker had no clue. The next moment a lock released and his cell door swung open. Igor, crazed look still in his eyes, winked at him and tossed him the keys. Luckily the throw was decent and Ryker somehow gripped the keychain in his shackled hands before it could fall uselessly to the floor.

Ryker freed himself. He was about to move out but then hunkered and cowered down, almost to his knees, when a thunderous boom clattered directly above his head.

Like before, he expected smoke. Fire, even. But no. He craned his neck. Bright sunlight. His confused brain took a couple of seconds to figure out why.

Part of the van wall in Ryker's cell, and the one next to his, had gone, along with a four-foot-wide portion of the roof. Jagged metal edges protruded. Ryker glanced across what he could see of the sky. The next moment, a huge crane arm lurched into view. The jaws crashed down onto the van a second time, clamped around the thick metal structure. The jaws squeezed together with a mechanical whir.

A horrific scream from the next cell tore at Ryker's insides. The van jolted and bounced as the crane arm lifted away, pulling a mouthful of twisted metal with it. Not just metal this time. Dangling from the jaws... A man's torso. Pulsing and quivering. The crane arm moved out of sight again.

Ryker took a step toward the hole. Looked outside as the van sped along a straight, desert-like road. A gigantic articulated lorry raced alongside, the crane arm on top. Surely the van could have outrun that thing. Which likely meant that, even though they were moving, they remained boxed in. Audaciousness, or craziness, Ryker wasn't sure which best described the tactics of the attackers.

'Free the others.'

A voice from behind him. Ryker turned back to Igor. His weapon was pointed at Ryker's chest.

He hesitated for only a second then moved forward. The van swayed left and right, making each step clumsy and difficult. Two more armed guards remained in the back, but where were they? Were they even still alive?

Ryker set about opening the other cell doors. Released the first of the remaining prisoners. He moved to the second. Threw himself to the floor when the roof above him peeled away. When he looked back up, to what remained of the cell and the prisoner in it, he shuddered. Another one dead. The man's headless body slumped, suspended strangely in the air by the one remaining chain he was shackled to.

'Hurry up!' Igor shouted.

Ryker got back to his feet. No sign of the crane lorry now. Where had it gone? Then the sound of gunfire echoed. Outside. But who was shooting, and at whom, Ryker had no idea. Two cars had made up the convoy with the van on leaving the prison. Were those cars still with them now?

Ryker moved to the next cell. He unlocked then opened the door, and was in the process of uncuffing the long-haired man there when a volley of bullets whizzed past his ear. Ryker pushed himself forward. Took the now-released prisoner with him. They landed in a heap on the floor. Ryker pulled himself off. A black-clad guard raced past. Ryker jumped up and to the door.

Another guard, right there, no more than two feet from him. No time for him to twist the gun to shoot...

Ryker lunged for him. An elbow to the guard's head sent him reeling. A knee to the groin sent him down. Another hammering elbow to the top of his head ended the fight and Ryker yanked the gun free.

He ducked instinctively at the gunfire right by him. He wasn't the target. He looked across to the back of the van. Igor was crumpled in the corner, rifle in one hand, two holes in his chest. Not quite dead, but he soon would be. The guard who'd shot him stood over him, at the ready to finish him off. Ryker lifted his weapon...

Above him, the crane arm reappeared. It swung down toward him at speed. Ryker dove forward. The arm smashed into the van. No attempt by the operator to grab using the jaws this time, the arm instead acted as a hammer, a pulverizer, and smashed into and through the van's structure. The hefty vehicle was nearly cut in two.

Screeching brakes filled the air. The back end of the prison van twisted and lifted from the ground. Ryker fell back. He grasped onto the open cell door to keep himself from flying. The severed end of the van crashed down, twisted around. Sparks flew as the two broken parts of the truck slid across the tarmac, the back grinding to a halt a few yards before the front.

A strange silence. Or, not quite silence, but at least an end to the raucousness. Ryker heard hissing. Whirring. Groaning. Engines still rumbled. Ryker pulled himself to his knees, keeping low for cover. The remaining prison guard was still alive. Igor was not. The gun lay out of the guard's reach. He went for it.

'Don't,' Ryker said.

But then flinched when gunfire erupted, all around him. The guard didn't heed the warning. Ryker had no choice. He pulled the trigger. Two quick taps. The first bullet hit the guard in his foot. The second in his thigh. Enough to subdue him.

'Behind you!'

The shout came from Ryker's left. The prisoner he'd just released.

Ryker hunkered down, spun the other way as the prisoner hurtled past him and dove for the black-clad figure who'd appeared from... Ryker had no clue.

Bullets flew from the guard's gun, raking up what remained of the van wall behind Ryker. The men tussled, Ryker had no clear target.

Bang.

A single shot. The prisoner rolled off. Handgun – from the guard's belt? – in his grip. A bullet hole in the side of the guard's neck oozed blood.

Ryker clenched his teeth. The casualties on both sides... He hadn't signed up for this.

The prisoner, his clothes now dirtied and bloodied, his long curly hair ruffled and messy, rose back to his feet.

To his left, Ryker spotted two eyes, visible behind the one remaining locked – and intact – cell door.

'What about him?' Ryker asked, before glancing at the keys on the floor between the two of them.

'I'm getting out of here,' the long-haired prisoner said.

Ryker said nothing.

Intermittent gunfire rattled all around them, though within the remnants of the van, it wasn't clear who was firing at whom, or where they were.

'You coming?' the prisoner asked Ryker.

He didn't answer. Instead, he raced forward. Lifted his arm. Clattered into the prisoner and sent him flying, off the destroyed edge of the van and to the tarmac below. Ryker lifted his gun.

Another double tap. To the chest this time. The black-clad figure two yards away crumpled. The Kevlar vest would at least save his life.

Ryker pulled his new companion back to his feet. He had a confident smile on his face.

'Now we're even,' Ryker said.

The man said nothing. Ryker pulled them to the ground once more as bullets whizzed by. He took a moment to survey the scene. The other end of the van was ten yards away, on its side. The driver and guard in there, behind the shattered glass, were dead.

The crane lorry, and another big rig, were at a stop nearby. So, too, the escort vehicles. Heads and gun barrels bobbed up here and there as each side took potshots at the other from their positions of cover.

'There!' the prisoner said, looking off to the right, where two black SUVs raced toward them, further along the otherwise deserted road.

The man moved off first, Ryker headed alongside him, both of them keeping low as they scuttled past the van, then the truck. Bullets intermittently pinged against the metal right by them.

They kept on going.

Screeching tires. The vehicles rocked to a stop. Doors opened. More armed men jumped out. Covering fire as Ryker and the prisoner raced over.

'In here!' one of the gunmen shouted over.

Ryker and the prisoner went that way. The prisoner jumped into the back seats. A thickly muscled arm blocked Ryker's way. Ryker looked from the deep-set eyes of the man they belonged to and back to his supposed new friend.

A gun barrel pressed into his back. The rifle was taken from his grip. He didn't resist.

The prisoner said nothing as he stared – unfeeling – at Ryker.

'Sorry, friend.' A voice from behind. Someone grabbed Ryker's neck. Went to drag him away.

'No,' the prisoner said. Then a pause, as though still contemplating. 'He's coming with us.'

No sooner had the words passed the man's lips than Ryker was tossed into the back of the SUV. The door slammed shut. The thirsty engine revved, the SUV swung around and Ryker was pressed back into his seat as they raced away from the carnage.

Next to him, the demeanor of Ryker's friend changed in a flash. Calmness gone, he rattled off an angry tirade – not Russian, but something close to it – to the two men in front. Plenty of insults, plenty of questions asked about the near disastrous and far from subtle escape. The tirade ended without a word spoken from up front in response.

Then silence, except for the noise of the powerful car's engine and the roar of fast-moving tires on tarmac.

'You did good, James Ryker,' the prisoner – former prisoner, at least – who Ryker knew as Roman Smolov said.

As with Igor, Ryker and Smolov had shared conversations, in their respective fenced-off areas in the prison yard, but had never seen each other face-to-face before.

Ryker turned to Smolov. The guy was calm, and confident, once more.

A smile now. It appeared genuine enough. In fact, overall, his appearance – beyond the blood and the prison garb – was perfectly normal. Ryker imagined all cleaned up he'd be a suave bachelor. Forty-something, gray hair here and there, but with a fresh and vibrant look. Distinguished.

'You did good,' Smolov said again. 'But that does still leave plenty to talk about.'

Ryker raised an eyebrow.

'*You*, of course.'

Silence once more. Ryker was the one to break it. 'What do you want to know?'

Smolov's smile broadened and he reached out and patted Ryker's thigh.

Ryker caught the driver's eyes in the rearview mirror. He couldn't quite read the look he received.

'Not yet, James,' Smolov said. 'Not yet. First, there's someone else for you to meet.'

'And that would be?'

A laugh. Or something close to one, at least.

'You need only know him by one name.' Another pause, before, 'Jesper.'

3

BLODSTEIN, NORWAY

March – present

On Ryker's last visit to Blodstein, winter had held a tight grip on the northerly area. Freezing conditions, snow and ice on the roads, in the hills. March wasn't exactly balmy, but it was at least more humane. Even on a dull day, the deep green of the pine forests in the hills, rising up from the fjord, mesmerized, and provided an altogether more welcoming feel. To the place, if not the people.

That was fine. He wouldn't stay long. His interaction with the locals would remain as perfunctory as possible. He wasn't welcome here. Not by many. He wasn't even sure himself why he'd come back – after his last trip, he certainly wouldn't have expected a return so soon.

But that was before...

He looked across the cordoned-off parking lot to the burnt-out shell of the factory. He'd already been inside. Nothing left to see, nothing to do here other than to look at the destruction. So why had he come? He knew what had happened. Did he really need to be here, to see and smell the embers?

He turned and strode back to his car. Hit the road. Not for long. Within a few miles, he turned off the main road and traveled toward one of the more upmarket streets in the area. A street with a small cluster of individual executive-style homes. Neat gardens, tall walls and gates, and ample foliage and trees hid the expensive houses from the roadside.

Mostly, at least, because one of the homes stuck out for all the wrong reasons. The one with police tape that encircled the front. A longer glimpse from the road told a similar story to the factory – no red brick, fancy sash windows, or neat roof tiles here. Everything that remained – which wasn't much – was blackened and charred.

Ryker shut down the car engine and stepped out. He moved under the tape and along the drive. He'd read as much as he could in the press about what had happened here, and at the factory, and at two other spots in and around the small town. Three days ago the fire here had taken a life. Five more bodies had been discovered at the other sites. Six murders in a town of only a few thousand people. Two others remained hospitalized, including the most senior policeman in the area.

A message. A strong message, from a man Ryker had never even met: Jesper. Yet a message that Ryker had received loud and clear, whether or not he was the intended recipient.

As he moved closer to the house, the smell of soot and ash and death lingered. He walked right up to the blackened front door where several lines of blue-and-white tape crisscrossed the fragile structure. He took one look behind him, then peeled the tape apart to give himself space to slip through and inside.

* * *

Half an hour later Ryker sat inside a very different house. He hadn't stayed long at the Bergs' former home. Little remained inside. The police had already removed anything of interest. Perhaps the attackers too, before they'd burned the place out.

This house was much smaller. A kitchen and dining area and separate living room downstairs. Two bedrooms upstairs, he presumed, though he hadn't been up there. Instead, after letting himself in through the poorly secured back door, he was on a sofa, the front door in view out in the hall. Darkness had fallen beyond the walls, and a chill in the house crept further into Ryker's bloodstream with each minute that passed.

Still, he didn't have to wait long. The distant car engine grew closer. Next, the headlights came into view, their arc wide enough to create a glancing shadow across the living room wall. The car pulled to a brief stop on the road, then swung around and onto the small drive.

A car door opened and closed. Light footsteps. A key in the door.

She stepped inside. Flipped lights. Closed the door. Pettersen. A local police officer. She looked... exactly as she had the last time he'd seen her. A little more worn out, perhaps. Understandable.

She was halfway through taking her yellow police coat off when she paused. Still facing the door, she spun on her heel. Fright in her eyes. She stared at Ryker. A few moments of strange silence followed before she calmly carried on taking off her coat. She held it in her hands as she continued to stare. He couldn't read the look on her face. Anger? Hurt?

'You're back,' she said.

He slowly rose from the sofa. Neither looked away from the other. Then, a little unexpectedly, Pettersen rushed forward, threw her arms around him, and buried her head in his chest.

They both held on. Only when her arms relaxed and she

pulled her head back did Ryker release his grip. She stepped away. Anguish. That was the look in her eyes now.

'I have to say, I thought it more likely you'd Taser me or something,' Ryker said with a laugh.

A half smile on her face, gone in a flash. 'What? For breaking into my home? Yeah, I...'

She trailed off and shook her head. He had no idea what she'd tried to say.

'Do you want a drink?' she asked.

'No,' he said. 'I'm not staying long.'

'I'm surprised you're back at all.'

'You know why I'm here,' he said.

'For a moment I thought it was to see me.'

'Aren't I?'

Her initial happiness – or relief? – at seeing him was all but gone and she sighed and slumped down on the sofa. 'You know what I mean.'

He wasn't sure he did.

'This isn't how I imagined it,' she said.

'Imagined what?'

'I thought... I wanted you to come back. Until... Now, I just don't know. Did six people really have to die just so you'd return?'

Was she trying to blame him for their deaths? Or just blaming him that he wouldn't have come to see her otherwise?

'How's Wold?' Ryker asked. Inspector Wold, her boss. One of the victims of the recent troubles, although at least he was still alive.

Pettersen shot him daggers. 'You really care?'

Ryker bit his tongue. She looked away. 'He's in a specialist unit in Trondheim,' she said, looking at the floor. 'He's breathing on his own now but the doctors still don't know if he'll make it.'

'And—'

'Look, James, what is going on here?' Anger now, her face all scrunched and lined. 'Two months ago, you simply walked away from us—'

'I helped here—'

'Did you? Listen to yourself. It's not complicated. Two months ago you turned up in our town, unannounced. Over the course of a few days, we had dead bodies here, there and everywhere—'

'I think you'll find most of those weren't down to me.'

'The mysterious Jesper? A man no one here has ever even met?'

Ryker said nothing.

'No one asked for your help before. We don't need it now.'

'I came here to—'

'To what? Hope I'd give you a lead so you could run off, seeking revenge for us? More blood, more death. How, where, when does it end, James?'

'I want to help.'

She huffed and shook her head. 'We don't need your kind of help. We don't want it.'

Ryker looked away from her. Despite himself, he was offended. A little hurt too. Her insinuation that he'd indirectly caused the fires, the deaths of the locals over the last few days...

'When did you last hear from Henrik?' Ryker asked.

Henrik. Other than Pettersen, Henrik was the main reason Ryker was back here. The reason he'd become involved in this town's affairs at all. A fourteen-year-old who Ryker had come across at random as the boy had tried to escape the clutches of a local gang. A fourteen-year-old who, unbeknownst to Ryker at the time, had a blood connection to the elusive Jesper and his gangsters from Russia and beyond, who were trying to take over the town, one business at a time. The local gang had attempted to use Henrik as a power play against the foreign invaders. That hadn't worked out well for either side.

'I haven't seen Henrik for two months,' Pettersen said. 'He left Blodstein the same day you did.'

Ryker took out his phone. The news story remained open in his browser window. He stepped over to Pettersen and turned the screen to her.

'Have you seen this?'

Her eyes flitted as she scanned the story. Her face dropped as she did so.

'Unknown teenager found murdered in Crete. What is this? You think it's Henrik?'

'Yes.'

'Because?'

'The description. No ID. Money and phone on him but nothing else. Most of the money was Norwegian kroner. The local police at first thought he must have been holidaying with his family, but no one came forward.'

A big jump to thinking that boy was Henrik? Possibly, but Ryker had more information than he'd let on. Did he not trust Pettersen, really? She shook her head but said nothing.

'You didn't know about this?' Ryker asked.

'Why would I be checking up on news from all over Europe? We have enough problems here. And... And it doesn't even make any sense. Henrik is Jesper's son, isn't he? Or that's what you told me. That was the whole point. They kidnapped Henrik to get at Jesper, whoever the hell he even is.'

Those last words were particularly apt. Who *was* Jesper?

'You haven't found out anything more about him?'

She glared at him but said nothing to start with. 'Even if I had...'

She didn't finish the sentence. Ryker got the point.

'Yes, I agree it's likely Jesper sent his army over here to cause us more pain...' she said. 'But why on earth would he kill his own son in revenge too?'

'That's exactly what I want to find out.'

She shook her head again. Disgust. That initial moment of longing, of comfort, when they'd shared a genuine embrace, was long gone now.

'Do you ever stop?' she asked.

'How can I?' His emotions showed through in his voice. Bitterness. Regret. Not at her. At himself, more than anything.

He put his phone away. She stood up from the sofa. Their faces were inches apart as they stared at one another intensely. She reached out with her hand and gently brushed his cheek.

'Tell me what you know,' Ryker said, realizing immediately he'd ruined the tender moment. 'Anything. Anything about the men who came here. Anything about Jesper. I will find them.'

'I'm sorry,' she said, her hand still to his cheek as she spoke, her touch soft and warm. 'I won't do it.'

'I want to help.'

She pulled her hand away and stepped back.

'You should go,' she said. 'Leave Blodstein. We don't need you here. *I* don't need you. I don't want to see you again.'

Ryker thought about responding, but honestly, he had no clue what to say. He was shocked by her words but also hurt.

Without saying another word, he turned and moved for the door.

4

___

HERAKLION, CRETE

Two weeks previously

Bright sunshine, nothing else but blue in the sky, the gentle breeze not even strong enough to rustle a leaf. Twenty degrees Celsius. A bearable temperature at least, in early spring. Olek Reva was only glad he hadn't been sent to Crete during the heat of the summer. He'd never enjoyed the heat; his body and his skin simply weren't used to it. He'd grown up in a small village halfway between Donetsk and the Black Sea, a temperate climate, with coldish winters where the mercury rarely rose above freezing. The hot but not super-hot summers where he came from saw most of the people who could afford holidays, and any youngsters who could afford a train or bus ride, travel the short distance to the Black Sea coast. Reva had rarely done that. In the summer, as a teenager, he used to skulk around the village instead or go on long rambling walks, usually alone, in the surrounding and heavily shaded pine forests. He'd become well used to spending time on his own back then.

Twenty degrees was fine, but he'd still rather sit in the shade than be out in the sun, and his pasty skin reflected that lifetime trend. Kids had joked at school about his complexion. Called him an albino. A freak. A monster. Perhaps the last was the closest to the truth, as those kids had eventually found out.

The car pulled up to the villa's gates. The driver looked around expectantly. Just a local cab driver from the airport. Reva's visit was unannounced. He'd wanted it that way. Jesper – his boss – had agreed. Both were unhappy with recent events and Reva was determined to figure out what, or who, the problems here were, and eliminate them.

Reva paid the driver a hefty tip, then grabbed his holdall from beside him – his only luggage for the trip of unknown length – and stepped out into the sun.

He squinted and held his hand up to his face and walked to the intercom by the solid wooden gates that, together with the high wall that ran off in both directions, gave little clue as to what lay beyond. Reva hadn't been here before, but he knew his host well and felt he knew exactly what to expect on the other side of the gates.

He pressed the call button on the intercom and waited. And waited. He pressed it again, bottling his already growing irritation. Yes, he'd come unannounced, but surely someone was here. There shouldn't ever be an occasion when a property like this – given the owner – was left entirely unoccupied.

Finally, a voice. He recognized it.

'Sylvia, it's me,' Reva said, looking directly at the little camera lens in the intercom box which was exactly the right height for his middling stature. Average. That's how he described his height. Not short.

Not many people would dare to call him that.

'Olek?' Sylvia responded, sounding feeble. 'Why... What are you—'

'Just let me in, you stupid bitch.'

A click before the gates swung open and Reva stepped inside.

Nice. He had to admit that Roman Smolov's home was very nice. Very Greek-looking. The wide, white-washed villa, terracotta tiles on top, hugged the Med and fitted its surroundings perfectly.

No sign of anyone by the house, or within the manicured grounds. Reva headed on. Made it halfway across the turning circle by the front entrance when the double doors swung open and a tall, broad man appeared. Crew-cut hair, clean-shaven skin. He wore khaki shorts and a white shirt that was tight on his muscled torso. A little too tight, as if he were determined to let people see how much gym work he did, rather than showing his toughness through his actions.

'You're eating too much, Alexei,' Reva said to the man, before moving up and shaking his hand briefly.

Alexei said nothing but put a hand to his gut, looking a little put-out.

'And too much time in the sun,' Reva added, nodding to Alexei's tanned arm, to go with his brown face and neck and what Reva could see of his legs.

In fact, not only was Alexei's skin heavily bronzed but it was silken too, as though he'd only just come off a lounger, all creamed up, and thrown on his clothes. Hard day at work with the boss's wife. Interesting.

'Where is she?'

'By the pool,' Alexei said.

'Anyone else here?'

Alexei shook his head and looked a little uncomfortable as he did so.

'Make yourself busy,' Reva said. 'I need to talk to her.'

Alexei nodded. Reva moved inside and plonked his holdall on the tiled floor. He headed through open and airy and tastefully decorated spaces into a lounge, or living room, or drawing room, or whatever else someone with lots of rooms they didn't use much would call it. Basically a room with lots of comfy seats and lots of little tables and a grand fireplace. A room that had wide patio doors opening out onto the ultra-sleek pool area.

Reva carried on, back into the sun. He squinted. He spotted Sylvia lying back on a lounger, soaking up rays. She wore a bright white bikini with spaghetti straps, leaving only a tiny fraction of skin covered. She looked good. Smolov had done well for himself like most men of money and power did.

Still, Smolov obviously wasn't satisfying her enough if she was screwing the errand boy.

Reva noted that Sylvia was about as far away from any parasol or shade as she could be within the garden. A deliberate sleight. He didn't go to her. Instead, he moved to the other side of the pool, grabbed a parasol, base and all, and dragged it unceremoniously across the tiles. Scratching, screeching, the movement left ugly streaks across the previously pristine porcelain. By the time he reached Sylvia, she was sitting upright on the lounger, sunglasses off, a deep glare directed at him.

He smiled as he set the parasol base down, his manner seeming to add to her annoyance.

'Sorry, did you want to be in the sun?' Reva said, looking down at her, the left side of her body now shaded. 'You know I'm not made for it.'

'Who'd have guessed it, looking at you.'

He sat down on the edge of her lounger, and she shuffled further up, away from him. Reva looked over to the villa and spotted Alexei, just beyond a window. He slunk back, into the darkness.

'I'm disappointed,' Reva said, looking back to Sylvia, his eyes moving from her ample chest to her angry face.

'With what?' she said.

'With you. I come all this way, hours of traveling, and I arrive and you haven't even the decency to meet me at the front door. You haven't even put any clothes on. Unless your intention was for me to find you like this.'

She said nothing to that.

'Instead, I find you lying out here like your world couldn't be more happy and perfect.'

'Perhaps I just didn't want to see you.'

'I think you've made that quite clear already. But I'm here anyway.'

'For how long?'

'I don't know yet.'

'Jesper sent you.'

'Was that a question?'

'I guess not. But *why* did Jesper send you?'

'Why do you think?'

She didn't answer, so Reva decided to help her out a little.

'Who knows when we're going to see Roman again,' he said. 'Jesper's worried – and I am too – that business here might suffer. I've come to make sure that doesn't happen.'

'You don't think we can handle it ourselves?'

'We? So who is in charge here right now while your husband sits behind bars in the Gulag?'

Sylvia didn't answer that either. At least she hadn't said herself. Reva wasn't sure he'd have been able to stop laughing.

'I'll be honest with you, the idea of coming to this place doesn't make me happy. But...' He reached out and put his hand on her knee. She flinched a little, tensed. 'It's been a while, and I am looking forward to getting to see more of you.'

He smiled at her and moved his hand from her knee and to the top of her thigh. He slowly moved his fingers up her leg to her waist, enjoying the feel of her soft skin. Enjoying the tension in her muscles, on her face. She tried so hard not to move, not to squirm, even though he knew she wanted to bolt and jump away from his touch.

He laughed. 'Put some clothes on,' he said, rising from the lounger and tossing a towel onto her. 'We've got work to do.'

5

ATHENS, GREECE

Present

The sunny weather did little to brighten Ryker's mood, which remained downbeat as he arrived in the Greek capital following his nearly two-day trip from Northern Europe. Preferring rail and road to air, Ryker's journey had been both long and dull. Even in 'retirement', he would always choose routes and modes of transport that minimized the breadcrumbs of his trail, as long as expediency wasn't essential.

Retirement. His being in Greece was not what most people would associate with that word, and the conversation with Pettersen back in Blodstein continued to play on repeat in his head. Yet how could he walk away from this? How could he ever walk away?

Ryker had visited the sprawling metropolis of Athens countless times in his troubled life, and the area he found the small apartment block in was familiar, located within easy reach of the world-renowned Parthenon. Every now and then he'd spotted a glimpse of the famous temple – high up on its perch in the near distance – in the gaps between the buildings off to the south.

More than one reason had brought Ryker to Greece. During his original trip to Blodstein in the winter, when he'd rescued Henrik, three outsiders had been in the town, causing mayhem. Valeri Sychev. Andrey Klitchkov and Konstantin Mashchenko. A mix of Russian and Ukrainian heritages, the three were all cronies of a secretive kingpin whom Ryker still only knew as Jesper. The three were now dead, but Jesper was very much alive and kicking, and judging by the shock revenge attacks and murders in Blodstein over the last few days, the boss was still reeling from the earlier events in Norway.

When Ryker had left Blodstein two months ago, he'd truly hoped it was for the last time. He hadn't intended then on heading off to Russia, or wherever, to track down Jesper. He wasn't the world's police. But his intentions had changed. First, the attacks in Blodstein. Second, the murdered teenager in Crete.

Henrik – supposedly Jesper's illegitimate son – had made clear his intention to Ryker of heading off to find, and kill, his father. It looked like he'd tried. It looked like he'd failed. A fourteen-year-old boy. Murdered by his own father, or at least his father's gang. How could Ryker move on from that without taking action?

Why would Henrik have traveled to Crete? Ryker had found from his own research – with the help of a couple of old 'acquaintances' – that Konstantin Mashchenko, when he wasn't killing on behalf of Jesper, spent much of his time in Athens. A link that Ryker was determined to investigate.

He waited for a moped to pass before moving across the street to the apartment building. Five stories tall, the block was narrow, much smaller than the buildings on either side of it.

Comprised of gray, sandy stone blocks, the outside of the building was heavily weathered, and judging by the state of many of the timber windows, hadn't seen significant upkeep for several decades.

Still, on the ground floor, the main doors to the building included a modern swipe card security lock, and Ryker timed his movement across the street based on seeing a young man approach the doors from the inner atrium. That man had walked off down the street, obliviously, the door still swinging shut, when Ryker slunk inside. A quick glance over his shoulder to make sure no one was watching. All clear.

He moved up the stone staircase, the steps bordered by a wrought-iron handrail. Nicely decorative fixtures, even if the many layers of touch-up paint on the metal were peeling and blistered and cracked, and the stone had worn down and become shiny – almost polished – from years of pounding.

Ryker moved up to the third floor. No sign of anyone else. He detoured from the stairs. Just two apartments on this floor. No sounds of anyone behind the door to 3a. He moved to 3b. He tried the door – why not? – then used the torsion wrench and pins from his jacket pocket to work the two locks. Less than three minutes later he moved inside.

He closed the door softly. An odor of oldness filled his nose – the same smell that permeated the communal areas of the building, but also something else... Shampoo? Shower gel? Life.

He moved through the small space, keeping his movements slow, his feet light. He didn't expect anyone to be home, but until he'd scanned the layout, he'd remain cautious.

Definitely alone. The home was a simple one-bedroomed apartment with bathroom and open-plan living space. Plenty of belongings still there. In fact, the apartment was, overall, neat and very tidy. The supposed occupant – Konstantin Mashchenko – was dead, so had no one been to clear this place out? Not friends, family, not the police? Not Mashchenko's employer who would certainly be wary of any incriminating evidence the former assassin had left behind?

That did make Ryker curious. Unless... the apartment already had a new tenant?

Ryker moved to the kitchen once more. Clean. No dirty plates or cups or crockery anywhere. He moved to the fridge. Opened the door.

Fresh milk. Cheese. Lettuce.

New tenant.

Ryker sighed. He was two months too late. Whatever had been here, linking Mashchenko to whatever else, was long gone. But then, two months ago Ryker hadn't been on this manhunt. Then he'd only cared that Mashchenko – not just an assassin but one with a bloodthirsty, sadistic touch – was no longer alive, could no longer hurt people.

Ryker wouldn't quit so easily. He pored over every inch of the apartment. He determined that the new tenant was a man, given the clothing, the name on recent mail, and the tray full of membership and loyalty cards that he found in the kitchen. He'd not come across the name before, but he'd do some checks. Certainly, he found nothing nefarious belonging to the new tenant... until.

A glint caught his eye. In the screw hole of the overhead fan in the living area. An old fixture that looked like it hadn't been used for years. Perhaps it didn't even work. Ryker pulled a dining chair over, stood on it, and reached up. Not a screw head at all, but a tiny wireless camera where a screw should have been. Still operating? He had no clue. He pulled it out and pushed it into his pocket.

A curious find. With renewed motivation, Ryker moved back through the rest of the apartment, paying even closer attention than before. He found himself in the bedroom. Found himself staring at the legs of the double bed. Wooden legs, on a wooden floor. A series of faint swirls spread out around the feet. Scratch marks from the bed shifting position. Either the bed belonged to a rowdy lover, or...

Ryker crouched down, lifted up the end of the bed, and swung it around a couple of feet. He spotted it within a few seconds. Classic. He pushed the bed further away, then shifted forward to the loose board. Lifted it up. A small box. Ryker pulled it out and opened the lid. Greek passport, a picture of Konstantin Mashchenko on the inside, except his surname in the passport was Nikolaidis. Certainly sounded Greek enough. Some cash. Not much. A bank card. Once again with the name Konstantin Nikolaidis. Bank of Cyprus. Interesting. Ryker replaced the board and the bed. He took the box and its contents with him.

He moved back out into the hall, to the front door. He stepped out, closed the door behind him, as quietly as he could. Quietly because, across the way, he'd heard the locks release on the door of apartment 3a. He turned away as the door behind him opened – as though he was standing there waiting. Then he spun around. A young woman. Younger than him, anyway. Early thirties perhaps, with long, wavy black hair. Casually dressed. Designer handbag. Designer sunglasses propped on her brow.

She paused when she spotted Ryker.

'*Yassou,*' she said, a little taken aback. *Yassou.* An informal greeting, roughly equivalent to 'hello'. Ryker wasn't fluent in Greek but he could get by, although his brain whirred as to which path he should take here.

'*Yassou,*' he said in return.

'Can I help you?' she asked, still in Greek.

'I'm looking for my friend,' Ryker said, trying his best in his non-fluent tongue. The slight pinch to her eyes showed she'd already figured he wasn't local. 'Konstantin,' Ryker added, to avoid any confusion as to which tenant he was referring to.

'Konstantin?' she repeated. A little confused now. Did she

know him? Did she know he was dead? 'I haven't seen him for a long time. Months, perhaps. There's someone else there now. He moved in only last week.' She laughed. 'I haven't even met him... I thought perhaps that was you.'

Ryker smiled and laughed. 'No, sorry, not me.'

She looked down at the box in his hand.

'You don't know where Konstantin went?' Ryker asked, trying to divert her attention.

She shook her head. 'I didn't know him well. And he wasn't here much.' Something about the way she said it. Was she scared of Mashchenko? If not, perhaps she should have been.

'Okay, well, thank you.' Ryker moved forward, toward the stairs.

'Did you come far?' she asked.

Ryker stopped. 'How do you mean?'

'You're not Greek. I think he wasn't too, despite his name.'

His name? Clearly, she meant Nikolaidis then.

'No. Not far,' Ryker said. 'It's not a problem.' He went to move again.

'What's your name?' she asked.

Ryker stopped once more.

'I'll remember it,' she added. 'If he comes back, or if anyone else comes looking for him, I can mention your name. I'm sorry, but I don't even have a phone number for him or anything.'

Ryker smiled. 'That's kind. I'm Carl. Carl Logan.'

'I'm Eleni,' she said.

'Nice to meet you, Eleni.'

A strange silence, a standoff, ensued. Until Ryker looked away and moved down the stairs. He'd made it all of four steps before he realized she was closely following. He looked behind him every now and then. A couple of nervous and awkward nods and smiles between them. They reached the ground floor. Ryker held the main door open for her. Waited to see which way she would go. She kind of just hung there.

'Have a good day,' Ryker said.

She nodded and smiled again. 'You too.'

Finally, she moved off. Ryker went in the opposite direction, the small box with the dead assassin's belongings clutched tightly by his side.

6

Ryker had a plan, and he wasted no time. More than two hours later he finally checked into a hotel, a basic three-star affair – three being generous – that was less than a mile from Mashchenko's former apartment. Two hours of sourcing, buying. Now he had the equipment he needed.

He sat down on the scruffy-looking maroon sheets of the bed and emptied out the contents of his backpack. Cheap laptop computer, new burner phone, wires, and the other over-the-counter devices he needed – card reader included. Nothing shoddy, though he'd needed to visit five different electronics stores before he'd gathered everything.

It took him another half hour to set up the equipment, and to download the necessary software from the hotel's painfully slow broadband, and then... He was ready.

Two and a half hours since he'd left the apartment. He needed only another five minutes to crack the PIN code on the bank card. With nearly ten thousand possible combinations, a four-digit PIN was about the most straightforward of modern passwords and encryptions to break. All he'd needed was the equipment and some free-to-download software.

Ryker checked his watch. Still time today.

He moved over to the window and peered down below. Habit. Nothing to see out there.

He headed out. Took the stairs. Stepped out into the sunshine. The sun was low in the sky, off to his right, directly between the buildings on either side of the road, and created long shadows that swept toward him. He held his hand up to shield himself from the glare. Took a moment to orientate himself. Straight ahead. He moved through the city streets, walking quickly but with his natural guard in place. He used the mental map from his earlier internet search to lead him to the nearest branch of the Bank of Cyprus. He arrived half an hour before closing. A single ATM sat on the outside. Three people in the queue. Ryker waited impatiently, looking this way and that.

Finally his turn. He inserted the card and typed in the PIN. Balance check. A little over twenty thousand euros. Not bad. He took out five hundred, half wondering whether the transaction would be accepted or not. Had Mashchenko's accounts been frozen? No. The cash popped out.

Ryker reinserted the card and entered the PIN once more. Recent transactions. The most recent, at least, because none were within the last two months, none since Mashchenko had lost his head from the blast of Inspector Wold's shotgun in Blodstein.

He took a printout, had his eyes glued to it when a lady behind him cleared her throat. He apologized and moved to the side, then looked at the printout again. Ten transactions. Some were more obvious – a few euros here and there for well-known shops, most likely food and drink, Ryker presumed. But he also saw three larger transactions: two transfers in, for a little over five thousand

and seven thousand euros, and one out, for nine thousand something. Not huge amounts, and not round sum amounts, which only looked all the more suspicious to Ryker. In modern banking, which was so well protected and scrutinized by computers and algorithms, all large round sum transactions set alarm bells ringing, and often required extra security checks, and extra forms for bank staff to fill. Were these transactions designed to fly under the radar?

Ryker headed inside.

The small unit was modern and functional. Plenty of corporate paraphernalia, plenty of bland gray panels, rough gray carpet underfoot. Two teller positions, both with nothing for security but a flimsy-looking plastic screen that rose a couple of feet from the tellers' desks. Probably a register for each teller, the small amounts of cash from the tills cleared to a single on-site safe each night, with regular collections or deliveries to maintain a modest float. Perhaps as little as ten thousand euros. After all, any bigger withdrawals would likely need twenty-four hours' approval or more. Not that Ryker was casing the place out for a future heist, but it was interesting that Mashchenko's bank of choice was such a low-key affair.

There was no queue inside and Ryker headed right up to one of the two female tellers. The older, and more stern-looking of the two. Why? Because he wanted to appear less suspicious himself, draw less attention, and the easy-going one would get rattled more quickly.

'*Kalispera*,' Ryker said to the lady. *Good afternoon.* She responded in kind, though with a slight look of distrust in her eyes. At his accent, he presumed.

'I have a question about my bank account.'

A more prolonged glare this time. Had he said the words correctly?

'Please, your card.'

She gestured to the card machine. He inserted the card and entered the PIN and she spent a few moments perusing her screen.

'Yes?' she said when she returned her gaze to him.

'There are some transactions I'm not sure of,' Ryker said, putting the printout onto the desk and turning it around for her to see. 'These two, money in, and this one, money out.'

An even more inquisitive look now, perhaps because of his clunky choice of words, but he had no idea what the word for *withdrawal* was.

'You think it wasn't you?' she asked, her words delivered slowly and mechanically. The way people often talk, in their own language, when speaking to someone they know is foreign, with intonations in all sorts of weird and wonderful and unnatural places.

'No, probably me, but I just wanted to check. Do you have any more information?'

She didn't say anything but typed away on her keyboard. A moment later the printer next to her whirred into life and three pieces of paper dropped out, one after the other.

'This tells you all we have. The bank, and the account that the payments came from. Or went to.'

Ryker took the papers from her and scanned through. Both receipts, from a sender listed only as KSL, had the same account details. For the payment, the recipient was listed as R. Kirilenko.

'This one?' Ryker said, pointing to the slip for that transaction.

'It's a foreign payment,' she said, looking back to her screen and typing again. 'I don't have any more information to give, but that bank is located in Ukraine.'

'And these two?'

A sigh now. But no more typing. 'Bank of Crete,' she said. 'There isn't one here. Only on the island.'

Ryker's brain rumbled.

'Mr Nikolaidis, is there a problem with these transactions?' she asked, concern on her face now, and she looked over Ryker's shoulder, as though ready to call out for help. That was exactly what he'd hoped to avoid.

'No, no, not at all. You know? I've remembered now. It's all okay.'

He smiled at her and walked away. A quick glance over his shoulder. No. No one was coming out after him. Why would they?

He paused for a moment outside. R. Kirilenko. A name he didn't recognize, but one he'd follow up on. And a payment to Ukraine? A solid link back to Jesper, perhaps. Then he had the money coming in from Bank of Crete to the assassin. Even more interesting, given the murdered teen found there only days ago.

He stuffed the papers into his pocket and moved back in the direction of the hotel. He slowed in his steps when he spotted a silver car across the street. Nothing particularly suspicious – plenty of cars were parked on both sides of the road. Except this one – an oldish Peugeot – had a distinctive dent on its front wing. Ryker had earlier spotted the vehicle outside the hotel. The dent had caught his eye, cast strangely in the sun's rays. He'd fleetingly looked at the license plate. Hadn't intended to memorize it, but he had anyway. This was definitely the same car.

Ryker looked left and right then turned to head across the road, moving straight for the Peugeot.

Two occupants, both up front. A man in the passenger seat. A woman in the driver's seat? Ryker wasn't quite sure because of the glare of the low sun. And because, when he was five yards away, the engine rattled on, and the car swung out into the road and sped off into the distance.

Ryker reached the footpath and turned. The silver car took a left and moved out of sight, leaving Ryker with plenty of questions as to who was following him and why, but absolutely no doubt that in his short time in Greece, he was already chasing exactly the right leads.

7

Ryker saw no more signs of the Peugeot, or of anyone else following him, as he made the short trip on foot back to his hotel. As he walked he thought through the various steps of his journey from Blodstein to Athens, his actions at each stage, trying to figure out in his head when the tail had first appeared, and why.

By the time he reached the hotel, it was time to test the theories.

He headed up the stairs – a little bit more cautiously than the last time – then walked slowly along the corridor. Prepared himself as he unlocked the door and pushed it open.

Everything was fine. At least insofar as he found no one else inside the room and none of his things were missing. Had someone been inside? If they had, they'd left no trace.

Still, he did a thorough search through the room, looking in nooks and crannies, behind the air conditioner vent, screw holes of various fixtures. He even gave a once-over of each of his electronic devices. He found nothing to suggest anyone had planted any sort of listening or recording device or software anywhere.

He sat back on the bed and sighed. Paranoia. He hated this

feeling. Yes, even after having left his old life as a clandestine agent, he still lived, by second nature, always that little bit more alert than perhaps necessary. He was well used to that. But this feeling right now was something different from an everyday background hum, and he didn't miss one bit this all-consuming paranoia, where he triple-guessed his every move, where he couldn't leave or enter a room without a meticulous search to identify anything amiss.

He picked up the tiny camera he'd found in Mashchenko's apartment. He used one of the newly purchased cables to attach the device to his laptop. Minutes later he'd done all he could. As he suspected, the camera had no capability for recording on its own – it was nothing more than a wireless transmitter. If he wanted to see anything of what the camera had captured he'd have to find the device, or devices, the camera had relayed data to. Not impossible, but not easy either.

The only useful data Ryker could glean from the camera itself was the IP address it had connected to in the apartment and the IP address it had sent data to. Curiously, the two IP addresses weren't the same. Did that mean someone else had spied on Mashchenko, rather than the camera being there for his own security?

Ryker got on the phone. Anton Silviu. Not a friend, not an ex-colleague even, and not someone Ryker fully trusted. No one fit that last category. Anton Silviu, who worked as a data analyst for the Italian government, had found himself in more than one compromising position in the past, which, naturally, the likes of Ryker and his old employers had taken advantage of. Blackmail? Kind of.

Now that Ryker was officially ostracized from his government's work, and hence from official connections, the compromised Silviu remained one of a handful of assets that he could turn to for information. How long that position would last, Ryker didn't know. Perhaps his bridges with the Italian were already burned down.

Ryker would find out soon enough.

'It's me,' he said when Silviu answered the call.

'I know. Only two other people have this number. And you're the only one who would be calling me from Greece.'

Ryker gripped the phone a little more tightly, though he wasn't sure why. Something about that way the Italian always spoke, as though he had the upper hand. As though he was all-seeing, all-knowing. Well, in a way...

Ryker didn't bother with any small talk. What was the point? 'I've two IP addresses. Can you find out everything you can about them?'

'Tell me.'

Ryker read them out.

'How soon?' Silviu asked.

'As soon as you can.'

'Give me one hour.'

'One more thing.'

Silence.

'You still there?' Ryker prompted.

A sigh. 'Yes.'

Ryker could imagine the exasperated, worn-out look on Silviu's face. Except he had no one but himself to blame for the position he found himself in.

'I have a name and address I'd like you to look into.'

'Go on.'

Ryker relayed the address.

'Didn't I tell you about this place already?'

'That was apartment 3b,' Ryker said. 'This is 3a.'

Another sigh. 'And the name?'

'Eleni.'

Silence.

'Silviu?'

'That's it?' Silviu asked. 'Just Eleni?'

'For now. That's it.'

One last sigh, then, 'I'll be in touch.'

The call ended.

* * *

It had gone 7 p.m. as Ryker idled along the streets of Athens. Darkness had arrived, street lights were on, cafés and bars and restaurants were bustling. The sound of traffic horns drifted through the night air. The artistically lit Acropolis drew the eye whenever a glimpse was given. The city felt so different at night. So vibrant. So much more dangerous too.

Ryker walked slowly, deliberately. Still no sign of the Peugeot. He remained convinced as to his deduction, so where were they? In another car? He didn't think so. On foot behind him? Certainly, he hadn't spotted anyone, but he was roaming foreign territory in the dark. However familiar the city was to him, it wouldn't be too hard for accomplished trackers to remain unseen.

He got lucky when he arrived at the apartment block. A woman carrying three bags of shopping stood wrestling with the doors and Ryker darted up to hold them open for her. She thanked him profusely then waddled up the stairs. Ryker waited a few beats before heading up too.

At nighttime, the block was louder than earlier in the day. TVs and music played behind closed doors. He heard shouting, laughing.

Much more quiet on the third floor though.

He first moved to 3b. No sounds or other indication that the new tenant had arrived home.

So he went to 3a, knocked, and waited.

Eleni opened the door. She looked a little bewildered when she caught Ryker's eye, her natural confidence faltering ever so slightly. She wore the same casual clothes as earlier. No designer bag or glasses this time.

'Carl,' she said, almost a question.

'Eleni.'

'Is everything okay?' she asked in Greek.

'I was...' Ryker smiled and sighed. 'Do you speak English?'

A pause, before, 'Probably better than your Greek.'

Ryker smiled. 'This might sound crazy but... it's my first night in Athens. I really don't know anyone and... perhaps...'

'You're asking me to go out with you?' she said, her suspicion clear.

Ryker shrugged.

'A complete stranger?'

'So far.'

'How do you know I don't have a partner?' she asked.

'I don't. And I never said it was that kind of a date.'

'I might have plans.'

'Do you?'

She didn't answer that.

'Look, I'm easy,' Ryker said with another shrug. 'It would be nice to have some company. And you can choose where we go.'

She held his eye for a moment. 'We could go out for a short time.'

'Whatever you like.'

'Give me five minutes.'

With that, the door closed. Ryker stepped back. Waited. Eight and a half minutes later the door opened again. She looked exactly the same, except the handbag had returned. So what had she needed the eight and a half minutes for?

'There's a bar not far from here,' she said as she closed the door again. 'Quiet enough to talk, busy enough for me to feel safe.'

Ryker looked at her, eyebrow raised.

She smiled. 'What? How do I know you're not planning to murder me?'

Ryker shook his head and smiled. 'How do I know you're not planning to murder *me*?' he said.

She didn't answer that before she brushed past him, holding his eye as she moved.

8

The bar was exactly how she'd described it. Modern, but not overly swish, with ambient lighting, plenty of tables and booths, low-level music playing. A hubbub from the fifty or so customers, who ranged in age from twenties to fifties, but all in all it felt relaxed and comfortable. Certainly safe.

Ryker bought the first round – a beer for him, a white wine for her.

'So what brought you to Athens?' she asked as he took a seat. She'd chosen a booth and had seated herself so she had full view of the room beyond. Ryker scooted around on the circular bench, closer to her, but his back remained facing a good portion of the room. Not his favored position.

'I'm tracking down some old acquaintances.'

'Acq...'

'Friends. Looking for some old friends.'

'My old neighbor?'

'He's one of them.'

'How do you know him?'

'Honestly? I don't know him well. Friend of a friend, if you know what I mean?'

She didn't answer, but her eyes narrowed a little as she stared at him. Suspicion? Under the circumstances, his vague answers, it would be strange if she weren't at least a little wary.

'What about you?' Ryker asked.

'What about me?'

'What do you do? For a job?'

'I'm a journalist.'

'Newspaper?'

'Freelance.'

'What do you write about?'

She looked down at her drink and smiled coyly. 'Whatever I can to pay bills. It's not that easy these days. What about you? What do you do?'

'Consultant. But I'm on a career break.'

Ryker took a large swig of his beer. Eleni nursed her wine, glanced over Ryker's shoulder a couple of times. After a few moments of awkward silence, she caught his eye.

'Sorry, I just need the restroom.'

With that, she stood up and walked off. Ryker half-turned to watch her as she moved across the bar to the stairs at the far side. When she was out of sight he turned back to the table. Her phone, which had been in her hand, was now gone. But her bag remained on the bench, reaching distance from Ryker.

Should he?

He decided no.

Eleni came back a few minutes later, a more relaxed nature than when she'd left. And more relaxed conversation followed. One, two, three drinks went down, each of them over the next hour or so.

'You want another one?' Ryker said.

She looked unsure. With three beers on an empty stomach, he certainly felt light-headed. But still fully in control.

'Just a small one,' she said.

Ryker got the drinks from the bar. She greeted him back at the table with a broad smile that showed off the dimples on either side of her mouth and pinched her eyes at the sides, seemingly making them sparkle all the more. With each drink, she'd become more relaxed, more confident. More sassy.

'I get the sense you move around the world a lot?' Eleni said. Likely in reference to the conversations they'd had about traveling.

'I have done in the past.'

'Where exactly is home these days?'

'You know, I don't think there is one place anymore.'

'Then where makes you most happy?'

'Anywhere I can find good company.'

He smiled at her. She didn't fully return the look.

'You were born in Athens,' he said.

'Yes, but I've lived in lots of other places too. London. St Petersburg. Budapest. And I traveled all through Central Asia when I was younger.'

'A well-traveled journalist.'

'And a well-traveled consultant.'

'Do you still have family here, in Athens?' Ryker asked.

She looked awkward. 'No, not now.' Then smiled and looked up, as if in thought. 'I know it's not your home, really, but the first time I saw London... Wow. I was twenty-two years old. I'd been to foreign countries but I'd always had this magical image of London. The red buses. Taxis. Big Ben. The palaces. Perhaps I was naive but I really thought everyone would be so... like in the movies. You know? And the Queen... I really wanted to meet the Queen.'

Ryker laughed. 'London does have its many plus points. But

when you live in a place for some time, I think you get to see different sides to it.'

She nodded. 'Yes, that's very true.'

'For instance, before I ever came to Athens, I had a vague idea of what to expect. Big city, lots of people. Money in places, poverty in others. Of course, I knew about the ancient sites, the history of the place. But...'

He looked away, deep in thought.

'You saw a different side to Athens?'

'You could say that. On my first night here I was with a colleague. We were sent here to speak to a man. A very important man, who was very difficult to get in front of.'

'That sounds strange.'

'It was. We found him after only a few hours, but it didn't really go very well.'

'In what way?'

'Well, basically, we were ambushed. My colleague was shot in the face. He was standing right next to me when it happened. As his body was still falling to the ground I had a sack thrown over my head and men tackled me to the ground. They transported me off to this derelict dump of a place. Tied me to a chair. Threatened to cut off my fingers and toes if I didn't reveal why I was there, who I worked for.'

The color had drained from her face. Ryker took a long drag from his beer.

'To cut a long story short, I kept my fingers and toes. I got out of there, but not without a few scratches. This is one of them.' He pulled up the sleeve on his right arm and pointed to the four-inch-long lump of raised flesh below his elbow. 'That, along with a couple of superficial bullet wounds. I could show you the scars for those, but I'd have to take my clothes off.'

He laughed. Eleni remained motionless.

'Do you know the worst of it?'

She didn't answer.

'I didn't even get to properly speak to the man we were sent here to see. Not before I stabbed him in the heart. I was on a boat out of Greece the same day I arrived.'

He finished his beer. Eleni took tentative sips of her wine. 'That wasn't really where I thought the conversation was going,' she eventually said.

'No,' Ryker said. 'But I thought it better to speed up the process a bit.'

'The process?'

'Being honest with each other.'

She glanced over his shoulder again.

Ryker turned that way, then back to her.

'You can just ask your friends to join us if you like.'

'My friends?'

'The man and the woman behind me, by the bar. The guy with the boring cream shirt, who's drinking Diet Coke and is so tense he looks like he's carrying twenty bags of cocaine in his rectum. The woman, calmer, drinking a soda water, I think, who... doesn't look dissimilar to you, in a way. About the same age, hair tied back rather than loose. Casual clothes. But she's got a much sterner look than you. More formal. And together they look like the most boring couple imaginable. They've barely spoken a word to each other the last two hours.'

Eleni didn't say anything. But she did look behind her. To the wall, where a blackened shiny screen gave a glimpse of the bar beyond Ryker, which was how he'd been able to pay attention to the couple without being obvious.

Eleni rolled her eyes when she looked back at Ryker. She picked up her glass and downed her wine in two big gulps.

'Shall we go?' she said.

'Another bar?' Ryker asked.

'No. Home.'

'Fine by me.'

He finished his beer. Eleni was already moving for the door. The two stooges remained seated, doing everything they could not to look at Ryker as he passed. His best guess? Some local police or intelligence unit. Eleni? Ryker remained unsure who she really was.

They walked back toward her apartment. Side by side. Slow steps. Eleni shivered and hunched her shoulders.

'It's cold out now,' she said.

Was it?

'So do you know them or not?' Ryker asked.

She leaned her head toward him, resting it on his shoulder, and looped her arm around his.

'I preferred it when we were lying to each other,' she said.

Ryker laughed. 'Really? You weren't that good at it.'

She looked up at him, offense in her eyes. 'Actually, most of what I said about my past was true, in a way.'

'It was? But you just said you preferred it when we were lying?'

She tutted. 'You know what I mean.'

Ryker glanced over his shoulder. No sign of the watchers now. What the hell was going on?

They shared little more chat before they arrived at her apartment building. Her apartment? Likely not, after all.

They stopped by the entrance. 'You want another drink?' she asked.

'Do you have a hit squad waiting for me up there?'

She laughed. Then shrugged. 'Would you like to find out?'

She opened the door and stepped inside the building. Ryker took one look behind him then followed her in. Up the stairs. To her apartment door. They passed no one on the way. Still no indication of anyone home at 3b. Eleni walked into her apartment and turned on the lights. Ryker followed her and closed the door behind him.

'What would you like?' she asked as she moved through to the living area.

'Something strong,' Ryker answered.

'Good choice,' she said with a cheeky smile.

Ryker followed her through. Her apartment mirrored Mashchenko's. Similar furniture too. Not much by way of personal items, photos and the like.

'How long have you lived here?' Ryker asked.

She rummaged in a cupboard in the kitchen, took out two tumblers and filled them both with a good inch or so of clear liquid before she turned back to Ryker. She handed one of the glasses to him.

'Who said I really live here?'

She downed her drink and grimaced.

Ryker decided to do the same. She hadn't spiked it; he'd watched her closely. Vodka. Warm. It burned his throat but in a good way.

'Another?'

'Maybe to sip,' Ryker said.

She sloshed more vodka into the glasses then moved toward the brown leather sofas, took off her heels as she went.

'Who do you work for?' Ryker asked.

She remained facing away from him. Stood close to the window, the curtains open, looking to the nightscape beyond.

'Eleni? Is that even your name?'

She turned to him. 'You don't know?'

He held her eye.

'I'm assuming you already checked my name,' she said.

'I haven't had long. I only found that there really is an Eleni Tzolis registered as the tenant here.'

'You think I might not be Eleni Tzolis?'

'Are you?'

'I checked you as well, you realize.'

Ryker took a sip of his drink. 'And?' he said.

'And you're not Carl Logan.'

'I'm not?'

'You look pretty alive to me. Carl Logan isn't.'

'There's only one?'

'So what is your real name?' she asked.

'Depends what you mean by real.'

She rolled her eyes. Downed her drink. Put her glass down on the side.

Ryker moved closer to her.

'You didn't answer my question,' he said. 'Who do you work for?'

'All work, no play with you, isn't it?'

He reached the window and looked down below. Where were the other two now? Perhaps she didn't know them after all. But someone was still watching Ryker.

'So what happens if I grab you?' Ryker said. 'Your friends barge in here?'

He caught her eye. Strangely, it seemed her confidence was growing.

'Find out if you like.'

Ryker finished his drink. Put his glass down next to hers. Then spun in a flash, grabbed her wrist. He twisted her around, pulled her wrist up into the small of her back. Pushed her up against the wall. Pressed himself against her.

Neither of them said a word. Eleni panted. Then smiled.

'Looks like you're on your own,' Ryker said.

'Happy now?'

Ryker released her and stepped back. She turned to face him.

'You want to know about me?'

The way she said it didn't feel like a question. More like an intro to something.

'Well, I want to know about you too.'

'What about me?' Ryker asked.

She looked at his arm. 'That scar. You said there were others. From that night in Athens. Scars that you couldn't show me with your clothes on.'

Ryker said nothing. She reached down and grabbed the bottom of her jumper, pulled the garment up over her head smoothly, and dropped it to the floor. She tossed her hair as she held his eye, pulled her hands behind her back to reveal everything the bra wasn't covering.

'You're very serious,' she said. 'Don't you know how to play?'

She reached up and unclasped her bra. Held it out, on the end of her finger, before dropping that to the floor too.

'I know how to play,' Ryker said.

'Then what are you waiting for?'

She turned and sashayed toward the bedroom. Ryker headed right after her.

* * *

'I'm really not like you,' Eleni said as they lay naked in the bed, Ryker on his back, just like he had been for a good while.

Eleni, on her side, had her warm body draped around him like a quilt. Her fingers danced across the scars on his chest.

'You're not?' he said.

'I'm not a fighter. Not a killer.'

'You think I am?'

'Look at you.'

He sighed. 'Then what are you?'

'An information gatherer, I would say.'

'And what information have you gathered tonight?'

'More than you might imagine.'

'And what information have you gathered on your old neighbor, Konstantin Mashchenko?'

'Now there's an interesting question.'

'That's why I asked it.'

She laughed. 'Sorry, Carl. But I said I'm an information gatherer, not sharer.'

'You seem pretty good at sharing to me.'

She hit his chest playfully. 'Only when I want to.'

'There are ways to get people to talk.'

She sat up in the bed. Looked at him almost excitedly. 'What would you do to me?'

He found her supreme confidence almost unnerving.

'Did you know Mashchenko is dead?' Ryker asked.

She shrugged and lay back down on him but said nothing.

'I'm not here looking for him,' Ryker said, 'but I am here to find whoever he worked for.'

'Good luck with that.'

'How do you mean?'

'I mean, good luck. That's all.'

'Can you help me?'

'No.'

'You don't know who he worked for?'

'I didn't say that.'

'Then will you talk to me about what you know?'

'No.'

'Because?'

'For one, because I don't know who you are. Not really. But I'm very sure you shouldn't be here. And secondly, if I told you anything at all, my employers would be very disappointed with me.'

'You care that much what they think?'

'Shouldn't I?'

This was going nowhere. Ryker shifted and gently pushed her off. She looked a little offended. He got up from the bed and fished for his clothes on the floor.

'I upset you?' she asked.

'No.'

'You have somewhere better to be?'

He didn't answer that. He finished dressing. She remained in the bed, no covers, her naked body on full display as if inviting him, showing what he was missing.

'I had fun,' she said.

'Think about what I said. I need information. If you have it, it would be easier to just tell me.'

She laughed but didn't say anything else.

Ryker turned for the door.

'Carl?' He looked back at her. 'What was his name?'

'Who?'

'The man you stabbed in the heart when you first came to Athens. What was his name?'

Ryker thought for a moment before he answered. 'I don't remember,' he lied, before turning and walking out.

9

HERAKLION, CRETE

Twelve days previously

Reva moved out of the villa and onto the patio, glass of Coke in his hand, the ice clinking with each step. He wore only swim shorts. The pool, at this time in the morning, was mostly in shade because of the copse of palm trees off to the east side, which made it by far the nicest time to swim. Needless to say, Sylvia wasn't yet outside sunning herself. She wouldn't be until sunshine bathed the pool area, and she wouldn't at all if she saw Reva.

He set his drink down and stood by the side of the pool and watched the rippling water for a few moments. Then he pulled the goggles over his eyes and dove in. Not a bad dive either. His body glided into the water, he went down, hands out in front like the tip of a spear until they touched the blue-and-white tiles at the bottom. He pushed to gently propel his body back to the surface. He completed ten laps at pace, front crawl, until he stopped to let his heart rate calm down. As he pulled the goggles from his eyes he realized he wasn't alone. He pushed his hands on the side of the pool and effortlessly climbed out. He stretched, water slipping and dripping off his body to the tiles below.

'Hi,' he said to the young girl standing in front of him, blue-and-white school uniform on, a satchel clutched in her hands.

'Hi,' she said. She stared at him curiously. Why? Was she scared?

'You're Clara,' he said.

She nodded. An odd name, Reva thought. Not very traditional. But then Sylvia had always looked down on her Ukrainian heritage. At least in Reva's eyes.

'I'm Olek,' he said.

'I know. Mom told me about you.'

'She did? She told you how we met?'

The girl looked confused. 'No, she told me you work with my dad. And she told me to stay away from you.'

Well, of course, she had. 'Yet here you are talking to me.'

No reaction on the girl's passive face. Had she come out deliberately to speak to him, or had she not realized he was outside, in the pool? She certainly looked like the proverbial rabbit in the headlights, though she must have had at least some of her dad's fire in her.

He hadn't yet come face-to-face with the youngster since he'd arrived. Partly because Sylvia clearly wanted to keep her daughter away from Reva, partly because Reva really had no interest in the thirteen-year-old.

Not yet.

'But I'm more than just your dad's work colleague,' Reva said. 'We go way back. I've known your mom a very long time too. You should ask her about that sometime.'

She seemed unsure.

'Does that hurt?' Clara asked, indicating the ugly scar on his belly – a gouge running crossways, over a foot long. A more than twenty-year-old reminder of how lucky he was to be alive.

'Not anymore,' he said.

'What happened?' she asked.

'You really want to know?'

She didn't answer but remained standing there, staring.

'Somebody tried to pull my guts out. Literally.'

Clara gulped, her eyes fixed firmly on the scar still.

'They managed, more or less,' Reva said. 'But I got a very good doctor to put them back inside again.'

He laughed. Clara said nothing.

'I'm fine now,' he said, 'but I didn't eat much sausage for a long time afterward.'

He laughed again, more heartily. Clara looked at him, looked like she didn't know what to say or do next.

'Clara, what are you doing?' Sylvia said, hotfooting it out of the house. 'You're going to be late.'

Clara whipped around to her mother. 'Sorry, I—'

'Just get out to the car, they're ready to go.'

Clara scuttled off without another word or another look to Reva.

'She's off limits,' Sylvia said to him, genuine worry in her tone.

'You really think so low of me?' he said, offended, if he were being honest, but acting as though amused by her comment.

'You have no idea,' she said with disdain before going to turn away from him.

'We need to talk,' Reva said, grabbing her wrist.

'About what?'

'About Roman.'

'Later, I have to take Clara. Then I have errands.'

She pulled out of his grip and moved for the house.

'I'll be waiting for you.'

And that was exactly what he did. He opened out a parasol and lay down, drying out as he waited. And waited.

Three hours later she finally resurfaced. No bikini today. Shame. Though the micro denim shorts and crop top revealed plenty enough.

'Can you not put some clothes on?' she said to him, looking at his bare torso, his toned but pasty and scarred physique, as though repulsed.

'Why?' he said.

'So I don't have to look at you like that.'

'My body offends you?'

'Everything about you offends me.'

He sat up in the lounger. 'Sit down.'

He patted the space next to him, but she turned and moved to the next lounger a couple of yards away. In the sun.

'I don't have long,' she said.

'For me you never do.'

'Can we cut the snipes now? I'm getting bored of it.'

'Fine by me.'

'What do we need to talk about? I thought Alexei was your new best friend. Isn't he telling you everything you need to know?'

Reva laughed. 'Yes, Alexei is very helpful, isn't he? Tell me, how long have you been sucking his—'

'You piece of shit. Don't you dare—'

'What? I'm the one in the wrong?'

She glared daggers at him.

'I'm right though, aren't I?'

She said nothing.

'At least you're not so dumb that you'd deny it to my face,' he said.

'It's nothing to do with you.'

'Isn't it?'

She got up from the lounger, as though ready to storm off. Reva shot up, too, to block her path. Stalemate. They both stood their ground, barely a foot of space between them.

'Roman is one of my best friends,' he said, feeling and sounding calm and in control, compared to her obvious hot-headedness.

'You don't know what that word means.'

Reva shrugged. 'I wouldn't want to hurt him unnecessarily.'

They stared at one another. Pure hatred in her eyes, but also fear.

'So... I'm sure I can keep my mouth shut,' Reva said. 'If you persuade me to do so.'

He reached out and put his hand on her waist and squeezed the little bit of flesh she had there. She grimaced at his touch but didn't move away. He pulled her closer to him and pushed his face toward her neck. Took a deep inhale of her scent. She smelled damn good.

'You'd really rape me?' she said, sounding strangely calm.

'You didn't have to use that word,' he said, pulling back a little, though his hand remained on her skin.

'But that's what it would be. Because I'd never touch you otherwise. I'd never have you touch me.'

Reva laughed. 'But you already have. Don't you remember?'

'No,' she said, twisting out of his grip. 'And isn't that the problem? I don't remember what you did to me. I only remember waking up next to you, no clothes on my body, your semen between my legs.'

'You're sure it was mine?' he said with a callous laugh. 'There were lots of men in the house that night.'

Now she looked angry. Fuming.

Without warning she reached forward and grabbed his scrotum. Hard. He winced, but only because he hadn't expected the move. He didn't mind the pain. It was worth it to see her face.

'Is this what you want?' she said through gritted teeth before squeezing even harder. 'Is this what you want from me? For your silence?'

He ground his teeth as the pain level ramped up. Too much. He swiped the back of his hand across her face. She let go and reeled back in shock and clutched at her reddening cheek. She looked up. But not at him. At the house. As though someone inside would save her. They wouldn't. No one would dare.

'I could have you anytime I want to,' Reva said, angry now. 'But you know what? I don't want you. I don't need a filthy whore. Another man's cast-off.'

'You're disgusting.'

She straightened up and went to walk past him but he grabbed her hair and pulled her along and threw her down onto the lounger. She cowered there, didn't fight back. Was Reva glad about that? He took a few moments to regain his composure. He hated her, as much as he lusted over her, but there was only so far he could take those two feelings. She was still Roman's wife.

'Tell me what happened,' he said.

She glared at him but said nothing.

'Tell me what happened to Roman.'

'I've already said everything I know.'

'Not to me you haven't. Not to my face.'

She looked away. At the house. Reva glanced that way. Just Vlad, another of Roman's crew, mooching beyond the open patio doors. He looked over. Looked like he knew he shouldn't be there.

'Leave us!' Reva snarled.

Vlad nodded and turned and scuttled off. At least it hadn't been Alexei there. Young Romeo wouldn't have known what to do if he'd seen Reva manhandle his plaything.

'Tell me what happened,' Reva said. 'I won't ask this nicely again.'

She took a deep breath. 'We were at a restaurant in the city.'

'Which one?'

'Rafael's. An Italian. We've been before. It's in a square near the marina. Quiet. Expensive.'

'Who was there?'

'A lot of us. Eight at the table, plus three drivers. We were entertaining the Egyptians.'

The drug runners from Africa. Reva hadn't yet met with them. Soon.

'Do you think they set it up?'

'I don't know,' she said. Very promptly. Very assuredly.

Did he believe her?

'We left the restaurant after 10 p.m., it was dark out. We walked to the car but before we got there two vans sped up to us. All these men got out, shouting.'

'How many?'

'I don't know. Six, seven.'

'Shouting what?'

'Police. Get down. Things like that.'

'You think they were police?'

'At the time? Yes. They had uniforms. All black. Helmets. Guns. Big belts. But only afterward I realized they didn't have police insignia anywhere.'

Reva thought about that for a moment.

'They spoke Greek?'

'Greek and English.'

'Nobody challenged them?'

'To start with a little, but they had guns. We'd been for dinner. I was wearing a skimpy little dress, we didn't have any weapons, we weren't expecting a fight. What was I, what were *we* supposed to do?'

'The excuses just roll with you, don't they?'

She glared daggers again. 'It wasn't just me there.'

'Then who? At that very moment.'

'Me, Roman, Alexei and Iya.'

Iya, the sole female among Smolov's main gang in Crete. Short in stature, not exactly a powerhouse build, but a tough-as-nails attitude and a combative opponent to almost anyone. Pretty too, but Reva was sure she had balls in those trousers. He'd be interested to take a look.

'Only the four of you?' he asked.

'Iya was our driver.'

'And Alexei decided to cozy along with his boss and his lover?'

She shook her head, that same disgusted look on her face as usual.

'The others had already gone. The Egyptians were parked somewhere else.'

'And what next? Alexei, Iya, Roman? They did nothing?'

'Iya tried. Alexei too. Both of them were hit. Threatened. They shoved us all to the ground. Made us lie flat. Faces down. I had a gun barrel pressed to my back. It all... happened so quickly. I was still trying to figure out what was going on. Maybe the others were too. Maybe that's why they didn't fight more. It all took only a few seconds, then I heard the engines revving again. The pressure went from my back. When I looked up they were all gone. Roman too.'

Reva chewed on her version for a few moments. He had to admit, it was remarkably consistent with what Alexei and Iya had already told him. Still, he really didn't like how it had all gone down.

'Who else knew where you were that night?'

'How should I know?'

'It's a simple question.'

'Everyone who comes and goes here probably knew. It wasn't a secret meeting. It was pasta and wine.'

'And you never heard anything after that? From anyone? The local police?'

'Nothing. I expected a call. The police. Or a ransom. Something. But I've heard nothing at all. Alexei called you straight away that night. The next day we were all on and off the phone to you and Jesper and whoever else for hours and hours. But I've had no contact with Roman or the people who took him since that night.'

Reva sucked in air through his nose then slowly exhaled.

'Do you know where he is?' Sylvia asked.

Should he tell her?

'Yes,' Reva said.

'And?'

'He's not in Crete anymore.'

'So?'

'You don't need to know anything more than that...'

'You don't trust me.'

'Hardly at all.'

She shook her head but didn't say anything to that.

'Is he safe?' she asked.

'He's alive.'

'Will I see him again?'

Her eyes welled. Reva didn't trust that the reaction was genuine.

'Do you want to?' he said.

'Of course.'

'Because to me it looks like you have it pretty good here now. Less... complications, with Roman gone. For you. And others.'

'Are you seriously saying—'

'That someone set Roman up? Yes. To be in the right place at

the right time like that, to know they had the drop on Roman, they
had to know his plans. Most likely they had to have the buy-in of
the local police too, to not just get to him, but to get him off the
island so easily.'

'You might hate me,' Sylvia said. 'You might think I'd do something like that, but it wasn't me. I love Roman. Even if I didn't... I
wouldn't do that.'

'We'll get him back,' Reva said, looking away from her. 'But if I
find out you, or anyone else here, had anything to do with it...'

He left the threat hanging. Felt anger bubbling when he saw
the determined look on her face. No fear now.

'Olek?'

Reva turned to see Alexei, standing there by the doors. He
looked at Sylvia. Like a lost puppy dog. His eyes all sorrowful,
hurting for his woman.

'Everything okay?' he said to Sylvia.

'Why wouldn't it be?' Reva said.

'Come on, it's time we got moving,' Alexei said to him.

One last look at his woman before he turned for the house.
Reva glanced at Sylvia.

'Enjoy the sunshine, while you still can,' he said with a wink,
before following Alexei into the house.

10

PRESENT

Ryker walked away from Eleni's apartment with strangely conflicting thoughts rumbling in his mind. Unexpected. That was the word that most closely described what had happened in her apartment. No doubt he'd enjoyed his time with her. He found her curious, sultry, playful, just a little bit sinister. Was that last one a good thing?

But frustration also bubbled away, because he wanted to know more, about her, who she worked for, what she knew of Mashchenko et al. The question was, how could he find out?

Ryker was also angry. Not at Eleni. At Anton Silviu.

He would call him. He would have it out with the Italian. But not yet. Not on the dark and unfamiliar streets of Athens while he knew people were watching. He had to keep his wits about him.

Where were those two from the bar now?

Ryker walked quickly back to the hotel, his skin clammy from exertion by the time he arrived. The reception area was quiet, just a solitary worker looking bored behind the desk. The shabby-looking bar remained open but there was only one customer drinking and one barman who looked as bored as his colleague.

Ryker moved for the stairs. Went up two at a time. Strode along the corridor. Opened his door and stopped dead.

'Bastards.'

He slammed the door shut. Hands at the ready, he moved forward. No. Whoever had been inside was already gone.

So, too, were all of Ryker's things. Well, not his spare clothes, but the laptop and other devices were all missing, the bed was a mess, drawers were turned out. He moved to the cupboard, opened the door, and looked at the safe. Still locked. He input the six-digit code and the door popped open. Ryker sighed. Empty. Passports, cash, the contents from Mashchenko's box, all gone.

He looked back at the room and sighed again. Silviu or...

Silviu could wait.

Ryker stormed out into the corridor, down the stairs, up to the reception desk. The young guy there – late twenties, early thirties, tops – bolted upright, looking from his phone.

'Can I—'

'Yes, you can damn well help me,' Ryker said in English. 'Someone's broken into my room.'

A second of doubt in the man's eyes – perhaps as he processed the English – but then his face dropped.

'A break-in?'

'My things were stolen. Computer. Tablet.'

'Are you... are you sure?' he stammered. His name badge read Nikos.

'Yes, Nikos, I'm sure.'

'You haven't lost your room key?'

'This one?' Ryker said, wafting it in the air.

'And you didn't give it to anyone else?'

Ryker didn't answer that, just glared.

'I'll... I'll call the police.'

Nikos went to pick up the desk phone. Ryker threw his hand out across the top, pushed the phone back down.

'Not yet you won't.'

'Sir?'

'You're going to show me CCTV. I want to see who did this.'

Nikos looked left and right, as though searching for someone to help him. He glanced over Ryker's shoulder, probably to the barman who was now entirely on his own, his last customer gone for the night.

Ryker took his hand from the phone and fished in his pocket.

'You're the only one on reception tonight?' Ryker asked.

'Since nine,' Nikos said with a nod.

'So this happened under your watch.'

'But—'

'You like this job?'

'I need this job.'

Ryker placed two hundred euros on the counter. Nikos stared at it like the devil was standing in front of him, asking him to sell his soul. Wariness, but Ryker saw the temptation in his eyes.

'Show me the CCTV,' Ryker said. 'If you do, I won't take this any further. No police. Your manager won't find out your mistake. You keep your job.'

Nikos swept the money away. The surprisingly deft move made Ryker wonder whether this was the first time the young man had taken a bribe.

'This way,' he said with a sigh.

Ryker followed him around and through the door at the back of the reception. An office. Nikos kept going, through to another room. A smaller office. Storage, mostly. But also a basic setup for CCTV monitoring.

'I don't know exactly how it all works,' Nikos said, staring at the equipment.

'It's fine,' Ryker said. 'I do.'

Nikos unlocked the screen with an admin password then Ryker set to work. Nikos hovered but said nothing. It didn't take long for Ryker to find the feeds he needed. Two were cameras located within the third-floor corridor. The first one looked across to the elevator doors and the entrance to the stairwell. Ryker started at 7 p.m. and flicked forward. Not many people about at all, and none that caught Ryker's eye. Until a little before 9:30 p.m. when the elevator doors opened and two figures stepped out. Hard to tell much about them because they both wore baseball caps, kept their heads low, and were casually dressed. But one was taller than the other and Ryker was sure they were a man and a woman.

'You think that's them?' Nikos asked.

Ryker didn't answer. He switched focus to the other third-floor feed which gave a view along the corridor. He flicked straight to 9 p.m. and wound forward to the man and woman. He shook his head in disgust when they stopped outside his door. The woman did the business with the key card. The man stood watch. He glanced along the corridor. Ryker hit pause with the guy looking straight at the camera. The angle was as good as Ryker could hope for, but the guy was too far away and the picture too grainy. He hit play again. They both moved inside. Less than five minutes later they came back out, hurried along the corridor back to the elevator.

Ryker sighed. He scrolled through the other cameras, settled on one that covered part of the main reception, looking down toward the elevator area, but with a decent view of the reception desk too.

There they were again. Strolling into the hotel a few minutes before the break-in, side by side. Ryker glanced at the reception desk on the screen. To Nikos. He didn't even look up at the intruders as they passed.

Ryker paused and turned and glared at the young man.

'I didn't... How could I know?'

'They also had a key card,' Ryker said.

'It wasn't from me!'

Ryker said nothing. He hit play. The couple moved up to the elevator and waited, heads down. Then, just as the man moved into the elevator and out of view, the woman looked up. Not fully, but enough. Why? Nerves? Or had she not spotted the camera?

Ryker rewound and played again. Hit pause at the right moment. Again, not a great quality image, but with the woman so close to the camera this time, it was good enough.

He recognized her. From the bar.

'That's all,' Ryker said. He stood up from the chair, turned to Nikos. The force in Ryker's demeanor caused Nikos to step back, almost quivering as though he wasn't sure of Ryker's intentions.

Ryker pushed his hand into his pocket. Nikos looked like he was going to wet himself. Ryker drew out his key card.

'I'm checking out,' he said as he tossed the card to the shaken receptionist.

Nikos said nothing as the card bounced off his waist and to the floor. Ryker brushed past him.

Time to find somewhere else to stay. Time to find out what the hell was going on.

11

Ryker was tired out from the day, from the journey from Blodstein, after which he'd still not rested, and the alcohol he'd consumed earlier with Eleni certainly wasn't helping. It would have been easy, sensible, to find another hotel and rest for the night, and start afresh in the morning. He had too much on his mind.

He strode back across the city to Eleni's. The streets were quieter than before. Most of the midweek revelers had called it quits already, with just a handful of bars in the area still open. No doubt plenty of late-night rowdy spots remained in the city, but not here.

He didn't see any sign of the Peugeot, nor of the man and woman, or anyone else following him. Perhaps the twosome were holed up somewhere going over their spoils. Ryker clenched his fists at the thought. It hadn't escaped his attention that they'd broken into his hotel room while he'd been having sex with Eleni. A setup? He certainly wouldn't rule it out.

He stopped outside the apartment building. Considered whether to wait for someone so he could sneak in through the open doors a third time, or just buzz her on the intercom.

He decided neither. Instead, he pulled out his phone and called Silviu. A more delayed answer than the last time.

'Ryker? It's late—'

'Who did you tell?'

A short pause. 'I... No one.'

'Bullshit. I've been under watch here in Athens pretty much since I arrived. No one knew I was coming here.'

'Neither did I! When we first spoke you were in Norway!'

'Don't play me, Silviu. You got me the information on Mashchenko. His address here in Athens. That's what started this.'

'Started what?'

'Who did you tell?'

'I told no one! And that's the truth... But...'

'But what?'

Ryker turned when he sensed someone approaching the doors from the inside. A group of three. Two men. A woman. Merry. Ryker stepped to the side as they came out. They paid him no attention as they tootled off along the street, jovial and loud.

Ryker moved inside.

'But what?' he repeated.

'There was an alert on Mashchenko. I honestly don't know why, or who put it there.'

'You didn't think to tell me?'

'I didn't even know until after! My boss called to ask me what the hell I was doing.'

'And what did you tell him?'

'I gave him an answer. That's all you need to know.'

'You owe me,' Ryker said.

A snort, then, 'Do I?'

The way he said it caused Ryker to clench his teeth. As though Silviu would have the audacity to say that, in that tone, to Ryker's face.

'The thing is, Ryker, as scary as you are, you're actually not the scariest person out there.'

What the hell did that mean?

'I still need the info on those IPs,' Ryker said, but the line was already dead.

He resisted the urge to toss the phone at the wall. Instead, he took a few moments to calm himself before he moved up the stairs and to the door to 3a.

Noticeably, there were lights on in 3b now – he could tell from the slivers of orange leaking from the gaps between the door and frame. He still had no further information on the new tenant there. Was he connected to Mashchenko and Jesper too? A safe house of sorts for traveling assassins?

Ryker knocked on Eleni's door and waited. Waited. He knocked again.

'I'm coming!' came the shout in Greek from the other side.

Eleni opened the door. Bathrobe. Her hair was pulled up, her makeup gone. Ryker actually found the more natural look even more alluring on her.

'You're back?' she asked as she glanced beyond him at 3b.

Ryker barged his way in. He moved through to the living area. Eleni followed him, arms folded, anger lines creasing her forehead.

'Did I do something?' she asked.

Ryker took his backpack from his shoulders and dropped it to the ground.

'Did you?'

He stared at her. She held his look. Neither blinked.

'My hotel room was broken into,' Ryker said. 'Those two from the bar.'

No reaction at all on her face. Way too cool. He wished he could read her better.

'They did it while I was here with you,' he added.

Now she shook her head in disgust. 'You think they're with me?'

'Either they are, or at least you know a lot more than you've told me.'

She didn't say anything.

'So which is it?' Ryker asked.

'You're looking for a place to stay?' she said, indicating his bag on the floor.

'Seems like it.'

'Then you'd better get rid of your fucking bad attitude if you want to stay here.'

She moved over to the kitchen. The vodka bottle was soon in her hand.

'You want one?' she asked, turning to him.

'Not really.'

'Well, I need one.' She poured two.

She handed Ryker his drink and sat down on the sofa. The ends of the bathrobe parted to reveal nearly every inch of her bare legs.

Ryker took the seat opposite, tried not to look, but how could he not?

'Just because I won't tell you everything, doesn't mean I'm playing you,' she said.

'Am I in danger?'

'Here, with me?'

'Here with you. Here in Athens.'

'No. And I don't know.'

'You don't seem too worried.'

'About you, or about me?'

'Either.'

She smiled and sipped her drink.

'I'm quite happy having you here to protect me,' she said.

She uncrossed and recrossed her legs.

'Protect you from who?'

She shrugged. 'Anyone.'

They sat through a few moments of silence. Ryker's anger and irritation dissipated as he sipped his drink and watched his host.

'Your new neighbor is home,' Ryker said.

'I know.'

'Is that why you're still here? In this apartment? Two months after Mashchenko took his last breath?'

'I don't know anything about Mashchenko's death.'

'That didn't answer my question at all,' Ryker said. 'So who is he?'

'He? It's not just a he. More than one person stays there. They come and go now.'

'A safe house?'

'Safe house? That's a bit dramatic. Mashchenko, not long ago, was here for a while, I think that's why you thought he lived there. But it's just a stopover. When people are in the city, doing business here, sometimes they stay there.'

'Doing business? Mashchenko was a violent assassin, not a corporate salesman.'

'That doesn't mean everyone is the same as him.'

'But they're still people of interest.'

'To me, yes.'

She finished her drink then stretched out and yawned. As she did so her bathrobe fell further open. Silk negligee underneath.

'I'm really tired,' she said. 'Can't we do this in the morning?'

'Do what in the morning? Talk?'

'Exactly. All work and no play makes Carl a dull boy.'

Ryker shook his head in disbelief. What was this woman? She pulled herself up from the sofa. Stared down at Ryker for a moment before she turned and wandered off to the bedroom. The bathrobe slipped off her shoulders as she moved. Ryker remained seated. She disappeared from sight.

Silence. Then she shouted out, 'If you're staying here, you're staying with me.'

Ryker sighed. Then got to his feet. He left his bag on the floor and moved to the bedroom.

12

Their bodies remained close through the night, and as Ryker awoke, Eleni remained cuddled up to him. Ryker stared around the room, too deep in thought to be bothered about trying to rouse her.

When she eventually opened her eyes, nearly half an hour later, she stretched out and sighed and placed a kiss on his chest.

'You sleep well?' she asked.

'Not much sleep really.'

'Sorry.'

He kissed the top of her head, though felt a bit foolish for doing so. Why?

'I need to get moving,' he said.

'Because?'

He didn't answer.

'So what next for the mighty Carl Logan?' she asked, a little mockingly.

'I will find those two who took my things,' Ryker said. 'You must realize how it's going to look if I find you work with them.'

She sat up in the bed, clearly annoyed. 'I've only just woken up. I mean, do you ever stop?'

'No,' he said. 'I wouldn't be here, in Athens, if I did.'

'I feel sorry for you.'

She huffed and slammed her head down onto the pillow.

'Perhaps it would be better if I was like you,' Ryker said. 'No cares in the world. Just doing what I want.'

For once her caginess eluded her, and she looked genuinely offended, exactly as he'd intended.

'You don't know the real me,' she said.

'I'd like to know more. Why else would I be here?'

'Why else?' she said with a playful grin now.

She sighed. He did too. Did Ryker feel awkward? Not really.

'Tell me what brought you to Athens,' Eleni said. 'Tell me the real story. Perhaps there's something I can do to help.'

He thought about that proposition. Was there really any harm in him being open with her about that?

'How about over breakfast?' he suggested.

She stared at him, as though not clear on his intentions. He had no ulterior motive though, he was simply hungry.

She didn't have a wide choice. They settled for coffee and eggs with toast, which Eleni prepared while Ryker showered and dressed. Eleni remained in her bathrobe.

'I was traveling in Norway,' Ryker said.

'Official business?'

'I have no official business anymore.'

The doubt in her eyes suggested she wasn't sure she believed that.

'There was a boy. His name was Henrik. I nearly crashed into him on his moped on a twisting road. He was frightened. But not because of the crash, I figured. A policeman turned up and claimed he knew him. He took Henrik back to their hometown. A tiny place called Blodstein.'

No reaction on her face to any of the story so far.

'Something wasn't right, so I went to the town and started asking questions about the boy. I didn't get any satisfactory answers. Anyway, to fast-forward to the end, Henrik had been kidnapped.'

'Kidnapped?'

'By a local gang, led by a prominent businessman. The day I saw him he was attempting to escape.'

'Why?'

'Why'd they have him? Because of who he was. The locals were getting squeezed by some out-of-town gangsters. Low-level stuff, I thought, except it'd been going on for years. A long story there, but basically the kid was the illegitimate son of the leader of the gangsters. A man named Jesper.'

A slight pinch in her eyes. She knew the name.

'I never met him, only his soldiers. There was a standoff. I was involved. The three outsiders who'd been sent to the town to cause trouble lost their lives, including your old neighbor, Konstantin Mashchenko. Some of the local gang were killed too, but Henrik was safe.'

Eleni shook her head in disbelief. Had she ever been close to violence like that, or had she always been on the sidelines, looking from afar? His guess was the latter.

'You're not eating,' he said to her.

She hadn't touched her eggs. She shook her head. Ryker took the opportunity for a couple of mouthfuls.

'You killed Mashchenko?' she asked, as though she couldn't believe it. He wondered again how much she knew about the dead man.

'No,' Ryker said. 'Actually, the local police chief did that. Shotgun to the head. But I was there when it happened.'

Ryker was on top of the assassin, grappling with him. He received a face full of blood and brain and skull for his troubles.

'In the end, Henrik was safe, and as far as anyone else knew, the fact he was Jesper's son remained a secret.'

'This all sounds... like a...'

She never finished the thought.

'That should have been the end of the story. I don't know Jesper. Clearly a bad guy, a career criminal and probably rich from it, but the story was over for me. I left town. Henrik did too.'

'Except now you're here?'

'Because of Henrik. He wasn't... a normal teenage boy. Perhaps it was his father's blood. I feared he wouldn't just walk away, take his chance for a fresh start.'

'Every time you mention him, it's in the past tense.'

'That's because he's dead.'

He let that hang. Eleni held his eye until Ryker looked down at his food. He chewed through another mouthful before starting up again.

'A dead body was found in Crete a few days ago. Unidentified. But I'm sure it's him. He went looking for Jesper. Wanted to kill him. I think he failed and paid the ultimate price. A few days ago Jesper sent another hit squad to Blodstein, in retaliation for what happened. Six more dead bodies there.'

Ryker clutched his knife and fork that little bit harder at the thought.

'And now you're here for revenge too?'

Ryker said nothing. Was that all it boiled down to? No, there was justice as well.

'An experienced man like you... You must know these things

never end well. Gang warfare. One killing leads to two more, leads to three more. Both sides lose. Where does it end?'

'Gang warfare? I'm not one of them.'

'No, but you're stuck in the cycle.'

'You're saying I shouldn't bother?'

'I don't know you very well, but I'd say you wouldn't listen to me anyway.'

Ryker huffed.

'Do you know who Jesper is?' he asked.

'No,' she said without thought.

'Honestly?'

'Why would I lie?'

'You've never heard that name?'

'No. Never.'

'Then what about Mashchenko? The others in that apartment across from here?'

'I'm here to watch them.'

'With what end goal?'

'I have no end goal. I told you before, I just gather information. I'm not the decision-maker. I'm not a trigger-puller.'

Ryker shook his head. Something about her blasé attitude riled him. He believed that she was on the right side of good and bad, but it was almost as though she didn't care. She just did what she needed, what she was told, without thought of what it all meant, where it all ended.

'Who did Mashchenko work for?' Ryker asked.

'I honestly don't know. But Crete?'

'Crete what?'

'There's a man who lives there. An associate. Whether Mashchenko's boss or what, I really don't know, but he's involved with the same people.'

'His name?'

'Roman Smolov.'

Not a name Ryker knew, and not a very Greek-sounding name.

He got to his feet.

'Where are you going?' she said.

'I think you know.'

He looked down at her. Disappointment in her eyes. He could ask her to go with him? Two pairs of hands were better than one. But... No, he really wasn't sure he could rely on her.

He moved over and kissed her on the forehead.

'I hope you'll come back,' she said.

He hoped so too, though he didn't say it. Instead, he got his things together, then set off.

Next stop, the island of Crete.

13

HERAKLION, CRETE

Nine days previously

Reva's first few days in Crete were certainly revealing. Mostly in a good way, but not entirely. Smolov ran a decent enough operation. Not overly surprising really, given he was one of Jesper's most trusted associates. Not a second in command, as such, but as close to one as anyone else who worked for Jesper came. Reva and Smolov, to the greatest extent, were peers, equivalents. That said, Smolov had been given his own foreign kingdom, while Reva preferred to stay closer to the top dog, work alongside him, a problem solver. The two roles suited both men perfectly well. Smolov got to feel more important than he really was, got to have the house with the fancy cars, designer wife, and life in the sun. Reva got a life with far fewer ties, most of the time got to do whatever he wanted, which mainly involved making himself and those around him who remained loyal very, very rich.

That was part of Smolov's problem. He'd settled for a nice life, rather than a boundary-breaking, fully productive life.

'Your operations are too disconnected from the mainland

here,' Reva said to Alexei. The poolside bar of the luxury hotel was quiet. In early March there weren't that many tourists, and the weather wasn't that hot, but Reva still preferred the hotel pool to Smolov's place. At the villa he only had Sylvia to ogle. She was nice on the eye, certainly, but out here, a couple of hundred yards around the bay, there were gold diggers with their sugar daddies aplenty.

'Too many fat Russians for you?' Alexei said, smirking as he followed Reva's eye to a hairy-chested, seriously pot-bellied man in his fifties, leathery brown skin, who was receiving lotion on his shoulders from a young woman who could quite easily have been a supermodel if she'd chosen a life of work rather than one of fucking horny old rich men.

'Definitely,' Reva said, taking a long drag of his beer before turning to Alexei. 'My point is, you're too far away from the real action.'

'We have plenty of action here.'

'Plenty? But you're on an island of less than a million people.'

'We go to the mainland all the time. We do plenty there.'

'Yeah? How many men work for you there? How many properties are ours, used exclusively for our businesses?'

'A few.'

'Why not hundreds?' No answer. 'The mainland is a trip by boat or air. Why the hassle? If you're not careful we'll get outmaneuvered there. You want to move gear from Africa into Europe, where do you go? A little island in the sea, or straight to the mainland?'

'We do both. There's a big enough market here in the summer to keep everyone happy. That's how Roman started here.'

Reva felt like biting back at that but didn't bother. He didn't need to be schooled on Roman. Alexei had still been pissing his pants when he and Roman had first started working with Jesper.

'But there's an even bigger market on the mainland,' he said. 'Three hundred million people all year round.'

'Jesper's already got plenty of action in Europe. You too. But it's a market with hundreds of other gangs. Out here, we're the only operators. Why risk that?'

Reva shook his head, disgruntled. He'd had plenty of talks with Alexei since he'd arrived. The young man was as close to in charge as anyone else with Smolov out of action. He wasn't stupid either, even if some of his life choices were beyond reckless. He had a decent sense for business at least, though he struggled to see the bigger picture.

'Three-quarters of what we organize goes to the mainland,' Alexei said.

Okay, so that wasn't a bad number, but still...

'But then you pass it on straight off and let others take the main profit,' Reva said. 'Plus, if we had a real base there, you'd be able to treble the amount we were shifting. Maybe more.'

Alexei shrugged as though it was all hyperbole. Perhaps he'd become too used to the easy life already. Running the culmination of another man's hard graft was hardly the same thing as building an empire from scratch.

'And moving people?' Reva said. 'Why aren't we making more?'

'It's becoming too difficult.'

'That's my fucking point. It's too difficult *here*. It's not as if there isn't a constant stream begging to come to Europe, but there's no sense in bringing migrants from Africa to Crete. What are they going to do here? They need to go straight to the mainland.'

'They do. But there are too many players, and the money's not what it was.'

Reva slammed his beer down on the bar top. 'Too many players? There shouldn't be anyone but us in this part of the world.

Then we charge what we want. Supply and demand. Right now there's too many others in the market.'

Alexei shrugged again. Reva was becoming a little riled by his lack of care. He finished his beer. Across the way the fat Russian had finished getting his lotion and returned to lying face down on his lounger, his huge butt sticking up in the air, his legs and back as hairy and fat as his front. How could his wife want that on top of her? Inside her?

Well, the answer was simple, really.

The Russian's supermodel wife sauntered over to the bar, her loincloth bikini revealing pretty much everything, her nipples poking through the thin fabric. She smiled coyly at Alexei as she removed her sunglasses and ordered her drinks from the barman. She glanced at Reva but then quickly away. Typical. Alexei was a handsome young man. Tall, athletic. Reva... He knew what he looked like.

Reva caught Alexei's eye. The young man smirked. Then Reva got up from his stool and moved up behind the woman. He put one hand on the bar and the other firmly onto her left buttock as he leaned in.

'I bet I've got more money than he has, if that's your thing,' he said to her in Russian, before squeezing her ass and holding his hand there. She pulled herself out of his grip and turned around. No playfulness, no anger even. She looked... scared as she gazed into Reva's eyes.

'Ignore my friend,' Alexei said. 'He doesn't get out much.'

Reva shot the underling a glare before returning his lustful gaze to the woman.

'What's your name?' he asked her.

She opened her mouth to speak but he put a finger to her lips to stop her.

'No,' he said. 'Tell me when you're on top of me.'

He reached forward and put his hand to her shoulder then dragged it down to her breast. She quivered.

'Hey!' the barman called over. 'What are you doing?'

English. Always fucking English, even though his name badge read Dmitri.

Reva took his hand back and glared at the barman. The next moment, fatty was sitting upright, looking over. His woman went to walk away but Reva grabbed her, swung her around and wrapped his arms around her and planted his lips firmly onto hers.

He pulled back. 'Tell me I'm not a better catch than him.'

The Russian shouted over, rose to his feet as Reva pushed the woman away. The guy wobbled over. His woman hid behind his flabby frame. Not hard. Ten people could have fitted there.

'What the fuck are you doing?' the Russian spat.

Reva didn't wait to see whether he was all mouth, or whether he actually intended to throw a punch. Instead, he grabbed his empty bottle from the bar, lunged forward, and smacked the glass against the side of the man's head.

Clunk. The glass didn't break. So Reva did it again, crashing the glass down onto the man's head like a hammer. This time the bottle did break and the man crumpled to the ground.

'Shit, that's enough,' Alexei said, the anxiety in his voice clear.

He reached out but Reva shrugged him off and threw a foot into a wall of flab on the Russian's belly. He screwed his face in disgust then hammered his heel onto the man's nose. The Russian groaned as blood poured. Everyone in the area looked on, horrified.

Reva smiled, squatted down by the Russian and grabbed his hair and pulled it back.

'I fucking hate Russians,' Reva said before spitting in the man's face and slamming his head to the slabs. 'Especially fat ones with too much money.'

A few more moans and gasps from the crowd. Reva straightened up. Looked at the Russian's woman. Caught her petrified eyes.

He moved toward her. She cowered away.

Alexei grabbed him by the arm and pulled him to the side.

'Come on,' he said. 'Before the police get here.'

Reva really wanted her, but fair enough. They'd had their fun. Reva blew the woman a kiss then he and Alexei strode out of there, down the steps and to the beach below. They moved at pace back along the bay.

'Why did you do that?' Alexei said.

'Why not?'

'Because we live right around the corner from there. People know me. Know my face.'

'Don't you pay the police?'

'Of course we do. But not all of them. And not all the hotel staff. Not all the tourists.'

'If you pay the police then the others don't matter.'

'And you don't even know who he is. What if he's connected?'

Reva came to a halt. Alexei did too. They turned to one another.

'Connected to who? You told me there weren't other players here.'

'There aren't.'

'Then if he's connected back home, perhaps now he knows who's in charge here and won't get any silly ideas about moving in.'

Reva headed off again. Alexei moved alongside.

'You didn't have to do that to them,' Alexei said.

'Them?'

'Yeah. Both of them. The man, the woman. You didn't need to do that. They weren't doing anything to you.'

'Maybe you should keep your thoughts to yourself. That mouth could get you into a lot of trouble.'

Alexei said nothing more. They arrived at the gate and the steps that led up the cliff to Smolov's villa. Reva reached for the handle. Alexei looked back to where they'd come from.

'No,' he said. 'People are watching.'

'So?'

'So we don't have to make it that obvious. You don't have to cause me problems. Please.'

Reva sighed and looked along the beach. Two police officers were in view in the far distance, on the beach by the hotel.

'Do you know those two?' he said to Alexei.

'I can't tell from here. Probably not if they're the lowly idiots they send on beach patrol. The ones we pay are higher up.'

'Then that's something you need to work on. The more police you have in your pocket the better. And the lowly ones are cheaper and hold more power than you might think.'

'Let's just keep moving,' Alexei said.

Reva thought about that for a moment.

'No,' he said. He opened the gate. 'If they want to come, let them come. It's time to properly take charge of this town.'

14

PRESENT

The ferry bobbed lightly on the crystal waters of the Med. Ryker leaned on the railing, looking ahead to the island of Crete, which drew closer all the time, the old harbor of Chania the destination. Of the hundreds of inhabited islands belonging to the modern-day country of Greece, Crete was the largest, the most populous, and the most important for the Mediterranean country's tourist industry – an industry that accounted for nearly a quarter of the country's entire economy. Even on the approach from the water, Ryker could see the draw of the island.

His first glimpse of the ancient harbor told a lot of the story of its rich but troubled past. To his left, at the edge of the pier that wrapped around the harbor, stood a painstakingly restored lighthouse, originally built by the Venetians in the sixteenth century, and later modified by the Egyptians in the nineteenth. On the opposite side of the harbor entry stood the Firkas Fortress, a simple stone-built structure similarly built by the Venetians. In front of him, the domes of the Mosque of the Janissaries rose proudly, one of many remnants of more recent Ottoman rule.

Rich and varied history, rich and varied civilizations. Almost a shame that the island was now seen by many outsiders as nothing but a beach destination. Even in early spring, the island was likely busy with tourists there to soak up the sun, and Ryker was only glad it wasn't midsummer when the hoards would have been several times larger.

He moved from the ferry port and to a rental shop. No car for this trip, he instead opted for a moped. He'd been to some of the Greek islands before and knew from prior experience that away from the cross-city routes, many roads were far more suited to two wheels than four.

Once out of the city and on the open road, Ryker was pleasantly surprised by what he saw of the natural landscape, with a sweeping mountain range dominating the eyeline from west to east, the undulating hills full of greenery. Jagged, rocky outcrops dropped toward the pristine-looking ocean that the main road snaked back and forth alongside, the water remaining in view much of the way.

His destination was close to Heraklion, the capital city of the island, and although he could have caught a ferry directly there – if he'd waited for longer in Athens – he was glad for the mini detour which certainly helped him feel more acclimated.

The city was still three miles away in front when his phone pinged to tell him he'd reached his destination. He pulled into a public parking lot by the beach and looked around. To his right, off in the distance, the shoreline of the city swept around, the buildings muddled by a haze. To his left, beachfront properties were dotted as far as he could see.

He made his way on foot onto the golden sand, taking his backpack and the few belongings he'd brought with him, having managed to arrange for some more cash from a money transfer shop in Athens. Nothing he could do yet about the stolen passports. He'd need to find a place to stay the night – if indeed he decided to stay at all – but for now it was straight to it, reconnaissance first.

Stretching into the near distance were several clusters of neatly arranged rows of sun loungers, different coloring schemes employed to denote which of the hotels beyond they belonged to. Most of the areas had their own dedicated beach bars too, though there were also stretches of bare sand between some of the plots, open for all, which, perhaps strangely, were the busier parts. Not that any of the beach was particularly busy. The sun loungers were 20 percent taken at most.

With his sunglasses on, cotton shirt and shorts, he at least blended in a little with the tourists as he walked along the sand. He passed by three, then four of the hotels, their relative class and expense denoted to a large extent by the quality of their beach gear, and the smartness of the attendants and bar staff. He flitted his gaze from the staff, residents, and the hotels behind them, and to further ahead where the land swept inwards and round into a narrow bay, a couple of hundred meters wide.

He headed on past a group of four scrawny teenagers, locals judging by their appearance, messing about with a ball as three teenage girls looked on goggle-eyed.

He stopped when he reached the edge of the bay and took his sunglasses off, making a point of wiping them on his shirt as he looked up and down the beach. At the nearest edge of the bay, a small bluff jutted out to the beach. A modest cluster of sun loungers sat below it, but at the top of the rock, he saw pristine-looking metal railings and a white-rendered hotel complex beyond – probably the most modern and swankiest-looking of all those on the stretch.

Beyond the hotel, though, as the bay extended inward, he saw no more hotels, but instead, a line of private villas. Some modern and sleek, some more traditional stone or white render, but all were big and undoubtedly expensive.

Ryker knew, from his research prior to arriving here, that one of those villas belonged to Roman Smolov. The man Eleni had given Ryker the name of as a lead, and one very key reason why Ryker was now standing in this spot on the beach.

The other reason was because of Henrik. Henrik, a fourteen-year-old boy who was now dead. Henrik, whose washed-up body had been found mere yards from where Ryker was standing.

He looked back from the villas and to where he'd just walked from, where the kids played further along. Then he glanced at the hotel in front of him, rising above everything else around. A prominent viewpoint for sure.

He set off in that direction.

* * *

The teenager's body had been found only a few days ago, on the beach, by a hotel worker. No sign of police tape or anything like that now. No sign that anything untoward had happened at all. Of course, that's exactly how the local police would want it, given the negative impact that such a ghastly crime – and sight – would have on holidaymakers, but still, Ryker felt aggrieved for the victim, as though the quick clean-up was a sign that his death, and life, was of secondary priority.

Not to Ryker.

At the edge of the beach a rocky, crazy-paved staircase wound upward into the cliff. Ryker headed up the steep incline. The stairs ended at the top of the bluff in a nicely lawned garden, with pretty shrubs and flowers in neat borders. The sound of chatting and splashing drifted over from beyond. Ryker followed the noise, which came from the other side of a wickerwork fence.

He came to an iron gate. Not security locked, but he found a guard – black trousers and white shirt, cap on his head – standing there, arms folded.

'Afternoon,' Ryker said to him with a nod and a smile.

A smile in return from the guy before he opened the gate to let Ryker through without a word spoken.

Not much of a guard. Obviously, Ryker didn't appear the threatening type, in the guy's eyes at least.

The pool area was busy enough. No kids. Perhaps because they were all at school back home, or perhaps because the luxury hotel was adults only. A dozen or so guests were dotted about the place, in and out of the water. In the far corner, at the cliff edge, Ryker spotted a beach bar with several stools. He moved that way, took his backpack off his shoulders then sat at one of the stools and ordered a local beer – a small one – from the sole barman.

The amber drink was cold and crisp, and a surprisingly low price given the location. Which probably explained why the vast majority of the other customers were also drinking, even though it was only early afternoon.

Ryker sat half facing the pool, half looking out over the bay below him. A spectacular view, and exactly as all-encompassing as Ryker had imagined when he'd looked up from the sand.

Two other men were at the bar. One in his fifties, one in his forties, sitting a couple of stools away from each other. Ryker didn't believe the men were holidaying together, but they were clearly familiar with each other from previous days spent there, given the on-off chat between them. Both were English, as Ryker assumed a lot of the hotel's guests were. Both of the men wore only their beach shorts. Both had bronzed skin – the younger one more red than bronze, really – and both had portly bellies from too many days sitting by the pool and drinking, perhaps.

Ryker listened in to the conversation as subtly as he could. The

younger man had a Midlands accent, the older one was from
Essex. Their chat sounded straightforward enough, mainly football and kids. Within a few minutes, Ryker had deduced that
there'd been an exciting match in the hotel bar the night before,
and both men had teenagers at home who were in various stages
of exam preparation.

After finishing his second beer – the second since Ryker had
arrived, at least – the wife of the younger of the men collected him
and they headed off for lunch.

The older man turned from his perch, looking out at the pool,
and then back to the bar. He ordered another beer. He glanced at
Ryker and nodded in greeting. Ryker nodded back. The man took
his beer and a couple of sips. Ryker waited for it...

'Nice day for it,' the man said with a chuckle that made his
belly wobble.

'Can't beat it,' Ryker said, raising his glass in a toast.

For the next few minutes, Ryker indulged the guy's apparent
enthusiasm for chit-chat, working through various topics from
marriage to kids to dogs, before he decided to get down to
business.

'So you were here the other day, when they found that kid?'
Ryker said, indicating down to the beach.

The man put on his glum face now. 'Yeah, terrible that.'

'Did you see anything?'

'How do you mean?'

'With the kid? Did you see what happened to him?'

'Nah, it wasn't like that. No one saw it, as far as I know. Basically, he was there in the morning. Washed up. It was actually one
of the guys from here who found him and called the police.
Christoph, one of the bar staff.'

'The guy who was just here?'

'Nah. Different one.'

'So what did you see?' Ryker asked and received the slightest look of suspicion in return. But he knew he'd read this situation exactly right. This guy was a loudmouth and a gossip. Even if he had seen absolutely nothing on that morning, by now he'd know as much as anyone else about what had happened.

'When I got out here, after breakfast, everyone was talking about it. Down there was ten, fifteen police, easily. A little tent. Loads of people standing around on the beach dying for a better look. Phones out, the lot. Macabre, if you ask me.'

'Did you go down there?'

'Nah, I'm not that nosy.'

He said that with a completely straight face.

'I stayed up here. Within a couple of hours, most of the police had cleared out. The kid's body, tent and all that, that was all gone before it went dark. You'd never know anything happened at all.'

Ryker clenched his fist at that comment.

'Did the police come up here at all?' he asked.

Definitely suspicion in the man's eyes now. Ryker needed to be careful if he wanted the full story.

'You're pretty keen on this?' the man asked. 'Not a journo, are you?'

Ryker laughed. 'No, I'm damn well not. Just interested, that's all. Shook me a bit when I read about it, knowing that it happened right where I was coming to stay.'

The man nodded as though he completely understood.

'No, a couple of the police did come up here, but only to speak to one or two of the staff. Like I said, it was Christoph who found it.'

It. Like the body was an inanimate object.

'I've got to say, when I read about what happened, it did kind of put me off coming, even if the story I read was pretty bland. When I heard about it being a murder, I expected he was stabbed or something and there'd been a fight. But you said washed up?'

The guy nodded and drank at the same time. Quite clever, really.

'Yeah. Washed up.'

'How do they know he didn't just drown, then?'

He looked around him now. Leaned in a little closer to Ryker as though what he was about to say was highly secret. Ryker hoped so.

'Odd, wasn't it? They didn't say much in the papers, not even here. Maybe they don't want people getting all worried. Or maybe because it was a kid. You know? No one wants to think about bad stuff happening to kids. But... the thing is, his wrists were tied up. Rope. So he definitely hadn't just got into trouble in the water. I don't know how he died, but I reckon, dead or alive, he was dumped in the water. No doubt.'

'Damn,' Ryker said. He shook his head in disbelief.

'I know, right? Especially for us dads. Just imagine.'

'Strange that they don't know who he is,' Ryker said.

'The staff here were all calm and everything, I mean, it's adults only, isn't it? But all along the stretch here, people were rushing about, asking questions, trying to find out who the lad was. Everyone expected he was a kid on holiday here with his family. At least at first.'

'At first?'

His eyes squinted. He didn't like Ryker's questioning now. Or was it something else?

'No one's come forward, so he definitely wasn't with a family here. But... I reckon I saw him.'

'The dead kid?'

A nod in response. 'I read the description of him, I talked to a few people here and there. Like I said, everyone was trying to figure out who he was, so I was just doing my part, trying to help out. The kid they found had long dark hair. Not that usual for a teenage boy these days really, is it?'

'I guess not,' Ryker said with a shrug.

'And I saw two of them like that, around the bay.' The man indicated behind Ryker.

'Two of them?'

'Looked like brothers. Not twins, but pretty similar. Both long hair, both skinny and tall. They were hanging around the beach on the bay. You get a lot of the local kids down here, particularly on the weekend.'

He shook his head, not overly happy at the fact, then had a drag of his beer before he carried on. 'It's a public beach, so you can't exactly stop them, but sometimes they're a nuisance. Big groups, loud music, parties and fires at night.'

'But those two kids?'

'Those two... just stuck out. Only the two of them. Not really dressed for the beach, I just thought it was a bit odd. That's why I remembered them.'

He looked Ryker up and down. 'Kind of like you, really.' He laughed and finished off his beer. Ryker laughed too, then did the same.

'And you're sure it was the same kid?'

A shrug. 'I mean, I didn't see the kid in the sand properly, but I haven't seen either of those two on the beach since. Coincidence?'

'So what's the theory?'

'Just two local petty criminals maybe. Got to be careful, you know? Maybe they got themselves into something they shouldn't have. Happens, doesn't it?'

'Certainly does,' Ryker agreed.

'You want another,' the guy asked.

Ryker got to his feet. 'No, not before I've eaten.'

'Was nice meeting you. What did you say your name was?'

'Carl.'

'I'm Ryan.'

He reached out for a handshake. Ryker took it.

'See you around,' Ryker said.

'You'll know where to find me.'

Rarely a truer word spoken than that.

15

EIGHT DAYS PREVIOUSLY

The police had come to the villa after the fracas in the bar. That fact alone told Reva a lot. Most of all, it told him that the police didn't understand their place here. Naivety, nothing more. Reva was a very persuasive man, however, and if anything he'd welcomed the opportunity to teach the officers some quick but essential life lessons. Survival lessons. A few calls here and there, the most important being to their boss – who Smolov was already paying off – and Reva squared out the situation and gained two new assets.

Two days later and it was time to further test the robustness of Smolov's operation, and the people involved in it.

Reva hadn't met the Egyptians before, face-to-face, but he knew of them. Drug runners, people traffickers, bad guys, but nothing Reva hadn't seen a thousand times before. For all their swagger they were essentially middlemen. As was Smolov, in a way, but the Egyptians came with a fearsome and brutal reputation. Still, nothing unusual really, given the nature of their business, but Reva had seen plenty of times in the past how fearsome reputations were built through propaganda rather than real action, and he didn't yet know where the Egyptians sat. Regardless, they were one of many available suppliers of illicit goods from Africa, the Middle East, Asia, South America, into Europe. If their supplies dried up overnight, it wasn't as though Reva and the rest of Jesper's wider organization wouldn't be able to sort an alternative. The Egyptians didn't hold the cards. Reva hoped they already understood that. If they didn't, then they soon would.

He was sitting in the wood-paneled library when Alexei and Iya brought the guests through. Four in total. Two of them in nicely tailored suits, one blue, one gray, waistcoats and all, and two of them in black suits – the muscle, with sunglasses on and pouts on their faces like they truly believed they were Secret Service agents.

Reva got up from his seat and smiled. The man in the gray suit, the shortest and oldest of the foursome, with piercing dark eyes, a Romanesque nose, and neatly trimmed stubble, stepped forward and reached out with his hand.

'You must be Olek,' he said in warm tones. English, of course. That was fine. Reva didn't speak Masri, so he could hardly expect them to speak Ukrainian.

'Hassan?' Reva said.

The man nodded. 'And this is my son, Ali.'

Reva shook Ali's hand too. He was tall, not that broad, with a youthful confidence and slicked-back hair. A playboy more than a gangster. Reva bet he drove a garishly colored Lamborghini or similar back home. Loved spending his time in the VIP lounges of the local nightclubs in Cairo, or other trendy spots, rather than actually getting his hands bloodied. Looking at the two of them Reva already doubted their brutish credentials, though he knew not to judge looks too flippantly.

'Please, take a seat,' Reva said.

Hassan and Ali did so, taking the dark leather sofa opposite Reva who sat back down in his green leather wing-backed armchair. Alexei perched on the arm of another sofa next to Reva. Iya remained standing on the other side of him, a little further away. The two Secret Service agents stood behind their bosses, by the now-closed library door. The bulges under their jackets showed they were both carrying. As were Alexei and Iya.

'You want some coffee?' Reva said, indicating the table that separated them, upon which sat a large cafetière and a selection of sweet tidbits.

'Baklava, my favorite,' Hassan said with a smile that revealed yellowed teeth. He reached forward and took one of the sticky morsels. 'And coffee, please, strong and black.'

Reva smiled again and reached forward and poured two coffees for the guests.

'No word on Roman?' Hassan asked as he sat back in his seat.

Reva eyed him for a moment. 'That's why I'm here.'

'He's not coming back?'

'Not yet.'

'But this is still his home?'

Hassan looked about the room, a look on his face that Reva couldn't read. Was he impressed with what he saw?

'This is still his home,' Reva said.

'But you're in charge now.'

'I'm looking after business here.'

Hassan and Ali both glanced at Alexei. No reaction on the young man's face, but Reva felt he knew what the looks meant. They were mocking Alexei. Mocking him because with Smolov gone he hadn't been handed the reins but, instead, had Reva thrust upon him.

'Where's Sylvia today?' Hassan asked.

'In the sunshine, where she belongs. She doesn't need to be part of our business.'

Hassan shrugged, as though he didn't agree. Or perhaps he just wanted to stare at her breasts.

'And where's your lovely wife?' Reva asked Hassan.

'At home too, of course.'

'Of course. You wouldn't even let her out without a male chaperone, I suppose. Certainly not without everything but her eyes covered in black cloth. Just imagine if another man looked at her and got a fucking hard-on from her eternal beauty.'

That did the trick. Hassan glared daggers. Ali clenched his fists on his lap. The two goons looked at one another like they couldn't believe what they'd heard.

'Are you mocking me?' Hassan said. 'My religion?'

'Yeah,' Reva said. 'You, your religion, your god, and your prophets. To be honest, I can't stand any religion. Yours included.'

Hassan's face twisted but he said nothing. Reva wasn't finished.

'It's nothing personal, but every religion is filled with ridiculous traditions, stories that are more fantasy than *Harry Potter*. But then, I think you don't really care that much about your religion either, do you? Or you wouldn't be here today, selling drugs and whatever else you can get your hands on for profit. Haram?'

Hassan said nothing but his face and body were tight with tension. His son simply stared on, lost and pathetic.

'So, to go back to your original question once more, Sylvia is not joining us today. She doesn't need to. Your wife isn't here today either. Ali's boyfriend isn't here today either, but maybe that's just because he hasn't told you about that yet.'

Reva blew the young man a kiss. Ali shot up from his seat, Egyptian expletives spewing from his mouth. The two goons took a step forward. Iya twitched – she'd have those two easily. Hassan held his son back with a simple arm across his chest and the fun was soon over.

Reva laughed. 'Sorry, Ali, I'm just having a bit of fun with you,' he said.

Ali glared but said nothing more. He straightened out his suit – obviously very important to do that after his brave stand – before retaking his seat.

'Roman is gone,' Reva said. 'I don't know how long for, but our business cannot be interrupted. Do you agree?'

He expected a straightforward answer. What he got was nothing.

'Is there a problem?' he asked.

'Many problems,' Hassan said in something of a snarl. 'To start, I don't like the circumstances.'

'What circumstances?'

'Roman. You know what happened to him, but you're not telling me. But I only see two options. One, a rival gang took him, which means he's probably already dead. Two, the police took him, which means your whole operation is under siege.'

Reva looked on. Hassan seemed pleased with his statement, growing a little taller in his seat. He leaned forward and took another baklava and stuffed it in his mouth, holding Reva's eye as he chewed.

'Or three,' Reva said. 'Roman was set up by someone who would gain from his disappearance. *You*, perhaps.'

Hassan didn't react, didn't stop chewing. The room remained silent until he'd swallowed.

'You think I took him?' Hassan said. 'You think I have him?'

'No. I know you don't have him. Because I know where he is. But I think it's possible you set him up.'

'So, I'm presuming by your statements, that the police, or some other authority, do have him then?'

'Yes. But not here.'

'Then I'm very disappointed. Because this was exactly as I feared. I'm not sure I can deal with you at all while this is happening. I'm not jeopardizing my own business, my family members.'

Hassan got to his feet, pulled at the sides of his suit jacket to unruffle the material. Ali rose up after his father. A good little boy.

'You want to know what I think?' Reva said.

'Not really.'

'I think you have a lot to gain from this.'

'From having to pull my business from this island?'

'With Roman gone, you get to move in and do what you want here. That's what you're thinking. Am I wrong?'

'You're accusing me of setting him up?'

'Damn right, I am.'

Silence in the room. Hassan and Ali were motionless.

'You have one opportunity,' Reva said. 'One opportunity to tell me the truth.'

'I did not set your friend up,' Hassan said. 'Goodbye, Olek.'

He went to walk away.

'Then our business continues,' Reva said. Hassan paused. 'It's the only way I can trust you. If you stop everything now, how does that look? Roman is gone, and you kill our business together just like that?'

Hassan said nothing, but he wasn't making a move to leave now either.

'Please sit down,' Reva said. 'I've got a proposition for you. A sweetener, you could say.'

Ali leaned into Hassan and whispered in his father's ear. Hassan nodded.

'Okay, we'll hear you out,' he said, before he and his son retook their seats, though both looked a little disinterested as though they were morally above Reva now. 'But if you continue to insult me, my wife, my son, anyone else I know, this won't end well for you. Friend.'

Reva laughed. 'Yeah, okay. Anyway, I admit, business here has been good, more or less. Roman did well for himself. But I want to expand.'

'In Crete? You've swamped this place already.'

'Not in Crete. On the mainland.'

'You don't have the reach there.'

'Don't I?'

Hassan's eyes narrowed. 'How much are you talking about?'

'Triple what you're sending to Crete now. To start with. Give it a few months then see if we can expand again.'

Hassan laughed. 'Triple? Just like that.'

'Just like that.'

'And you have the money to pay for this? I'd need it upfront.'

'You don't trust me?'

'I don't know you. And you haven't shown yourself in the best light so far.'

'This is my best light, believe me. You don't want to see me any darker.'

Did his English make sense? He couldn't fully tell from the passive look on Hassan's face.

'Triple,' Reva said. 'We can start next month. Twenty percent discount for the extra volume.'

Hassan laughed, his son smiled. Reva remained stony-faced, and after a few seconds, his guests' faces fell too.

'You're serious?' Hassan said.

'Why would I joke?'

'You want extra merchandise?' Hassan said. 'I can do that. But it's extra work for me. More manpower, more backhanders, more organization. You want extra, you pay extra.'

'No,' Reva said.

'Yes. Twenty-five percent uplift per kilo. That's the best I can do.'

'Hassan, you might not like me, but I'm not a fool. When someone buys in bulk, you give them a discount. There isn't a business in the world that doesn't understand something so simple.'

'Yes, there is. My business. You want extra, you pay for it. Twenty-five percent more for every kilo. Or we stay where we are.'

'No deal.'

'So you want to stay the same?'

'No. I want you to do what I'm fucking telling you. Triple the supply. Twenty percent discount.'

Hassan rolled his eyes and shook his head and got to his feet. 'This is going nowhere.'

'Is that a no?'

'It's a no.'

'You walk out on me today, that's it,' Reva said. 'There's no going back for you.'

Hassan's face soured once more. 'Are you threatening me?'

Reva said nothing.

'Do you know what I could do to you?' Hassan said. 'Your family?'

'Bad threat,' Reva said. 'It shows you haven't done your homework on me. My parents are long dead. My brother is an asshole and I'd be happy for you to torture him to death. My wife...' He waved his hand in the air, showing the lack of a ring. 'She's already dead. Strangled. Years ago. Want to know who killed her?'

'You're not as clever as you think you are.'

'You're not as tough as you think you are. Or you wouldn't be standing there making schoolboy threats. You'd already be trying to tear my head off.'

'Our business arrangement is over,' Hassan said. 'But me and you... We're not finished.'

Reva shrugged. Hassan turned for the door, Ali by his side. Together with the two goons, the four marched away.

Reva got to his feet. Looked at Iya, then at Alexei. 'Come on,' he said to them.

The Egyptians were already stepping into their hired Mercedes by the time Reva reached the front door. The car started up with a raucous rev and the driver put his foot down, gravel kicking up as the Merc sped away to the gates.

Reva looked at Alexei and Iya, standing by his side, to Vlad, who had already been standing guard at the front.

'No problems?' Reva said to Vlad.

'None.'

'Let's go see.'

The four of them set off for the gates. The brake lights of the Mercedes illuminated and the car rolled to a stop. Vlad pressed the button on the fob and the gates slowly opened as Reva and the others marched forward.

The Mercedes pulled out of the open space and moved out of sight onto the road beyond the wall. Out of sight, but still right there. The flashing blue of the police car lights lit up the area beyond the wall. Reva smiled to himself. Moved a little faster. He couldn't miss the look on Hassan's face.

By the time he reached the gates, the Egyptians were already out, all being manhandled by the swarm of Greek police. One of the policemen opened up the trunk and shouted to his colleagues. He reached inside with a gloved hand. Pulled out the brick of coke – one of five that Vlad had stashed there. He reached in again. Pulled out the gleaming black assault rifle – again, one of several. He rattled off in Greek to his colleagues who stood looking smug.

Reva cast his eye to Hassan. Two cops on him, his hands in cuffs as they marched him to a police car. He shot evils at Reva but said nothing. Soon he was inside the car.

Reva caught the gaze of one of the policemen. One of those who'd turned up at Roman's house the other day after the incident at the hotel bar. He nodded. The policeman quickly looked away, no recognition.

'I told you, they hold more power than you might think,' Reva said, glancing at Alexei. The big guy just nodded. 'Come on, let's get back inside. We need to find a new supplier.'

16

PRESENT

Ryker took more from his chat with Ryan than the talkative holidaymaker probably realized. He'd been on the island for only a couple of hours but already the information he'd heard, and what he'd seen related to Henrik's murder raised aggravating possibilities. At the very least, the police's work to date suggested incompetence or apathy, but perhaps the more extreme case – and perfectly likely under the circumstances – was that he'd stumbled upon a cover-up. Members of the police were either complicit in Henrik's murder or knew who the culprits were and would protect them.

He walked back down the steps to the beach, in two minds as to whether to head right, around the bay and toward Roman Smolov's swanky villa or...

He went left. To the teenagers he'd seen earlier. Take the low-hanging fruit first, so to speak. The group of boys remained on the sand, messing around, kicking the ball about. Not so much a game of football, as an opportunity for them to show off to their captive audience: the three girls, who had moved closer and were having a jovial chat with one of the lads – the one who saw himself as the charmer, given his confident stance and manner.

The three remaining boys with the ball noticed Ryker first. A glance from one, then another. Then double-takes when they realized Ryker was making a beeline for them. By the time he was five yards away, all messing and chatting had stopped and seven sets of dubious eyes stared at him.

'Afternoon,' Ryker said.

'What do you want?' one of them asked in neat English. Ryker guessed on an island where foreign tourism was so important and so ingrained in everyday life, it wasn't at all unusual for the local children to be taught the language of their biggest market at an early age.

'We're not doing anything wrong,' one of the girls piped up.

'I just want to talk,' Ryker said, holding his hands up.

The kid with the ball, the tallest and stockiest of the mostly weaselly looking bunch, stepped forward.

'About what?' he asked.

Ryker looked around him. A few other eyes had turned his way. Holidaymakers on sun loungers, probably wondering why the foreigner was talking to the kids, perhaps hoping he was giving them a hard time and asking them to move on.

'The kid who was murdered,' Ryker said.

Their faces dropped. None of them were any good at poker, apparently. Ryker noticed plenty of glances between them too.

'Did you know him?' Ryker asked.

'No,' said the kid with the ball, his answer accompanied by a few shakes of heads from the others.

'You sure? He was about your age. There's a good chance he was local, given none of the tourists here is missing a child.'

No response at all now, just pursed lips and head shakes. The girls, grouped together, looked as if they were about to try and edge away from Ryker, the stranger. He couldn't blame them really, regardless of whether they were hiding something or not.

'I heard he had a friend,' Ryker said. 'Similar age, appearance. They were seen hanging around here together, on the bay. Both around fourteen. About as tall as you.' He nodded to the kid with the ball. 'A bit skinnier, with long dark hair. Did you see them?'

At the mention of that, their faces dropped further. Now the girls did turn. Without a word to either their male companions or to Ryker, they dropped their heads and walked away.

The boys too, looked like they'd had enough, turned from Ryker and to each other, as though pretending he wasn't there. Or that they weren't. Very odd.

'Is there a problem here?' came a stern voice from behind Ryker.

That explained the change in mood. Even before Ryker turned he guessed who had addressed him.

He ended up face-to-face with two uniformed police officers. A man and woman. Both were youngish. The man had slicked dark hair and aviator sunglasses. His dark blue uniformed shirt looked a size too small resulting in it stretching out over his athletic torso. He definitely liked his own looks. The woman was as tall as her colleague but slimmer, a little less cockiness in her look, but no less formality in her stance. It was the man who'd spoken. Even more accomplished English than the local kids.

'I asked you a question,' Mr Slick said. He unfolded his arms. His right hand, fingers twitching, hovered at his side, just inches from his holstered sidearm, as though this was the Wild West and he was ready for a quick draw. Quite a reaction to a man talking to a group of teenagers.

Ryker glanced over his shoulder. All seven of the kids had cleared out.

'And you are?' Ryker said to Mr Slick.

'Why were you harassing those children?' the woman asked.

'I didn't realize I was.'

'We've had complaints,' Mr Slick said. 'You've been walking along this beach, harassing people, asking questions about a murdered boy.'

Ryker raised an eyebrow. 'Have I?'

'What?'

'Sorry, are you saying I've done something wrong? Talking to people?'

Mr Slick sighed and shook his head.

'Perhaps you could come with us.'

'I'm quite happy here.'

'Who are you?' the woman asked, more conciliatory than her colleague.

'I'm no one. Just an interested party.'

'Just tell us your name, smart-ass,' Mr Slick said.

'Interested party? Interested in a dead boy?' the woman asked.

'Yeah. Aren't you?'

'Okay, you're coming with us.'

Mr Slick reached forward as though to grab Ryker's wrist. Not a sudden move. Not to catch him out. Just a show of authority. Ryker was caught in two minds. Resist or comply.

With the many onlookers, the numbers seemingly much larger now than a few minutes ago, Ryker decided on the most straightforward path. No point in attacking two police officers in broad daylight.

Still, he whipped his hand away and stepped back from Mr Slick, which caused both of the officers to flinch and put their hands to the grips of their guns.

Ryker lifted his hands, palms out. 'I'm not going to cause a problem,' he assured. 'But I'm not under arrest, am I?'

'No,' the woman said eventually.

'Then why don't you both relax a little. You really don't want to take those guns out.'

'Please can you come with us, off the beach,' the woman said.

'I can do that. My moped is parked that way.'

Ryker indicated over his shoulder.

'Get moving, then,' Mr Slick said, his fingers brushing the butt of his sidearm.

Ryker gave him the benefit of the doubt and turned and walked. The officers moved either side of him, slightly behind.

'You haven't identified yourselves yet,' Ryker said. He looked at Mr Slick.

'Identified ourselves?' the woman said.

'Sergeant Robertson,' the man responded without further prompting.

'Senior Constable Georgiadis,' the woman said.

Ryker had already deduced their ranks from the stripes on their uniforms. But Robertson?

'Not a very Greek-sounding name,' Ryker said to him, though with his dark hair and olive skin he definitely looked local enough.

'Nothing to do with you,' he said.

And he definitely sounded English, Ryker now realized. He'd been thrown by the look initially.

'What are we going to do with him?' Georgiadis asked her colleague in Greek.

'Let's just get him away from here first,' came the response from Robertson, similarly in Greek.

Should Ryker spoil their fun and let them know he understood them? No. Not yet.

'Have I actually done anything wrong?' Ryker asked.

'What's your name?' Robertson said.

'James Ryker.'

'Well, James Ryker, we've had enough trouble on this beach

this week. We're only here to keep the peace. We don't need people causing scenes.'

'I don't think I was, really.'

'You think you're pretty smart.'

Ryker said nothing to that. They arrived at his moped.

'This yours?' Robertson asked.

'Rented.'

'Where are you staying?'

'Haven't decided yet.'

'Can I suggest you don't stay near here.' He moved around the moped and looked at the license plate. 'Back in Chania, perhaps.'

'You haven't even asked why I'm here,' Ryker said. 'Why I've come here, asking questions about a murdered boy.'

That shut the guy up. He stood straight and folded his arms. With his aviators on it wasn't possible to know for sure, but Ryker imagined he was receiving a death glare.

'So?' Robertson prompted.

'So?'

'So, why are you here?'

'The murdered boy is still unidentified, isn't he?'

'Yes.'

'I think I know him.'

Arms unfolded again. A quick look between the two of them.

'We need to do this properly,' Georgiadis said to him, in Greek once more.

'You're a relative?' Robertson asked, ignoring his colleague. Or perhaps not.

'If I can see him, I'll be able to tell you.'

'No,' Georgiadis said. 'You can't just see him. If you think you have information about who he is, we'll take that from you first.'

Robertson nodded in response, though Ryker was sure some of the man's confidence had waned all of a sudden. Why?

'Shall we go somewhere to talk, then?' Ryker suggested.

'Not the station,' Georgiadis said to Robertson, once again preferring Greek.

'Yeah,' Robertson said. 'We can talk to you.' He looked around. 'We'll do it right here.'

Ryker guessed it was quiet enough. And at least they weren't trying to lure him somewhere bad.

'Go on, then,' Georgiadis said. 'Talk.'

'His name is Henrik Svenson. He's from Norway. Fourteen years old.'

'A fourteen-year-old from Norway?' Georgiadis said. 'Who was he here with?'

'He came on his own.'

'A fourteen-year-old?'

'It happens.'

'Why'd he come here?' Robertson asked.

'To see his family.'

'And who is his family? No one here reported him missing. No one from Norway has claimed this kid might be theirs.'

'I'm here, aren't I?'

'You're not Norwegian.'

'And you know that how, Sergeant Robertson? Who sounds like he's from Bristol.'

'Dual nationality, Mr Ryker.'

'Exactly.'

Robertson glowered.

'So you're his family? From Norway?' Georgiadis said, sounding a bit confused.

'No. I'm a friend of his family.'

'You claim to know him, yet his family hasn't come forward?' Robertson said. 'Either here or in Norway.'

'I've come from Norway,' Ryker said. 'I'm pretty sure I already said that. And his family here didn't know he was coming, so they won't know he's missing. And as you haven't let me see the body yet, I can't confirm whether or not it's actually him. Are you getting it now?'

Neither looked impressed by Ryker's summation.

'Except you arrived here in Crete today,' Georgiadis said. 'You drove from Chania to here, and the first thing you did was roam the beach asking questions about a murdered boy. You didn't go to Henrik Svenson's family. You didn't go to the police.'

She had him there.

'How do you know I only arrived today?' Ryker asked.

Georgiadis shrugged and nodded to Ryker's backpack.

'A guess,' she said.

'A good one,' Ryker responded. 'I didn't go to his family here because I don't know them.'

'You said you were a family friend.'

'I didn't say a friend of every single member of his family. And I didn't go to the police because I'm not convinced I can trust them.'

Robertson scoffed. 'Excuse me?'

'Are you part of the investigation team?' Ryker asked.

'No. We're not.'

'Then perhaps it's unfair for me to group you with your colleagues, but from what I've heard, I'm not happy with what's going on here.'

'And what's going on?'

'Potentially a murder by an organized crime gang. Potentially a body washing ashore because of a mistake.'

'A mistake?'

'Yeah. I think Henrik was held captive. His hands were bound, weren't they?'

'Were they?' Robertson said, though his attempted bluff sounded feeble.

'Maybe whoever was holding him didn't mean to kill him, I really don't know, but I'm thinking he tried to escape and ended up, dead or alive, in the water.'

'You've got a good imagination,' Robertson said.

'I have. And wait, it gets better. I'm pretty sure his death would have been ruled an accident or suicide, even. Except remember that rope on his wrists? Probably the worst place for him to wash up, on that beach, because you've got scores of people on the scene straight away. Camera phones, and so on. Impossible to keep that part about the wrists out of the official story, so suicide was a no-go.'

'Why would anyone want to lie about it?' Georgiadis asked, and she sounded genuinely curious.

'Did you know Henrik wasn't alone?' Ryker asked her.

She said nothing. Neither did Robertson.

'He traveled here from Norway on his own. But when he got here he made a friend. Why? I don't know. But the two of them were seen lurking on the beach together, in the bay, in the days before the murder.'

'You know this how?' Robertson said, taking his sunglasses off to reveal two dark eyes full of both intrigue and suspicion. Okay, so maybe these two weren't as dumb as he'd first thought and perhaps weren't as closed-minded either.

'Because I bothered to ask around,' Ryker said. 'Unlike your colleagues from the investigation team.'

'Who says they didn't ask?' Georgiadis said.

Ryker didn't respond to that.

'I'm interested in how you two came to be with me at all,' Ryker said. 'I get the whole point about beach patrol, wanting your tourists to see the pristine side of your island rather than the seedy underbelly. But I don't buy it.'

'You don't buy what?'

'That you two just happened upon me as I was talking to a group of teens on the beach. So, who asked you to come here? Who tipped you off?'

They looked at one another again, but neither said a word in response. The fact he'd spotted what he assumed was their vehicle in the same parking lot as Ryker's moped was just another in a number of oddities about their presence which he didn't like. Of course, he'd wondered all through his trip from Athens whether the watchers from there would be lurking in the shadows still. Whether they'd somehow use a connected network to follow his moves.

The latter looked the most likely now. Although, whatever the purpose of them watching his movements, it did all seem... a light touch. Certainly compared to measures Ryker had been subjected to in the past. There were no cloth sacks over the head here. No silent transfers in the back of a van to a dark, grimy location for any manner of 'interrogation'. And Ryker really had seen all manner of that.

'The thing that gets me the most,' Ryker said. 'Is that I know why Henrik came here. And by extension, I know why he's now dead.'

'And that is?' Georgiadis asked, sounding more nervous than at any other point.

'He came here to find his father. His father is not a nice man, if you know what I mean.'

'Not really,' Robertson said.

'But his father isn't here. Only an associate of his is. He lives right around the corner, in the bay. Roman Smolov.'

Yeah. Robertson definitely knew the name. Georgiadis looked away so Ryker couldn't see her full reaction, but that move alone said it all.

'Henrik Svenson came here to see Roman Smolov,' Ryker said.

'A career criminal. Organized crime. He's Ukrainian. You know him?'

'Who are you?' Robertson asked.

'I told you my name.'

'That's not what I meant.'

'I'm just trying to understand why my friend was murdered here.'

'Your friend. A fourteen-year-old boy,' Georgiadis said, his tone clearly insinuating he saw something suspicious about the idea.

'Yes,' Ryker said. 'So now I've laid everything out for you, perhaps you can call your colleagues and arrange for me to see the body. So I can confirm that it is Henrik Svenson. Or not.'

'What do we do?' Georgiadis asked Robertson, in Greek of course.

'Your jobs,' Ryker said, himself switching tongue. 'You only need to do your jobs.'

She glared at him. Anger. But it was she who had tried to be sneaky.

'Where are you staying?' Robertson asked.

'You already asked me that. I haven't decided.'

'Then you'd better decide,' he said. 'We'll help you get there. Make sure you're checked in. Then you'll sit and wait for us to get back in touch.'

'You want to keep watch on me?'

'I certainly do.'

Ryker shrugged. 'Do you have any recommendations?'

Robertson looked Ryker up and down, somewhat disapprovingly, then glanced over his shoulder.

'Yeah,' he said. 'Follow me. May as well keep this simple.'

They set off toward the hotel right in front of them.

17

The Hellenic Paradise Hotel was definitely not a paradise. It was barely a hotel. At least it was Hellenic. Basic was a kind way to describe it. No clifftop pool here. No pool at all. But then it had the beach right there, and the ocean beyond the fifty or so neatly arranged sun loungers. Their blue-and-white striped cushions matched the Greek flag, though the blue was faded and the white murky, the tired look matching most of the internal decoration of the hotel.

Ryker's room was poky, a little chilly, with pebble-dashed walls with off-white paint – perhaps bright white when originally painted – and a classic tiled floor. Threadbare curtains framed the view outside. Not a view to be wowed by. Ryker's second-floor room looked over the road, with nothing but a paltry glimpse of the hills beyond, over the tops of the buildings opposite. Apparently, all the sea-view rooms were taken.

Still, he saw little point in spending more money than necessary. The Royal Venetian, where Ryan the gossiper was staying, was likely at least twice the price. At least twice as nice too, though.

A dark-wood bed, dark-wood cupboard and side table, and an

aging shower en suite finished the look. No in-room safe here. Given the theft in Athens, Ryker had only brought with him the bare minimum of personal possessions – cash, a single change of clothes, and a new burner phone he'd purchased near the ferry port in Athens.

Robertson and Georgiadis had accompanied Ryker into the reception. Had stood watch while Ryker organized the room – for one night only. Had shepherded him to the stairs – the hotel had no elevator. Once in his room, he wondered how long they'd hang around for.

Not long. All of five minutes later he spotted them walking across the public parking lot, which he had a good enough glimpse of if he stuck his head and shoulders out of the window – although he couldn't see his moped from that angle, nor the near end of the lot closest to the hotel.

Ryker stayed inside for only twenty minutes. He hadn't come to Crete to sit and wait on others.

He moved back down the stairs, through the airy reception area. No sign of the police. Not on the inside, at least. Robertson and Georgiadis had gone, but parked all of ten yards from the hotel entrance he spotted a police motorbike.

The rider – a man, Ryker thought – remained on the bike, helmet on, though the engine was off as he played with his phone. When he spotted Ryker he quickly put the phone away and put his hands to the handlebars as though at the ready, no attempt at subtlety. His head remained up, pointed in Ryker's direction as Ryker moved across the parking lot. But he didn't go to his moped. Instead, he walked to the road, took a quick look left and right, then darted across to the other side.

Behind him, he heard the motorbike rumble into life. He glanced over his shoulder as the bike rolled toward the parking lot exit, the rider's feet hovering an inch above the ground as though he wasn't yet sure if he needed to give chase or not.

Ryker kept going straight ahead, into the tiny parking lot of a restaurant on the other side of the road, the space big enough for only three vehicles. At the end of the plot sat a six-foot-tall fence. Beyond that, a hill of jagged rocks and worn-looking shrubbery rose into the distance, several hundred yards of nothing much.

When he reached the fence Ryker stopped and turned. The policeman came to a stop again, feet on the ground, one hand on the radio attached to his shirt. Probably asking for advice as to what to do next.

Ryker smiled, turned, and scaled the fence, then began his ascent.

After a couple of hundred yards, he looked behind him again. Glorious. The way the hill swept downward to the sea, the way the shoreline curved in and out from left to right. The natural landscape was breathtaking, and all in all, from high up, it was clear the authorities had done a good job of keeping the developments of the area low-key and low in scale. No mammoth high-rises, no ugly monoliths. The hotels and resorts and homes that lined the coast – whether new or old, high-end or not – all blended.

But the view wasn't really why Ryker had turned at all. His eyes refocused on the policeman. He hadn't moved from the spot. It wasn't as if he could follow on his vehicle, and whoever he'd spoken to had obviously told him not to bother chasing on foot.

He smiled, turned, and carried on up the hill. A strenuous walk, the incline becoming more steep and rocky in places. He looked behind him every now and then but didn't stop walking until the coastal properties were out of sight below him, beyond a ridge – about a mile away, he believed.

He looked all around him. Nothing much out here, other than a few farms dotted about, a few clumps of trees. He'd already looked on the GPS map on his phone before leaving the hotel so had a vague idea of his route, so as to not come into trouble with any farmers and their shotguns. He edged west, and soon after found a descent back to the coast, the deep blue water shimmering and stretching out to the horizon.

As he turned a corner, following a partly worn dirt track, he spotted two figures a couple of hundred yards away, walking toward him. He kept his eyes fixed on them, trying to decipher what he was seeing. Not police – at least, not uniformed police. A man and a woman. For a fleeting moment, he wondered whether it was the twosome from Athens... No. These two were older. The woman had silvery hair, the man was nearly bald. They both wore walking gear – hiking boots and thick socks, khaki shorts, T-shirts.

Ryker carried on toward them, keeping his focus, but not expecting a threat.

'Afternoon,' the man said in English when Ryker was five yards from them.

He smiled and nodded. Ryker did the same. They carried on their way. Just a couple of holidaymakers bored of the beach, or perhaps expatriates.

Further down the hill, Ryker spotted his destination. The villa had a prime location within the bay, taking up the highest point in the arc of land. It wasn't the biggest though. Amongst the half-dozen properties, he saw at least two that were larger, more sleek, and more modern-looking too – split-level white boxes interspersed with huge windows all over. Very nice, but probably a nightmare to keep cool in a place like Crete, at least without expensive air-conditioning whirring non-stop. But the villa Ryker headed for was quite different. A much more traditional-looking, white-rendered building with red-brick trims, single-story, with narrow, arched windows, and an inner courtyard. Within the luscious-looking gardens, he spotted a long but plain rectangular pool, and a tennis court. A tall wall ran around the perimeter, grand double-gates marked the entrance along a narrow descent from the road. Ryker stopped and looked behind him. No one following. He pulled to the side, behind a rock, and crouched down as he took his backpack from his shoulders. He took out the binoculars – one of the very basic items he'd brought with him.

No sign of any cars on the property, though he noted the separate garage block with three rolled-down doors, so it was certainly possible that vehicles were parked up inside. No signs of anyone either. The tennis court was empty, the pool too, no one in the gardens that he could see.

No police car or uniforms in sight, which was on the one hand a good thing, though also made Ryker a little dubious. He'd given Roman Smolov's name to Robertson and Georgiadis, so wouldn't they have expected Ryker to end up here having evaded the sentry at the hotel?

Ryker put the binoculars away, put a cap over his head so any cameras on his approach to the property wouldn't capture his face, and got moving once again, edging with just a little bit more caution than before. He reached the road, no fence or wall or anything to separate him from the tarmac, still no signs of the police or anyone else at, or around, Smolov's home.

Ryker darted across the road, down the narrow drive, and to the closed gates. An intercom. A single CCTV camera. Ryker kept his head low and moved along the wall, away from the gates. The wall rose above him, seven feet high, but clearly designed for aesthetics as much as security, with no barbed wire or any other similar deterrent. Ryker moved on until he was in a quiet spot where trees and undergrowth covered his presence from the road and the neighboring properties, then he reached up, grabbed the top of the wall, and scrabbled his way up. A quick look below and beyond as he perched, then he dropped down, landing with a light thud in a flower bed, sinking into a crouch.

The plan from there? Improvise, to a certain extent. Ryker wanted to find and get in front of Smolov. He wanted to confront him, not just about Henrik, but about his boss, Jesper, who Ryker still knew next to nothing about, but who was undoubtedly the endgame of Ryker's mission. He knew little of Smolov, but Ryker had dealt with badder apples than this, he was sure, and he really didn't care whether he got in front of Smolov on his own or the Ukrainian's terms. He'd deal with either. And if the guy really wasn't here, then Ryker would simply do all he could to pry, and figure out what he could about the shady foreigner.

Ryker took a good look around him. The villa entrance, large turning circle in front, was thirty yards away, the garage block to the left, the tennis court to the right. The swimming pool was out of sight now, at the back of the property, overlooking the bay beyond.

Ryker rose from his spot and moved for the garage. Better cover in that direction, if someone was watching. From where? Well, he'd spotted three more CCTV cameras dotted about the place, though they were mainly focused on the area immediately around the buildings. If he kept to the foliage as long as he could before moving to the garage block, he'd remain out of view. Was there someone inside, watching from the windows? Possible, but he saw no indication of that.

He soon reached the garage and pulled up against a side window. A quick glance. Space for three cars inside, but only one there – a bright yellow Ferrari. Did that mean someone was home after all, or was the pricey car just a weekend runabout and the homeowners had headed out in another vehicle?

Ryker walked around the back of the garage and to the far side. The ocean came back into view, as did the swimming pool where the water gently rippled. No sign anyone had been in it recently, given the tiles all around the pool were entirely dry.

But one of multiple sets of patio doors at the back of the house was open, and as Ryker stood and listened, he heard voices inside. Talking, or was it a TV or radio?

Ryker took a chance and made a dash from the garage and to the corner of the villa. He kept his head low, aware of the camera above him on the eaves, though even if they couldn't see his face, if someone was watching the feeds in real-time they would know he was there. Likewise, if the cameras were motion-triggered. But would they be set like that if someone was home?

Ryker didn't know. He'd remained cautious and ready.

From closer up, the voices were a little more distinct. A man and a woman. Their chat was boisterous and playful, and in a language familiar to Ryker in sound, even if he couldn't speak it all that well – Ukrainian.

Giggling, then the next moment the woman dashed out of the open doors and Ryker pulled back a little. The woman swept out onto the patio tiles, nothing but a bikini and a sarong that did a poor job of covering her nicely bronzed skin. In her forties, she was short and stocky, but in good shape, her dyed blonde hair flapping as she bounced along. Following after her was a much taller, much broader man. Boxer shorts. A leather belt flapped around his neck. A little weird, Ryker thought. He had one black sock pulled up his left ankle. Ryker could guess by the giddy looks on both their faces where the rest of his clothes were. He also knew exactly who the man wasn't: Roman Smolov. Even if he was pretty sure the woman was Mrs Smolov. An interesting turn.

'No, no, you've had enough,' she said to him playfully, swatting his wandering hands away like he was a troublesome fly.

Ryker pulled further around the corner, not that either of them had paid him the slightest attention.

'They'll be back soon,' she said, hitting his arm when he grabbed her butt and pulled her close, kissing her shoulder.

'Alexei, come on! Seriously.' She shoved him away and looked just a little bit annoyed and Ryker noticed a moment of doubt in the big guy's eyes. 'And I need to do my swim. I don't look this good just from lazing around.'

'No. It's from screwing me. That's all the workout you need.'

He went in again but she pushed him back once more, then both stopped dead, staring at each other. Ryker soon caught on why. Car engine. More than one.

'They're early,' Alexei said.

The woman laughed at him, as though amused by his predicament. Was he not meant to be there at all? Or was he simply meant to be dressed and not screwing her?

Alexei darted for the house. Ryker listened with keen interest as he watched Smolov's wife. She didn't go for a swim after all. Instead, she adjusted her sarong so it covered a bit more flesh, then made her way inside.

Ryker crept along the side of the house. By the time he reached the front, the cars were in sight, coming through the open gates. A big black BMW SUV, and a big silver Mercedes S-Class.

The cars crunched to a stop on the gravel turning circle. Two men and a woman got out of the front car. With smart casual clothing, they weren't exactly ridiculously obvious as gangsters or heavies or whatever they thought they were, but they really weren't that subtle either, with their overly formal stances, their big sunglasses, and their swagger. One of the men had a noticeable bulge under his shirt – a barely concealed gun. Out of the second car came two more men, plus a girl. Possibly a teenager. She looked hacked off by something. Perhaps having to be chaperoned by a hefty entourage. Smolov's daughter?

The front door to the house opened and out came Alexei.

Dressed now, though he looked a little flustered – at least to Ryker. Given his clothing – smart navy shorts and a cream long-sleeved shirt – Ryker guessed he was yet another in the crew.

One noticeable absentee from the gaggle? Smolov himself. So where was he?

'Let's get inside, then we need to call him,' one of the men said to Alexei.

With that, they all disappeared into the villa, with the exception of the woman and one of the men from the silver car. Ryker watched them for a moment. Nothing was happening there, they simply stood and ignored each other and both were soon on their phones.

Ryker turned and moved toward the back of the house once more. He stopped when he spotted Smolov's wife. She was spread out on a lounger, facing the house. Facing him? He took a step out into the open. He hadn't come here to hide. She didn't flinch.

'Can I help you?' she asked Ryker in English. Entirely calm. Not exactly what he'd expected.

'Maybe you can,' Ryker said, stepping closer to her.

'Who are you?'

'I'm looking for Roman Smolov.'

'He's not here.'

'You're his wife?'

'Am I?'

Ryker said nothing.

'I asked who you are?' she said.

'An old friend.'

She laughed. 'Yeah, okay. You realize there are several people in that house. Most of them armed. Perhaps you should turn around and go back wherever you came from.'

'You don't seem very bothered about me being here.'

'Why would I be? I already explained the position. Your problem, not mine.'

'What about Alexei? Is he your problem?'

Even with her big sunglasses on, he could tell she didn't like that comment.

She stepped up off the lounger, reaching under the cushion as she did so to pull out a handgun which she pointed to Ryker's chest. He didn't budge. Didn't flinch, even if the way she held it suggested she wasn't unused to the weapon.

'Sorry, I didn't catch that?' she said, taking confident steps toward him.

Ryker put his hands up.

'I mean, I'm pretty sure you did,' he said. 'But, what you do with men like Alexei, in your own home, is really none of my business, right?'

'Damn right.'

'So what do I care? Do what you want. But I do care about Smolov. I need to talk to him.'

She carried on walking until she was all of three yards away.

'About what?'

'About a murdered teenager from Norway.'

A slight twitch in her face. What was that?

Then movement behind Ryker. 'Is everything o—'

The female sentry from the front. Was she armed too? Ryker really didn't know. He didn't wait to find out either. Instead, he drove forward. Smolov's wife was caught in a quandary. She didn't fire. At least not until Ryker had already barged into her, and pushed her gun hand away from him. The shot boomed. The bullet flew harmlessly away. Ryker grabbed her arm, twisted, kicked low onto the side of her leg to cause it to buckle. He swiped the gun from her grip. Moved up behind her, kicked her in the back. She fell to the floor. Ryker lifted the gun and pointed it at the other woman.

Not armed. But not looking particularly scared either.

'You're in a lot of trouble,' she said.

She remained perfectly calm. Unlike Mrs Smolov. She propped herself up on the ground, turned to Ryker, her face lined with rage.

'Alexei! Vlad!' she screamed, the force so hard her voice cracked.

Commotion inside. An immediate response to her call for help.

Ryker darted forward, toward the other woman, who stood her ground, as though ready to counter-attack. A surprise to Ryker. Then he fired the gun. The bullet thwacked into the slab inches from her feet, she lost her focus and Ryker shoved her to the ground as he blasted past.

He sprinted away from the house, toward the wall. Behind him, talking, then shouting. Shouting at him. Footsteps. He glanced. Four men. Two with handguns. One had a shotgun.

Boom.

Ryker ducked instinctively. In the clear.

The wall was ten yards away. Sirens beyond. What the hell? Another gunshot – a handgun this time. The bullet smacked into the white render in front of Ryker, sending a plume of dust into the air. Ryker leaped for the wall, practically ran up it, swiveled, and fell to the other side.

He ran and hurdled through trees and undergrowth, in two minds as to where to go. The police sirens got louder. He was sure he could lose them if he headed up the hill once more. But where to then?

Ryker reached the road. Flashing lights. To his left. Two cars blasted across the tarmac toward him. He tossed the gun – the police were much more likely to immediately shoot him if he was armed – and took his chance. He sprinted across the road. Made it all of five yards on the other side before screeching tires filled the air. Car doors opened. More shouting. A mixture of Greek and English.

He didn't doubt their threats. Seconds later, as Ryker scrambled, two gunshots rang out. Both bullets landed within a foot of him.

He stopped. Turned. Four police officers. Robertson and Georgiadis among them. All four had their handguns pointed at Ryker. Beyond them... No sign of Smolov's crew whatsoever. So where were they?

'Come down, Ryker,' Robertson shouted out. 'You won't get another warning shot.'

Ryker sighed. It wasn't worth the risk in testing whether Robertson was bluffing or not. Even if they stayed put and didn't follow on foot, Ryker had a good hundred yards or so of open ground to cover before he was out of sight of the road.

He put his hands into the air and slowly walked toward them. Still no sign of Smolov's lot anywhere.

Ryker reached the officers and Georgiadis did the honors of swiveling Ryker around and slapping the cuffs over his wrists.

'You're under arrest,' she said.

'No shit.'

Robertson gave him a crooked smile and grabbed his arm to pull him toward the patrol car. He opened the door and pushed Ryker's head down. Ryker let them have their moment and sank down into the seat without resistance. The door slammed shut. Moments later they were heading away, toward the capital. As they went past Smolov's home the gates were open. Smolov's wife stood there with Alexei, the other woman, and one other guy. No guns in sight now. Smolov's wife had an evil grin on her face.

Ryker looked away. He glanced at a bystander. Of course, there'd be a bystander ogling. But then Ryker did a double-take and his eyes rested there. The bystander was on a moped. At the side of the road. Kind of hidden by foliage, but not really. What had caught Ryker's attention?

The license plate. Not just a moped. *His* damn moped.

'What the hell?' he said out loud.

'Shut up,' Robertson said, disinterested.

As the police car drove past, the rider pulled the helmet off. Not only *his* moped but a face he recognized. Young-looking, thin, long dark hair.

Not a ghost, but Henrik Svenson.

18

SEVEN DAYS PREVIOUSLY

It turned out Reva didn't like the Tunisians any more than he liked the Egyptians, but at least the deal was done. He traveled back to the villa in the Maserati GT, Alexei driving the smooth V8. Only the two of them had gone to the meeting. Reva's decision. The less muscle the better, he'd decided. Word had obviously gotten to the Tunisians about Hassan's fate, so an ultra-cautious approach was necessary. It had worked. The meeting had ended with hand-shakes and an agreement, even if there remained room for improvement on the terms.

Reva's phone buzzed in his pocket as they headed back through Heraklion and toward Smolov's villa. Jesper.

'All good?' the boss asked.

'It's done.'

'With the extra too?'

'Of course.'

'Then you can't stay there much longer. I'll need you back closer to me to organize everything else.'

Strangely, Reva felt a little disappointed to hear that. In his short time on the Greek isle – to his surprise, really – he'd warmed to the place. Perhaps because everything seemed so easy here. Certainly compared to back home where real, brutal conflict was ever-present.

No, if he stayed here too long, he'd only become soft, like the rest of them.

'I'll fly to Athens tomorrow,' Reva said. 'Send me six men. We'll use our properties there to start everything rolling.'

'Okay. But don't waste time there. Get them ready, then come home. I need you back with me soon. We need to get Roman back.'

'I understand. But I want to find who betrayed us first.'

'You're sure someone did?'

'If not, then I still want to know what happened. We can't just forget.'

'Keep me updated.'

The call ended.

Silence, but Reva sensed his companion glancing at him every now and then.

'What?' he said.

'Any problems?'

'Just drive.'

He looked out of his window and neither said another word until they arrived at Smolov's villa. Alexei opened the gates and rolled the car through, then brought it to a stop.

'What is it?' Reva asked.

'Something's wrong.'

Reva looked around the grounds in front of the car. Three other cars were parked up by the house. So plenty of men about, somewhere. But he could see no one on guard. That was the problem. Where were they?

'There,' Alexei said as a flash of black bolted between the open space beyond the house and the garage.

Alexei drove on at pace. Stopped by the other cars. Both men jumped out and set off for the side of the house. Shouting drifted over. Banging. More shouting. A cry of pain.

'Hassan's crew?' Alexei asked.

'They wouldn't dare,' Reva said through gritted teeth. Though in a way, he hoped it was. He'd love the chance to show Hassan his true dark side.

They passed between the house and the garage. Three of their men. No, four – Reva spotted one in the trees too. No sign of Sylvia. But Iya was there, closest to the house.

'What is it?' Reva said to her as he and Alexei came to a stop.

'Over there,' she said, pointing to the trees.

A moment later and two more men came into view, dragging a little bundle of a thing that was kicking and shouting.

'Shut him up,' Reva demanded and one of the men smacked the scrawny kid on the ear to quieten him down.

They marched the runt over. A boy. All of fourteen, fifteen.

'What is this?' Reva asked the men, before turning to Iya.

'There were two of them,' Iya said. 'Inside the house when we got back. They gutted Leo as they were fighting us off.'

Two kids? Against how many adults?

'He's dead?' Reva asked.

Iya nodded. Reva looked at the boy.

'Thieves?' he said to no one in particular.

'No,' Iya said. 'They were looking for Roman.'

'How do you know that?'

'Because the little bastard had a knife to my throat when he asked me where Roman is.'

'This little bastard?'

Iya paused as she scrutinized the kid.

'I'm not sure.'

'Who are you?' Reva asked the boy.

No answer as he stared at the floor. One of the lumps holding him twisted his arm further behind his back, causing the boy to cry out in pain.

'Who sent you here?' Reva said.

Nothing from the boy still. A cool character given his position.

'Take him inside. Find out everything you can about him.' Then he looked around. 'And get down on the beach, find the other one and bring him here.'

'Is that a good idea?' Alexei said. 'Causing a scene on the beach, again?'

'Just do as I tell you.'

Nobody moved.

'I said, get him inside!' Reva shouted as he turned to Iya. 'He killed one of ours. You get him to talk. Or I'll do it myself. My way.'

Iya said nothing, though the look of disquiet on her face was telling. She motioned to the goons who dragged the boy toward the house as three others headed off for the steps to the beach. Reva fixed his gaze back on Alexei. The big man's look of embarrassment said it all.

Perhaps these lot were missing their boss more than Reva had realized.

Time to show them what real leadership looked like.

* * *

Two hours later and the kid was barely conscious. They hadn't gone too hard on him. Not yet. Not so soon. Reva had only been in the room with the boy for a total of thirty or so minutes in that time, leaving the grunt work to the grunts. But they were getting nowhere simply beating the boy.

Reva and Vlad were the only ones in the room now. Vlad

nursed his knuckles; the kid's head was bowed, his body limp on the chair he was roped to.

Reva caught Vlad's eye and shook his head, disappointed. He'd not met the man before this trip, and all he'd seen so far was a lump of muscle with nothing between the ears. Useful, to an extent, but a man who couldn't think for himself never lasted long. Sooner or later, no matter how good the instructions from above, they found themselves needing to make their own decisions, and that's when they came unstuck. Often fatally.

The boy moaned and tried to lift his head. Reva stepped toward him and crouched down in front. He reached out and used a single finger under the chin to lift the boy's head up.

'Why aren't you talking?' Reva asked, his voice soft.

The boy said nothing, wouldn't look him in the eye. Well, he only had one eye that he could use to do that, the other was swollen shut from the beating, but he instead chose to look down, at the floor.

'You're young,' Reva said. 'This isn't your world. I can make this last for days. Weeks. Do you understand that? Can you imagine what I can do to you? Better to do what you can to help us, to help you.'

Nothing.

'Do you really believe we'll stop at hitting you in the face with fists?'

Still nothing.

Reva used the same finger to turn the boy's head to the right, toward where the table was laid out with the tools Reva had asked for. Tools as of yet not used.

'This isn't a joke,' Reva said. 'I'm not bluffing, or simply trying to scare you. If you don't help me, then let me be clear. I will take you apart. Fingers, toes to start with.' He paused. The boy's body trembled. 'Skin, limbs next. Did you know I was a field surgeon in the Ukrainian army?'

Some sort of incoherent murmur.

'That's actually true. I'm not joking. I've seen real conflict. I know how to fix horrible wounds. Severed limbs, stab wounds, lacerations, snapped bones. I can break you, take you apart, without killing you.'

The boy said nothing but he quivered with fright.

'We don't even know if he understands English,' Vlad said.

Not helpful. Reva shot him a look and Vlad looked away apologetically. The point was valid enough, but English was a decent bet for communication, Reva had decided, even if they had no clue who the kid was, or where he'd come from.

'Can you even imagine the pain you'll feel as I slice you apart?' Reva said.

'P... Please.'

So he did understand.

'Why did you come here?'

No answer.

'Who sent you? Hassan? The Egyptians?'

No answer, no nod or shake of the head, but something in the boy's eye suggested no. He'd not heard the name before. Egyptians meant nothing to him.

'Russians? The FSB?'

Did they operate so underhandedly that they'd now send kids to do their dirty work?

'N... No... No.'

The boy shook his head, each word seemed a struggle. Mainly because it looked like his jaw was broken from Vlad's poor attempt at getting him to talk.

'What's your name?' Reva asked.

But he got no answer. Instead, the boy sobbed, tears rolling, spit drooling, snot bubbling from his nose. Reva looked down and spotted the widening patch of liquid underneath the chair.

He stood up and stepped back. Turned to Vlad.

'Time to step this up. Get him on the table. Give him the adrenalin shot. That'll wake him up for the next step.'

The kid only had a little fight left. Some gentle persuasion would tip him over the edge.

Vlad looked unsure, but moved forward and worked on the ropes on the boy's ankles. The kid moaned and writhed pathetically in response.

'Fuck, his legs are soaked,' Vlad said, disgusted.

Reva shook his head. Then the door burst open behind him. He whipped around to see Alexei. Out of breath, red-faced.

'The other one. We think we found him.'

Reva spun back to Vlad. 'Wait for me.'

Then he turned and raced out of the room, after Alexei, up the steps from the basement, through the villa to the pool area. It was dark out now but the security spotlights lit up the area like it was daytime.

'Where?' Reva said.

'He was in the trees. Iya and the others set off to the beach after him.'

They moved for the steps. Reva paused when he reached the top. He looked down at the beach below. Difficult to see in the darkness. Some of the beach areas, by the hotels, were delicately lit with lanterns and string lights, but much of the space in front, the vast expanse of water, stretching into the distance, remained inky black.

'Come on,' Reva said, moving down the steps.

He could see no one on the beach, the only sound was his own breathing and the roar of waves. He looked up and down the bay.

'There,' Alexei said, pointing to his right.

Sure enough, Iya came striding out of the dark toward them. Alone. She didn't look happy. Her nose streamed blood.

'He got away.'

'How?' Reva said, clenching his fists.

'It's dark. I didn't see him. He hit me. A bat or an oar or something.'

'You were the only one? Where are all the others?'

As if on cue, two other lumps appeared from the other direction.

'Anything?' one of them asked.

Reva didn't even answer. He turned for the steps and stormed up them. The others all followed.

'He came back for a reason,' Reva said to no one in particular. 'To save his friend, perhaps, or to finish what he started.'

'Which is what?'

'How the hell should I know?'

They reached the top. Reva paused and turned and looked around, back out across the dark bay. All appeared calm and serene down there.

'Brave kid,' Reva said. 'All of you, stay on watch out here. If he comes back, no more mistakes.'

He turned away from them and moved for the house, back through to the stairs for the basement. He paused. A bang below. Moaning.

Vlad? He hadn't waited. Reva bounded down the stairs, ready to have it out with the guy. He reached the door, opened it, then stopped.

Vlad was on his feet. Chest heaving from exertion. A slash across his cheek wept blood. The boy lay on the floor. Curled up. Not moving.

Vlad looked over. 'I'm sorry,' he said.

Reva said nothing.

'He jumped me. He tried to get away. I just... I...'

'You what? Killed him?'

Vlad said nothing, but the look in his eyes said everything. The boy was dead.

19

PRESENT

The police interview room was little different from the countless other police interview rooms Ryker had seen over many years. A little more tired and worn perhaps than some of the others, but really just a garden variety, plain, boring room. A simple metal chair for Ryker, two others the opposite side of the Formica-topped table in the middle of the room. A barred window behind him. Locked door in front. Large mirror to his right, which surely had an observation room beyond. Nothing exciting, nothing too disturbing either. Certainly not a room that brought Ryker any great fear for his immediate safety. This was no barbaric interrogation chamber. But that didn't mean he was in any way comfortable or content about being there.

The door opened. He'd been sitting for fourteen minutes on his own, contemplating – mostly about the fact that Henrik was still alive. *Relieved* that Henrik was alive, but confused as to who the dead boy was, and how it all connected – to Smolov, Jesper, himself – which he was sure it did.

Two police officers walked in. Robertson, plus an older, plain-clothed woman. Short, squat. Very serious-looking face. Her hair was pulled back tightly, the skin on her face stretched because of it. She had thin-rimmed metal glasses perched on the edge of her nose. She looked like a school headmistress from a bygone era.

A uniformed guard, who remained outside, closed the door and the two officers took the seats in front of Ryker.

'James Ryker?' Robertson said.

'Yes.'

'As you know already, I'm Sergeant Robertson, and this is Second Lieutenant Xenakis.'

So she was ranked higher than Robertson, and her seriousness certainly projected an air of seniority and superiority.

'How is your cell?' Robertson asked.

On arriving at the police station in Heraklion, Ryker had been put into the holding cell for all of half an hour before a guard had brought him to this room.

'Square,' Ryker said.

Xenakis smiled. 'Mr Ryker, do you understand why you are here?' she asked. Her accent made it difficult for Ryker to understand her.

'Please, tell me,' Ryker said. 'I was merely visiting an old friend. Roman Smolov. I'm sure this is all a misunderstanding.'

'Roman Smolov?' Xenakis said. 'This is nothing to do with him.'

'We've arrested you for the murder of Henrik Svenson,' Robertson said.

Ryker glared at the man. What was this?

Robertson carried on, giving Ryker a rundown of his rights. He barely took it in. His brain was too busy.

'As you're a foreign national you have the right to request that we inform your embassy or consulate,' Xenakis said.

'The nearest is the British consulate here in Heraklion,'

Robertson added. 'They can provide you with more advice on the
provision of legal counsel or interpreters.'

'That's fine. I think I understand you two perfectly well,' Ryker
said.

'Right now, yes, but not all our colleagues speak English,'
Robertson added.

'So you don't want us to do that?' Xenakis asked Ryker.

'I'd rather you told me why you think I killed Henrik
Svenson.'

'We'll get to that,' Robertson said. 'First—'

'Actually, I think I'd rather start with that,' Ryker said. 'The
thing is, Henrik Svenson isn't dead. And I'm pretty sure, even in
Greece, you can't arrest someone for murdering another person if
that other person isn't dead.'

Xenakis looked from Ryker to her underling. She leaned over
and whispered in his ear.

'But, Mr Ryker, we do have a murder,' Robertson said. 'And you
know that. It was you who identified the victim, to me, as Henrik
Svenson—'

'Identified? I think I provided you with a name. I *asked* if I
could see the body, to confirm if the victim was, in fact, Henrik
Svenson.'

'Mr Ryker, I'm not sure you're listening—'

'No, you're not listening to me. I didn't kill Henrik Svenson.
He's not dead. I didn't know that earlier when we first met, but I
know that now. How? I saw him today. When you arrested me. He
was right there, sitting on the damn moped I drove here from
Chania.'

Frowns and a confused shared look between the two officers.
Ryker sympathized. His brain remained confused by the whole
thing. Ryker had thought Henrik dead. Instead, the boy was alive
and in Crete, and not only that but he knew Ryker was there too.

Had the audacity to steal Ryker's moped and watch as Ryker was carted away by the police. What on earth was the kid playing at?

'I agree there's a dead teenager,' Ryker said. 'I read about it in the news, and I came all this way because I thought it was Henrik Svenson. But it's not. And I didn't do it. I wasn't even here when he was killed. I arrived today. So either you two are talking shit, or, if you actually have any evidence at all to link me to a murder, it's because I'm being set up.'

Silence.

'So which is it?'

'Let's start with some easy questions,' Xenakis said. 'Can you please confirm your name?'

Ryker sighed before he answered. 'James Ryker.'

'That's your legal name?'

'Yes.' Now at least. James Ryker had all the officiality it needed. A new identity put together for him by his old employer.

'And your occupation is?'

'Retired.'

That drew curious looks from across the table.

'Retired from what?' Robertson asked.

'Consulting.'

A slight shake of the head from Robertson. He didn't believe Ryker at all.

'And what is the purpose of you being in Crete?'

'Personal business,' Ryker said.

'Personal? Can you explain?'

Ryker full-focused on Robertson now. 'Didn't I already? I came to Crete because of the body you found. I thought I knew who it might be. A friend of mine.'

'Henrik Svenson?'

'Yes.'

'You arrived today in Crete?' Xenakis asked.

'Yes. By ferry.'

'And before this, when were you last in Crete?'

'Not for many years.'

'Are you very sure about that?'

'Very sure.'

Xenakis sighed and shuffled about with the papers she'd brought into the room before pulling a single sheet out which she pushed across the table to Ryker.

'This is you?' she said.

Ryker looked down. A photo of a passport. His passport. Name: Carl Logan. The passport that was stolen from him in Athens.

'Is this you?' Xenakis asked again.

'It certainly looks like you,' Robertson added.

'Perhaps it's my long-lost twin.'

'Funny. This passport was found yards away from where our murder victim washed up.'

Ryker laughed. The officers didn't look impressed. 'Seriously?' Ryker asked. 'You think if I was going to murder someone, I'd be dumb enough to bring along a passport? A passport, with a false name. Dumb enough to drop that passport?'

'There are plenty of dumb criminals,' Robertson said. 'Believe me.'

'And the boy washed up on the beach, but you've no idea where he was killed, where he was put into the water. Do you? Why would my passport – the killer's passport – be found where he washed up? It makes no sense. You say this passport was found near the victim? In the sand, I presume you mean? When?'

Robertson glanced at Xenakis. 'It doesn't matter—'

'It does matter. Because I know that passport wasn't uncovered there when the body was found.'

'You know that how?' Robertson asked.

Ryker shook his head. 'I didn't kill that kid.'

'Then how was this passport, of you, found near to the body?'

'*You* say it's me.'

'You're saying it's not?'

'Regardless, that passport wasn't found near the body. Not really. At most, it was found near the same spot where a body was found a few days before. You're telling me that links directly to the murder? How many other people have been on that beach these last few days?'

They both looked at him sternly, but neither made an attempt to answer the question.

'I already said I arrived in Crete today,' Ryker added. 'I didn't kill that kid.'

'Do you have proof of where you were the day he was killed?' Robertson asked. 'Taking into account the time in the water, we believe he was killed six or seven days ago.'

Ryker thought about that for a moment. Of course, he didn't have definitive proof of where he was six or seven days ago. Certainly not on him. Could he try contacting hotels? Car companies? Train stations? There'd be something. Someone who remembered him. A CCTV image of him. But he remained reluctant about sharing too much. Just like he wasn't going to share that the passport of Carl Logan was his. That Carl Logan was an alias. That the passport had been stolen from him in Athens. He could hardly explain to the police that he'd come to Greece to exact bloody revenge, could he?

'If this is all you have, then I suggest you just end this now and let me go,' Ryker said. 'Save yourselves the effort.'

'This isn't all we have,' Xenakis said.

She searched for another piece of paper. She placed that one on top of the passport picture, a snide grin spreading across her face as she did so. Ryker glanced at the picture but not for long.

'Can you tell us what you see there?' Robertson said.

'It looks like a USB thumb drive,' Ryker said.

'It is. Do you recognize it?'

'Not particularly.'

'It has your fingerprints on it.'

Interesting that he said that, but that he hadn't said it about the passport? They'd taken his fingerprints when they'd checked him in at the station. All of an hour ago. Quick work for matching fragments with any certainty.

'Okay?' Ryker said.

'This device, with your fingerprints on it,' Robertson said, looking confident and a little bit smug now, 'was found on the victim. In his pocket.'

'Impossible,' Ryker blurted. He kind of wished he'd kept his mouth shut because the shocked reaction drew an even greater rise in confidence from the two officers.

'Impossible?' Xenakis said. 'Why is that?'

If that really was his thumb drive, part of the equipment stolen from him in Athens, he hadn't even bought that item when the murder took place. Found on the dead body? Ryker was under no doubt now that this was nothing but a crude setup. But by who? And why?

'We've got our forensic team working to find out what data is on the device,' Robertson said. 'Of course, we think it could be crucial to the investigation, in understanding who the victim is and why he was killed.'

'Mr Ryker, can you explain how this item, with your fingerprints on it, came to be in the pocket of a dead teenager?' Xenakis asked.

He ignored her and remained focused on Robertson. 'On the beach today, how exactly did you and Georgiadis come across me? Who told you to be there?'

Robertson frowned and quickly glanced at his boss. 'I don't have to—'

'Then when I was at Smolov's villa. Once again you turned up just at the right time. How?'

'This has nothing to do—'

'With Roman Smolov?'

A pause. 'That wasn't what I was going to say.'

'Good. So we both agree this has everything to do with him.'

Robertson smirked – kind of. 'I wasn't going to say that either.'

'What's your relationship with Roman Smolov?' Xenakis asked Ryker. He'd been about to ask Robertson something similar.

'There is no relationship,' Ryker said. 'I've never met him.'

'Then why were you on his property today?'

'I took a wrong turn.'

She shook her head. Exasperation? Then leaned back in to Robertson and whispered away. Greek, Ryker could tell, though it was too quiet for him to make out the gist of what she said. He wished he hadn't given the game away so early to Georgiadis and Robertson that he had an understanding of the language, but then he hadn't expected events in Crete to spiral quickly into him being wanted for murder.

'Okay, Mr Ryker,' Xenakis said when she'd finished relaying whatever to her colleague, 'we can stop this interview now unless you have anything to add.'

'I'm fine,' Ryker said.

Xenakis gathered the papers. She and Robertson got to their feet.

'If you change your mind about wanting us to contact the consulate for you, please let someone know.'

Ryker nodded. The officers headed for the door. Xenakis knocked and waited.

'Actually, just one last question,' Ryker said as the door was opened by the guard on the other side. Both Robertson and Xenakis half-turned. 'Is it blackmail or greed?'

They turned more fully. Annoyance, but also questioning on their faces.

'Excuse me?' Robertson said.

'Well, it's pretty clear to me that someone, somewhere in your force is corrupt,' Ryker said. 'Could be blackmail, could be greed. So I'm just asking, is it one of you or both of you that's working on the instruction of Roman Smolov?'

The angry glare from Robertson was far more forceful than the look Xenakis gave. Though Ryker wasn't sure which reaction told him more. He'd keep it in mind.

Moments later they'd both left the room, and the door slammed shut.

20

Several hours passed with Ryker alone in the holding cell, during which time he received a single basic meal, pushed through the flap in the door to him. Outside his barred window, nighttime had arrived. He listened to the sounds of the city beyond. Not a big, boisterous city at all, though with the amount of tourists on the island, it certainly had a vibrant enough nighttime scene, he imagined. That said, before long the sounds of the city – traffic noise, mostly – died down, while beyond the closed cell door, in contrast, the station became more noisy at times, with shouting and banging. Perhaps late-night revelers who'd taken things too far, or young hoodlums – thieves, joyriders – caught in the act. As Robertson had said, there were plenty of dumb criminals around, and it was common for them to come out at night when they believed they could get away with their crimes.

Alone in the cell, Ryker had plenty of time to think. He wished he'd had more distraction because the more he thought, the more angry he became. One of his key focuses remained on the twosome from Athens. Not only had they stalked him there, not only had they broken into his hotel room and stolen his things, but they'd used those stolen items to try and implicate Ryker in a murder. The murder of Henrik Svenson? Obviously not, because the teenager was very much still alive. Another facet of the mess that Ryker didn't fully understand but which irked.

Ryker had no doubt the events were all connected – Henrik being in Crete, the murder, the thieves in Athens, Smolov, Ryker being set up – but Ryker's brain simply couldn't figure out how.

What he remained confident of was that the Hellenic police couldn't possibly carry on the charade for long. Ryker hadn't murdered that poor teenager, whoever he was. The phony evidence wouldn't stack up in front of a prosecutor, never mind a judge and jury. Did Robertson and Xenakis already know that? Someone within the police certainly should. So if trial and conviction weren't realistically on the cards, then what was the endgame?

A knock on the door. Ryker looked up as the flap opened. Two eyes peeked in.

Georgiadis.

'Good evening,' she said to him.

'Is it?'

'You're comfortable in there?' she asked.

'Not really.'

'I bet you didn't think your day would go like this.'

He said nothing. Why had she said that?

'I'm just finishing my shift. Back home now for a hot meal and a comfy bed.'

'I'll happily join you if you like,' Ryker said.

She laughed. 'Thanks for the offer, but I have better company waiting for me.'

'I doubt it.'

'Sleep well, James Ryker.'

The flap closed again and Georgiadis was gone. Ryker sat up on the hard mattress, his back against the cold wall. His brain fired with disparate thoughts.

Sleep well?

Not a damn chance.

* * *

The sun was up, its warming rays landing on Ryker's bed, making it nearly impossible to stay asleep. He really wished he could, having found so little shut-eye during the night. A combination of noise, the hard bed, and his continued rumbling thoughts meant he'd tossed and turned for several hours, only finally reaching a fully deep sleep somewhere around five in the morning. Awakening a little before eight he felt groggy, his body leaden.

No more sleep, but nothing else to do, Ryker remained on the bed for well over another hour before the door to the cell finally opened.

He wondered with interest who he'd see standing on the other side. Georgiadis? Robertson? Xenakis?

Just a guard. He spoke in Greek, sullen tones, telling Ryker to get up, to come with him to see his visitor. Ryker did as he was told. The corridor smelled of coffee and cooked meat – obviously, the station staff were having an early morning treat. Ryker's stomach grumbled.

The guard escorted him to the same interview room as the previous day and opened the door. The room wasn't empty. Sitting with his back to Ryker, a man. He stood up, turned as Ryker entered.

The man was tall and lean. Smart linen trousers. Shiny brown shoes. A fitted white shirt, the top two buttons undone. In his late twenties or early thirties, he had a clean-shaven face and neatly styled hair. Together with his tanned skin, he looked exactly like a young Brit who'd landed himself a cushy job abroad that allowed him to spend a lot of time in the sun, and a lot of his money on designer gear. Real estate agent, Ryker might have said. Definitely not police.

'James Ryker?' the guy said, reaching for a handshake as the door closed shut.

Ryker turned. The guard was gone. Ryker took the hand. 'Yeah.'

'I'm Bruno Hitchens. From the British consulate in Crete.'

Ryker tried hard not to roll his eyes. 'Okay?'

'Shall we sit?'

His Scottish accent was neat and polished. Edinburgh, Ryker believed, but definitely a well-off part of the city.

Ryker moved around the table. Two paper coffee cups sat on top. A white paper bag too. Ryker took the seat opposite Hitchens, sat back in the chair, arms folded. Hitchens sat forward, forearms on the table, hands clasped together.

'I wasn't sure if they'd have fed you yet,' Hitchens said, indicating the cups and the bag with his head. 'I got you an Americano. White. And a croissant. If you want it?'

Ryker reached forward and pulled the bag closer to him. He used two fingers to open the bag and peek inside. His belly growled.

He left the croissant and took the coffee cup and had a sip. Lukewarm, and way too milky for his taste, but it was better than nothing.

'Thanks,' Ryker said before taking a bigger sip. No point in letting it go even colder. 'I didn't ask for the consulate to be contacted.'

'No. But we became aware of your situation anyway.'

'How?'

'I'm not entirely sure. But I was asked to come here to see you.'

'And your job is?'

'This.'

'This? Prisoner liaison?'

Hitchens laughed. 'That's not my official title, but you're probably aware we get a lot of British tourists here, so... naturally—'

'You get a lot of idiots getting themselves arrested. Most regularly after them having too many beers.'

Hitchens laughed again, a little more nervously this time.

'Yeah. That's part of it. But it's not very often we get British nationals arrested for murder.'

'Good to know.'

'Probably not so good for you.'

'Though obviously, if you look at the concoction they're calling evidence, you'll see it's a load of bull. So—'

Hitchens unclasped his hands and held an open palm up to halt Ryker.

'Sorry, Mr Ryker, I don't have the authority to interfere in the legal proceedings against you. No one at the consulate does. That's not our purpose. My role is simply to monitor and report on your well-being, and to make sure you're aware of what is happening to you, and that you have all of the assistance that can be afforded to you by local law.'

Ryker said nothing to that. Just sighed. He drank some more of his coffee. He really wanted to pick up the pastry, but wouldn't yet.

'But, having said that,' Hitchens continued, 'there is something I wanted to talk to you about.'

'Which is?'

'Your identity.'

'Because?'

'You're claiming to be James Ryker.'

'Not claiming. I am.'

'The police said they found no ID on you. I've had a look in our systems and... I mean, I think I found which James Ryker, but...'

'What's your question?'

'What exactly is it you do?'

Ryker's eyes narrowed as he stared at the young man. 'I'm retired.'

'Really? From what?'

'Why's that important?'

'Because part of the evidence against you—'

'I thought you said you wouldn't, or couldn't interfere in the legal proceedings?'

'Well, yes, technically, but that doesn't mean that I'm not allowed to be privy to the police's work, especially if they ask for information.'

'So they asked you to check up on me, basically.'

The nervous rub to the back of his neck and picking up his coffee to delay gave away the answer.

'What exactly have the Greek police asked you for?' Ryker said.

'That's not how it is. But I've been made aware of the passport they found connected with the murder you've been arrested for. The passport, which I have to say is... Well, it's you, isn't it? Except with the name Carl Logan. Very official-looking. And the passport is actually properly registered, useable, except... The identity doesn't really exist, as far as I can see.'

Ryker said nothing. Instead, he finished his coffee, reached forward, and took the croissant from the paper bag. He sank his teeth in and tore off a big mouthful. Hitchens eyed him suspiciously.

'The thing is, I spent a couple of hours yesterday digging, trying to find out about James Ryker, and Carl Logan, and... It really doesn't look right to me.'

'This is really good,' Ryker said, holding up the part-eaten croissant. 'Thank you.'

He took another big bite.

'There are plenty of Carl Logans. Alive and dead. But none that match your description, the date of birth on that passport. I haven't shared this with the Hellenic police because, well, I thought I'd better run it all by you first. It's all a bit...'

His eyes narrowed as Ryker shoved the final third of the croissant into his mouth. They sat in silence as Ryker chewed then swallowed.

'It's all a bit what?' Ryker asked.

'Who are you, exactly?' Hitchens asked.

'I'm James Ryker.'

'Because if there's something... If you're someone who's... If there's someone I can contact to help—'

'Bruno Hitchens,' Ryker said.

A raised eyebrow in response.

'That's your name?'

'Yes.'

'Tell me about yourself.'

'What... What do you want to know?'

'Why Bruno?'

He smiled now, though looked just a little embarrassed. 'My dad was a boxing fan. You know, Frank—'

'Yeah, I know who he is. You don't look much like him.'

Hitchens laughed. 'Yeah, there is that.'

'What else? Why and how the consulate in Crete?'

'Why? Because... Well, basically... It's a job, isn't it? And I like traveling.'

'So you became a consulate worker? Visiting prisoners. Why not go backpacking?'

'I... Honestly? I couldn't afford it. I studied law at university, had a mountain of debt.'

'Law? But you're not a lawyer.'

'Not exactly.'

'Why not?'

'You're a bit older than me, but it's a bitch out there even for grads,' Hitchens said, in such a way as to make Ryker realize he'd hit a nerve. 'Like a lot of my friends, I struggled to get a job after university. At least one that didn't simply involve me sacrificing everything working sixty-hour weeks in a city.'

'So how did you end up here?'

He looked at Ryker more suspiciously now, as though he couldn't understand why it was him being interviewed.

'I don't see the relevance—'

'Just humor me.'

Hitchens paused, sighed, then said, 'I couldn't find a full-time job I wanted, so I spent ski seasons in the Alps, brushing up on my French while I was there. I spent summer seasons repping on the Med, brushing up on my Greek and Spanish, and... I guess with my legal background and my language skills and my desire to work somewhere other than the UK, I somehow ended up here.'

'This is your first posting?'

'Second. My first was Majorca. This one's better.'

Ryker nodded. That was enough questions. Did he believe Hitchens? Actually, he kind of did.

Why did he care? This wasn't the first time Ryker had found himself in jail in a foreign country on a false charge. It wasn't the first time he'd had an apparent British government employee come to him unannounced for his 'welfare'. The last time that happened Ryker had been in a shabby Mexican jail overrun by gangs, mostly those linked to warring drug cartels. In Mexico on semi-official business, Ryker had been locked up following a sting operation for 'crimes' he'd previously committed on Mexican soil as part of his work for the JIA. The stooge who'd been sent to him that time – a woman named Willoughby – had, like Hitchens, claimed to be a simple consulate employee. She had in fact been a junior intelligence officer – junior, but very smart and conniving, in a good way – sent by Ryker's bosses to figure out if he was spilling about who he was, who he worked for, and to figure out if it was worth the effort in trying to save him.

They decided it was – not that Ryker had ever explicitly asked for their help in getting him released. Nor would he ask this time. Could he make a phone call to London, to old contacts, to have strings pulled to help him get out of jail? He could certainly try. But he really was retired now. He didn't want those ties to his old life to exist, never mind have to rely on them when things got tough. Perhaps more than anything, he didn't want to have to show that desperate hand before he had even figured out who was trying to frame him and why.

As for Hitchens? Was he really a prisoner liaison, or an intelligence agent and a very good actor? Ryker's instincts told him it was the former. That made him both glad and a little bit sad. Glad that he wasn't being worked on by an operative who was secretly trying to determine his loyalty and worth, but sad that perhaps this time there really was no one from his old life who cared.

'Now you have my life story,' Hitchens said, 'perhaps you could tell me—'

'What do you know of Roman Smolov?' Ryker asked.

'Roman Smolov? I've never heard of him.' His confusion at the sudden question seemed genuine enough.

'No?'

'No. Should I have?'

'I was arrested right outside his house. Actually, I was trespassing on his property.'

'You were arrested for murder. The teenager who was—'

'Who was murdered while I was thousands of miles away. I came here because I thought I knew the victim. Turns out I was wrong. But I know Roman Smolov is involved. He's Ukrainian. Organized crime. Murder, drugs, extortion, that kind of thing.'

'I'm sorry, Mr Ryker, this is really way beyond what I'm doing here.'

'Is it? It was you who was asking about the passport for Carl Logan.'

'Yes, because—'

'That evidence was planted.'

Hitchens paused now. 'You're saying... By the police?'

'At least some of them, yes.'

'I don't... I really don't know what the protocol is for that. That's not why I'm here.'

'Perhaps you should find out what the protocol is, then. Someone in the police is framing me. Someone in the police is working for organized crime.'

Hitchens stared at Ryker but said nothing. He was way out of his depth.

'Do you understand what I'm saying to you?' Ryker asked.

'Not really.'

'Then I suggest you go back to the consulate and relay what I've told you.'

'Yes. I will.' Hitchens got up. A determined look on his face as though it was all his idea. 'Is there anything else I should know?'

'You seem like a smart man. I'll leave it in your hands.'

Hitchens looked like he didn't know if Ryker was being serious or not.

'I'll be in touch,' Hitchens said, before turning for the door.

The guard opened up and Hitchens disappeared. Ryker got to his feet to leave but the guard motioned for him to stay put.

'No,' he said. 'You have visitor. Different.'

Ryker, curious, retook his seat. The door remained open. The guard stood there, looking out of Ryker's sight, down the corridor. Ryker heard footsteps. Two sets on the hard floor.

He expected Robertson and Xenakis to appear.

It wasn't them at all, but it was a man and a woman. A man and woman Ryker recognized.

The watchers – the thieves – from Athens.

21

SIX DAYS PREVIOUSLY

Reva stood on the sand, across the bay from the gathering of people on the other side of the water. A white tent now shielded the grim discovery from the public, the cluster of nosy bastards growing in numbers all the time, as did the police presence. Nearly a dozen blue-uniformed officers moved around, most with sunglasses on, arms folded, looking about the place as though they were in charge, while just one or two of them talked to unsettled – or perhaps simply overly eager – tourists.

To his left, he spotted Alexei and Iya walking toward him. He decided to set off and met them halfway. Iya looked despondent. Alexei worried.

'I've tried with everyone but there's nothing we can do about this now,' Alexei said. 'Too many people have seen already. There's a news crew down there as we speak, cameras and all.'

Reva sucked in a lungful of sea air and slowly expelled it through his nose as he looked across at the mess on the other side once more. A simple dead body. A scrawny little dead body at that. Not a hard task to deal with, even for a dunce like Vlad. How could he mess up so badly?

'Where is he?' Reva said.

'Who?'

'Vlad?'

'Where you asked.'

'Come on.'

He set off for the villa. The quick march up the steps from the beach left them all out of breath. They walked around the pool area. Sylvia was there, sunning herself as always. She lifted up her sunglasses and caught Reva's eye.

'Problems?' she asked with a sly grin.

'Any problem for me is a problem for you too.'

She didn't respond. He really wasn't in the mood to delve further and continued striding for the house. Alexei and Iya followed him to the basement, down the stairs. Through the door.

Reva stood, staring at the bound and naked man on the chair, trying to calm his breathing and his anger.

Vlad looked back at him. Terrified. Quivering, just like that teenager had.

'You fucked up,' Reva said to him.

'I'm... sorry,' Vlad said.

Fucked up more than once, Reva thought but didn't bother to say. First of all in killing the kid in the first place. The ham-fisted idiot had strangled him when the teenager, having worked on the rope tying his wrists with a razor blade he'd concealed somehow, whipped that blade toward Vlad as he went to move him. A surprise, yes, but Vlad could and should have floored him with a couple of punches. Instead, he'd throttled the kid. That was not an accident, as claimed by Vlad, but pure, simple incompetence. And to then dispose of the body so lazily... How had Smolov even come to employ someone like this?

'Please?' Vlad begged.

Reva looked at Alexei and Iya by his side. Both looked doubt-ful. About what?

'What do you two think?' Reva asked them.

They looked at him but neither said a word in response.

'Alexei, what should I do with a man like this? A man who's put us all in jeopardy?'

He glanced to Iya, then to Vlad, then back to Reva. 'I think... I think he needs to be punished.'

Reva nodded.

'But everyone makes mistakes,' Alexei added. Reva wished he hadn't.

'Punished how?' he asked.

Alexei looked at the forlorn figure. Reva could see the sympathy in his eyes. 'Cut his payments for the next six months. Demote him. Make him work to prove his worth.'

'What a kind-hearted soul you are,' Reva said. Alexei looked offended.

'Better than causing more problems for ourselves,' Alexei said. 'We've already got police everywhere. Even the ones we paid off will turn against us if we give them a reason or the option. They have no real loyalty to us. They only fear us as long as we're on top. You want another dead body? It's only more risk for us.'

Vlad moaned at the mention of *dead body*. Reva thought about Alexei's words for a few moments. Of course, his points were perfectly valid, but that didn't make him right.

'And you?' Reva said to Iya.

'I think some people aren't cut out for this.'

She delivered the statement without any hint of feeling at all. Reva liked her. Not cold or disassociated, just very cool, and savvy.

Reva nodded, his mind made up.

He stepped over to the table. Picked up the serrated knife. He moved to Vlad. Looked down on the captive.

'Please...' Vlad whimpered.

'You know what I could do to you?' Reva said. 'You know how much I could make you suffer?'

Vlad slowly nodded.

'Good. Then be glad about this.'

Reva reached out and slashed across with the blade. A vicious swipe. A two-foot-long gash opened up in Vlad's torso. As if in slow motion the thick skin and the flesh beneath parted and parted. Blood oozed, then innards poked through and slopped out. Reva stared into Vlad's eyes which were wide with fright, but nothing – no scream, no pleading – came from his lips. Vlad looked down. Looked at his own abdomen, open, guts spilling onto his lap and dropping to the floor.

Then Vlad looked up. Pleading now, in his eyes at least. Reva dropped the knife and it clattered to the floor. He unbuttoned his shirt. Held it open. Vlad's eyes fixed on Reva's long, jagged scar.

'A horrible sight,' Reva said to him. 'To see yourself inside out. It happened to me once. Not a situation like this, but as you can see the wound is the same.'

Vlad's body trembled but he didn't say a word.

'It might not seem like it where you are, but believe me, it's possible to save a man even in your position. It's possible because I was saved.' He paused then laughed. 'I'm here, after all, aren't I?'

Still not a word escaped Vlad's lips. His face had turned pale, his blood loss already massive. He was fading.

'The point is, my friend, some people are worth saving,' Reva said. 'I was worth saving.' He buttoned up his shirt again. 'You... are not.'

Vlad's head slowly bowed.

Reva turned. Iya remained stony-faced. Alexei looked shocked but quickly pulled himself together when he realized Reva was staring.

'You want us to clean it up?' Alexei said, sounding brave and calm.

'Not yet,' Reva said. 'Get on the phone. Find all our police assets. Get them over here. I want them to see. I want them to understand.'

Alexei nodded.

'Start with the new ones. What are their names again?'

'Robertson,' Alexei said. 'Robertson and Georgiadis.'

* * *

An hour later and Reva headed back for the basement, the two police officers in front of him. Georgiadis remained calm and collected. Strange, he didn't really know her at all, but her confident manner, her edgy attitude, reminded him so much of Iya. When did the young women of the world get so bullish? Robertson, on the other hand, looked like he would shit himself. Every couple of steps he looked back at Reva, as though he expected an ambush.

'Why are we going down here?' Robertson asked, nerves in his voice.

'This isn't a trick,' Reva said. 'But I need to explain what's happened.'

They reached the bottom and the closed door. The officers looked around at him expectantly.

'It's okay, open it,' he said to them.

They turned back. Robertson reached forward and opened the door. Took a half step and paused. Georgiadis glanced inside then spun on her heel, pulling her gun from the holster on her side.

'What the hell?' she shouted. She pointed the gun at Reva but couldn't keep her eyes on him. Instead, she flitted them back and forth between him and the body and the bloody mess inside the room.

'Put that away,' Reva said to her.

'He's dead,' Robertson said, sounding as calm as Reva now. Or perhaps just detached.

Strange, how the roles had switched so suddenly. Perhaps Georgiadis wasn't so tough after all. Her usual bravado was simply because she'd never seen or known true nastiness before.

She looked at her partner, then slowly lowered the gun. She didn't put it away, though. Reva moved past her into the room, stood to the side so the officers retained an unobstructed view of the corpse.

'What is this?' Robertson said, a little bit angry more than anything else. 'A threat?'

'An explanation,' Reva said.

'Well, go on, then,' Georgiadis said, her natural confidence returning, though she was doing everything to avoid looking at the dead body. She holstered the weapon. 'Explain.'

'The boy found on the beach this morning.'

'We should have known,' Georgiadis said, looking at her partner with a disgusted shake of her head.

'Last night that boy, and another, broke into this home. They were confronted and one of my friends was killed in the process.'

The officers both gave him their full attention now, though neither said anything.

'One of the boys got away. Tricky little bastard. But we caught the other.'

'So you killed him?' Robertson said.

'*He* killed him,' Reva said, indicating Vlad. 'A mistake. We held that boy here because we wanted to know who he was. Who his friend was. Why they came here. But Vlad messed up.'

'So you tossed the kid's body into the sea?' Georgiadis said. 'Not very clever.'

'Not very clever at all,' Reva said. 'Which is why Vlad has paid for his mistakes.'

Georgiadis gulped, then looked a little embarrassed, as though she realized her reaction showed her weakness.

'Why are you showing us this?' Robertson asked.

'I already said, to explain.'

'Because you don't want us looking too hard into who killed the boy on the beach?'

'Oh, you can look as hard as you like. As long as you don't look around here.'

'What are you saying. Exactly?'

'The boy's death was unfortunate, but he brought it on himself.'

The officers didn't say anything. Reva knew Georgiadis was wavering. She wanted out.

'Do I need to remind you of how you came to be here?' Reva said to her.

'No. You threatened the lives of my family,' Georgiadis answered. 'My sister. My mother and father. And his wife and baby boy.'

Reva smiled and looked at Robertson. As at the start, she was now displaying far more composure than he was.

'It's an unfair way to characterize our relationship,' Reva said. 'It's not all threat. You'll benefit from this too.'

'I want double,' Robertson blurted.

Reva focused on him. 'You really think—'

'Double,' Georgiadis said. 'This is a bigger ask. You wanted us to turn a blind eye to things in this area. To give you information. Not to stifle active murder investigations.'

Pass on information? Turn a blind eye? Had they really been so naive? But then, really, Reva had only offered them peanuts before.

'You deal with the boy for me,' he said. 'Make sure the investigation doesn't touch me or my people, and you have a deal.'

Georgiadis went to leave.

'I need to know who the boy is,' Reva said. 'I want to know why we were attacked. If you find anything, tell me. If you find his friend, tell me. And find someone to take the fall.'

'That's not what—'

'It's fine,' Robertson said, putting his hand on his colleague's shoulder to stop her protest. 'We'll be in touch. But please, no more bodies. Don't make this impossible for us.'

'Don't worry,' Reva said. 'Not all of us are as useless as Vlad. Some of us know exactly how to dispose of bodies. We can make anyone disappear. Anyone at all.'

He winked at Georgiadis. Moments later the officers were heading up the stairs. Reva took one last look at Vlad, then turned and moved out after them.

22

PRESENT

The man and woman – fake smiles on their faces – sat down in front of Ryker. They looked different somehow to the last time Ryker saw them in the flesh, in the bar in Athens. More confident and in control than Ryker remembered. Or was it just that he realized now that he'd misread the two of them back then. They weren't simple surveillance, moderately trained agents of some low-level organization. These two had reach and power. How else could they pull so many strings?

Both were younger than Ryker. Both wore office gear – smart trousers, open-necked shirt and blouse. The woman's face was plain, very ordinary really, dark-brown eyes and just a slight Slavic edge to her bone features. The man's face was likewise pretty ordinary – a face that wouldn't stand out in a crowd. Slightly rounded, with deep-set green eyes.

Perhaps their plainness was one reason Ryker had underestimated them before.

'Good morning,' the woman said after a strange silence. She spoke in English but her accent immediately gave her away: Russian, Ukrainian. Perhaps one of the Baltic states. 'My name is Natalia Petrova, this is my colleague, Denis Zhirov.'

'You want me to call you those names?' Ryker said.

'These are our names, yes.'

'Unlikely.'

'Excuse me?'

'You're hardly going to walk in here and give me your real names, are you?'

Petrova glanced at her colleague as though confused by Ryker's comment. 'These are our names.'

'Okay, fine,' Ryker said.

'And what about you?' Zhirov asked. 'Is it James Ryker, Carl Logan, or something else?'

'Call me whatever you want.'

'Very well. Let's stay with James Ryker.'

'How did you two get in here?' Ryker asked, looking from Petrova to Zhirov. He wasn't yet sure which one was in charge. Perhaps neither.

'It's not really important to you,' Petrova said.

'It's very important to me, actually. Like it's very important to understand why you were following me in Athens. Why you raided my hotel room there. Why the items you stole from me have ended up in the hands of the Hellenic police, implicating me in a murder that happened when I was thousands of miles away from here.'

Petrova's face remained passive. Zhirov looked like he was enjoying himself just a little.

'You want us to answer all of those questions?' Petrova asked.

'It'd be a good start to understanding why you're here.'

'Maybe, but why don't we start at the end, and why we're here,' Petrova said. 'We're here to make you an offer.'

'You're going to get me out of jail?' Ryker suggested.

Petrova smiled, just a little. 'Yes and no.'

'How can it be both?'

She shrugged. 'We want to get you out of this jail. But we want to put you in another one.'

She spoke as though her words, her proposition, were the most normal thing in the world.

'Okay, okay,' Petrova said, her face brightening a little more. 'I can see I confused you. Perhaps it was better to start at the beginning after all.'

'I think you're right,' Ryker said.

'We heard about what happened in Norway,' Zhirov added.

'Heard about it?'

'We were never there,' Petrova said. 'If that's what you were wondering.'

She was right. Ryker had immediately wondered that. 'But the men you were fighting against there—'

'Valeri Sychev, Andrey Klitchkov, Konstantin Mashchenko,' Zhirov interjected.

'—they are all men we've been watching for some time—'

'When you say *we...*' Ryker butted in.

'I mean both of us,' Petrova said, 'and the people we work with.'

'And you work for?'

Petrova paused. Straight face once more. 'I'm sure you know.'

'The FSB?' Ryker suggested, referring to the notorious Russian foreign intelligence agency that he'd had too many run-ins with to count in his past.

'Close enough,' Zhirov said.

Which likely meant they worked for an offshoot of the FSB. An even more cloak-and-dagger unit that was held accountable to no one, by no one. Kind of like the unit of British intelligence that Ryker himself had worked for.

'So you were watching those three in Norway,' Ryker said to Petrova. 'Carry on.'

'Not just those three. Everyone involved with them.' She shook her head disconsolately. 'I have to say, you caused us some problems.'

'Did I? Those men were all scum. Murderers. Torturers. Extortionists. They're all dead now. Because of me. I did you a favor. Unintended, but there you go. You should be thanking me.'

'Are the people of Blodstein in Norway thanking you?' Zhirov asked. 'Or are they still mopping up the blood of their relatives because of your actions, and what happened after.'

Ryker clenched his fists as tightly as he could under the table. Zhirov's words were a deliberate attempt to rile Ryker, and he hated to admit it, but it worked. An image of Pettersen – weary dissatisfaction on her face – flashed in his mind. The things she'd said to him the last time he saw her pretty much confirmed Zhirov's point. Ryker thought he'd done good in Blodstein. He'd gotten rid of the bad guys, helped save Henrik, the town. But look what had happened since.

'I don't disagree with you,' Petrova said to Ryker. 'They were all horrible men. Wicked. We've been following their movements for a long time.'

'Not very well if you've been letting them get away with murder.'

'No,' Petrova said, shaking her head. 'You know how it works. It wasn't just about those men, and what they did. We needed to know why. We needed to understand who was at the top. You must know this, a man of your experience. Removing the smallest branches doesn't make the tree fall down. You have to cut the trunk.'

'And you know who the trunk is?' Ryker asked.

'We'll get to that,' Petrova said. 'After you left Blodstein the first time, we started to do some work to understand what had happened there. At first, we feared there was a big problem. A rival perhaps, who we didn't know about. Then came the retaliation. Then came the murder here. And then *you* came, asking questions of Mashchenko.'

Just as Ryker had feared. When he'd asked Silviu to dig into Mashchenko's past, the FSB was alerted. Had Petrova and Zhirov already been in Athens at that point, or only because of the alert?

What about Eleni? Was she just a surveillance operative for the Greek authorities, or was there more to her story too?

'So when I turned up in Athens, you were already there, waiting for me,' Ryker said.

'Precisely,' Petrova said. 'But we never were there to harm you. Only to understand.'

Ryker scoffed at that. They were trying to set him up for murder. That was pretty harmful.

'Do you understand why I did what I did in Blodstein?' Ryker asked.

'Not really,' Petrova said.

'Because you can't help yourself,' Zhirov said, almost a sneer. 'You're like a dog who sees another dog. You have to chase and chase. Bark and bark. Why? No reason. You just do. You have no self-control.'

Ryker clenched his fists again.

'There was a boy,' Ryker said. 'Henrik Svenson.'

'Yes, we know about him,' Petrova said. 'He's why you came to Crete.'

'He's why I went to Athens first. I want to find whoever caused that mess in Blodstein. I want to know who they are. I want to look them in the eye—'

'And then you want to kill them, blah-blah,' Zhirov interjected. 'You're a cold man, James Ryker. A little bit boring, and predictable, but definitely cold.'

Ryker sucked in a lungful of air and tried his best not to rise to Zhirov's taunt.

'The murder that took place here,' Petrova said.

'I didn't do it,' Ryker said.

'I think we all know that—'

'Well, yeah. It was you who planted the false evidence with the police here. It has to be you.'

Both of them stared at Ryker. They weren't going to admit to that, even if it was plainly obvious. Although their lackluster reaction left just the smallest chink in Ryker's theory. Was it not them, but someone else trying to set him up?

'Do you know who killed him?' Ryker asked.

'No,' Petrova said. 'And that is the truth. We weren't here. But, like you, we think we know *why* he was killed. Henrik Svenson came to Crete asking too many questions. Questions which got him killed.'

'Except the dead boy isn't Henrik Svenson,' Ryker said.

A twitch on Petrova's face. She hadn't known that. Perhaps Ryker should have kept the point to himself. Had he placed Henrik in danger? No, these weren't Henrik's enemies.

'The boy who was killed here wasn't Henrik,' Ryker said. 'I don't know who he is, and I don't know why they killed him. Mistaken identity, perhaps.'

'But you think you know *who* killed him.'

'Do you?'

'Actually, we know who *didn't* kill him,' Zhirov said.

'Me, you mean?' Ryker said, catching Zhirov's eye.

Zhirov laughed. 'Well, yes, but someone else also.'

'Who?'

'Smolov,' Petrova said. 'We know you, like Henrik Svenson, came here looking for Roman Smolov, but he didn't kill that boy.'

'You know that how?'

'Most likely people who work for him carried out the murder, but it definitely wasn't Smolov. He's not even in Crete.'

'Then where is he?'

'Roman Smolov is in jail. In Russia.'

A smile crept up Petrova's face now. From plain and passive, it made her face look sinister. Not a nice transformation at all. With the look, Ryker's mind put some more pieces of the puzzle together.

'You want to take me out of this jail, and put me in another one,' he said. 'Not to punish me, but so I'm with Smolov?'

'Exactly,' Petrova said.

'But why on earth would you want to do that?'

Petrova laughed again. 'Perhaps it's not so obvious really, after all. Smolov isn't our friend. Far from, it in fact. But... Well, quite simply, we want to put you in prison with Roman Smolov, so you can help him to break out.'

23

Ryker chewed on the quite frankly ludicrous proposition for a good few seconds. Petrova and Zhirov both watched him with intent.

'You two set me up for murder,' Ryker said eventually. 'Why the hell would I ever want to help you?'

'You'd rather stay in jail in Crete?' Zhirov said.

'You know what? Perhaps I would.'

Not that Ryker really thought that would happen, long term. As he'd already mused previously, did the Greek authorities really have enough evidence to pursue a case? The Russians surely must have seen how flimsy the ploy was if they were behind the setup.

'No deal,' Ryker said.

'No deal?' Petrova repeated. She looked seriously surprised. 'You haven't even let me tell you the whole plan.'

'I don't need to hear any more. It's stupid. It's insane. And whatever your intentions with Smolov, it has absolutely nothing to do with me.'

'This has everything to do with you,' Zhirov said.

'How?' Ryker said, glaring at him.

'Please, can I at least finish?' Petrova asked.

Ryker sat back in his chair and sighed. 'It's not like I've got anything better to do.'

'You didn't ask why we want Smolov out of prison,' Petrova said.

'That's because I couldn't care less.'

'Are you sure about that?' Zhirov said.

'From what I know of Smolov he belongs in prison, so why would I want him free? And why would *you* want him free? I expect it took a lot of work to get him out of Crete, into a Russian prison. Now you want to recruit me to help you break him out again? If you want him out of prison then just let him go. Put him on a plane back here and be done with it.'

The room went silent. Both of the Russians stared at Ryker. Petrova was back to passive. Zhirov looked at Ryker a little mockingly. The longer Ryker spent in a room with the guy, the more he wanted to punch him in the face.

'What do you know about the man named Jesper?' Petrova asked.

Ryker gritted his teeth.

'You have heard that name, haven't you?'

Ryker said nothing.

'There is something of a problem here, though,' Petrova said, then shook her head and turned her hands over, all a little theatrically. 'We've heard the name too. But for all our power and reach, we really don't know much about the man himself.'

'The FSB never were ahead of the game much.'

Neither showed a reaction to Ryker's flippant comment.

'What we do know is this,' Zhirov said. 'Jesper, Smolov, the men you killed in Norway, are nothing but terrorists. They fund campaigns across the Caucasus, into Georgia, Ukraine. Anti-

Russia campaigns. They kidnap and kill political figures. They drive up hatred and rebellion.'

'You might have thought they were just organized crime,' Petrova added. 'Criminals out to make themselves rich, but that's not it at all. Yes, they are funded through drugs and extortion and corruption, but the purpose of their funds is political.'

Ryker still said nothing. His brain whirred. He thought back to Blodstein, to the dead men. Sychev, Klitchkov, Mashchenko. When he'd first spoken to the locals about them, the Norwegians had said they were Russian, but they weren't. They'd spoken a language not familiar, but not entirely unfamiliar to Ryker: Balachka. A fluid dialect, essentially a blend of Ukrainian and Russian, spoken by the Cossacks of the north Caucasus. Modern-day enemies of the expansionist regime in Moscow who themselves were known to use underhand tactics to sow discontent in old Soviet states, and in disputed territories like Chechnya, with the ultimate purpose of retaking lands lost during the Soviet dissolution. Smolov, similarly, was Ukrainian, a country still engaged in conflict with Russian-backed rebels over large swathes of Ukrainian territory.

Ryker laughed. A little mockingly. 'Jesper is an enemy of the state,' he said.

Petrova and Zhirov were both stony-faced now.

'A terrorist?' Ryker said. 'That's how you view him? The way I see it, is that it's your government that's playing games all across that region. Funding rebel groups. Stamping down on dissident political views. Hampering free speech. The very fact you have Smolov in prison through clandestine actions backs that up. Georgia, Ukraine, Chechnya, Moldova – it's the same story in all of those places.'

Petrova and Zhirov looked offended. 'Jesper *is* a terrorist,' Petrova said. 'If you want, I can show you exactly what he's done.

Car-bomb attacks, drive-by shootings, people, whole families disappearing without trace in the night. In the past year alone there have been tens of deaths linked to Jesper and people associated with him. Women, children are victims of his too. You can disagree on our politics, but you can't possibly disagree on indiscriminate killing.'

She had a point there. If any of it was true.

'As they say, one man's terrorist is another's freedom fighter,' Ryker said.

'After everything he caused in Blodstein, you'd still side with Jesper?' Zhirov asked.

It did seem contradictory to everything Ryker was doing. But still, he simply didn't trust these two...

'Do you even know who he really is?' Ryker said. 'Or do you only have a name?'

'That's why we need your help,' Petrova said. 'Because we have to know more. We have to know everything about Jesper and his plans. You can help Smolov get out of prison. He'll take you to Jesper. Earn his trust. Find out what they're doing. Work with us to prevent more unnecessary deaths.'

'You two are insane.'

'No, we're really not,' Petrova said. 'But perhaps you need some time to think this through properly. You're perfect for this—'

'I'm not exactly one of them.'

'No? You like well-known sayings? How about "the enemy of my enemy is my friend"? You don't need a fake story to get in with them, to earn their trust, and to become one of them. You need to only be you. James Ryker. Ex-British intelligence, right? You *hate* Russia.'

Ryker tensed a little, though didn't show it. How much did they know of his past?

'I don't hate Russia at all. I just hate some of the politics, and some of the people.'

He glared at Zhirov as he said that, though he felt the same about both of them really.

'We'll give you some time to think,' Petrova said. She motioned to Zhirov and they both got up from their seats.

'I don't need time to think,' Ryker said. 'The answer is no.'

'We'll give you the time anyway,' Petrova said. She knocked on the door. 'We'll see you soon.'

Moments later they were gone.

* * *

They didn't give Ryker much time for contemplation back in his cell. He was quite pleased with that, all things considered, because every thought he did have about what had just happened in that interview room, about everything happening around him involving the agents from the FSB, made him mad. Seriously mad. Blood boiling mad. He needed to find a way to keep his head calm and rational.

A cruddy meal later and Ryker was back in the interview room. Tired, worn out. He wondered who would appear at the door. Bruno Hitchens was perhaps his preferred option. At least the consulate worker's intentions were straightforward enough.

No. It wasn't Hitchens. Georgiadis and Robertson.

'The dynamic duo,' Ryker said to them as Robertson closed the door. They both gave him an odd look before sitting.

Robertson appeared a little troubled by something. Georgiadis looked a little bit smug. Kind of like how she'd acted the previous night. What was with her? Of course, Ryker had mulled plenty about who within the police force was corrupt. Who was working with the Russians to implicate Ryker in a crime he couldn't have possibly committed. How far up the chain did the deception go?

Surely the ploy required input from someone with more seniority than these two. Yet Georgiadis' manner...

'How are you doing today?' Robertson asked.

'Wonderful,' Ryker answered. 'Never had so many people wanting to speak to me.'

Robertson looked like he didn't know how to take that comment.

'Where are the Russians now?' Ryker asked.

A frown from Robertson. Nothing much from Georgiadis.

'Which Russians?' Robertson asked. 'You mean Smolov and—'

'No, I don't mean Smolov. He's not Russian. I mean the two Russian FSB agents who were in here talking to me earlier this morning.'

Robertson looked at his colleague then back at Ryker. 'I don't know anything about that. I haven't been at the station all morning.'

'What about you?' Ryker asked Georgiadis.

'Same,' she said.

'FSB?' Robertson asked. 'You mean, like...'

'Secret agents. KGB. Yes, that's exactly what I mean.'

'This is... This is... Okay,' Robertson stuttered, and his confusion did seem genuine enough. What the hell was going on? 'Let's park that. I'm going to find out what on earth you're talking about. But that's not why we're here.'

'So why are you here?'

'We have some progress in our investigation.' Robertson shuffled the papers he'd brought with him. Kind of like how Xenakis had the day before.

'Where's your boss today?' Ryker said.

'My boss?'

'Xenakis.'

'She's more senior than me, but she's not technically my boss.'

'I didn't ask for a rundown of your corporate structure, I just asked where she is.'

'Not here,' Georgiadis said.

'Anyway,' Robertson continued. 'We've taken two new witness statements over the last twenty-four hours, and, to put it simply, this doesn't look good for you, Mr Ryker.'

Robertson spread out four pieces of paper in front of Ryker. Two witness statements, handwritten. Dated only that morning. The statements were in Greek and Ryker struggled to understand them fully. Understanding the spoken language was one thing, but he'd never come close to mastering the Greek alphabet.

'This is... There's nothing I can see in here apart from a vague reference to a man seen on the beach,' Ryker said.

'A man matching your description,' Georgiadis added.

'What? Tall? Dark hair?'

'It's a bit more than that,' Robertson added. 'Both witnesses, independently, talked about seeing a man arguing with two teenage boys. A week ago today. Around 9 p.m.... The facial descriptions match you. So, too, the clothes.'

'At 9 p.m.? Wouldn't it be dark on the beach?'

'Not pitch black. Not in this spot, close to lighting.'

'You just happened to find these two witnesses since my arrest? Just happened to get witness statements with virtually identical wording.'

'I'm not sure what you're suggesting,' Robertson said.

'I think you damn well do. And the more you talk, the more I'm pretty sure both of you are directly involved in this scheme.'

'There is no scheme,' Georgiadis said with a tone that showed she felt entirely in control. 'We showed both of these witnesses a picture of you. *After* we'd taken the statements. Both of them said they believe you are the same man they saw.'

'Where were you that night?' Robertson asked.

'Denmark,' Ryker said.

'Where in Denmark?'

'Esbjerg. You know it?'

'No.'

'It's nice.'

'I'm glad to hear it. Do you have any evidence you were there?'

'Not to hand.'

He'd paid in cash for a hotel. Had traveled to the city on public transport.

'You're not making this easier for yourself,' Robertson said.

'Aren't I? I've given you a pretty clear indication of what's happening here. The fact you won't listen to my version tells me a lot.'

'This is what we're going to do,' Robertson said, pulling the papers back toward him. 'We'll set up an identity parade. We'll ask these two witnesses and some of the others we've spoken to already to take part. We need to do it today. After that, there'll be a charging decision. If charged, you'll be remanded and taken to the main jail in the city where you'll await a court appearance.'

'Good luck with that,' Ryker said.

'This could be your last chance to get on record anything you want to tell us before you're charged with murder.'

Ryker said nothing. Robertson and Georgiadis got to their feet. The door opened for them. The same guard on the outside. Ryker thought about it. He'd thought about it every time he'd been in this room. Every time that door was open.

How far would he get if he tried to run? These two officers, the guard. He would send them down to the ground in seconds. After that lay the corridor, and a secure door to the waiting area. Lastly, the front entrance. How many armed officers would he have to pass? Difficult to say. Two minimum at the front desk, but if he timed it badly maybe half a dozen overall.

Still, he'd get out of the building for sure.

But what then?

No. Not yet. One way or another he'd get another chance.

'Next time I see you,' Ryker said before the officers left the room, 'I want some answers on those two FSB agents. If I don't get something satisfactory from you both, then I'll know for sure it's you who's setting me up. You won't want that.'

The look of disquiet on their faces showed they'd received the veiled threat loud and clear.

Looking a lot less confident than before, Georgiadis and Robertson walked away.

24

Ryker carried on along the corridor with the guard, back toward the holding cell, still in two minds as to whether or not to make a move. A move which would surely see him free, at least in the short term. But what would be the long-term ramifications? Particularly as, with the police armed, he couldn't guarantee there'd be no collateral damage.

Continuing to contemplate even as they turned the corner toward Ryker's cell, his mind was finally made up when he spotted the two figures further along. Petrova and Zhirov, standing outside Ryker's cell. As much as he'd love to get one over on those two, this wasn't the time or place. Plus, he was intrigued – as much as he was apprehensive – about what they were doing there, waiting for him, so soon after them last seeing him.

'Busy day for you,' Petrova said as Ryker and the guard approached. She stood in the center of the corridor, arms folded. Zhirov leaned against the wall – pure nonchalance.

'I thought you wanted to give me some time,' Ryker said.

Petrova didn't respond to that. Instead, she turned to the guard and rattled off something in Greek. 'Put him back,' or something like that, Ryker figured.

The guard said nothing but opened the cell door and ushered Ryker in. Zhirov peeled from the wall and followed Ryker inside. Ryker tensed, ready for action, as though Zhirov was about to attack him. Poison? Tranquillizer? Or just a good old beating?

None of those came. Ryker relaxed, a little.

'Leave us,' Petrova said to the guard. He looked unsure, but Petrova stepped into the cell and closed the door behind her. A moment later the lock turned.

'Interesting,' Ryker said.

He stood in the far corner, Petrova by the door, Zhirov off to the left. With the bed on the other side, barely any space lay between them.

'No need to be scared,' Zhirov said, pleased with himself.

'Nothing to be scared of,' Ryker said.

Standing up, Ryker was a good three or four inches taller, broader too, but he wouldn't underestimate Zhirov. Nor Petrova. They were both FSB agents and he had no clue what training they'd had, what combat capabilities they had.

'We heard about the developments with the police investigation,' Petrova said.

Ryker kept his mouth shut. His brain rumbled with thoughts. He'd assumed the Russians were behind the setup here. But was the answer more complex than that? Was the setup actually orchestrated by Smolov's crew, having paid off the local cops? A straightforward enough explanation, except for the FSB agents being here. Clearly, not all parties were in on it together, as the FSB and Smolov were antagonists to each other. Most likely the Cretan police – definitely 100 percent neck deep in the setup – were the middlemen, different officers being controlled by different strings from above. Whether they even truly realized that, and who'd win out would depend on who held the most power and persuasion.

'Your position is looking worse all the time,' Petrova added.

'Why are you here?' Ryker asked.

Petrova looked at Zhirov, then back at Ryker. Then she smiled. That same wicked smile he'd seen on her in the interview room. 'I heard this story, a few years ago now. About a car accident in America.'

'Okay?'

'A husband and wife were traveling along a desert highway. You know the type. Long, straight road, nothing either side except for desert and rocks.'

'I know the type.' He'd driven them plenty of times. Some of the best times.

'So they're all alone. No other cars for miles around, and, I guess they're feeling a bit naughty. The woman unzips her man's trousers, goes down on him, right there on the highway as they're speeding along.'

Zhirov smirked. Ryker wasn't sure why, other than because he was a childish buffoon.

'She's going at it, he's loving it. Really loving it. How do I know?'

'Because it was you giving it?' Ryker asked.

Her face screwed up in offense.

'No, because the guy, maybe he closed his eyes or something, but the next thing the car is out of control, swerving left and right. He couldn't correct it and...' She motioned with her hand. 'It flips right over. Bang, bang, bang, along that deserted highway until it comes to a stop. Blood pouring, gasoline pouring. Smoke going up into the blue sky.'

Petrova paused. Zhirov looked over at her as though he wasn't sure why. Had he heard this story before?

'I don't know who called the police,' Petrova continued, 'but just say eventually two cop cars turn up. One from the west, one from the east. You see, the road goes over the state line. One cop turns up from Arizona, and the other from... I can't remember for sure, Utah or something. The Arizona cop takes one look at the car, realizes both the occupants are dead, then goes up to the Utah cop and the two of them go at it, arguing over what happened, over whose jurisdiction the crash is in. Neither can really be bothered to take ownership as who cares really? The tire marks from when the guy pumped the brakes start in Utah, but go right over the state line. The car itself is now in Arizona, but the woman's torso, somehow or other – I mean she didn't have her belt on, did she, because she was giving head – ends up in the desert in Utah. You can imagine the scene.'

'Yeah,' Ryker said. 'You've done a pretty good job of setting it for me.'

Petrova smiled again. Zhirov glared, as though Ryker had flirted with his woman.

'These two cops,' she said. 'They just stand there arguing and arguing. They really hate each other; it's not the first time they've had battles over jurisdiction. They keep on arguing until the ambulance turns up.'

'From which side?' Ryker asked.

Petrova looked up, as though searching for the answer. 'I don't actually remember. But the paramedics rush to the car. The man is still alive, after all. He's sitting there, crushed in the driver's seat, with his wife's head in his lap, her mouth still around his you-know-what.'

'Probably a bit limp by that point,' Zhirov said, smiling at his own quip.

'Hanging off, I think,' Petrova said, deadpan. 'Her teeth went right into it. Anyway, the paramedics are all in a panic trying to get him out, the cops join in too. They put their differences aside, realizing their mistake, but within a couple of minutes, they all have to give up. They run away into the sand just as the whole thing goes up in a huge fireball.'

Petrova motioned the fireball with her hands too. She certainly had a mind for drama. The silence that followed suggested she'd finally finished.

'Is any of that true?' Ryker asked.

'Hundred percent,' Petrova responded.

'Doesn't even matter,' Zhirov said. 'The point of the story still stands.'

'And that's what?' Ryker said. 'You're Arizona, and she's Utah. Two incompetents pissing about rather than getting the job done themselves.'

Zhirov's death glare showed the comment had riled him.

'No,' Petrova said. 'Me and him are both Arizona, and you're Utah. Not incompetent. But two natural enemies.'

'They weren't natural enemies,' Ryker said. 'Just two cops who let bullishness and arrogance get in the way of their duties.'

'But by fighting, rather than acting, that man died,' Petrova said. 'They could have saved him if they'd put their differences aside and worked together.'

'Fine. So I understand why you're telling me this. Except in our situation, you're not asking me to save someone. You're asking me to go into prison in Russia to break out a career criminal so I can assimilate myself in their gang.'

'But don't you get it?' Petrova said, sounding frustrated, as though Ryker's inability to see her view meant her whole story had been pointless. Which, in a way, Ryker felt it had. 'You *will* save people. By getting to Smolov, then Jesper, we'll be able to prevent more deaths. This is our chance, *your* chance to save lives. Let's put our differences aside.'

Ryker thought for a few moments. Then shook his head. 'Sorry,' he said. 'Your argument, your proposition, still doesn't cut it with me. I'm only in jail right now because you two set me up.'

'It's not that simple,' Petrova said, further adding to Ryker's confusion as to who was doing what in the background.

'I don't owe you anything,' he said. 'When I get out of here, I'll find Jesper myself.'

'When you get out of here?' Zhirov said, a devilish grin on his face. He looked at Petrova.

'We're down to the final roll of the dice then,' Petrova said. 'I hoped we wouldn't be.'

The tension in Ryker's muscles renewed as Petrova reached into the pocket of her suit trousers. Would she really pull a weapon there and then?

No. Only a piece of paper. Though Ryker didn't relax at all. The mood in the room, the stoic look on Petrova's face, made him realize he had nothing to feel relief over.

She unfolded the paper and held it out to Ryker. He didn't move forward to take it.

'You don't want to see?' Petrova said.

'I'm sure you'll tell me what it is.'

'It's an extradition notice,' Zhirov said, loving every second now. 'Signed, sealed, delivered.'

'You're leaving Crete today,' Petrova said. 'We're taking you back to Russia.'

'That's not possible,' Ryker said. 'Do the British co—'

'They have no say in it,' Zhirov said. 'You're an ex-spy. Your government wants nothing to do with you.'

Was there a way he could get in contact with Hitchens? Would Hitchens even know what to do?

'You're on your own,' Zhirov added.

Ryker remained focused on Petrova rather than the taunting

Zhirov. If he looked at that man's face he wasn't sure how much longer he could control himself. Petrova shrugged.

'He's right,' she said. 'In a few hours from now, you'll be in Russia. But the choice of what happens to you when you arrive there remains up to you.'

'Our people have good memories,' Zhirov said. 'A lot of people know what you've done to us in the past.'

'I doubt that,' Ryker said. 'Most of the people there who knew me at all are dead now.'

Zhirov flinched. For a split second Ryker thought the FSB agent would come for him. No, he obviously thought better of it.

'Again, my friend is right,' Petrova said. 'You – or Carl Logan, more specifically – are still a wanted man in Russia. Espionage, murder. You won't ever be released. You'll end up in a Gulag thousands of miles away from anything—'

'Rotting like all your other political prisoners?' Ryker finished for her.

Petrova shrugged, calm as anything, as though none of this caused her any issue at all.

'The choice is yours,' she said. 'We're taking you today. The murder investigation here will move on. It's done for you here. You can come to prison in Russia as Carl Logan, and you'll spend the rest of your life behind bars. Or come to prison in Russia as James Ryker, and we'll make sure you get out again.'

'But I'll be tied to you. To the FSB,' Ryker said, shaking his head.

'Only as long as we need you.'

'And after that?'

Petrova looked at her watch. 'Right on time,' she said.

A moment later the lock behind her released and the door swung open. Not just one officer but three stood in wait there.

'Transport is here,' one of them said to Petrova, before eyeballing Ryker.

'So which is it?' Petrova asked him. 'Logan or Ryker?'

The guards came forward, handcuffs in the grip of the one at the front. Ryker found himself caught in two minds once more. The odds were seriously against him, but wasn't it worth trying, at least? Didn't he have to?

'Which is it?' Petrova said as the guards grasped Ryker's wrists and slung the cuffs over.

'I'm James Ryker.'

Petrova smiled. 'Good choice.'

25

TWO DAYS PREVIOUSLY

No news was good news. Perhaps Reva had to take comfort in that age-old adage. The police in Crete had made no progress in the investigation into the dead boy – either publicly or privately. Why hadn't they simply found some random tourist to take the blame or a foreign worker who they could later deport quietly, to solve the matter? On the other hand, there'd been no suggestion in the now dwindling press reports of the murder, that the killing was linked to organized crime. Absolutely no mention of Reva or anyone else connected to him, Jesper, Smolov, or their operations. That was good. What wasn't as good was that the police had also provided him with absolutely no information on the dead boy's identity, nor that of his now absent friend.

At least the basement was cleared, and Vlad's remains gone for good.

'Isn't it about time you found somewhere else to be?' Sylvia said.

Reva, sitting on a seat under a parasol, turned to her. Summer dress on, her pink bikini showing through the thin fabric, she sat down on a lounger two away from Reva. He downed the rest of his Coke can.

'You want rid of me?' Reva asked.

'Yes,' she said. 'I don't want you anywhere near me, or my daughter, or my home.'

'Yet every time I sit out here, you always turn up.'

She rolled her eyes and pulled her sunglasses from her hair and put them on. Perhaps to better hide her poor poker face.

Reva laughed. 'You can pretend with me, Sylvia, but we both know, that if Roman wasn't around, you wouldn't say no to me. You'd be in my bed whenever I asked. That's who you are. You need a man. You need someone to look after you.'

'Except Roman already isn't around, is he?' she said. 'And you really think I need looking after?'

Reva looked about the place. 'You're telling me you worked for this?'

She huffed and sat back on the lounger.

'My point is, why are you still here?' she said. 'I thought you were going to Athens.'

'You want to come with me? I can show you—'

'No, Olek, I don't want to go with you. I don't want to even look at you. Do you really think this is a game between us? That shows me exactly how dumb you are. In your head, you think you're charming me with your tough guy attitude. In reality, everything about you disgusts me.'

He ignored her little jibes. He was more concerned about how she knew of his plans in Athens. Who'd told her? Alexei, most likely. That man really needed to think more carefully about his loyalties.

'I'm taking lover boy with me,' Reva said. He hadn't originally planned to, but the guy was becoming a liability here. He had one last chance now to prove his true worth.

Reva studied Sylvia but she showed no reaction to the statement.

'When he meets those city girls, he'll know what he's been missing.'

'Olek, if you think that is going to make me jealous, then you really don't know me at all. Alexei can do what he likes.'

Reva laughed. 'So cold.'

'Now please, leave me alone.'

Reva got up from his seat. He walked over to Sylvia. She didn't move at all. With her sunglasses on he couldn't see her eyes but he knew she was looking at him. Hadn't looked away since he'd stood up. The way a rabbit watches a suspected predator as it decides whether or not to make a mad dash for safety.

He stood over her. Looked up her long legs, to her chest. He wanted to touch her. To grab her. Why was he so drawn to her? He hated her, just like she hated him, but...

She shuffled up in her seat and folded her arms, as though trying to cover herself more.

'What?' she said to him, sounding less in control now than moments before.

He grew a little taller, felt a tingle in his groin. He thrived on her vulnerability.

Footsteps behind him.

He turned. Groaned inwardly. Who else?

'Alexei,' he said.

'Olek. Everything okay?'

'Yes, fine. Come on, let's get out of here.'

He turned and strode toward him.

'But I was going to stay here—'

'You're coming with me,' Reva said. He wasn't leaving those two alone.

'Sure.'

A little glance to his woman before Alexei turned and walked with Reva into the house.

* * *

An hour later they were sitting on the terrace of the bar in Heraklion, an ice-cold beer each on the table in front of them.

'I spoke to one of our people in Athens,' Alexei said.

'Who?'

'No one you know. Just someone who keeps an eye out for us.'

A strange answer. Why would Alexei hold back on him?

'And?' he asked.

'And they reckon there's some heat in Athens. On Konstantin's place.'

'His place? You mean—'

'The block we own there. Two of the apartments are used as hangouts.'

'Heat from who?'

Alexei shrugged. 'It's not too clear, really. But a duo. From what I heard, sounds like something semi-official. Not police. Not a rival. Most likely intelligence services.'

'The Greeks wouldn't bother us,' Reva said. 'We pay them too well.'

'My thought too.'

'So you think it's the FSB?' The Russians were the next best guess.

'I think we have to be prepared for it. Particularly given what's been going on here recently.'

It did make some sense, especially given Smolov's under-handed capture.

'You don't think those two boys—'

'Were working with the FSB?' Reva said. 'It has crossed my mind. And if you're telling me there's heat in Athens too...'

'We all need to watch our backs. More than ever.'

Reva's phone buzzed on the table. He picked it up. Jesper. No pleasantries. Jesper never called for chit-chat.

'What is it?' Reva asked.

'Give me an update,' Jesper said.

Reva had done so only yesterday, and really nothing had changed since. Still, he went through the list.

'This isn't good, Olek. I'm hearing a lot of bad news.'

'From who?'

'From everyone.'

Reva paused and thought again about Alexei's claim of heat in Athens.

'I'm going to the mainland tomorrow. The first shipments from our new partners arrive—'

'No,' Jesper said.

'No what?'

'It's not the right time.'

'It's already arranged.'

'The goods are on the water?'

'Not on the water, but on the way certainly.'

'Then it's not too late to cancel. They'll find someone else for the goods this time.'

'That's not exactly the point—'

'It's exactly the point. I want nothing going into Athens. Nothing going into Crete. Not until we figure this out. The risk isn't worth it.'

Reva said nothing. He looked over at Alexei. The younger man watched him curiously. He was party to only half the conversation but could he tell what Jesper was saying? Was he enjoying this moment?

'Olek, do you understand me?' Jesper asked. 'The business in Athens needs to stop. For now.'

'And I suppose you want me to give the bad news to our new partners.'

The Tunisians wouldn't be happy. Would they want blood? Possibly. Certainly, they'd want compensation. Money for nothing.

'It's your arrangement,' Jesper said.

Reva clenched his teeth.

'Finish what you can in Crete today. Tomorrow you come back here, to me. You're needed.'

Reva continued to stare at Alexei. His mind tumbled with thoughts: the immediate conversation he was about to have with the underling. About how he was heading home. How Alexei would be 'in charge' once more. Unfettered access to Sylvia. And what about her? He could imagine the snide look on her face when she found out Reva had been called home. The thought made his blood boil. Was there a way to truly leave his mark here first?

Had Alexei planned this? Gone to Jesper behind Reva's back with the knowledge he had from Athens, just to get Reva pulled away?

'Olek, are you still there?'

'Yes. You want me to come home?' His voice sounded weak. Alexei somehow grew in stature as he looked on.

'That's what I said. I'll see you soon, old friend.'

The phone call ended.

26

PRESENT

They initially traveled in a police car to a small port on the outskirts of Heraklion, where Ryker and the two FSB agents were transferred to a small boat that set off across the Med. Four other men were on the boat, all in black uniforms – combat gear with no identification. None of them spoke. Ryker had no clue if they were Greek or Russian or what.

Still in cuffs, Ryker sat back on the bench he'd been plonked on and watched his captors with interest. They traveled northeast, Ryker decided, by the position of the sun – toward Turkey? After about an hour at sea one of the guards shared out bottles of water. Ryker couldn't take his himself, with his hands tied behind him, so Petrova pushed the bottle to his lips. Ryker only took small sips, most of the liquid dribbling down his chest, such was the difficulty of having someone else feed him water on a bobbing vessel.

He took enough. Both for refreshment and for the tranquilizer to take effect. He knew within seconds that was what they'd done. The world before him blurring and fading, Zhirov's smile growing, Ryker drifted off.

* * *

He had no clue how long he was out for. Anywhere from a couple of hours to... Anything above that really, if they'd topped up the dosage through a needle while he was out. Whatever the answer, they were still traveling when he awoke. A road vehicle. Ryker was lying on his side. A barely cushioned bench. The car, or van, traveled on poor-quality road, the vehicle bouncing around, Ryker's body jolting and smacking against the bench and the side of the vehicle. His hands remained cuffed behind him, but he was also in darkness with a cloth sack over his head, hot and stuffy.

'You're awake,' came the voice from in front of him. Ryker tried to pull himself up. His body ached, his neck in particular. He'd obviously been stuck in an awkward position for some time. 'I could tell you were awake by the way you were breathing.'

Petrova. Sounding as calm and in control as ever.

'Where are we?' Ryker asked, the words coming out in a slur.

'Nearly there now.'

'Russia.'

'Yes.'

'What part?'

'The nearest city to here is Chita.'

'Nearest?'

'A few hours' drive away. Do you know Chita?'

'No.'

'Okay. So we're currently a few hundred kilometers east of Irkutsk. Chita is further east from here. We're two or three hundred kilometers north of the border with Mongolia.'

They were in deepest, darkest nowhere.

'Why the sack?' Ryker asked.

'It's just the way we do things here.'

Ryker said nothing to that, though he would be lying if he said he wasn't anxious. He'd been stuck in far-flung Russian prisons before. Both officially and unofficially. His most horrific experience had been his last, when he'd spent several months in a Gulag in frozen Siberia. Unofficial incarceration, on that occasion. At the hands of the FSB – his current captors. He'd suffered horribly. All manners of psychological torture had been employed to try to 'break' him. And he had broken. Those dark memories came right to the fore now. That last time he'd faced certain lifetime imprisonment, with his own people having left him for dead. Eventually, he'd managed to orchestrate his own escape, only to find his own people no longer trusted him. His life with the JIA, his relationship with the people there, had never been the same after that. If they hadn't bothered to save him back then – and he didn't even work for the JIA anymore – what chance did he have of rescue this time? None. Likely no one would even know where he was.

All these years later did he still have the fight in him to achieve his own escape again?

If Petrova kept her word, he wouldn't need to. If. Unfortunately, he simply didn't yet know whether Petrova's words and actions were one big deceit. Was her plan all along simply to bring Ryker here for him to see out his miserable days?

He'd find out soon enough.

He flinched when he heard her shuffling. Seconds later someone pulled the sack from his head. No sudden influx of light. It was dark outside. No lights on the road. Just the headlight beams of the four-by-four bouncing through the dense pine forest that surrounded them.

There was nothing around here. Nothing for miles. Those painful memories surfaced once more. He caught Petrova's eye. No smugness there, she looked almost sympathetic.

'Don't worry,' she said. 'This is just for show.'

Her words, her manner were genuinely reassuring. Ryker

looked around the space inside the vehicle. A driver and another man were up front, beyond a thick plastic divider. In the back, it was just Ryker and Petrova.

'Where's your friend?' Ryker asked.

'He's busy,' Petrova answered, looking out of her window. 'Here we go, this is it.'

Ryker looked out the front window. A wide, arched entrance came into view. Two big brick pillars either side, tall wooden gates in between. With barbed wire twisting across the top of the wall that ran off from the pillars in each direction, it reminded Ryker of the pictures he'd seen of World War II concentration camps. Well, this probably had been a Gulag back then. Signage warned that the area was private, mentioning various forms of punishment for trespassers, ranging from fines to shooting. As if there were hikers in these woods who might otherwise accidentally try to walk through.

Before they reached the gates, the vehicle became bathed in bright white light from a spotlight in a guard tower beyond the wall. The driver slowed to a stop and the gates swung open. Out marched two uniformed guards – military-style fatigues – with assault rifles slung over their shoulders. Forty or so yards behind the guards, sporadic orange lighting provided a glimpse of the grim and bleak low-rise structure of the prison.

The passenger up front got out and opened the door by Petrova.

'Come on,' she said to Ryker.

She stepped outside. Ryker followed. As he did so the heavens above opened and thick drops of rain pelted down onto the dirt ground.

The two guards from the prison came behind Ryker, grabbed his arms, and marched him forward, through the open gates. Petrova walked ahead of him, up to a man standing further beyond the gates. Legs apart. Arms folded. A cap over his head from which water dripped down onto the already rain-soaked ground. He and Petrova held a brief conversation. The guards brought Ryker to a stop a few yards from them though the rain drowned out their words. After a while, the man's hard face showing no reaction at all, Petrova turned and walked back to Ryker.

'This is it,' she said to him, with more than a hint of apprehension. Did she doubt her own plan?

'What now?' Ryker asked.

'Now you do as you're told. Make this easy for yourself. I'll be in touch.'

With that, she walked off. The engine of the 4x4 started up, and Ryker heard the clunk as the gates shut behind him. The guards marched him up to the man who hadn't moved a muscle. Up close, in the thin light, his features were gnarled.

'Welcome,' he said, his voice hoarse and as hard as his looks. 'Welcome to the last place you'll ever see.'

27

Out of the rain, the guards hauled Ryker through grim corridors to a simple square room. Not a cell. Just a plain, old, windowless room. The only furniture was a table upon which sat Ryker's prison clothes. Underwear. Trousers. Top. All three light brown and baggy.

'You really want to watch me?' Ryker said to the guards who had said nothing to him but who stood glaring at him once they'd released the cuffs on Ryker's hands.

No reply. Ryker got dressed and the guards took him back along narrow and poorly lit corridors. He tried his best to remember the route, tried to picture the layout of the structure in his head. They moved through a locked and barred door, where a guard stood sentry, and onto a corridor with a stretch of cell doors, five on each side. The guards shoved Ryker into the final cell on the right. A cell that was as dark and grim and slimy as any Ryker had seen. Cold concrete walls, cold concrete floor and ceiling. As for furniture, he had a toilet and a concrete bed that had a worn-down sponge mattress and a single grimy sheet.

'Enjoy,' one of the guards said as he slammed the door shut with a thunk.

Darkness. The windowless room had a single light fixture – Ryker had spotted it as he'd walked in – but it wasn't on. The only illumination he had were the slivers coming through the tiny gaps in the door frame, though the corridor out there was hardly bathed in bright light either.

Ryker sat down on the cold, hard bunk and sighed. Had he just made the biggest mistake of his life?

No. There'd been bigger. He groaned at that thought. Out loud. A strange thing to do, he realized. Perhaps just the first signs of distress.

'Welcome, comrade,' came a faint Russian voice through the wall behind Ryker's head. 'What's your name?'

'My name is James Ryker,' he responded in English.

A pause. Then a laugh.

'English. You must have been a very naughty boy,' the man said, continuing in Russian.

Ryker decided to switch:

'Would you believe me if I said I was innocent?'

Another pause. Perhaps because he was surprised at Ryker's fluency. Then another laugh.

'Every man in here is innocent. If you look at it a certain way.' Ryker felt he knew what he meant by that. There were no regular prisoners here, no one who'd gone through an open and objective trial process. This prison was where the government hid its enemies, away from watchful eyes, enough steps removed to provide deniability.

'You want some advice?' the man said.

'Not really.'

He laughed again. 'That's okay. If you change your mind, let me know. Just call out.'

'What's your name?' Ryker asked.

'My name? Just call me Igor.'

The click of locks disturbed Ryker's unlikely sleep. The door to his cell burst open and in strode the guards. They yanked Ryker off the bed and to his feet. A fist to the gut knocked the wind from him. A blow to the back of the head sent his head spinning. The cuffs on his wrists put an end to any thought of an immediate counter-assault.

His mind groggy and his limbs heavy, the guards pulled Ryker out of the cell block, along the corridor... No, they weren't going back the same way as before. Instead, they headed through double doors and to a staircase. Up to the next and final floor. A smaller corridor here, suggesting the top floor only sat upon part of the ground floor structure. Through some double doors. Carpet. Proper lighting. Through another door to an office.

The man from outside. Standing in front of a battered, old, dark-wood desk. Same pose as before.

The guards twisted Ryker's wrists behind his back. Kicks to the back of his knees caused his legs to buckle and the guards forced him down.

Then silence. Ryker stared up at the man, who in turn stared back down.

'I don't know who you are,' the man said in Russian. 'I don't care who you are. I don't care what you did. You're here. That means you're under my watch. That means you do what I say.'

Ryker said nothing.

'This isn't a prison. No one cares you're here. You won't make friends here. You won't get a TV or a radio or a phone or books.

Your life is mine now. This is my kingdom. I'm the king. Do you understand me?'

Ryker still said nothing. He winced when he took the blow to the back. A sharp, hard thwack that sent a stinging pain up his spine. A baton?

'When he asks you a question, you answer it properly,' one of the guards behind Ryker said. 'Yes, Colonel.'

'Do you understand me?' the colonel asked again.

'Yes... Colonel,' Ryker said.

'Good. Let me explain the rules. There are only two. Rule number one, you do what I say, and what my men say. If you obey rule number one you get one hour out of your cell each day. You'll also get two decent enough meals a day. But, rule number two, keep your cell clean and don't smear shit around the place and we won't piss and spit and shit in your food in return.'

'Not all the time, anyway,' one of the guards behind Ryker said. The colonel smiled a little at the quip but kept his focus on Ryker.

'Am I clear?' the colonel asked.

'Yes, Colonel,' Ryker said.

'Good. Now take him back. Give him a real introduction. He looks far too comfortable.'

The guards yanked Ryker back to his feet. Tugged him out of the room, back toward the stairs. 'A real introduction'. Ryker could guess what the colonel meant by that. Most likely a beating. Fists, feet, batons. Nothing serious or long-lasting. That didn't make the prospect any more appealing. They reached the stairs, Ryker deep in contemplation about how to react. Take the beating? Squeal like a pig and beg them to stop? Or fight back and show them he wasn't like the other prisoners.

'Watch your step,' the guard behind Ryker, on his left, said.

Right before they let go of Ryker's wrists and shoved him in the back. With his hands behind him, Ryker could do nothing to stop from falling. He tumbled forward, head first. Managed to twist his body, pull on his neck, to stop his skull from cracking onto the concrete step. Instead, his shoulder took the brunt of the first blow. But it was only the first of many as his body bounced and twisted and banged and smacked down the stairs. By the time he landed in a crumpled heap at the bottom, every part of his body roared with pain.

Above the agony, he heard the guards' laughter.

'And that was your real introduction. Hope you enjoyed it.'

Ryker said nothing as his head slumped to the floor.

28

'Any broken bones?' Igor asked.

Ryker didn't know how long he'd been back in the cell. Several hours. One meal. Most likely daytime had arrived outside now, but in the cell, he had no way to tell, he saw and felt no distinction at all.

'No,' Ryker said.

'You were lucky.'

'I don't think so.'

'Not long ago a man broke his neck.'

Ryker said nothing. He balled his fists to channel his anger. The simple gesture caused a wave of pain up his arm.

'What did you do, to end up here?' Igor asked.

'I told you, I'm innocent.'

Igor said nothing straight away, then, 'But what did they say you did?'

'Espionage, murder.'

'But you didn't do it.'

'I didn't.'

'But someone thinks you did.'

'Someone set me up.'

'Do you know who?'

'No.'

Another pause from Igor. 'So what's the story. Tourist? Journalist?'

'Wrong place at the wrong time.'

Igor chuckled. He liked to do that. Ryker hadn't yet seen his closest jail mate in the flesh, but from his husky voice, and his manner, Ryker imagined a middle-aged man, relaxed and with a smiley face. Average height, a little plump. Glasses. A little bit of a studious look. He wondered how close to the truth that was.

'Sorry, my friend, but I'll be honest with you,' Igor said. 'I don't believe you.'

'About what?'

'Your story. I know this place. I've been here a long time. They don't send just anyone here. They don't make mistakes like that. Every man in this place is here for a very good reason. Even if we don't agree with that reason.'

Ryker said nothing to that as his mind whirred.

'If you're truthful with me, I'll be truthful with you,' Igor said.

'I have been truthful,' Ryker said. 'I shouldn't be here.'

Igor said nothing.

'When they took me,' Ryker said, 'I was interrogated by two officers. Over and over. They kept asking me the same questions. Kept on saying the same names.'

No response from Igor now.

'Are you there?'

'I'm here. They asked you about names? Which names?'

Ryker thought before he answered. Should he do this? Was there a risk Igor was a stooge and Ryker taking this step would land him in deeper shit with the colonel? Would Ryker even blow his own cover somehow?

'A few names,' Ryker said. 'I don't remember them all. The one they said the most was Roman Smolov. They wanted to know if I knew Roman Smolov.'

Silence once more from Igor. But not for long. 'Roman Smolov?' he said, his voice a little deeper and less friendly than before.

'Yes. Do you know him?'

'I know him. Why are you asking about him?'

'I wasn't,' Ryker said. 'I don't know him. Just a name. I don't even know why I was being asked about him.'

'Yes, well—'

BANG. BANG.

A thunderous double rap on Ryker's cell door.

'You two. That's enough,' came the guttural voice of a guard.

Ryker held his breath a few moments, listening with keen interest until he heard the footsteps tapping away.

'Roman Smolov is here,' Igor said, his voice quieter, almost inaudible now. 'He's in the next block. I can get a message to him if you want.'

That wasn't what Ryker wanted at all.

'No. I told you, I don't even know him.'

'If you say so,' Igor said. 'Speak soon, James Ryker.'

29

She rose up from the bed. Reva watched her luscious, naked body, her skin glistening with perspiration as she moved to the chair by the dressing table. She took her panties from the seat and slipped them on, facing away from him, then took the jeans from the back of the chair and pulled those on too. She picked up the jumper.

'Come over here,' he said to her.

She turned to him. Not a smile on her face. Not much of anything, really. She moved back to him, looked at him quizzically.

'Sit down.'

She hesitated then did so, resting on the edge of the bed. He pushed himself up and shuffled next to her. The jumper remained clutched in her hands. All of his clothes lay on the floor still. If he'd been a younger man he would have had her one more time before she left. Not today. He couldn't afford to wait that long.

'I have to go,' she said, not looking at him.

'Okay,' he said. 'But I'll see you again soon.'

She said nothing. She went to pull the jumper on but he reached out and held her forearms close to her thigh to stop her. He let go and her hands stayed there. He reached up and drew his finger along the lines of reddened flesh around her neck. Imprints. Hand imprints. His hands.

'It's okay,' she said. 'I'll cover up. In a couple of days, it will be gone. He won't find out.'

He thought about saying something to her. Sorry? No, not that.

'If he—'

'He won't find out,' she said. 'I promise. Please, just... Please?' He got it. She was wary. If her husband found out, the guy would be upset. Angry. Vengeful. Would he be more bothered that someone had hurt his wife, or that someone had screwed her? Reva didn't know. But he did sense her worry. Not of what her husband would do to Reva, but of what Reva would do to her husband. He liked the easy sex with her, but that's all it was. He didn't want a jealous husband banging on his door, causing problems. The blood would be on her hands if that happened.

'Be careful,' he said to her.

She nodded and got up from the bed. She pulled on the jumper, didn't once look back at him. Soon she was gone.

Reva showered then dressed. Women remained on his mind as he did so. Since coming home he'd quickly fallen back into old routines. He hadn't slept alone on one night. But was he truly satisfied? No. He didn't like to think about it, but did he really gain from such one-sided relationships? Not that he was looking for more, certainly not love, but he questioned the type of woman he'd become used to bedding here. Easy. Boring.

His mind inevitably drifted back to Crete. Iya. Even Georgiadis. Most of all Sylvia, who surely felt a power trip at Reva having been called home so abruptly. Any one of those women provided a challenge he didn't receive here. Despite everything, he missed the Greek isle.

So long as Smolov remained behind bars, then that place still needed him. He'd find a way to go back.

He arrived at Jesper's compound a little after 3 p.m. The sun was shining, it was warm out, but in the rough-looking countryside of eastern Ukraine, the place felt so very different to the coastal position of Smolov's place on the Med. Nothing luxurious here. More a fortress than a villa. The outer perimeter wall of the compound – what had been a livestock farm until two decades ago – was rendered white, much like at Smolov's villa in Crete, but here the render was cracked, missing in places, paint bubbled here and there. A roll of barbed wire topped the wall. An old water tower just beyond the wall had been converted into a sentry post, and as the gates opened and Reva drove through he saw another two armed guards there. The armed guards patrolled all hours, every day. This was Jesper's home, but there was little homely about it in the traditional sense.

Reva parked up next to the other vehicles and headed for the front door of the mammoth but plain-looking house – two stories, nine bedrooms, but the structure was simple and blocky and the masses of tarmac and rubble together with the unkempt garden that surrounded the home only confirmed that this was not the lap of luxury. Not that Jesper couldn't afford a nice home. In fact, across the globe, through various offshore arrangements, he owned several designer pads. Except he couldn't use those anymore. Not now. This place was as good as it got for Jesper. As near a recluse as a man could be.

Reva passed another two guards on the way to the door. They nodded in greeting. Inside the dim, musky entrance hallway yet another armed man.

'He's waiting for you in the kitchen,' the man said.

Reva didn't say anything but headed on through to the aging kitchen that looked exactly like the home it belonged to. Spacious, but plain. Farmhouse style, perhaps, but all the cupboards and units were banged up, the oven and fridge and other electrical items were grimy-looking and out of date. Jesper was sitting at the round pine dining table, a coffee cup in his shaky hand. He was alone. Despite the warm temperature outside he wore a thick woolen cardigan. He was hunched over in his chair, his wispy gray hair falling over his face. The truth was, to Reva he looked a mess. Not the man he used to be, to look at anyway, even if he remained more powerful than ever amongst his own people.

'Ah, you're here,' Jesper said. He sat up a little straighter and put his cup down and made a move to stand.

'No,' Reva said. 'You stay there.' He moved over to Jesper and leaned in and kissed him on his leathery forehead.

'You're enjoying being home?' Jesper said with a bit of a grin.

'No place like it,' Reva said.

'Which one were you with this time?' Jesper asked, though Reva sensed no answer was necessary. 'Always the same with you.'

Reva said nothing, but something about the accusatory tone didn't sit well with him.

'Tell me,' Jesper said as Reva took the seat next to his boss. 'What have you found out?'

'I don't like what's happening in Crete,' Reva said. 'The police are giving us the runaround.'

'I thought you said they were ours?'

'They are. They were. But...' He trailed off and sighed. 'They arrested a man. A man who was lurking on Smolov's property.'

'You told me about this. You told me you thought he was FSB.'

'No. I said it wouldn't surprise me. He claimed to be English, but the police couldn't give me any useful information on who he was, or why he was there.'

'But they pinned the murder on him, you said.'

'Initially, they were trying to, yes. But now he's gone.'

'Gone?'

'I'm getting all this second-hand. The police released him, but they won't tell us why, or who he was. The police are doubling down. They've destroyed all of the concocted evidence they were putting together. Covering their backs, but making it harder for us at the same time.'

'They released him, or they don't have him anymore? There is a difference.'

'You think they found out who he was?' Reva asked. 'That he was an agent of another country – FSB, perhaps – and were forced to let him go?'

'Possibly. Or someone else could have taken him. A prisoner exchange.'

'And exchange with who? And in exchange for what?'

'You're looking to me for answers?'

Jesper delivered the question calmly enough, but Reva knew by his tone that he was far from impressed with the situation.

'What do you know about the man?' Jesper asked.

'Nothing.'

'No name even?'

'Just that he was some drifter, a homeless guy. Nothing more than that.'

'And where is this man now?'

'Exactly.'

'You think they killed him to protect themselves?'

'Probably not. But like I said, they're not cooperating with us now. If I was back there, in Crete, I could get the answers we need more easily. The guys out there are lost without Roman or me.'

'No,' Jesper said. 'It's of little consequence, really. Forget about Crete. That's not your job now.'

'Then what is?'

'Crete is Roman's problem.'

'Roman isn't there either.'

'Then it's time to change that,' Jesper said, before looking beyond Reva and smiling. 'Ah, you're here.'

Reva stood and turned and watched the new arrival – a woman – saunter over.

He didn't know her. He wanted to change that as soon as he looked into her sassy eyes. She smiled at him. A playful smile.

'I'd like you to meet a friend of ours from Athens,' Jesper said. 'The one I told you about.'

'Right,' Reva said. She held out her hand and Reva took it. When he went to release the grip, she held on for a split second longer. Not tightly, and just long enough to make him notice. Long enough to allow her to smoothly slide her fingers away from his at her choosing.

'Olek,' Jesper said. 'Meet Eleni.'

30

Days passed. Ryker was sure it was days, although the lack of natural light and the boredom of captivity made it much harder to keep track of time. He'd been to the yard for exercise three times, which he took to mean three days, but the gaps between the exercise slots didn't feel equal at all, adding to his doubts about how long he'd been in the Gulag.

His injuries from the fall down the stairs were healing nicely, which gave another indicator of the passage of time. A few aches and pains remained, but nothing serious. He tried what he could to get his body moving during those exercise periods, but the space provided outside, a fenced-off area all of ten yards square, with no equipment at all, was hardly conducive to that.

Igor had gone quiet. Ryker knew he was still there, next door, but their chats had been few and far between, and only banal in nature. No more mention of Roman Smolov. No more questions about who Ryker was or what he'd done. Ryker was both relieved and disappointed by that. Relieved that he hadn't blown his own cover mentioning Smolov, but disappointed that nothing had moved on.

A bang on his cell door broke his chain of thoughts. The door opened. Too soon for food; he'd eaten the gruel they served not long ago.

'You've got visitors,' one of the two guards said.

Ryker went through the usual routine as the guards rough-handled and cuffed him. He'd already come to realize that the less he resisted, the less they smacked him with their batons. Still, he received the obligatory one or two whatever approach he took.

They moved Ryker on through. He expected them to retrace the steps from the first day, back to that plain room, or one near it, where he'd first got dressed in his prison garb. Instead, they moved for the stairs, then toward the colonel's office.

Visitors?

The door to the colonel's office opened. No. He had no visitors in there. Just the man himself. In front of his desk. Normal pose. Had he even moved since Ryker last saw him in there?

Ryker was soon on his knees. The whole thing a carbon copy of the first time he'd been in the room.

'Two people are here to see you,' the colonel said, clearly annoyed about the fact.

Ryker said nothing even though a cheeky quip had sprung to the tip of his tongue.

'Did you hear me?'

'Yes, Colonel,' Ryker said.

'I don't like visitors here. I don't like my prisoners talking to anyone who doesn't belong here.'

Once again Ryker kept his mouth shut.

'I don't know these two well, but I know who they are, who they work for. Good people.'

Ryker still said nothing.

'But I'm asking you, why are they here?' the colonel asked.

'I don't know,' Ryker said. A whack on his back. He grimaced. 'I don't know, Colonel.'

'You don't know? You've been here for four days, and already they're coming here to check on you. Ask you questions? I don't like it.'

'I didn't ask them here,' Ryker said.

The colonel lunged forward and slapped Ryker's face with the back of his hand. A slap, but a ferocious one, all of the weight of his upper body behind it. Ryker fell to his side, his face smacking onto the carpet.

'I didn't tell you to talk!' the colonel screamed into Ryker's ear before he was pulled back to his knees.

The colonel walked back to his position, resumed his stance. Was calm again. As calm as he got, anyway. 'I know who they work for, but I don't trust anyone. Be careful what you tell them. And if you're playing games with me... Next time you see me in here you won't be walking up those stairs on your own. Do you understand me?'

'Yes, Colonel.'

'Get him out of here.'

The guards hauled Ryker to his feet and shepherded him out.

* * *

The room the guards took Ryker to was as bland and soulless as Ryker's cell. The bare concrete walls were pockmarked and had dirty streaks here and there, stains from water ingress or perhaps leaking pipes. There was no window, no two-way mirror even, just a flickering bulb overhead and a CCTV camera in one corner.

The guards folded Ryker into the bolted-down chair and attached the cuffs on his wrist to the metal bar protruding from the functional but sturdy table. One guard remained, standing at the closed door, arms folded. A couple of minutes later came a knock, and in they strode, guard in tow.

Ryker said nothing to Petrova and Zhirov as they walked around the table and took the seats on that side.

'Leave us,' Petrova said to the guards without looking at them.

A clank as the door closed behind Ryker. He looked from the twosome and up to the camera in the corner.

'It's not on,' Petrova said.

'You're sure?' Ryker asked.

'One hundred percent,' Zhirov said.

'You trust the colonel?'

Zhirov smirked.

'He might seem like a powerful man to you,' Petrova said. 'After all, in here—'

'He's the king,' Ryker finished for her.

Petrova looked at him and nodded.

'A king among fleas,' Zhirov said.

'The camera isn't on,' Petrova said. 'That's all you need to know.'

Ryker didn't say anything as he stared at them both. Would it even matter if the colonel was listening and watching? In theory, Ryker was on the same side as him anyway, so what would it matter if the colonel knew Ryker's incarceration was a scam? He was there to get to Smolov, there to ultimately get to Jesper, an enemy of the Russian state. Perhaps in the near future, Jesper would be under the care of the colonel because of Ryker's work...

'How is it here?' Petrova asked.

'Is that a serious question?'

She looked a little offended, perhaps because of the genuine bitterness in Ryker's tone.

'I thought you were a tough guy?' Zhirov said. 'You've only

been here a few days. No broken bones. No missing body parts. What's your problem?'

'You want me to kick you down a flight of concrete stairs?' Ryker asked. 'Then perhaps we can discuss toughness a bit more objectively.'

Neither of them said anything. Did they already know of the colonel's initiation? A twinge of doubt flashed in Ryker's mind. That same doubt that had lay just below the surface ever since he'd first heard Petrova's proposition. What if they were simply setting him up? What if they had no plan to get him out?

No. If everything they'd said was a charade, then they wouldn't have come to see him, would they?

'When do I get out?' Ryker asked. 'How, and when?'

Petrova and Zhirov shared a look.

'We're working on it,' Petrova said.

Ryker gritted his teeth rather than question that. Had they got anywhere at all in their plan? Were they delaying deliberately or had they hit snags that they didn't want to admit to?

'There's a man in the cell next door to me,' Ryker said. 'Igor. What do you know about him?'

'You're making friends already?' Zhirov said with the usual sly grin.

'Have you ever tried it?'

'We know about him,' Petrova said. 'We knew they were putting you next to him. He's been here for a long time.'

'Is he of interest?'

'To us? No. He's not part of this.'

'But he does know Smolov.'

Petrova looked a little unsure about that.

'You've been asking questions about Smolov?' Zhirov said. 'Are you that stupid?'

'No,' Ryker said. 'I wasn't asking questions. But we got talking about Smolov anyway. Really there isn't much to do other than talk. You can find out all sorts about a man.'

'And?' Zhirov said, challenging in his tone. 'What have you learned about Smolov?'

'He's not even in the same block as me,' Ryker said. 'How am I supposed to get close to him, to befriend him and gain his trust if I haven't even met him?'

'Look, Ryker, you let us worry about how this works,' Zhirov said. 'Don't go doing anything stupid. You mess up in here, and we can just leave you to rot if we want.'

Ryker held his eye on Petrova, not wanting to rise to Zhirov's continued heckling.

'He's right,' she said, to Ryker's irritation. 'I don't want that to happen, but we only came here today to check in and make sure you're okay. The reality is that the less you know, the better. Keep your head down, don't aggravate the colonel, or the other inmates.'

'And don't blow your cover,' Zhirov added.

The two of them got to their feet.

'Stay safe,' Petrova said, putting her hand on Ryker's shoulder as she spoke.

Zhirov just glared.

Moments later they were both gone.

31

Not much sleep, not much to eat, not much exercise, not much sunlight, but one thing Ryker was afforded plenty of in the Gulag was time for contemplation. Hours a day he'd sit alone in his cell, quietly thinking. His life. His mistakes. The colonel. Igor. The guards. Smolov, who Ryker was still yet to meet.

Could he find a way to force the introduction?

Most of all, Ryker contemplated his escape. If Petrova and Zhirov didn't come through, then Ryker certainly wouldn't languish forever on the inside. The biggest question wasn't even *how* to force his escape, but how long he would wait before doing so.

That thought remained with him as he sat in the blazing sunshine in the yard for his measly allocated slot. Altogether, the outside space of the prison was likely overall sprawling, but through the use of fences and screening it was subdivided into multiple small square spaces of isolation. Like cattle pens. One inmate per square. Guard towers provided watch, and more guards always seemed to be close by on foot, patrolling the other side of the fences.

Ryker's brain stopped whirring when he noticed movement to his left. The outline of figures moved beyond the screening. He rose from his seated position, stepped over to that spot. He pushed his ear close to the fence. He was well used to the routine by now. Several inmates were allowed out at the same time, though the times for each were staggered. Most likely because there were only so many guards, who worked on a continuous cycle of one out, one in. Igor always came out after Ryker. Always into the square to the east of Ryker's. But he should have been out minutes ago. So why the change?

BANG.

Ryker reeled back from the fence which shook and wobbled from whoever or whatever had hit it from the other side.

'Who are you?' came the unfamiliar voice from beyond the fence.

Ryker didn't say anything.

'I know you're there. I can smell you.'

Still Ryker didn't say a word.

'You smell like shit. Pig shit.'

Ryker took a deep inhale. 'Smells like fresh air to me.' Though actually, he could definitely smell the man he was talking to, he realized. Nothing like shit, but definitely a musky, sweaty odor – only to be expected given a combination of the outdoor heat, the grubby clothes, and the semi-regular showers.

'You like pig shit?' the man asked with a laugh.

'Not really.'

'No? Well, I guess I do. I grew up on a pig farm. My father was a pig farmer. His father too. We bred them, reared them, slaughtered them. I started to clean out for them when I was six years old. I've known pig shit my whole life.'

'You definitely know your shit.'

Ryker wondered if the translation made sense. The laugh suggested maybe it had.

'You know what? I changed my mind. I don't like the smell of pig shit, of any shit really, though it does remind me of home. I think that's a good thing.'

'Maybe.'

'Shit is shit. But pigs themselves? Decent animals. Clever. You can train them, a certain amount. But what's the fucking point of training a pig? Much nicer to have a dog or a human if you want a companion.'

'If you say so.'

'I do. But, that's not to say pigs don't have their uses.'

'Eating them?'

Another laugh. 'Yeah, I know my way around a pig, that's for sure. There's a cut for every occasion. One of the things that surprises me the most is how good it tastes even when you know what they eat. You know, a pig will eat anything.'

'I've heard.'

'Flesh, gristle, bone, hair. And it's not just what they eat, it's how much they eat, and how they eat it.'

'Greedy as a pig,' Ryker said. Another expression that perhaps wasn't well known in Russian.

'You're English,' the man said. 'I know that saying.'

'Good deduction,' Ryker said.

'What's your name?'

'Doesn't matter to you.'

'It doesn't?'

'No.'

'But my name matters to you?'

'Does it? I don't even know your name.'

'Roman Smolov.'

Ryker had guessed as much.

'You do know my name,' Smolov said, sounding less amicable now, 'because it was you who used it.'

So Igor had betrayed Ryker after all? But did it even matter if he had, because wasn't this – him meeting with Smolov – only what Ryker needed, and wanted to happen?

'I did use your name,' Ryker said.

'Why would you do that? How do you know me?'

'Which of those questions should I answer first?'

An agitated sigh. 'How do you know me?'

'I don't.'

'Then why are you asking questions about me?'

'I wasn't.'

BANG.

Ryker flinched at the unexpected whack on the fence. The rattling continued as the fence recovered. Ryker waited for an angry retort to his blank statement but none came so he decided to carry on.

'I wasn't asking questions about you,' Ryker said. 'I told Igor that the FSB was asking *me* about *you*. They mentioned your name to me. More than once.'

'Why would they do that?'

'You'd have to ask them.'

'Who?'

Ryker thought for a moment. Should he say?

'Their names are Petrova and Zhirov. That's all I know.'

Silence from Smolov now.

'Do you know them?' Ryker asked.

No answer. Ryker thought about repeating the question, but Smolov beat him to it.

'Have you ever killed a man?' the Russian asked.

'Yes,' Ryker said.

'You didn't even need to think about that.'

'Because I have a good memory. And it wasn't a hard question.'

'But many men, and women, who have killed, have trouble saying it out loud. They feel shame. Or remorse.'

'Sometimes I do,' Ryker said. 'But most of the people I've killed deserved it.'

'Most of them?'

'Everyone makes mistakes.'

'But it sounds like killing isn't new to you.'

'It's not. But that doesn't mean I like it.'

'I was sixteen when I killed a man for the first time.' Smolov let the statement hang. Ryker didn't say anything. 'I still worked on the farm then. I was big, strong. A real laborer. Do you know what I did to him?'

'Fed him to the pigs?'

Another laugh from Smolov.

'I thought you'd say that.'

'You set it up very well.'

'You're right. And those pigs would happily have eaten a whole body, I'm sure. Maybe they did in the past. I never asked my father. Or my grandfather. But see how easily you were fooled into thinking one thing? Into saying something without truly thinking it through. I have to ask myself, can I trust a man like that? Can I trust him even in a place like this, to keep his mouth shut when he needs to?'

'You don't have to worry about me. Like I said, I don't even know you.'

'But those two agents, talking to you. The ones who visit you here. They know you. They know me.'

Another pause. Did Smolov want Ryker to say something to that?

'I think we moved off subject there,' Ryker said. 'So if not the pigs, then how did you do it?'

A pause before Smolov continued.

'His name was Andrei. He was a friend of my sister. He was a nice guy, friendly to me because he knew her, and because he knew my reputation. He knew I wanted to be the tough guy. He was older and bigger than me, but that isn't everything, and he would never have dared to challenge me.'

'He hurt your sister?'

'No. He slept with her one time. Her first, not his. But he didn't treat her badly. She was like that. She got what she wanted. She was a slut back then, in truth. But he was good to her. He wasn't so good with his money. He owed me.'

'How much?'

'That's not important. Enough. A couple of bottles of vodka, a few joints. Whatever. He owed me. He kept giving me weak excuses. Until one night, when he came to the farm to see my sister, I told him he wasn't coming inside unless I got my money. He had nothing on him, so I said my sister was in the barn and we walked over there. Inside, I hit him over the head with a shovel. Knocked him unconscious. I tied him to a chair.' Another pause and a scratching sound before Smolov started up again. 'I had this sewing needle in my pocket. I don't know why really. It'd been on a side table in the house and I'd picked it up and was playing with it. So I prized Andrei's eyelid open with one hand, so I could see his pupil, and, quite gently really, I pushed that needle right through the hole, into the nerve or whatever else it is behind there. Nearly the whole thing disappeared. He woke up, of course. He screamed. He called me everything he could think of calling me, shaking his head furiously with the end of the needle still protruding from his eyeball. Very freaky. But he said some very hurtful things. About me, my sister. My whole family really. So I went back to the house, took my mother's craft scissors, and I cut off his tongue to stop the words from rolling.'

Smolov paused once more and Ryker said nothing as he waited. He was well aware the story wasn't over, and that Smolov likely hoped Ryker was shocked by what he'd heard. He was. But perhaps not as shocked as Smolov wanted him to be.

'His words stopped, but not his screams, and I was worried my father would hear. Or my sister. Or anyone within ten miles.' A callous laugh. 'So I stuffed the tongue back in his bleeding mouth. Pushed it in as far as I could until all that came out of him was a choke and a... hiss. Strange really, the sound he made. I remember it so well, but it's hard to describe. Then he went silent.'

He said those last words solemnly. Smolov himself had talked about shame and remorse. Did Smolov feel either of those things when reminiscing about Andrei, his first kill?

'I hadn't wanted to kill him. Only to teach him a lesson. But I was young and dumb. I thought about giving the body to the pigs but... I liked those beasts too much, somehow it didn't seem fair on them to make them part of my mistake. Instead, I used a handsaw to cut Andrei into pieces and I went into the forest and spent several hours burning piece after piece. I buried the ashes, teeth, bits of bone that the fire hadn't destroyed. No one ever found out what I did.' Another pause and a sigh. 'Have you ever smelled burning flesh?'

'Yes,' Ryker said.

'Horrible, isn't it?'

'Yes.'

'I was so hungry all the time. My brain told me to be disgusted but my stomach only wanted that roasted meat.'

Ryker closed his eyes to try and push his own memories away.

'You know, after that I didn't eat meat for a week,' Smolov said. 'Not until my father nearly choked me shoving pork fillet into my mouth, he'd become so mad at my refusal. Practically the same as I did to Andrei with his tongue.'

Both men went silent. Ryker continued to think through the story, to think about what it meant about the man he was talking to. The man he'd been sent to prison to help escape.

Ryker heard the shuffling of feet. The guards. Coming for him.

'Next time you'll tell me something about you, yes?' Smolov said. A demand, rather than a suggestion.

Ryker said nothing. The guards opened the gate and came toward him.

'Speak to you soon, James Ryker,' Smolov said. 'And remember my story. Don't let that tongue get you into trouble.'

Smolov gave a hearty laugh as the guards pulled Ryker away.

32

Two days passed. Two lackluster days, like most days on the inside of a prison where inmates were isolated from human contact for more than twenty hours a day. At least Ryker suffered no horror treatment, no torture, not even any real beatings.

No sign of Petrova or Zhirov either...

Igor's quiet streak continued. Ryker knew he remained in the cell next door because of the guards' movements, the feeding and exercise routines, and because of the intermittent shared greetings, but Ryker and Igor hadn't engaged in a real conversation in days.

The sun blazed in the sky once more during Ryker's time in the yard. He sat in the sun, rather than the shade. Even though it was almost unbearably hot, he owed it to his skin to get some much-needed sunshine. Ryker spent the vast majority of all times in the yards sitting rather than exercising. A few push-ups here, a few sit-ups there, but no point in over-exerting himself when the temperature outside was so hot, compared to the ever consistent much cooler temperature on the inside. Really, there wasn't much he could do in the small outdoor space that he couldn't do in his cell at any other time anyway.

Activity next door. Igor? No. Something about how he heard the guards moving. The prisoner too.

'Here we are again,' Smolov said after a few moments of silence. He spoke in English this time, though his heritage remained clear in his accent.

'Yeah,' Ryker said as he got to his feet and moved closer. 'So who decides that you get to be here now. Igor? You? The guards?'

A short pause before Smolov answered. 'Interesting question.'

And that was as close as Ryker got to an answer.

'Remember, I want you to tell me something about you this time,' Smolov said.

'I'm not talking to you about me killing—'

'That wasn't what I was going to ask. I'm not sadistic.'

Ryker wasn't so sure about that.

'Then what?'

'Think about this one. Think hard if you need to. But I want to know what makes you hurt. What fills you with pain and regret. Tell me about a moment. A moment where you made a big mistake. One you wish you could change and that still haunts you.'

In truth, there'd been many such moments, and myriad thoughts flashed through Ryker's mind. All painful, some more than others. Some he'd never tell a living soul about, the memories remained too raw, the sense of loss too great, the sense of failure even greater. One thought stuck. Not the worst, but close to it.

'You have it?' Smolov asked.

'Actually, it's quite an apt story,' Ryker said.

'Apt?'

'Relevant. This isn't the first time I've been in prison. And this happened right after.'

'Now you've got me interested. Tell me more.'

'I'd been inside for a long time. There was no getting out. Not through official routes. If I was ever to see the outside world again, I knew I'd have to fight for it.'

'You escaped?'

'I did.'

'Just you.'

'Just me.'

'Why didn't you take anyone with you?'

'I didn't want to.'

'There was no one you could have helped?'

'No one I wanted to help, and no one who could have helped me.'

Smolov went silent as though contemplating this. Did he approve?

'How did you do it?' he asked.

'I fought. It's one of the things I'm good at. I learned the layout of the prison. The guards and their routines, and I simply waited for the opportunity. It wasn't easy, and I found myself hundreds of miles from safety once past the walls, but I got away. I never went back to that place.'

'This was how long ago?'

'Years.'

'Except you are back in prison now.'

'Different prison. Different reasons. Different country.' That last one was actually a lie, but Ryker wanted to throw it in there, to play down his past ties in Russia as much as he could.

'It's a nice story, but it's not the one I asked for,' Smolov said.

'It is. Because I'd been away for so long, by the time I met up with my people, they didn't trust me anymore. They couldn't believe I got out like that. So easily.'

'It does sound very easy, the way you described it.'

'Much harder in real life, believe me. But if you want something enough, you can make it happen.'

'Good point. You mentioned your people. Who are they?'

'You don't need to know the details. But there was one man in particular. He was like a father to me. At the time, for much of my adult life, he was more important to me than anyone else.'

Ryker realized his words were tinged with bitterness as the genuine emotion of those events came to the fore. Would Smolov see that as a sign of weakness?

'He was one of the first people I knew who I met on the outside. I wanted to see him, to explain. We sat down for coffee. Neutral territory. Simple, right? But I knew he didn't trust me anymore. He couldn't even look me in the eye. Even after everything I'd suffered, horrible injuries, brutality, there was something about that moment, about his manner with me, that hurt more than anything else.'

'He abandoned you,' Smolov said. 'You were no longer good enough.'

'Almost. But even more than that, he thought I was the enemy. That I'd turned against him. Nothing I would have said or done would have changed that. We could never have turned back to how we were before.'

'That was the last time you saw him?'

'The last time I saw him alive. As we left the café, a single bullet was fired from the building opposite. He was dead before he hit the ground.'

'Who did it?'

'Our enemies. Our real enemies. The very people he thought I was working with. They'd followed me. Waited for me to bring him out into the open. I caused his death. And he died thinking I was a traitor.'

Smolov sighed. Ryker shut his eyes and tried to push the emotion back inside.

'You got your own back?' Smolov said. 'On your enemies.'

'I always do.'

'They're dead now?'

'That's the best way of getting revenge.'

A short pause before, 'I think we're very alike.'

Perhaps they were. Ryker didn't want to believe it though.

'You're good at spotting opportunities?' Smolov asked.

'I try.'

'I hope so. Tonight is your last night in this prison. Tomorrow there's a transport truck coming. It's taking me, you, and four others out of here.'

'Why?' Ryker asked.

'Why what?'

'Why me?'

'Because I say so.'

'Why now?'

'The colonel runs this prison, but he doesn't run the world outside it. Funding has been cut. They can't run this place with so many inmates. They have to move us somewhere else.'

'Where are we going?'

'Just be ready.'

'Ready for what, exactly?'

'For anything. For everything.'

The sounds of the guards approaching.

'Don't let me down,' Smolov said.

'I won't.'

* * *

The next hours passed by more slowly than usual, Ryker's anticipation causing time to drag. At least that's what he thought. He was sure he should have been fed by now. Was sure morning had arrived, but perhaps the guards, the colonel, were punishing him.

The food never came. The rations were measly anyway but Ryker's belly grumbled and groaned, painfully at times. His head swam too, he'd had barely any sleep.

'Not long to go now,' Igor said. Quietly, but loud enough for Ryker to hear. It was the first time Igor had spoken to Ryker in hours. Since before exercise the previous day.

'What do you know?' Ryker asked.

'Enough.'

Ryker didn't know what to think, who to believe anymore. He'd seen Petrova and Zhirov in the prison only one time, and on that occasion, they'd given him no details as to how or when the escape would take place. Now it all felt like it was going to come so easily, with Igor and Smolov pulling strings with whoever else on the inside and out.

Doubts whirred in Ryker's mind. What if this wasn't an escape at all? What if it was a trap?

'You must know more than that,' Ryker said. 'The fact Smolov, rather than you, has been outside with me took some organizing. Why?'

'You'd have to ask him.'

'And now this? So who's really in charge in this prison?'

'No one. Everyone.'

Ryker said nothing in response, and nothing more came from Igor before the sounds of the guards' feet echoed gently into Ryker's cell, getting louder with each step. Not the usual sound. More guards than normal. This was it. The footsteps stopped. Then banging on the door. Barked instructions for Ryker – and Igor next door – to stand up, at the back of their cells, hands above their heads.

Moments later Ryker's door burst open. Two guards rushed in.

Shackled him. A few whacks with their batons to his arms and legs and sides even though Ryker didn't resist at all. When his legs gave way from a blow to the back of his knees the guards dragged him out.

He spotted Igor in front, the same position. No talking en route. The guards moved quickly, purposefully, until they were outside where they tossed Ryker and Igor to the ground. Ryker clambered to his feet. The prisoners were ushered into a line. Six in total. Smolov among them. Ryker could tell which one he was because of the confidence in his pose. But Ryker's eyes rested on Igor. He'd never before seen his companion – of sorts – in the flesh and had drastically misread his looks. Igor was taller than Ryker, broader too. A little younger than Ryker, even though he had a bald head and messy salt-and-pepper stubble. His nose was wide and deep-set bloodshot eyes made him look both ferocious and as though he was in perpetual pain.

'Nice to meet you,' Igor said with a smile before his face screwed up when a guard whacked him across the back with a baton.

'Look to the front!' the guard shouted.

Ryker did so, too, but took a blow to the back anyway. He gazed beyond a guard in front of him to the transport truck – a big, bulky-looking thing. Well-armored, but not exactly modern construction.

'You'll be on the road a few hours but don't expect any luxuries,' barked the guard in front as he marched back and forth along the line of prisoners. 'There's no food. No toilet. If you want a piss then do it where you stand.'

'Only if you clean it up afterward,' Igor said.

The guard glared but didn't otherwise react.

'And it's going to be hot in there. You can see what it's like out here today. Global warming or whatever you want to fucking call it but that beast is like an oven.'

'You must have really annoyed the colonel then if you were chosen to take us,' came a heckle from further down the line. Ryker didn't recognize the voice and didn't look to see who'd said it.

The guard glared that way.

'*You* don't get any luxuries,' the guard said, to no one in particular. 'But we do have a sweepstake. Who'll be the first to piss their pants? Who'll be the first to beg like a bitch for water?'

No one said anything to that, though Ryker sensed the anger and tension from his fellow inmates.

'Follow me,' the guard said before turning to Ryker. 'You first.'

Ryker stayed on the spot.

'Move!' the guard screamed at Ryker, who paused for only a heartbeat before moving forward to the transporter.

He had one foot up on the step to the inside when he glanced over his shoulder. Not to the other inmates, but to the prison building. The top floor, where at the windows, sure enough, the colonel stood, arms folded, glaring down.

He didn't look pleased. In fact, he looked incensed. Ryker hadn't known him long, but it was the look of a man who felt wronged and who wouldn't forget the sleight. A man bent on getting his own back.

Ryker knew the look well. He'd seen it often enough in the mirror.

He looked away from the colonel and stepped on board.

33

Reva walked slowly, quietly, along the corridor. Like a lion stalking its prey. Except it wasn't prey on his mind. He passed a closed door, another. Came to one that was ajar, a few inches. Not the first time it had been like that. Hence why he'd moved so quietly.

He edged closer to the gap, slowed his breathing. Gazed inside. An unmade bed. A pile of clothes on the floor. The sound of running water – the shower – drifted over from beyond the door to the en suite. Nearly closed, though the gap was too small to see beyond.

Damn it.

He thought about creeping into the room. Moving up to the en suite door for a better look. Or just to barge in and get this over with. He'd been on edge for days, thinking about this. About her. He'd not had sex in nearly a week. Out of choice. As though saving himself would make him more relaxed and rational.

No, it definitely wasn't having that effect on him.

The shower stopped. Reva heard faint voices behind him. He whipped around. Looked down the corridor. No one there. The voices faded.

When he faced back to the door... He saw her. She moved out of the en suite, a towel wrapped around her chest and waist. Her smooth, damp skin glistened. She walked to the pile of clothes on the floor. Remained facing away from Reva as she bent down to pick up her panties. The towel rode up as she did so. Reva's underwear bulged at the sight.

She dropped the towel. Half turned. Slipped the panties on.

'Can I help you with something?' she said, staring into space.

Taken by surprise, Reva paused, thinking. Hadn't quite made up his mind before he pushed the door open and slipped inside. He pushed the door closed behind him.

'It's rude to spy on people,' Eleni said, turning to face him now, no embarrassment or modesty in her confident stance. Her pert breasts seemed to stare at Reva. He wanted to rush over and grab her. 'So?'

'So what?'

'What do you want?'

'Why don't you put the rest of your clothes on.'

'But I thought this was what you wanted to see?' she said, putting her hands on her hips. Her breasts jiggled as she did so.

They both went silent. Then Eleni giggled and grabbed her bra from the floor and whipped it on.

'You're such a boy,' she said to Reva.

He snorted and shook his head.

'I bet this is how you used to act with your mother. Spying on her in her bedroom when she got dressed.'

Reva ground his teeth. The smile on Eleni's face grew, the confidence in her pose heightened.

'I'm right, aren't I? She was the first woman you saw naked?' She laughed. 'Did you jerk off to her? Did she *know*?'

Reva launched himself for her, snarling. He grabbed her by the neck and lifted her off the floor and pushed her down onto the mattress. She grimaced, but a moment later her confidence returned.

He'd dent it for good.

'Is this the only way you can get laid?' she said.

He pushed his lips onto hers. Grabbed at her breast. He stared into her eyes. The disinterest, the coldness. He pulled back.

She glared at him. 'Was that it? After all the build-up? After the way you ogle me every second of every time you see me?'

'You stupid fucking bitch.'

He balled his fist and sent it rushing for her face. But he hadn't expected her to move like she did. She blocked the shot. Slid out from under him. Grabbed his wrist, pulled it behind and into the middle of his back. Pushed to breaking point. He squirmed. Ready to haul her off and punish her.

'Ah-ah,' she said.

He felt the blade against his neck. Where the hell had that come from?

'You'll pay for this.'

'For you trying to rape me? What would the others here think if I told them? Jesper?'

She took the knife away, released his wrist, jumped up. So too did Reva.

They both glared at each other as they squared off. She looked him up and down. Fuck, he hated her, almost as much as he hated Sylvia. He wanted her even more badly.

'You know, perhaps if you'd just asked me...' Eleni said, pulling her jeans from the floor. 'But now we'll never know.'

'Don't be so sure.'

A knock on the door.

That smarmy bastard, Alexei. Why had he been brought here again?

'We're almost ready to go,' he said to Reva.

'Have fun, boys,' Eleni said to them both. 'I'll keep the boss entertained while you're gone.'

Alexei looked like the clueless chump he was. Reva said nothing more as he moved for the door.

34

Traveling in convoy, the two black SUVs raced away from the scene of carnage, the destroyed prisoner transport truck, the abandoned crane, the multiple dead bodies. Nobody inside Ryker's vehicle spoke for several minutes, the tension palpable. The two armed men up front both looked dead ahead, barely even moving, such was the concentration. Smolov mostly looked out of his window as the pine trees blurred by.

'Did you know that was the plan?'

A pause before Smolov answered. 'How do you mean?'

'You told me to be ready, but you gave me no information about what would happen.'

'And?'

'And I've never seen anything so crazy.'

'I did you a favor.'

'You did. But we're only here now because of luck. That plan... It was bloody and reckless.'

He didn't even want to think about all the men who'd lost their lives. He'd tried his hardest to deliver no fatal shots unless absolutely necessary, but still...

'Why are you concerned with a few Russian guards? And a few criminals you know nothing about?'

'Criminals? Most of the men in that prison were like you and me. You know that.'

'You and me? You think we're the same?'

Ryker didn't answer that.

'He that is hard to please, may get nothing in the end,' Smolov said.

Ryker kept his mouth shut as he contemplated the proverb. He'd heard it before though couldn't recall where. Was it even apt here? Or actually were the words a threat from Smolov, who held Ryker's eye for several seconds before he looked away, out of his window again.

'Where are we going?' Ryker asked Smolov after a few more minutes of increasingly tense silence.

No answer.

'Out of Russia?' he suggested.

'Who says we're in Russia at all?' Smolov answered.

A strange response. Who says? Petrova and Zhirov had. Not that Ryker felt he could really trust those two.

'You're from Ukraine,' Ryker said to Smolov.

That got his attention. Smolov looked over. A bloodthirsty doubt in his eyes.

'I can speak Russian fluently,' Ryker said. 'Ukrainian I can understand a little. The language I heard you and these men speaking is a mixture of them both. Surzhyk, I think. Either you're from eastern Ukraine or somewhere on the other side of the border with Russia.'

Smolov said nothing. Up front, the driver glared at Ryker in the rearview mirror. Just as well the road ahead was straight as an arrow.

'My point is,' Ryker said, 'I was told that prison was near Chita.

East Russia. The nearest countries there are Mongolia and China. But to drive to your home, to the Ukrainian border, you're talking...' Ryker tried to calculate it from a mental map. 'Four thousand miles, give or take a few hundred.'

Smolov nodded and smiled.

'To drive that distance?' Ryker said. 'Days. Four, five, and that would be really pushing it.'

'We are heading west. And we are leaving Russia. But we're not driving the whole way. You're right, it would be crazy to do so.'

'Then what's the plan?'

'Have you ever been to Mongolia?'

Actually, Ryker hadn't. Which was saying something as he'd been to well over a hundred countries in his time.

'No,' Ryker said.

'Then it's your lucky day.'

* * *

Two hours into the drive and Ryker battled to keep his eyes open, despite the turmoil in his head. He remained on edge, uncomfortable. Not just about how the reckless escape had gone down, but about what came next. He was exactly where he wanted to be. On the inside, traveling to see Jesper. The man he'd come on this long and twist-filled quest to seek vengeance against. But he found himself on a very different playing field from when he'd set off from Norway. Jesper remained an adversary, and Ryker was now indebted, intrinsically tied, to the FSB. He didn't like that. His ties to the Russians also meant he was deceiving the man sitting next to him. A powerful man in his own right, and one who Ryker couldn't afford to underestimate. One who Ryker had to keep the trust of if he were to in turn gain the trust of the man he worked for: Jesper.

'The border with Mongolia is over two thousand miles long,'

Smolov said, without looking at Ryker. 'Two thousand miles of mostly forest and mountains.'

Ryker stared outside as Smolov spoke. He'd never been to Mongolia before, but he had fled Russia before. The last time he'd made a crossing into Kazakhstan, one of Mongolia's near neighbors, and a country that shared an even longer border with the monstrously sized Russia.

'Do you know how many official border crossings there are between the two countries?' Smolov asked.

'No,' Ryker said, though he guessed the number would be very small.

'Ten,' Smolov said. 'Ten crossings in over two thousand miles. There are literally hundreds of miles of open space between most crossing points.'

'Mainly inaccessible space, I'm guessing,' Ryker said. 'The Sayan Mountains included.'

Smolov now looked at him and nodded. Either impressed with Ryker's knowledge, or a little dubious about it.

Moments later, without warning, the driver veered the car off the tarmac road and into the forest. The vehicle bounced over the rough ground, sending Ryker and the other occupants up off their seats. Ryker reached out and grabbed the handrail above his door to steady himself. Smolov smiled at him.

'And now for the detour,' he said.

They carried on, twisting through the forest, the vehicle banging and jolting, for what felt like an age. Not a road as such, but not an entirely made-up route either – with the number of ravines and steep rises and falls, taking a completely uncharted path would have been another needlessly reckless step. Although the GPS screen showed their location, the driver wasn't following a route on the device, and Ryker had no clue how he knew where he

was going, how he knew where the thin trail they stuck to – mainly
– would lead them.

Nearly an hour later the driver slowed and looked around at
Ryker and Smolov and smiled.

'Welcome to Mongolia,' he said in half-baked English.

'Not long to go now,' Smolov added.

Which was a little bit of an understatement because they traveled onward for a whole hour more before they reached tarmac,
and another hour more until they pulled off the single-lane and
virtually deserted road onto a dirt track. Ryker looked out of the
windscreen with keen interest as they rounded a corner, came out
of the trees into a long and thin clearing. An airstrip. Not very well
used, not very well kept. The runway, stretching into the distance
in front of them, was straight enough but certainly not smooth,
with a large hump in the middle, and another at the far end. The
tarmac was cracked, with weeds poking through here and there. A
grassy verge lay on either side of the runway though there'd been
no attempt at maintaining it recently and the grass had grown two,
three feet high, with even bigger weeds poking out over the top. A
single low-rise building sat to the side of the runway. Decrepit.
Windows largely boarded up. Weeds everywhere, including a six-
foot monster poking out of the gutter of the flat roof.

The mini control tower, sitting atop the building, had fallen
through the roof on one side, the whole structure tilted bizarrely,
but somehow still standing.

Ryker saw no vehicles. No cars, no plane.

'Where the hell are they?' Smolov said as the driver rolled the car
to a stop at the side of the building. The second car pulled up there too.

The driver checked his watch. He said nothing.

'They were supposed to meet us here at two,' Smolov said.

The dashboard clock read two forty-seven.

Had the plane already left? Ryker wondered. The pilot getting the jitters because of the late arrival?

'Give me your phone,' Smolov said.

The passenger up front dug his phone from his pocket, unlocked it, and handed it to Smolov without saying anything.

Smolov typed a number in from memory and put the phone to his ear. He waited. Said nothing. Ryker wound down his window. Doing so drew a glare from the driver, though Ryker didn't know why.

He looked outside. Listened.

'It's coming,' Ryker said.

He craned his neck out of the window. He couldn't see it, but he could definitely hear the craft. Not a big plane. A single prop, he thought. He glanced at Smolov who pulled the phone away from his ear again.

'Pull the car into the trees,' he said to the driver. 'Just in case.'

The driver nodded and started up the engine then reversed for the trees. The second car followed suit, both vehicles stopping just far enough into the woods to shield them from the open but still provide them with a decent view of the airfield.

Not long after and the plane finally came into view, dropping from left to right onto the runway. The little craft bounced on the tarmac, twisted a little before disappearing behind the building. Ryker sensed everyone in the car holding their breath as they waited for the plane to taxi around. Finally, it came back their way.

'It's them,' Smolov said.

Had he noted the aircraft number?

Smolov reached for his door.

'Stay here,' he said to Ryker.

The driver stayed too, but Smolov and the front passenger stepped out, as did the driver and the two passengers from the second vehicle. The five made a slow and slightly cautious approach to the plane as the door on the side of the aircraft opened out into a miniature staircase.

Ryker eyed the man who stepped out. He didn't recognize him. He realized, too, that eyes were on him. He looked over at the driver. A guy so big he barely fitted in the seat of the oversized SUV. Did he have a brain to match his brawn?

'What?' Ryker said.

The guy muttered something under his breath. Ryker didn't catch the words. He looked the other way when he heard engine noise. Not the plane. The propeller at the front was at a near stop, the individual blades visible as it slowed.

Movement off to the left, the way they'd come in. Ryker tensed. He sensed the driver, now looking out front, do the same. In fact, his hand reached to his side where Ryker knew a handgun remained stashed.

Out of the window, Ryker spotted the truck come out into the clearing. A fuel truck. Smolov and his party didn't seem at all phased by the arrival and the driver relaxed, as did Ryker.

The fuel truck came to a stop by the plane and two guys jumped out and were soon in the process of refueling.

'A bit late, aren't they?' Ryker said, but he got no response.

Ryker refocused on the men by the plane. Only two had emerged. The first was the man who'd opened the door. Just another grunt type. Big, stocky, plain clothes. The second man was different. More noticeable, but only because of his... strangeness. While Smolov had something suave and inherently likable about him – a lively character – this man was shorter, still stocky, but with oddly angular features to his face. He had paler than pale and mottled skin that, in texture if not color, reminded Ryker of the superhero character the Thing from the *Fantastic Four* – a beast with rock-like plates for skin. A head-turning look, but not a handsome man at all, even if he did display an air of supreme confidence in the way he walked.

Jesper?

'Who's that?' Ryker asked the driver.

No response.

'Jesper, isn't it?'

The driver turned and glared but still said nothing.

Ryker really hoped it was. He reached for the door handle.

'Hey—'

'I'm getting out,' Ryker said to the driver before he could finish his protest. 'You can come with me if you want, but I'm getting out.'

The driver continued to glare but said nothing more. Ryker stepped into the fresh air. So, too, did his chaperone. Ryker ambled toward the group by the plane. A few handshakes, a few manly embraces and slaps on the back for Smolov. A few smiles, but not many.

As Ryker neared, more and more of the group glanced his way.

Smolov turned and shouted out to the driver. 'Get back to the car.'

The driver stopped and grabbed Ryker's arm.

'No. You come here,' Smolov said to Ryker, switching to English.

The driver let go and grumbled and Ryker carried on his walk, keeping a close watch on the bunch in front, but mostly on Smolov and Thing.

The crowd parted and Ryker moved closer to the man from the plane.

Please let it be Jesper, he willed. He could end this here and now. The man held Ryker's eye. He looked seriously riled up. On edge.

'Who is this?' the man asked no one in particular, in his first language.

'He saved me,' Smolov said, in English once more, a smile on his face. 'His name's—'

The man turned to the two grunts by his side.

'Take him to the trees. Shoot him in the head and bury the body. And hurry up.'

The man turned away, as though disinterested. The two grunts nodded and moved forward as Ryker tensed and half-stepped back.

'Wait,' Ryker said.

Everyone paused. His brain scrambled for something. Anything. Because he didn't doubt the seriousness of the man's command.

But what on earth could he say, without giving up too much, without giving his own cover away, to persuade this man to not have him executed out here?

'I can help you,' Ryker said, realizing how pathetic that sounded.

'We don't need help from someone like you,' the man said, glancing at Ryker before turning back to Smolov.

The two men carried on toward Ryker. One had a handgun in his grip, by his side. The other had an assault rifle, double grip. Ryker thought quickly. Two options. Fight now, or wait for a moment.

He chose the latter. Two against one, in the woods, was far easier than two against many out in the open.

As the men approached, the one with the rifle pulled his weapon up and swung it for Ryker's face. Ryker had just enough time to reel back and the blow glanced across his cheek and eye socket. His head spun, but he managed to stay on his feet. The men grabbed him, one arm each, and dragged him toward the trees. The chatter of the group behind Ryker faded. In front, the driver continued to his car, without a care. Ryker's head quickly recovered, but he continued to drag his feet, letting the men take his considerable weight. They wanted to execute him? They'd have to work for it at least.

They pulled him just beyond the parked cars. Tossed him down onto the pine needle-covered ground, dry as a bone underneath.

No warning. No order for him to get to his knees. He heard the rattle and click as the man with the handgun – behind Ryker and to the right – prepared himself.

Now or never. Ryker transferred his weight, got ready to spin onto his back. But then paused. The shot never came. Because the men had heard the same thing he had. A rumble. Heavy-duty engines. More than one. Fast approaching. Increased chatter from the group of men not far away.

'Do it,' the man behind Ryker, on his left side, instructed his friend.

Now Ryker moved. He rolled onto his back, and grabbed a handful of needles and dirt as he did so. He flung the handful as hard as he could. Not a precise move, not a vicious attack, but enough to throw the shooter, if only a little. Because he did still shoot. The gunshot boomed as Ryker jumped to his feet. The bullet sailed a few inches past him, into the dirt. Ryker reached out, grabbed the gun and wrist, twisted into an arm bar. He pushed down on the forearm while pushing up against the shoulder. *Crack.* The man yelled in pain and Ryker prized the gun from him and used his body as a shield from the rifleman.

Ryker turned the handgun. A double tap before the guy with the bigger gun had even decided whether he had a shot or not. Both shots hit home. One in the knee, one in the thigh. Ryker cracked the handgun against the head of the man he was holding and let go and he crumpled to the ground.

The man he'd shot lay on the ground, writhing. The rifle just out of his grip. Ryker darted forward and kicked him in the face, hard. After that, he didn't move. Ryker dropped the handgun, picked up the rifle, spun. Expected to see some of the other men there, armed and ready to attack.

He did see them, but they weren't coming for him. They were racing out on the airfield.

Ryker flinched and ducked when an explosion rocked the ground beneath him. A grenade?

He couldn't be sure.

The next second, all hell broke loose.

35

Gunfire sounded out and echoed all around, coming from every direction, it seemed. Smolov and his men were under attack. Ryker grabbed the handgun from the ground, put it in his waistband, then rushed forward. He couldn't properly see the new arrivals until he passed the last tree and came out onto the edge of the clearing. He threw himself to the ground, into the long grass.

Two armored trucks had arrived from the road. A Jeep raced out of the trees off to the right, at the far edge of the runway. Five, six men had already leaped out of the two vehicles in front of him. Black-clad. Heavy-duty weapons.

Russians. They'd tracked them across the border. How?

Clearly, someone from the FSB hadn't told them about the escape plan.

Ryker had no time to contemplate. Or did he? He remained in cover. There were two vehicles behind him. He could backtrack to those. Turn around and escape through the woods. Or he could hide, wait it out, see who won the fight before he decided his next move – it wasn't as though he belonged to either of these sides really.

But still... He'd come this far.

A blast of fire nearby and the driver from Ryker's car, halfway between the trees and the building, went down in a heap. Smolov and Thing – Jesper? – and most of the other men who were still standing had bolted from the plane and were in various states of cover by the building.

Ryker heard a crack and a fizz and he spotted the projectile hurtling from left to right. The round from the RPG smacked into the already stricken control tower. The ensuing explosion obliterated the failing structure and sent shrapnel flying.

Ryker snaked within the tree line, moving closer to the building and Smolov and the others. Then noise behind him. Yet another engine. From nothing, all of a sudden the growl of the engine filled his ears and a Jeep bounced up over a hidden ridge, all of ten yards from him. Ryker dove to the right, spun, lifted the rifle, and fired. Four, five, six rounds erupted from the barrel. All of them smacked into the windscreen of the vehicle and a spattering of red sprayed onto the bullet-ridden glass as the Jeep bounced past him. The vehicle came out of the woods, swerved viciously left, then right. The driver, seriously injured or already dead, never managed to regain control and the Jeep flipped and rolled three times until it came to a stop – on its roof – in the grass.

Two of Smolov's guys crept closer, gave a signal back to their boss, then eyes turned toward Ryker's hiding spot. Would they come after him?

Too late. The other Jeep pulled to a stop at the far side of the building. Smolov's men looked that way instead and a tit-for-tat firefight ensued. Ryker refocused to the bossmen who were taking heavy fire from the men from the trucks on the other side.

Ryker spun on his heel and darted for the SUVs in the woods. He looked in the first one. No key. In the second one... Bingo.

He jumped in, put the rifle on the passenger seat, started the engine. He paused for just a moment. Forward, or back?

He released the parking brake, put the auto gearstick into drive, and thumped the gas pedal. The SUV rocketed forward, pinning Ryker back. It banged and crashed as it came out into the open. He raced for the nearest of the armored trucks, by which three men stood, firing toward the airstrip building. They spotted him. How could they not? Ryker ducked as they opened fire on him. Bullets raked the metalwork, splatted into the windscreen. After a few hits too many the glass exploded, showering Ryker with shards. He remained ducked, his line of sight barely an inch above the steering wheel.

The impact was imminent. Even if he hit the brake hard the crash couldn't be avoided. Ryker didn't want to avoid it. He grabbed the rifle. Thrust it down. Smacked it into place, wedged between the accelerator and the seat. He looked up. The men all dove left. Ryker turned the wheel ever so slightly that way then opened the door and jumped out. He landed shoulder and hip first. Painful, but he rolled into it as much as he could, turning over and over in the grass... *SMASH.*

Screams and shouts. Another bang. An explosion? Ryker recovered and poked his head up from the grass. An inferno. The smell of fuel vapor wafted over. Another explosion and the armored truck the SUV had wedged into was thrust into the air and crashed back down with an almighty thump.

Ryker pulled the handgun from his trousers. He didn't know how many bullets remained in the magazine, and he had nothing to reload with.

Movement to his right. Two men, crouched low, edging through the grass toward him. Ryker was about to turn the gun on them when he realized they weren't attacking him. They were backing him up.

'This way,' Smolov said, grabbing Ryker's arm and pulling him around in an arc, keeping their distance from the fireball.

'There's only two left,' Smolov said.

'There,' his companion added, pointing to the left, to the trees.

But as he said it Ryker heard the distinct noise. A whizz, close by, then the thwack of the bullet. No time to react. The bullet hit Smolov in the chest and he fell to his back.

'Shit!' Ryker said, looking over to where the shot had come from. Smolov's friend darted that way, upright, roaring and firing as he went. Ryker spotted the shooter by the trees. A good position, but the ambitious assault won out. The shooter went down in a pool of his own blood.

'Get me up,' Smolov said to Ryker.

Ryker looked at him. Blood streamed from the hole on the right of his chest. The bullet had missed his heart, but he wasn't in the clear. A collapsed lung was possible. Massive blood loss was even more likely unless they could stem the flow with whatever medical kit they could find.

Ryker gritted his teeth in anger and frustration as he grabbed Smolov under the arms and pulled him to his feet.

Smolov's friend rejoined them.

'There's still one more,' he said.

Almost as soon as the words had passed his lips, a scratching, clunking sound drifted over. The remaining armored truck. A man in the driver's seat tried desperately to start the engine up to make his getaway.

Smolov pulled that way and Ryker helped him along, even though he'd rather they cleared out.

'We should go,' Ryker said. 'There could be more.'

'Tell them to get the plane ready,' Smolov said to his friend. The guy dashed off. Smolov and Ryker continued to the truck.

The would-be driver glanced over at them through the open

door. He thumped the steering wheel in frustration. His leg hung outside, blood streaking down it from a hole in the clothing on his side. A bullet had slipped under his Kevlar. A lucky shot for the shooter, unlucky for him.

He stopped his fruitless battle with the machine and, panting in pain, turned to Smolov and Ryker.

'Do it,' he said to them.

Ryker looked at Smolov who pulled away from his grip, grimacing as he did so.

'You want to?' Smolov asked.

Ryker couldn't be sure of the intention of the question. A test of loyalty? Not that Ryker had anything to prove after the battle they'd already been through, did he? But he really didn't want to execute a man. A man he didn't know. A simple soldier or policeman or whatever he was.

Ryker hadn't answered before Smolov shook his head and pulled the gun up in his bloodied grip and fired a single shot that hit the man in the neck. The guy clutched at the wound as blood spurted. Smolov watched with keen interest. Ryker tried not to look. Behind them, the whop-whop of the plane's propeller starting up drifted over.

'Come on,' Ryker said.

Smolov practically fell into Ryker's arms and he ushered the injured man toward the plane, and what was left of Smolov's crew – which it turned out comprised only Thing and two others.

The boss glared at Ryker the whole way.

'Did you bring them here?' he said to Ryker when they were two yards away.

'No,' Ryker said. He looked at Smolov. 'Most likely we both did.'

'There might be a tracker,' Smolov said. 'We need to ditch these clothes.'

'Or you have a mole,' Ryker suggested.

Thing's eyes pinched at that suggestion. 'We're going,' he said to Smolov.

'Okay, but he's coming with us,' Smolov said.

Thing seemed to chew on that, glaring at Ryker the whole time.

'We can talk as much as you want about who I am, why I'm here, when we're in the air. But don't you think we should go now?'

Still, the man said nothing. Smolov groaned in pain, then laughed.

'Don't worry, Ryker, it's nothing personal. He hates most people. Let me do the introduction so we can go. James Ryker, I'd like you to meet my very good friend, Olek Reva.'

Reva said nothing. Ryker said nothing before he grabbed Smolov and pulled the injured man toward the waiting plane.

36

'You're doing a good job there,' Ryker said to Reva as he stitched up the wound on Smolov's chest.

Reva glanced over, something of a snarl on his face, but then got back to work without saying a word. They'd been in the air for over an hour. Smolov remained languid, reclined on a chair, drifting in and out of consciousness. The paltry drugs available in the on-board med kit were nowhere near enough to properly stem his pain, nowhere near enough to properly put him to sleep either. They'd draped his body with a sheet. He wore nothing but his underwear beneath that. Both he and Ryker had stripped off their prison clothes before the plane had left, though they'd found no trackers stitched into any of the fabric. Ryker had changed into the clothing intended for Smolov, that Reva and the crew brought with them. Linen trousers, a light blue shirt, loafers. Everything a size or two too small, but Ryker had little other choice, and the attire was several steps up from the prison uniform at least.

'This will have to do,' Reva said as he cut the thread. Ryker couldn't be sure if he was speaking to him or Smolov. The other two goons who'd made it off the airstrip alive were at the other end of the cabin, not out of earshot in the small space, but not paying any attention. 'The bullet avoided the lung, at least on entry, but it's broken apart. I got most of it out, but not all. We'll have to wait to get to a proper doctor, and hope the fragments don't do more damage.'

'Where did you learn those skills?' Ryker asked him.

Reva shot him a look. 'Any idiot can stitch a wound.'

'Perhaps. But not all of them can operate on a bullet wound with that calmness and precision.'

'Let's just say I've had a busy life.'

Ryker held his eye, hoping he got more.

'As have you, I think,' Reva added. 'Judging by the scars you carry.'

Ryker had been well aware of Reva's curious eyes on his body as he'd undressed and redressed. One of many silent assessments the man had made of him.

'What about you?' Ryker asked, referring to Reva's lined and mottled skin. The result of trauma – fire, perhaps? – or something else?

Reva glared and Ryker thought he would get nothing but the silent treatment.

'These aren't scars,' was all he said as he ran his hand over a cheek. Anger, mostly, evident in his tone, but also just the faintest hint of shame and... weakness.

Ryker looked away. Knew best not to push what was clearly an unhappy subject. Smolov's eyes were shut once more, his head tilted to the side. Reva packed up his tools, tossed the dirtied and bloody scraps into a plastic bag.

'If there was no tracker on those clothes,' Ryker said, 'then how did the Russians follow us to the airstrip?'

'You're asking me?'

'I am. Could any of your men—'

'Many of my men are now dead. If anyone betrayed us... You're the only candidate I see.'

Reva sounded pretty confident about that, about the loyalty of the men he'd brought with him for the rescue. Ryker knew from past experience that you could never really trust anyone fully, especially not low-level soldiers. They were expendable, which was exactly why they were put in harm's way so recklessly. Which was exactly why eventually they could turn, given the right pressure and persuasion.

'Where are we going?' Ryker asked.

Reva paused to renew his glare. He didn't need to, Ryker already got the point. Reva hated him, Reva didn't trust him. Reva would push Ryker out of the plane there and then if given half a chance. The only reason Ryker remained alive was because of Smolov. Which was a worry, given the man's current state.

'You're very interested in us all, aren't you?' Reva said. 'Asking questions all the time.'

'I've just escaped a Gulag where I was being held without charge. There was a high chance I might never have gotten out of that place. So yeah, I'm full of questions, now I've got a shot at freedom that I never thought I'd get. Questions about who I'm with, where we're going, what we're doing.'

Reva's look of disdain remained but he let out a long sigh as though slightly eased by Ryker's words. Which part?

'Why were you there?' Reva asked.

'In the Gulag? Because of my past.'

'Which means?'

'Which means I have a lot of enemies in Russia. In Moscow.'

'You're going to tell me all about that?'

'I'm happy to share, like for like.'

'What do you want to know?'

'Are we going to see Jesper?'

Ryker tensed at the cold-blooded look Reva gave him. Smolov stirred a little. At hearing the name of his boss? His head tilted further toward Ryker. His eyes opened slightly.

'You know Jesper?' Reva asked.

'No,' Ryker said. 'I don't know anything about him. Only that Smolov said that's who we were going to see.'

Reva looked at his friend as if for confirmation, but Smolov, although his eyes remained open, said and did nothing.

'You know *who* Jesper is?' Reva asked.

'No.'

Reva renewed his snarl, an indication he didn't like the answer.

'So you only heard that name from Roman?'

'No,' Ryker said. 'I heard it from the FSB too.'

Reva showed no reaction to that, but the two goons did. Both shuffled a little, as though desperate to look and see what was going on, but too wary to do so.

'You've been speaking to the FSB about Jesper? About us?'

'Well, who do you think put me in the Gulag?'

'Why would anyone be asking you about us?'

'Good question,' Ryker said. 'I thought you might know?'

Reva's eyes narrowed.

'Perhaps Jesper can help us with the answer,' Ryker added.

Smolov made a noise. Was he trying to laugh? Ryker thought so, because of the slight upturn at the sides of his mouth.

'I knew... you two would get along.'

Ryker smiled. Reva got up from his seat and stormed off to the cockpit.

* * *

The plane journey was long. Together with a midway refuel in Kazakhstan, they were in the air for several hours, arriving on the

ground in Ukraine well into the night. Everyone was tired and
groggy. Smolov, strangely, seemed more alert than before. Ryker
hadn't wanted to sleep on the plane, largely because he was fearful
of having his throat slit by Reva the second he closed his eyes, but
inevitably tiredness – physical and mental – had won out more
than once. Still, it hadn't been a good sleep, and Ryker longed for a
soft bed and warm sheets more than anything.

Two cars waited for them on the private airfield. Ryker traveled
with Reva and Smolov. They shared no chat on the way. Ryker's
body clock was all over the place – a combination of the long and
weary journey, but also the after-effects of the time he'd spent in
the windowless cell in the Gulag. The time on the dashboard read
3.23 a.m. as they turned off the lit single-lane highway and onto a
much more rural and rough road. With nothing around them – no
street lights, no lights from buildings – Ryker became even more
disorientated as they carried along, a good half an hour until they
took another turn onto an even rougher surface. Ryker couldn't see
but the road noise suggested a simple dirt track.

Finally in the distance in front of them some lights. As they
neared, a bright spotlight blared, giving a glimpse of gates and a
barbed-wire-topped wall.

'You look nervous,' Reva said to Ryker.

Ryker shrugged.

'You English have a saying. Out of the frying pan, into the fire.'

'We do,' Ryker said.

Reva smiled. The first time Ryker had seen that look on the
man's face. It didn't look good. Like a weather-beaten gargoyle.

'You're probably wondering why you chose to come here. Why
you didn't just run when you had the chance.'

Ryker held Reva's eye now. 'It never crossed my mind.'

Reva laughed and looked away and wound down his window
to shout to people unseen. The gates swung open and they drove

on through. Ryker noted the men with guns. Noted the outline of
the building in front of them. In the darkness, he couldn't see the
whole structure but he could see that it was plain and blocky. Not a
rich man's luxury escape, that was for sure.

The cars parked up, Reva got out. Ryker assisted Smolov, who
remained wrapped in sheets.

'He's waiting for you,' one of the armed men said to Reva.

No response. Reva walked off to the house. Ryker helped
Smolov along.

'I might finally get some clothes,' the injured man slurred.

'I might finally get some that fit,' Ryker said.

They headed on into the house. House? Not really a home,
Ryker saw little homely about it. Few knickknacks or personal
items, everything basic and functional and a little bit worn. The
house smelled of dust and cheap soap. A strange combination.

Reva had moved out of sight, but Smolov seemed to know the
way, ushering Ryker – who held the injured man under the
shoulder – along.

They reached an open doorway that led to a poorly lit lounge.
In front of them, a withered, old man stood by an unlit electric
fire. Five foot five, if that, scrawny, with wispy gray hair. He wore
thick, baggy trousers and a thick woolen cardigan and although
he was standing up, his shoulders were hunched and he had his
hand on the side table next to him as though to help him stay
upright.

Reva stood by the old man's side.

'Jesper, meet James Ryker,' Reva said.

Jesper held Ryker's stare for a moment. No warmth in his
features. He looked at Smolov.

'What is this?' Jesper crowed. 'Get the man some clothes, he
looks like he's broken out of the mental asylum.'

Smolov laughed but didn't say anything. Another man

appeared from behind Ryker and took Smolov and they moved out of the room together.

'James Ryker?' Jesper said. Both remained where they were, opposite ends of the room, the wariness from both parties clear for all.

'Yes,' Ryker said.

'I heard you saved Roman. Twice.'

Ryker nodded. 'And I helped *him* out a bit too,' he said, indicating Reva, 'though I'm not sure you'll get him to admit to it.'

Ryker smiled. Reva did not. Neither did Jesper for a couple of seconds, but then his face brightened and he looked at the man standing next to him and thumped his arm. No strength in the shot, but Reva looked chastised enough from the gesture.

'No,' Jesper said, 'he definitely won't admit to something like that, but I believe you.'

Reva shook his head but still didn't say anything.

'I don't know who you are, but I'm glad for what you did. It's late, everyone is tired. You can stay here tonight. Tomorrow we'll talk.'

Ryker heard footsteps behind him. He stepped to the side and turned to face the new arrival. Expected to see another grunt there. Instead, he saw a woman. A woman he knew. His head churned but he didn't move.

She glanced at Ryker, no recognition in her eyes, then moved over to Jesper. She whispered something in his ear. Ryker remained tensed, tried his hardest to show no reaction. Tried to show that he wasn't thinking of bolting, of attacking, a pre-emptive strike to prevent whatever they were planning.

He did neither. Instead, he remained standing, a little stunned. The woman finished her conversation with Jesper then turned back to Ryker. She caught his eye. Moved toward him.

'Ryker, I'd like you to meet Eleni,' Jesper said.

'Hi,' she said to him. She sauntered right up to Ryker and held out her hand. He shook it. They released in unison, then she walked off and out without another word. Ryker realized Reva was staring, a deep suspicion in his scowl.

'Olek will show you to your room,' Jesper said. Then he laughed. 'And we might even find you some clothes that fit you in the morning.'

Reva moved forward.

Jesper went to sit down. 'Goodnight, James Ryker.'

37

Ryker had become well-used to sleeping in squalid conditions – jail cells, rickety huts, jungle shelters, frozen wastelands – but he'd never not welcome a warm, soft bed. The room Reva showed him to was small and relatively plain. A simple shower en suite, a single bed, a pine wardrobe that had nothing in it. A small sash window, the timber of which had rotted in places. Certainly not a secure room, if Jesper and crew were concerned about Ryker running.

Ryker didn't run. Instead, he showered, stripped off, and had the best night's sleep he'd had in weeks. Not entirely intended, either. He'd wanted to remain cautious. Had secured the bedroom door with the simple lock within the handle. He'd thought about pushing the wardrobe in front of the door too, but ultimately had lain down on the bed to think, before tiredness once again got the better of him.

He awoke when he heard the rattle of the door handle. In a deep sleep, it took his brain several seconds to process where he was, what was happening. By the time he bolted upright in bed, the figure was already in the room, right over his bed.

Ryker flinched, ready to attack...

'Ssh,' Eleni said, putting a finger to her lips, and a hand to Ryker's bare shoulder.

He looked at her for a few seconds before glancing around the room. Daylight outside, seeping through the thin curtains. No clock in here, so he didn't know the time, but something about the smell, the stillness and chill in the air suggested it was early.

'Who are you?' Ryker said.

'You've forgotten about me already?' Eleni replied.

'I didn't mean it like that.'

She smiled and sat down on the bed. Ryker shuffled further up and pulled the sheets with him.

'I've already seen all that,' Eleni said with a cheeky grin.

'What are you doing here?' he said.

She didn't answer. She reached out again. Ryker wasn't sure of her intention, but he grabbed her wrist, twisted, jumped up, swung her around, and onto the mattress, him on top, her arms pinned by her head.

'This isn't a game,' he hissed.

She still looked pleased with herself.

He squeezed her wrists hard and the look on her face slowly melted away to passivity, then just a little bit of fear.

'You lied to me,' Ryker said.

'Did I?'

Ryker pushed down on her wrists, causing her to writhe.

'Does that make you happy?' she said. 'Does it make you feel powerful to know you're hurting me?'

He released his grip, then let go and got up from the bed, standing back from her, his modesty not a concern, though he did now spot the neat pile of clothes on the floor by the bed. Brought by Eleni?

She stood up and looked him over as she nursed the reddened skin on her wrists.

'You need to explain,' he said. 'Am I in danger?'

'Look at where you are. Of course you're in danger.'

'That's not what I meant. I think you know that.'

'They don't know about you,' she said. 'As far as I know. But then, I'm not sure I know much about you really either.'

'You haven't told them? About me and you in Athens?'

'Why would I?'

If she did, Ryker was a dead man.

'I don't believe you're one of them,' he said.

'Because?'

'Because you wouldn't be playing games like this if you were.'

'That's quite an assumption. Perhaps I really like games.'

'Who do you work for?'

She moved forward, her sore wrists apparently no longer a concern, her natural confidence and allure winning through as she sauntered toward him.

She came close. Looked up at him. What would he do if she reached up to kiss him...?

'Just keep playing along,' she said. 'If we both keep our heads, we can both leave here happy.'

'You know why I came here,' he said.

'To kill Jesper?'

'Is that why you're here too?'

'No,' she said. 'The opposite.'

'You're here to protect him? Reva? Smolov?'

'Yes,' she said.

'Then why aren't I already dead?'

'Because that would be such a waste of talent.'

She reached up and pecked him on the cheek.

'And I enjoyed our time together in Athens too much.'

She smiled and turned away.

'Get dressed. It's time for breakfast.'

She moved for the door.

* * *

Ryker headed down the stairs fifteen minutes later. The clothes fit fine, even if they were obviously used. He wondered who they belonged to. One of the dead men from the prison escape crew?

Eleni, Jesper, and Reva were the only people in the kitchen when Ryker arrived. No sign of any other henchmen. Perhaps they were fed already and on guard duty outside. Guarding from what?

'Good morning,' Ryker said as he moved toward the pine dining table which had seats for eight.

Reva and Jesper were in a quiet conversation and both looked up but didn't say anything to Ryker. Jesper kind of smiled in acknowledgement. Reva didn't. Eleni gave Ryker a flashing grin.

'Sit down, dig in,' she said.

Ryker took a seat across from the other three and took an empty plate from the middle of the table. There wasn't a huge selection of food on offer. Some bread, preserves, cheese, and cold meat. Coffee. Ryker put a bit of everything on the plate and poured a big coffee from the pot.

He took a sip. Lukewarm, but strong. He took a bite of the bread. It was bordering on stale. Perhaps it was meant to be that way, he didn't know. He chewed through it as the now whispered conversation between Reva and Jesper finished.

'Good sleep?' Jesper asked, before indicating Reva to top up his coffee.

'Very nice,' Ryker said. 'Much better than a concrete slab in a windowless room.'

Jesper laughed, then coughed. 'Yes, I suppose. I realize there is little luxury here, but really it depends on where you come from.'

'Help yourself to the food,' Reva said as Ryker reached forward for more meat – a pork salami of some sort.

'Thank you, I will,' Ryker said, pretty sure that Reva's comment had been sarcastic.

The table went silent for a few moments. Ryker ate and studied his host. He'd thought a lot about Jesper the last few weeks. Before that even, he'd been fighting off Jesper's assassin and gangsters in Norway. Vile men. Vicious men. Men who robbed and blackmailed and tortured and murdered. He'd built up an image in his head of Jesper as a criminal kingpin. A man wealthy through his illicit endeavors, living a rich life. A powerful and uncompromising man. Jesper was a withered old thing. He looked harmless. But then, was that just age? Everyone got old eventually.

But then the lifestyle too... Ryker couldn't reconcile the man he'd pictured, the man he'd so badly wanted to find and kill, with the man sitting in front of him.

On the other hand... He gripped the knife he held a little more tightly. Reva looked mean and hard, a tough adversary. Ryker would take him first. Then Eleni. He wouldn't underestimate her – it was clear she was full of surprises. And Ryker didn't have to kill them both, only put them out of action so he could get to Jesper.

But what would Ryker do? Slit the guy's throat and run? His ultimate aim would be achieved, but Ryker wasn't sure he'd achieve satisfaction. Not without even hearing the man out. Not without a confession of what he'd done and why.

Ryker put the knife back down. Reva continued to glare.

'How's Roman?' Ryker asked, looking across each of the faces in front of him.

'He's sleeping,' Reva answered. 'But he's fine. We're bringing a doctor to see him today.'

'You're concerned about him?' Jesper asked.

'If it wasn't for him, I'd still be stuck in that prison. So yes, I'm hoping he's okay. I'm hoping in a few days I'll be sharing beers with him as we watch the sun set.'

Reva practically growled at the suggestion. Jesper didn't react at all.

'Perhaps you two can go and get the others ready,' Jesper said to Reva and Eleni. 'I'd like to chat with our new friend some more.'

Reva continued to glare as he got up from his seat. Eleni looked pleased with herself. Why? Because Ryker was so obviously in danger? Whatever role she was playing, she needed to realize she was in danger, too, if she was deceiving these people in any way.

Moments later, Ryker and Jesper were all alone. If there were ever a time to strike and run...

'I asked Olek to look into your past,' Jesper said.

'I assumed you would.'

'Not much to find.'

'No.'

'Which makes me even more curious.'

'What about you?'

'Me?'

'If I were to look into your past, would I find anything? Is Jesper even actually your name?'

The old man laughed. 'I suppose it would be hard to google only that. You wouldn't find anything at all related to me.'

'So what is your real name?'

'Jesper is how I've been known for a long time now. That's all you need to know.'

Ryker sipped again at the tepid coffee. At least the caffeine helped spur his brain on.

'But you do need to tell me more about you,' Jesper added. 'This is my home. You've come to me, not the other way around.'

'I'm nobody,' Ryker said.

'Not quite. Not if you have enemies in Moscow, the FSB. Olek told me about that.'

Not a surprise.

'Yes,' Ryker said. 'That's true. But I have a lot of enemies in lots of different places.'

'Which once again begs the question of who you are.'

'Your English is very good,' Ryker said. 'The words you choose, the articulation, the accent. You were either taught by an English person, or you've spent time there.'

Jesper's eyes narrowed a little, a hint of suspicion. He drank from his coffee cup.

'Yes, I spent time in England. But not for many years. When I was younger than you even.'

'You worked there?'

Jesper laughed, then clapped his hands in mock applause. 'Well done for turning the conversation back around, but for now, we're concentrating on you.'

'I'm a no one,' Ryker said, shrugging his shoulders. 'A mercenary. A gun for hire. I've hurt and killed a lot of people on the orders of others. I've made more enemies than friends in the process.'

'A man loyal to no one but himself.'

'No, I do have some loyalties. I'm loyal to people who I like. People who treat me, and others, well.'

'A moral crusader?'

That term had been levied against Ryker plenty of times in the past. He hated it, though he wasn't sure why. Perhaps because it made him – his life, and his vision – sound so simple.

'I'm particularly interested in how you're on the wrong side of the FSB,' Jesper said.

'Aren't most people?' Ryker said, smiling.

Jesper didn't smile or laugh.

'I already told you,' Ryker said. 'I used to do jobs, for money. I was very good at it. I got paid a lot, I got used by semi-official groups, doing unofficial work.'

'The British government?' Jesper asked.

Ryker nodded. 'At times.'

Jesper inhaled then sighed. An air of dissatisfaction in his manner. As though he wasn't happy with Ryker's lackluster explanations of his past.

'You say you're a moral man,' Jesper said.

'Actually, you said that.'

'Perhaps I did. Are you a political man?'

'It depends,' Ryker said.

'On what?'

'On individuals. On who's doing what.'

'On who you believe is in the right?'

'There isn't always a right and a wrong.'

'We can definitely both agree on that. Do you know where you are?'

'Ukraine, I was told.'

'Do you know where?'

'No.'

'Have you been to Donetsk before?'

'No.'

'It's the nearest big city to here. I come from nearby there. Roman does too. Olek from further east. But we're all from the same region, broadly. But none of us is welcome in our home anymore.'

Ryker didn't say anything. He expected that Jesper, after his pause, would carry on with his explanation.

'Do you know of our recent history?' Jesper asked.

'Some of it.'

'We're at war. We have been for years. Perhaps not an all-out, front-line, every-day-is-a-bloody-day battle, but it's war none-theless. For several years now our homeland has been occupied by militants.'

'The Donetsk People's Republic. DPR.'

Jesper nodded. 'So you do know about this.'

Ryker shrugged.

'The DPR in Donetsk, the LPR rule over the lands further east in the Luhansk region. The Crimea was taken from us too. A whole portion of our country annexed by a quiet war machine. Quiet on the international stage at least. You heard about this, but did you ever care?'

'I felt it was wrong. I never did anything to intervene.'

'Of course. You're just one man. But neither did any other government around the world, which is why Moscow was able to get away with its disgusting behavior, and continues to do so.'

'They never admitted involvement in the DPR and LPR.'

Jesper scoffed. 'What do you believe?'

'Does it matter what I believe?'

'It matters a great deal to me. Russia backs, financially and militarily, all of the occupying groups. And they use their FSB and other secret units to hold back any rebellion.'

'And the Ukrainian government? Ukrainian army?' Ryker asked.

Jesper pursed his lips and shook his head. 'On our side, in theory. But what are they supposed to do? Attack their own people in those cities? Start a war with Russia? Any aggression by our own forces only makes the situation worse.'

'So it's left to the likes of you. I think that's what you're saying.'

'Why do you think I'm here, in a place like this?'

'You're hiding?'

'Not hiding, but this wouldn't be my choice. I was a very rich man once. I traveled the world. Five-star hotels. Luxury yachts, private planes.'

Ryker clenched his fist a little at the comment. So Jesper had once been the criminal kingpin Ryker originally thought him to be, only politics and circumstance had caused him to alter his perspectives.

'Fighting such a strong enemy doesn't come cheap,' Jesper said. 'I still control numerous operations across the world, but all the money... It comes here. It comes to help us fight back for our homeland. And believe me, we need a lot of money to make this work.'

Despite his age-related jitters, Jesper spoke so confidently, so certain of his morals and his ethics. Except the point remained – his operations, around the world, may have supported a just cause, but the means of obtaining that wealth didn't. Those means had brought Ryker to Jesper's table. For revenge.

'So what's the plan?' Ryker asked. 'What are you doing here, exactly? And I'm presuming the fact I'm alive, in your home, means—'

'I've always had a fascination with insects,' Jesper said.

Ryker paused.

'Ever since I was a boy. I grew up in the countryside. We were poor. We didn't have any material items, but I had the world around me to keep me entertained. I loved animals, I loved insects. I'd travel through fields and forests, collecting different species. I'd take them home, feed them, watch them, see what happened when I mixed different species together in the same space.'

Ryker thought back to his own childhood. An unhappy time. Growing up in the bowels of London, he'd never found solace in the world around him like Jesper had. He'd never seen countryside until he was in his teens. Only concrete and trash and violence.

'Ants are my favourite creatures,' Jesper continued. 'Strong, so resourceful. Clever, too, in many ways, although like many animals they have only one goal. Survival. Protection and continuation of their colony.'

Jesper finished the coffee in his cup. Looked at his watch.

'Do you know what would happen if you put rival ant species into the same container? A hundred of each, with plentiful food. Black ants, red ants together?'

'No,' Ryker said.

Jesper shrugged. 'Nothing much. Both groups would nest, both groups would collect food. Both groups would thrive so long as they have enough space and enough resources. Sounds peaceful, no?'

'I guess.'

'But what happens if you shake that container? If you inject danger into their mini world?'

'They fight?'

Jesper nodded. 'They do indeed. Their survival instinct kicks in, they have to fight. There's now a threat. They don't know it's a human hand doing the shaking, so what do they do? Who do they fight with?'

'Each other.'

'Of course. Who else? They kill each other, they perhaps *eat* each other, and it doesn't matter the losses. As long as that container is shaking, disrupting their world, then they'll continue, fighting, dying, until there is only one species left.'

'You're saying that's what's happening here?' Ryker asked. 'Two rival peoples, but groups who are intrinsically not real enemies.'

'That's exactly what I'm saying. The people of Donetsk, the people of the DPR and the LPR even, they're not our real enemies. We can fight them, to save ourselves, to try and reclaim what is ours. Many will die, eventually there may be a winner, but our real enemy?'

'The people shaking the container.'

Jesper smiled. 'Precisely. It's those people shaking our world that we have to stop.'

'That's your objective here?' Ryker asked. 'To attack Russia?'

A tap on the door behind him. He turned. Reva.

'We're ready,' Reva said to Jesper.

Ryker turned back to his host.

'Unfortunately we're several men short,' Jesper said. 'Because of what happened yesterday. But you're here.'

Ryker waited for him to say something else, but he didn't.

'We need to go,' Reva said.

Jesper still didn't say anything. Ryker held the old man's eye and got up from his chair. Then he turned to Reva and received a customary glare.

'Good luck,' Jesper said.

Ryker moved for the door.

38

The two black SUVs, one a BMW X5, the other a Toyota Land Cruiser, rode in tandem across the shoddy tarmac. Ryker, across the back seat from Reva in the BMW, looked out of his window at the surroundings, still trying to place exactly where they were – Ukraine, Crimea? – as much as where they were going and why. Seven men were on this mission. Each of the other six was armed, one way or another. Three carried heavy-duty carbines, the rest had handguns. Ryker? Nothing.

'Who are we meeting?' Ryker asked without looking from the window, beyond which a cluster of disused ugly concrete apartment blocks blurred by. So far, Ryker had seen little life out here. Empty apartment blocks, empty factories, weed-filled grounds. Many of the buildings had mottled walls where the many small holes may have been damage from years of weathering, but could equally have been bullet holes. Ryker had been to many war-torn countries in the past, both those in the midst of conflict and those struggling to rebuild in the aftermath. He wasn't quite sure where this place fit in that scenario. Certainly, he saw no patrols of soldiers on the streets here, no tanks, no roadblocks. In many ways, it was more like this area had simply been abandoned, though Ryker knew that wasn't the whole story.

'Who are we meeting?' Ryker asked again, turning to Reva now.

A deep frown on his brow, Reva faced Ryker.

'You don't need to know,' he said.

'I don't? Then why the hell am I here?'

'Because Jesper asked for it.'

'You don't approve?'

'Do I look like I do?'

'No. You look like a man who does whatever his boss tells him to, without a second thought. A lapdog.'

Reva's cheeks pulsed as he clenched his teeth.

'Seems a bit strange to me,' Ryker said. 'You left other people back at the house, Eleni included. They could have taken my place, and you could even have given them a weapon and the full story so they could actually help.'

'Perhaps you should have taken this up with Jesper before we left.'

'I wasn't really given a chance.'

'No. Me neither.' Reva sighed. 'You're here because you're capable. And I guess you look the part. We need numbers. We need to make sure these guys know we're serious so we don't get screwed.'

'And *these guys* are?'

'People who can help us.'

Ryker thought about that for a few moments.

'So what do I do?' he asked.

'Nothing. Stand by the car. Keep a lookout. Don't say anything, not a single word, unless you see something.'

'Something?'

'A problem.'

Reva turned away. After a few seconds of staring at the back of Reva's head, Ryker turned too. Despite Reva's clipped responses,

Ryker had a fairly decent idea of what they were doing. A meeting, most likely an exchange. An exchange of what, Ryker didn't know, but he'd bet the two parties weren't close, perhaps more enemies – or rivals? – than friends. Each side in it for themselves, and each side barely trusting of the other. A pressure cooker situation.

But then, Ryker also didn't trust Reva's intentions. If he really wanted Ryker's help here, then why give him so little information? Why give him no weapon? Ryker was here because of Jesper's – and to some extent Smolov's – insistence. Reva wasn't hiding the fact he didn't like his boss's decision, and it hadn't escaped Ryker that perhaps Reva was intent on setting Ryker up for a fall.

Reva had asked Ryker to be a lookout. But it would be Reva and the other men he traveled with that he'd watch most closely.

The journey lasted a little over half an hour more before the SUVs slowed. They rounded a corner into a square, of sorts. Four tall buildings surrounded the space, each a slight variation of cheap, Soviet-era concrete block. Each was beyond repair and abandoned. The inner square at one point was perhaps a grassy field for kids to play in, or a parking lot, or a landscaped area with patios and other features for residents to enjoy. Now the space was covered in debris and rubble and weeds.

The drivers parked the SUVs in one corner, facing the center, but with an exit point directly behind them, where, if the need came, the drivers could quickly reverse out, swing the vehicles around, and race off to safety.

Reva glanced at his phone as the engine shut down.

'They're almost here.'

Reva's eyes pinched when he realized Ryker was staring at the phone screen and he quickly put the device away, though Ryker hadn't been able to glean anything.

Car doors opened and soon all seven men stood on the outside, drivers included. The three men with the carbines hung around the hoods of the cars, their weapons down by their sides. Reva stood at the front, alone. The other two men waited with Ryker by the sides of the vehicles, looking around, up, and down.

Ryker could sense the tension and trepidation of the crew, and even though he remained in the dark as to the true purpose of the meet, he knew they were only one moment away from carnage, whoever they were waiting for.

A rumble in the near distance. The deep growl of diesel engines. One, two, three vehicles came into view directly across the square. An open-topped Jeep, flanked by two other hard-topped versions. No insignia on the grimy and muddy metalwork, but they looked like military vehicles, of sorts. So, too, did the armed men who stepped out. Not army uniforms exactly, but they wore heavy boots and black-and-brown combat-style outfits. No concealed weapons here; every man had an assault rifle or carbine in their hands, or a holstered sidearm on display.

So who were they? They reminded Ryker of the group who'd attacked them at the airstrip. Not official military, that was for sure. Part of a local militia? Perhaps. That, or they were an offshoot of the military or a special ops unit from an intelligence agency. But from which side? Ukraine? Russia? Were they here officially – at least officially in the sense of who they worked for – or were they traitors?

Reva looked around, nodded, then stepped forward on his own. Ryker kept a keen eye on the newly arrived group. A line of three came forward. None of them looked particularly like the head honcho. All were relatively young – mid-twenties to mid-thirties. They didn't look in the least nervous. The two on the left carried assault rifles, double-handed grip, but the barrels were pointed to the side. The one on the right had his empty hands down, the fingers of his right hand brushed against his holstered sidearm. Was he the boss?

No, the one in the middle started up a conversation with Reva. Too far away, and too quiet for Ryker to hear a single word. As the conversation carried on, Ryker looked across the buildings surrounding them. Nothing of interest there. A few moments later and Reva turned and marched back toward his companions. Ryker watched him. The men clustered together as he approached. Ryker moved closer too. Beyond Reva the three men from the other side remained in no man's land, staring over.

'Problem?' Ryker said as Reva arrived. He caught Ryker's eye. Looked pretty annoyed that Ryker had asked the question. He said nothing to Ryker but looked across the rest of the gang as he rattled away in his own tongue. Ryker caught the gist of it. Whatever Reva was here to procure hadn't arrived yet. They needed to wait. Though it wasn't clear to Ryker whether that meant waiting a few minutes now, or heading back and waiting for hours, days, before returning. The fact the three men from the other side remained in the middle of the square suggested the former.

A few nods and murmurs from the men – a mixture of discontent and agreement.

'So we're waiting?' Ryker said to Reva. 'For what?'

Reva held Ryker's eye again. 'We wait. But not for long. If they're not here soon, be ready to move.'

If they're not here soon. So was it a person, or people they were waiting for, rather than goods of some sort?

Reva went to turn away. Ryker glanced upward suddenly. A subconscious reaction, though his consciousness soon caught up with him. He'd seen something. Movement. A glint of light perhaps, in one of the broken windows of the building off to his right.

'Hold on,' Ryker said to Reva. Several heads turned his way, Reva included.

Ryker said nothing and Reva retreated to him, a look some-where between anger and angst.

'I saw something,' Ryker said, trying to be discreet so as to not alert the armed men across the square. If this was an ambush, then with people in sniper position they'd soon have the upper hand, and if they knew Ryker had spotted their men up high, the next course of action would likely be all-out attack. 'Up in the building to my right.'

Reva didn't look up there, just continued to stare at Ryker.

'You're sure?' Reva said.

'Sure I saw something, yes. Could it have been a pigeon? A torn curtain flapping in the wind? Yeah.'

'But it could have been somebody.'

'It could.'

'You know which window?' Reva asked.

'Seventh floor, fifth from the right.'

Reva turned ninety degrees to talk to the two men standing there, though Ryker knew the conversation was only to provide Reva the opportunity to glance up. He finished talking and faced Ryker again.

'Move away. Go up there.' The man next to Reva handed him a phone. Reva handed it to Ryker. 'If there's a problem, send a message. Don't jump the gun. I don't want to die because of you.'

Ryker didn't say anything as he stuffed the phone in his pocket.

'Be quick. We're not staying for long.'

With that, Reva turned and walked back toward the men in the middle of the square. Ryker kept his eyes on them for a few seconds before using Reva's distraction – if that was his aim – to slink off, moving behind the SUVs to try and be as inconspicuous as he could. Although if there really was a watcher up there on the seventh floor, surely they would see him?

Once shielded by the building that rose up beside him, Ryker increased his pace. He jogged to where two entrance doors to the block were broken inward, hanging on their twisted hinges. A padlock and chain clasping the doors together dangled uselessly in place. Ryker squeezed through the gap. Mustiness. Damp. The plain walls of the stairwell were green and black in places. Slimy wetness oozed from the concrete. Ryker moved for the slippery stairs. Moved up at speed, though tried to remain as quiet as he could. Certainly, he heard no sounds and saw no obvious signs of anyone having been there recently.

He reached the seventh floor. A gloomy floor where many apartment doors remained in place and closed, providing little natural light to the long, eerie space. Ryker moved forward with more caution. Every other step his feet sloshed through a puddle. Water dropped onto his head. He thought about the windows on the outside. The spaces between the doors on this floor. Fifth window in? Third door, he decided, based on his guess of two windows per apartment.

He stopped at the door. Ajar. He pushed it open slowly. Not quietly though. The door creaked on its hinges. Scraped on something underneath. Stuck in place after just a few inches of movement.

No point in being subtle now.

Ryker shoved the door. Whatever had lay propped there – deliberately or not – clanked out of the way, and Ryker barreled into the open space. A tiny apartment. Two rooms. He bounded forward to the one on the left – the fifth window, he hoped. A cramped, grimy space. Broken glass, a single flapping curtain...

A flicker of movement to his left, by the door. Ryker ducked and lunged. Crashed into the figure. Spotted the tripod and camera, on their sides on the floor. A watcher, rather than a sniper? Interesting. No time to dwell.

Ryker drove forward, and the man backward. He exhaled

painfully when Ryker crashed him against the solid wall. Ryker winced when the man hammered an elbow down onto his back. Growled when he took a painful strike to the kidney. Grimaced in pain when the man sunk his teeth into Ryker's shoulder.

Ryker launched his knee into the man's groin. Did it again then pushed his fist into the man's throat causing him to release his teeth and cough and splutter. Ryker pulled himself away. Got back to his feet.

The man was far from finished. He jumped up as Ryker back-stepped, giving him space for the counter-attack. The man had no gun. Not on him, anyway. One lay uselessly by the chair by the window. An assault rifle propped there. Because of the angle of the chair, Ryker hadn't spotted it when he'd first walked in. The man had obviously dragged his camera and tripod out of view when he'd heard Ryker coming but had strangely left the weapon in his hurry. Perhaps because he couldn't afford the noise. Yet.

In any case, the gun was too far away. And Ryker realized the man had another weapon anyway. A glinting knife. He lunged forward. Ryker sidestepped, reached down, scooped up the tripod, took two, three quick steps back as the man swooshed the knife through the air. Ryker stumbled. The man came forward again, the knife arced. Ryker was in trouble. He lifted the tripod up. The blade of the knife raked across one of the legs. Sparks flew.

Ryker spun. He snaked behind the man, pulled the tripod up against the man's neck to throttle him. Ryker yanked and strained. The man coughed and spluttered. But he still held the knife. He swiped it backward. Ryker edged to the side to avoid the blow. But he had so little room to maneuver, and despite being choked, the man didn't seem like he was about to give up his weapon.

Ryker bent at the knees then swung and heaved the man to the side, tossing him away and to the ground. The knife came from his grip and clattered across the worn wood floor. He landed in a heap by the broken window where air whistled in from outside. By the broken window, where the assault rifle now lay within his reach.

With renewed strength and focus, the man went for the weapon. Grasped it. Clambered to his feet as he pulled the barrel toward Ryker.

Ryker had little option. He tossed the tripod. A puny weapon in comparison, but it at least caused the man to flinch and pull the barrel away. Ryker shot forward. Twisted on his standing leg. Lifted the knee on his other close to his chest and then kicked out with the bottom of his foot, using the uncoiling power and momentum of his leg muscles to propel the man backward... and straight out into the open air.

Ryker darted for the window, instantly aware of the ramifications. He reached the gaping window and looked out and down, just as the man's body crashed to the ground below.

A moment of strange silence followed as Ryker glanced from Reva to the other armed men.

A beat later, the shooting started.

39

Ryker wasn't sure who started firing first. Or who they initially fired at. But within a few seconds his head filled with the sounds of rattling gunfire, and both panicked and angry shouting. Bullets whizzed by him, splatted into the concrete surrounding the window. Ryker reeled back just in time as yet more bullets flew. He had to get out.

He raced across the room. Was nearly at the door when he had a sudden second thought. He retreated and grabbed the camera from the floor. No time to look now, but would the pictures, or video on the device provide him with anything useful?

He moved for the exit, into the corridor. Paused. Voices among the shooting. He couldn't be sure if the sound was drifting in from outside, or if the voices were from men already in the building, coming after him.

Ryker went left. Away from where he'd entered. Further away too, from Reva and Jesper's crew, and closer to the other party. He reached the stairwell at the far end of the building. Looked down. Voices. But he still couldn't tell if they were coming from inside. Ryker moved down, quickly but cautiously, his heart rate ramping each time he got close to the next floor, as though expecting a sudden onrush of armed fighters from the corridor there.

There wasn't, and Ryker soon reached the bottom unscathed but then jumped back when a vehicle flashed past beyond the gaping hole where double doors to the outside used to be. He held his breath. The vehicle was out of sight. Whoever had escaped hadn't seen him. The gunfire had quietened down too, the time between bursts lengthening. The sound of screeching tires and revved engines took up some of the space in between.

Ryker moved for the exit. Stepped outside. Looked into the distance where two Jeeps raced away. Only two. So was one still there, the other side of the building? Ryker flinched when two gunshots echoed. He wasn't the target but someone remained out there.

He turned and raced along the face of the building, back to the corner where he'd first entered. He slowed once more. Peeked around the corner, then scooted back when he heard the engine. One of the SUVs, the BMW. It blasted past. Part of him thought about jumping out and waving them down. Instead, he pulled further back out of sight until the vehicle had moved out of his view.

Why had he done that?

Silence. Then the distant murmur of men talking. Ryker moved around the corner of the building, back toward the square and where Reva and the crew had been not long before. Both of the cars were gone. Two bloodied bodies lay on the ground near where they'd been parked. Reva wasn't one of the dead men. Across the other side, one of the Jeeps remained. Four bodies there. Two men with assault rifles checked them.

One of them looked Ryker's way. Spotted Ryker, who cursed under his breath and raced across the space to the corner of the next building. No shots came but the men shouted out. Ryker kept running, around the outside of the building, away from the square, across an open stretch of derelict land. He spotted trees up ahead. Low-rise buildings too. He sprinted and weaved as quickly as he could. Soon found himself on a twisting street. He couldn't be sure if the buildings were occupied or not but they were much older than the concrete monoliths he'd come from. Remnants of an old town or village he thought, the winding roads and alleys predating the long, straight tarmac seen in metropolises born during the automobile era.

He ran through the streets. Still no shots came. No sound or sight of anyone behind him, although because of the bend in the road, he could only see ten or fifteen yards. He pulled into a side street. Stopped and pressed himself up against a wall. Waited. Listened. He didn't know how many armed men were out there, after him. He didn't even know who they were, and if they really were his enemy. He also didn't know this place or have a vehicle to escape in. What was his plan? Run on foot endlessly?

No.

He heard footsteps. Cautious. One set? Certainly no voices now. He readied himself. Looked to his left. He could try to slink off in that direction. Or he could lie in wait, ready to pounce.

He chose the latter. But perhaps only because he'd left it too late to do anything else. The footsteps stopped. The person was only a few yards around the corner. Ryker could hear him – her? – breathing.

'Ryker, it's me.'

A man. It took Ryker a moment to place the voice. Not Reva. Not Smolov or Jesper.

It was Zhirov.

He came out into the open. A confident yet sly as-always look on his face. Plain, casual clothes, but with a noticeable bulge on his side, beneath his shirt. His hands were empty.

'They're still looking for you,' he said.

'They?'

'I'll help you get away from here.'

'Why?'

'Because you're in danger of screwing up everything.'

'How are you even here?' Ryker asked.

Zhirov looked over his shoulder, seeming a little more nervous than before.

'Come on, this way,' he said, moving off without waiting for a response from Ryker.

After a moment of hesitation, Ryker followed. They crossed the street, walking at pace. A couple of shouts somewhere behind, the sound of a vehicle too, but Ryker saw no one. They carried on for a few minutes, turning left then right.

'Where are we going?' Ryker said.

Then Zhirov stopped. A car engine. The vehicle pulled into sight just in front of them from an intersecting street.

'Come on,' Zhirov said, jogging over.

Ryker didn't hesitate this time. Partly because he could already see through the driver's window that Petrova sat behind the wheel.

Zhirov and Ryker both jumped in the back. Petrova put her foot down and they were away. She drove quickly, a little nervously, a little recklessly, her eyes flitting between her mirrors and the road ahead. Every now and then, as she looked in the rearview mirror, her eyes met with Ryker's, but no one said a word.

They moved away from the town, or whatever it was, and into open but bland countryside, heading back toward Jesper's place, Ryker knew. Eventually, they pulled up behind an abandoned building, away from the road. A small functional-looking building. Perhaps a café rest stop at one point in the past, now it was nothing more than an empty, decrepit shell.

Petrova shut the engine down but no one made a move to get out.

'Are we going inside?' Ryker asked.

'Not right now,' Petrova said, turning around in her seat. 'But remember this place. We'll take you back close to Jesper's. You'll have to walk a couple of miles on your own as we can't get too close but remember this place. It's safe here. We come past all the time. If you need to hide out, if you need to escape, come here and we'll find you.'

Ryker let the words sink in.

'What the hell is going on?' he asked her.

Zhirov scoffed. 'You're supposed to tell us that,' he said.

Ryker decided to wind back the story a little.

'Did you know how they were getting us out of the Gulag?' Ryker said to Zhirov. 'How many people died in that farce?'

'Farce? You're out, aren't you? Smolov too. And you're inside with Jesper now, just like we said you'd be.'

Ryker shook his head – disgust – but said nothing.

'That's done now,' Petrova said. 'No point in dwelling. What we need to know is what has happened since then. We don't have much time. You need to get back there soon before they get too suspicious.'

Ryker hesitated for a moment but then talked. There wasn't really much to say. He'd been in Jesper's home hardly any time. Didn't know the man at all.

'What did they tell you about today?' Zhirov asked.

'They told me nothing,' Ryker said.

Zhirov and Petrova waited, as though expecting Ryker to say something more.

'Nothing?' Zhirov prompted.

'That's what I said.'

'They took you to an armed meeting like that and told you nothing?'

'Yes.'

Ryker knew Zhirov didn't believe him.

'Perhaps more importantly,' Ryker said, 'why were *you* there?'

Zhirov shook his head and looked down at Ryker's lap, to the camera he was still clutching.

'That yours?' Zhirov asked.

'It is now.'

'Can I see?'

Ryker looked down, turned the camera to look at the little screen on the back.

'I think I'll hold on to it for now,' Ryker said. 'To help with my story when I get back.'

Zhirov looked away, unimpressed.

'The men you were meeting with are Ukrainian separatists, but they have support from the Russian military,' Petrova said. Ryker looked at her now.

'So they're your allies?' he said.

'Not exactly. Those men are betraying us. We believe they're selling weapons to Jesper and others.'

'Weapons Russia itself has smuggled into Ukraine on the quiet, to feed to those rebel groups, to give them distance from the fact that it's the Kremlin keeping the civil war here in full flow,' Ryker said, in such a tone as to draw a look of disdain from both of his Russian companions.

'This isn't about politics,' Petrova said.

'No? I'd say it's more about hundreds of thousands of people being displaced, thousands more being killed. For what?'

'Even more will be killed if Jesper gets his hands on those weapons,' Zhirov said.

'We know they're planning something big,' Petrova added.

'They've been pulling in basic weaponry for years to fight off the separatists. Guns, grenades, military vehicles, but this is different. They're planning an attack. We believe the targets are civilian. They're planning to use Russian-made bombs and weapons to make it look like it was us.'

'They'll kill their own people, just to smear Russia,' Zhirov said.

'We won't let innocent people die,' Petrova added.

They sounded sincere enough, though Ryker really didn't know what to believe anymore.

'How did you know about that meeting?' Ryker asked.

Once more he got no answer.

He looked down at the camera again. Flicked the power button. Quickly scrolled through the pictures. Fifty-six images. All taken within a five-minute period. Most were of Ryker, Reva, and the others from Jesper's crew, but some of the later ones were also of the military men.

Ryker's brain fired.

'He was working for you?' Ryker asked Petrova.

She didn't answer.

'This is bigger than you realize,' Zhirov said.

'His death was unfortunate,' Petrova said. 'I know you did what you had to do.'

How did they even know Ryker was the one who'd done it?

'You had another watcher?' Ryker said.

'His death was unfortunate,' Petrova said again, ignoring Ryker's question, 'but it doesn't mean the deal is off. We need them to find that the dead man was FSB. They have to know the deal wasn't an ambush.'

'Wasn't it?' Ryker suggested.

'No. Our men were only there to observe. To gain evidence of who it is that's betraying us. Jesper has to know it wasn't the separatists setting him up. They'll try to exchange again. They need this.'

'You want the exchange to take place?'

'The exchange, yes. The attacks, no.'

'You need to find out their plans,' Zhirov said. 'We need to know exactly what they buy, where they put it all, and we need to know the targets.'

Ryker thought for a few moments. 'So you can stop the attacks? Or just so you have the evidence of who carried them out when they happen?'

Would the Russians let the attacks go ahead, let innocent people die, just to gain an upper hand on their enemy? Ryker really didn't know.

'What do you think?' Petrova asked, sounding a little offended, though her answer wasn't exactly a firm rebuttal.

Zhirov rummaged in his pocket, then offered his hand to Ryker. A thumb drive, a USB cable.

'I know from the equipment you had in Athens that you're familiar with how this works,' he said.

Ryker took the items. 'With how what works?'

'Computer imaging. Taking a direct copy of a hard drive—'

'Yes, I know,' Ryker said.

'The software is already on there. Get what you can. You have a phone to review the data?'

'I do now.'

'Good.'

Petrova started the engine up.

'We'll take you back,' she said. 'Find us some answers, both about their plans but also about Jesper. We have to know more about him.'

'You obviously know where they are now. Why not just send a squad in to take him out? Why the games?'

'Because as powerful as he is, Jesper is just one man. We don't just want to remove him from the picture here, we have to tear down everything he is, everything he represents. We have to pull the walls down from the inside.'

'You want to turn the very people he's trying to fight for against him?' Ryker said.

'We want to end the fighting for good,' Petrova said.

'And you're going to help us do it,' Zhirov added with a sickly smile.

40

Ryker traipsed along the empty road, the grass by the verge tall but frazzled by the dry summer weather, his thoughts burning at pace.

He took the turning down the rough track that led to Jesper's compound. He remained in the center of the dirt until he heard an engine in the distance behind him. He moved into the trees to the left of the road, a narrow wood that widened ahead of him. He stopped behind the thick trunk of a beech tree and watched the road. Saw the SUV approaching – the same BMW he'd earlier traveled in. So where'd they been? Still looking for him?

As before at the failed exchange, Ryker stayed out of sight as the SUV went past. He couldn't see who was inside because of the tinted windows. He stayed in position until the sound of the engine faded away, then set off again, staying in the trees now, the same conflicting thoughts returning as he moved forward. Stay or go, those were the two main camps. Go, and forget all about what he knew of this place and the people. Walk away from Jesper, Reva, Petrova, Zhirov, Eleni, whoever was pulling the strings of all of those parties in the background, let them sort out their own squabbles.

Squabbles? No, their problems with each other were hardly a squabble. The conflict in Ukraine was real, people were dying, yet Ryker wasn't exactly in a position to bring it all to an end, was he? The international community, the UN, multiple governments had failed to do so over several years so how was he supposed to?

That didn't mean he couldn't help, yet the thought of helping the Russians, whom, given a free choice, he certainly wouldn't side with over the disputed territory, didn't sit right at all, even if their target – Jesper – remained the reason Ryker was there in the first place.

For him this wasn't about Russia, Ukraine, a war over land; this was about simple revenge. Ryker wanted to punish Jesper. He couldn't afford to lose sight of that.

Stay or go? He'd stay. He couldn't walk away now.

Ryker stopped dead mid-step when a noise filtered through from behind him, bringing a halt to his rumbling thoughts in a flash. He listened. Looked around. What was it? A twig crunching underfoot? Or just a small branch or nut falling from a tree? A squirrel?

He heard it again. Definitely a footstep. He crouched and turned.

The figure came into view, ten yards away.

'Hey,' he said.

Several months since Ryker had seen him. Still young, still scrawny, but his features had a certain maturity to them now. Or was it just the effects of hardship since they'd last properly seen each other?

'Henrik,' Ryker said. 'I'd say I'm surprised to see you.'

Except after the day he'd already had, and the weeks that had preceded it, he really wasn't sure he was surprised about anything anymore.

'You don't seem it,' Henrik said, taking a couple of cautious steps toward Ryker.

'I'm glad you're okay,' Ryker said.

'Am I?'

'Well, I'm glad you're alive.'

Henrik said nothing as he came to a stop. He had a strange look of disquiet on his face.

'You did what I couldn't,' Henrik said. 'You found Jesper.'

'Me? Except you're here too, aren't you?'

'Not on the inside.'

Ryker looked around, wary of watching eyes, ears listening. But they were deep among trees here, still half a mile from Jesper's home.

'How on earth did you get here?' Ryker asked. The look on Henrik's face suggested he wasn't about to answer that, though the boy's movements continued to surprise Ryker, and not necessarily in a good way. His brain flicked back to the day in Crete when he'd been arrested outside Smolov's. Henrik sitting on *his* moped, watching on. The kid didn't just have resolve, he had an unerring audacity.

'Where are you staying?' Ryker added, then felt a little foolish for the question. Staying? As though this were a holiday and the kid had himself a room in a quaint little hotel somewhere.

Yet Henrik still smiled at the question. 'I'll show you,' he said.

With that, he turned and walked off, further away from the road, further into the woods. Ryker followed him, a few steps behind, wary, but more curious than anything. Of all the people around him, Henrik was probably the person whose intentions were most clear-cut, and therefore the person who Ryker could most easily trust.

They headed over a small rise, and there below them, snug against a rocky outcrop, Ryker spotted a blue and orange tent.

He shook his head. 'You're camping. Out here. Right under their noses.'

Henrik looked a little offended. 'What did you expect?'

'I really don't know.'

Henrik carried on down to the tent. Ryker followed. He noted the pedal bike too. Thick wheels, a decent off-roader. A backpack, a couple of plastic bags filled with trash. No evidence of a fire, though Ryker knew from experience that Henrik – a kid brought up in the pine forests of northern Norway – was an ace at outdoor living. He'd have had no problem starting a fire out here, but likely wouldn't given the proximity to his enemy. At least at this time of year, the nights weren't too cold.

'How long have you been here?' Ryker asked.

'Only as long as you,' Henrik said, sitting down on a log.

Ryker's brain fired. He shook his head, a strange feeling creeping over him.

Henrik looked up at him and half-smiled, but the look then fell away.

'I know what you're thinking,' he said.

'You do?' Ryker wasn't sure he even knew himself.

'I didn't use you. I couldn't have known this was how everything would turn out.'

At least of that Ryker was certain.

'Did you see what they did in Blodstein?' Henrik said, anger and bitterness showing through both in his tone and his screwed-up face.

'I went back there.'

'But you weren't there at the time. I still was. I saw... Butchered. People I knew, butchered because of... because of...'

'Because of Jesper. Not because of what we did.'

'Are you sure about that?' Henrik asked.

'Yes,' Ryker said. 'Otherwise, we both wouldn't be here now.'

Henrik closed his eyes and shook his head.

'Last time we spoke, I told you I'd go after him.'

'You did. And I warned you not to.'

'How could I not after what he did?'

Ryker sighed but said nothing for a few moments.

'The other boy in Crete—'

'I didn't mean for that to happen,' Henrik said, looking down at his feet, his words tinged with both anger and regret, though it wasn't clear who the anger was directed at.

'I heard about the boy,' Ryker said. 'I thought it was you they'd killed. That's why I came to Greece. To Crete.'

Henrik still looked down. They both went silent. After a few moments, Henrik lifted his head. The look he gave Ryker was far from friendly. When he'd first met this boy, first rescued him, there'd already been an edge to him. A survival instinct, a fighter's instinct, but Ryker had no doubt that side of him had grown, had darkened too.

'You think I wanted him to be killed?' Henrik said. 'You think I let them catch him, let them kill him because I knew the dead body would be a calling card for you?'

'Did you?'

Was Henrik that cold? His eyes twitched. An ever so slight shake of the head, though Ryker wasn't sure if that, too, was a twitch rather than an answer to the question.

'He was my friend,' Henrik said. 'We met at a hostel in Greece. He was as lost as I was. He was helping me.'

'Why?'

'Because friends do that.'

'Did he know what your aim was? Really? Did he know your past?'

Henrik didn't answer straight away. 'I told you already. He was my friend.'

'Either way, I came,' Ryker said. 'And now here we both are.'

Henrik looked pretty annoyed but didn't say anything more.

'So what now?' Ryker asked.

'Who are the people you were with?'

Ryker thought back through the day. The failed exchange. Petrova and Zhirov scooping him up afterward. Had Henrik somehow seen it all, his presence unknown to everyone? Certainly, he had something inconspicuous about him, given his small frame, his young years. It wasn't as though people who didn't know him would see a threat, yet Ryker knew he was both capable and fearless, particularly given his years, but still...

'Who are they?' Henrik asked again. 'The people you're working with? The man and woman.'

'It doesn't matter. They're not the reason I'm here.'

'Jesper is?' Henrik said. Then his face dropped again, twisted into bitterness. 'My father.'

A strange sensation washed over Ryker. Jesper. Henrik's father. Henrik, the illegitimate son. That biological link was the very reason Henrik had become embroiled in violence in the first place, back in Blodstein. In the aftermath, Henrik had vowed revenge against the father he'd never known or met. After the subsequent more recent events in Blodstein, Ryker had vowed – to himself, at least – to assist. Yet as far as Ryker was aware, Jesper didn't know anything about Henrik. Had no idea he had a son. A son who was bent on killing him.

'Tell me about him,' Henrik said.

'There's not much to tell.'

'That's not true. I've come all his way but I still know so little about him. What does he look like? How old is he?'

'He's an old, frail man,' Ryker said.

Henrik seemed disappointed, whether because of the image

the description conjured, or simply because of the lack of depth in Ryker's words.

Ryker checked his watch. 'I need to get back.'

'Are you going to do it?' Henrik asked, getting to his feet. 'Are you going to kill him?'

'Not yet,' Ryker said. 'Not until I know what's happening here.'

'Good. Because when the time comes, I want to do it. You know that.'

Ryker really didn't know what to say in response.

'I'd tell you to go home,' Ryker said. 'Or someplace else at least. Stay safe. Live a life. But I know you wouldn't listen to that.'

'No. I wouldn't.'

'You have a phone?' Ryker asked.

Henrik took one out of his pocket.

'What's the number?'

Ryker memorized the number Henrik gave and called Henrik's phone to complete the exchange.

'Stay in touch. And please, don't do anything stupid. Give me some time.'

'Time for what?'

'Please. Just... Stay here, if that's what you need to do, but don't put us both in danger by jumping the gun.'

Henrik said nothing. Ryker turned and was about to walk away.

'I'm glad you're here,' Henrik said. 'I'm glad we're both here. But don't think I have to answer to you. If you're not going to do it, if you're not going to kill Jesper, then you can be absolutely sure that I will.'

Ryker carried on. For all the doubts in his mind, one thing he did know for sure: he believed Henrik 100 percent.

41

Ryker returned to the road. The wall and gates to Jesper's compound rose into view in the near distance, anger the emotion dominating Ryker's mind, though he couldn't be sure who it was mostly aimed at. Zhirov, Petrova, Jesper, Reva, Eleni, Henrik? They'd all lied to him, one way or another, or at least played him. Perhaps the only person who hadn't was Roman Smolov. Yet with what Ryker knew of him, the mid-level gang leader was hardly a beacon of honesty and legitimacy.

He was several yards from the gates when he heard voices beyond. A head bobbed into view on the guard tower. A gun barrel pointed his way. An instruction was shouted.

Ryker didn't heed the order to stop and carried on.

'Open the damn gates,' he bellowed at the top of his voice.

Silence for a few seconds before the gates opened. He paid no attention to the armed guards on the other side, strode on through toward the house. Noted the two SUVs from earlier, both parked up.

He shook his head and carried on, was a couple of steps from the house when the door opened and out popped Eleni, a snide grin on her face.

'The wanderer returns,' she said.

Ryker brushed past, knocking into her shoulder a little harder than he'd intended. She tutted but didn't say anything and didn't follow. Ryker carried on through the house, following the faint sound of voices. He stopped in the doorway to a sitting room. As bland as any other room he'd seen in the place. Three sofas, two armchairs, an empty coffee table, four people. Jesper, Reva, two others. Those others got to their feet the moment they saw Ryker and moved on out past him as he came into the room. Reva glared. Jesper looked disinterested. Ryker hovered.

'Where've you been?' Reva asked, no attempt to hide his hostility.

'Where do you think? You left me on my own, ten miles from here.'

'What are you holding?' Jesper asked, looking at Ryker's hand.

He held the camera up, then tossed it to Reva who just about managed to catch it. Reva immediately turned it over and looked at the screen on the back. Ryker gave him a couple of seconds.

'From the guy you threw out the window?' Reva asked.

'I didn't throw him.'

'No? Whatever you did, you fucked everything. The deal is screwed. We don't know how we're going to get things back on track now. Plus two of ours are dead. I've just been on the phone to Anton's wife. She has two young girls at home. You want to help her support them now her husband's a corpse?'

Did Reva expect an answer to that? The keen eyes on Ryker suggested perhaps he did.

'I'm sorry,' Ryker said, 'but that guy was watching us. And it was him or me.'

Reva and Jesper both said nothing to that.

'Look at the photos,' Ryker said. 'He was there to surveil. It wasn't a sniper. And he was there to surveil both parties, not just us.'

That got Jesper's attention. He leaned forward in his chair and reached out to Reva who handed him the camera.

'Someone else is watching you,' Ryker said.

The look of mistrust from Reva couldn't have been stronger. 'Someone else?'

'I could help you figure this out if you gave me more information,' Ryker said. 'If you gave me *any* information about who we were meeting earlier and why.'

'Yeah. That's James Ryker, all right,' Reva said. 'The man who wants to know everything. And why is that?'

'That's enough, you two,' Jesper said, putting the camera onto the table. 'Did you get an ID? Anything else from this man?'

'I didn't have a chance before he fell out of the window,' Ryker said. He faced Reva. 'What about you? Did you have a chance to search the body before you ran away, leaving me stranded?'

Reva's lack of an answer was enough.

'Take some men. Go back there,' Jesper said to his henchman. 'If we can find who that spy is, if we can show he wasn't with us, we might be able to salvage our deal.'

Reva didn't move for several seconds, then rose from his seat without saying a word.

'You want me to come?' Ryker asked him.

'No,' Jesper interjected. 'You'll stay here where we can keep a close eye on you.'

Reva moved up to Ryker.

'We'll all be keeping a very close eye on you from now on,' he said, his voice just above a whisper. 'And I'll be here waiting when you fuck up.'

He slapped Ryker's shoulder before moving out.

ROB SINCLAIR

'Go and get some rest,' Jesper said to Ryker.

Ryker stood his ground. 'How's Roman?' he asked.

Jesper paused before answering. 'Not awake. But we're still hopeful he'll pull through.'

The room fell silent and awkwardness quickly set in. Ryker turned for the door. Had reached it when Jesper spoke again.

'Next time I send you out with my men... No mistakes. If you go missing like that again... I'll give Olek what he wants, if you know what I mean.'

Ryker did.

He headed on out. Moved through the building to the kitchen. Fixed himself a snack – bread and cheese, a glass of juice. He finished it all off, then made his way upstairs. Initially, he'd been intent on going to his bedroom, but he decided on a detour to the room where he knew Smolov was. A sentry sat on a chair outside, his head tilted back against the wall as he dozed. Not very convincing as a guard, though it was a little odd that Smolov had a guard at all. Who was he being protected from inside Jesper's home?

The guy woke up as Ryker neared, looked suspicious.

'Just checking he's okay,' Ryker said.

The guy stood up as Ryker moved to the closed door.

'He's fine,' the man said, putting his hand in front of Ryker's as he reached for the handle. Only a gentle intervention, but Ryker decided not to push it.

The two squared off in silence for a few seconds.

'Let me know if he wakes,' Ryker said.

'I'll let Jesper know. If he wants, he'll let you know.'

They glared at each other for a few more seconds before Ryker turned and walked away. No point in starting something, though with Smolov remaining out of action, Ryker's unease in this place grew all the time. Smolov had been Ryker's way in. With him out of the picture, it was as though Ryker's enemies circled like sharks, waiting for him to trip, waiting for one of them to sneak a small bite before they all attacked en masse.

He thought back to the conversation he'd had with Henrik minutes earlier. Shouldn't Ryker just take the chance now, with Reva and the others out of the picture, to go and finish Jesper and then clear out? Henrik wouldn't be happy that he'd not dealt the fatal blow, but at least both could say it was mission accomplished.

'Busy day?'

Eleni came out of nowhere.

'Are you following me?' Ryker asked, not breaking stride.

'What if I am?'

'Please don't.'

She reached out and put her hand on his shoulder to stop him.

'This way,' she said, indicating off to the corridor on the left. 'There's something I want you to see.'

Intrigued, Ryker followed. He looked behind every couple of steps. No one there.

They passed by several rooms – all bedrooms? Ryker wasn't sure, in his short stay he'd not been to this area before. They came to a closed door. Eleni opened it and beckoned Ryker in. He stepped inside. A little confused, a little disappointed. Just a bedroom.

A bedroom that smelled a lot like Eleni.

The door closed behind him. He turned to see her pressed up against the wood, a sultry pout on her lips.

'I've been waiting for this ever since Athens,' she said. She took a step toward him. Ryker held his ground.

'Are you serious?' he said as she pressed up against him and raised a finger to his cheek. She gently swirled it over his skin before reaching up and kissing his lips. He didn't respond and after a few moments, she pulled back, looking disappointed.

'This isn't a game,' Ryker said.

'I didn't say it was.'

'Then what are you doing?'

'Fuck, you're so serious.'

'This *is* serious.'

'This is life. Do you never look for enjoyment out of it?'

The look of disappointment, tinged with anger, slowly melted from her face.

'Do you never look for danger?' She moved up to him again, that naughty smile back on her face. 'Yeah. I know you do.'

She planted her lips on his once more. He hesitated, but only for a moment more before finally opening his mouth and kissing her back, slowly for a few seconds, but then with passion and vigor. She murmured. Her hands fell down his back. He wrapped his around her and pulled her close.

Not long after, she was pulling at his belt. He didn't stop her. She stepped back to let him finish the job, undid her jeans at the same time. She pulled her top over her head to reveal her bare chest below. Ryker moved forward. She turned around and slid her panties down to her ankles, stepped out of them, and to the door. Ryker moved up behind her. He thrust his hips forward and Eleni gasped. Her hands spread out against the door as she pushed back against him and the two of them rocked back and forth.

'That's more like it,' she purred. 'That's the James I know.'

42

'You look disappointed,' Eleni said as they lay on top of the bed, the thin white sheet lazily covering their naked bodies. 'Disappointed with yourself,' she added with a curious look.

'I'm not disappointed,' Ryker said, though he felt he knew what she'd meant.

He'd not intended to sleep with her here. Doing so hadn't been on his mind at all. That didn't mean he regretted doing so. That didn't mean he'd made a mistake, or that he felt foolish.

'What are you thinking?' she asked.

'Take a guess.'

'I really don't know.'

He looked over at her.

'Who are you?' he asked.

She didn't say anything. Turned away, as though disinterested.

'Who do you work for? Because I know you're not just one of them.'

'One of them? What does that even mean?'

'Look, Eleni, I like you. I think you're probably a good person.'

She laughed, but it wasn't friendly.

'It's just as well I already slept with you,' she said, 'because you really aren't that charming once you open your mouth.'

'I don't really give a damn.'

'See what I mean?'

He was tiring of her nonchalance. 'I'm not into politics,' he said. 'I never have been. I think you're here on someone else's say-so, carrying out orders. CIA? MI6? Possibly. Some other organization I've never heard of? Equally likely. You told me you were here to stay close to and protect Jesper. That means you're working for some organization that sees him as an asset. Most likely an organization that sees his enemies as their enemies. But you're a doer. And that's fine. I used to be too. But now I get a choice—'

'You don't think I have a choice?'

As she looked back at him he noticed a certain hurt and vulnerability behind her eyes that showed he'd hit a nerve.

'My point is, I get why someone – a foreign government – would be interested in Jesper. The situation here, in Ukraine, is complex. All sides have their claims, all sides have support, on one level or other, from outside the country. You know what? I don't really want to get involved in any of that.'

She laughed, sarcastically.

'You can think what you like of me,' he said, 'but I'm here because Jesper is a bad person, and so are the people around him. And they're planning bad things.'

'Like what?'

Did she know anything of the attacks Petrova and Zhirov had mentioned?

'Civilian targets. Civilian casualties. The exchange I went to this morning was to procure an arsenal of weapons from Russian-backed rebels.'

She seemed confused by that. Just an act, or had she really not known?

'I don't know the details but my guess is they'll use those weapons to attack their own people, for the simple purpose of turning the tide against Russia.'

'That... that's not what...'

'If you don't know then that's fine. But there must be things you can tell me. About Jesper. Who is he really? What's his story? Who does he have funding him? Who are his key enemies? Anything you can tell me will help.'

She said nothing. Ryker sat up in the bed a little, reached out, and grabbed her wrist.

'Eleni, you need to tell me what you know. You don't owe these men anything. Do the right thing.'

'The right thing?' She whipped her hand away and stood up from the bed. 'You have no idea.'

She stormed off toward the en suite bathroom.

'When I come out you need to be gone,' she said, before closing and locking the door behind her.

Ryker stayed on the bed for several seconds, a little dumbfounded, a little annoyed. He looked over to the dresser where Eleni's phone and laptop lay. Was he tempted to try and get access? To take them with him? Very. He didn't.

Instead, he got up and slipped his clothes back on. He heard the shower running. Looked at the bathroom door. He sighed then made his way out. All quiet along the corridor. His belly rumbled aggressively. He looked at his watch. He'd been in her room for more than two hours and it was dark out now. He wanted to shower and rest, but first, he'd eat again.

He moved downstairs and to the kitchen. Passed a couple of goons on the way who gave him a customary glare. Jesper was in the kitchen, at the table, three others with him, talking quietly, playing cards.

'Busy afternoon?' Jesper said as Ryker headed for the fridge.

'Kind of,' Ryker said.

'Just help yourself,' Jesper added. Ryker wasn't sure if the head honcho was being sarcastic or not. He didn't really care.

He helped himself to... More of the same, really. A plate of meat and cheese and bread. Is that all they ever had? He knew keen eyes were on him the whole time, but he paid them no attention.

He took a large mouthful of hard bread then turned to face the others as he propped himself against the worktop.

'Any news on Olek?' Ryker asked.

'He's been back a while, actually,' Jesper responded, without looking up from his cards.

'And?'

'And the guy's body was gone.'

Not a surprise. Petrova and Zhirov would have cleaned up. Even though the body would have helped Ryker's cause, they had their own asses to cover.

'So where does that leave us?' Ryker asked.

'Us?'

Jesper fixed his eyes on Ryker now. Ryker didn't respond.

'It leaves me with some groveling to do,' Jesper said. 'I don't like to have to do that.'

Ryker was about to say something back when a figure appeared in the doorway. Reva. He immediately set his eyes on Ryker and wandered over. He grabbed a glass from the cupboard next to Ryker and inhaled sharply then smiled.

'I can smell what you've been up to,' he said before turning to the tap and filling his glass. 'Was she good?'

Ryker clenched his teeth. He didn't look over but he realized Jesper and the others by the table were all staring.

Reva looked back with a snide grin on his ugly face.

'You're not her first in here,' he said, 'and you probably won't be the last. The boys need entertainment.'

Ryker wanted to launch himself, but he held his ground, said nothing. Reva seemed a little disappointed by that. The next moment another man appeared in the doorway. The guard from outside Smolov's room. He looked worried. Seriously worried. Ryker tensed.

'It's... Roman,' he said, as nervous as he was out of breath. 'He's dead.'

Murmurs of disquiet from the table at the far side of the room. Reva downed his water and clanked the glass onto the wooden worktop. He turned to Ryker.

'Oops,' he whispered with a wink.

43

Along with a hefty crew, Ryker made his way to Smolov's deathbed to confirm the inevitable. Definitely dead, though the question of how would remain a mystery. There'd be no official postmortem. The doctor who'd treated Smolov said simply that he'd succumbed to his wound. Died in his sleep. That really wasn't an answer as far as Ryker was concerned. Had Reva drugged him? Smothered him? Had someone else do it on his order?

What was clear was that few people appeared particularly surprised, and none seemed distraught by Smolov's demise. Jesper had said next to nothing. Did he know the truth? Did he approve of it, or was Reva's move – which Ryker truly believed Smolov's death to be – a signal of a pending threat to Jesper's reign?

And with Smolov gone, and the debacle of the previous day, Ryker felt his days on the inside with Jesper were numbered. A very small number.

He eventually headed to his bedroom, caught a couple of hours of mostly restless sleep, and awoke at 1 a.m. when his phone alarm gently pinged.

Still dressed, he made his way out of his room. All quiet. As he'd hoped at this time of night. Since he'd arrived in this place he'd not exactly been a prisoner – he had no twenty-four-hour armed watch restricting his movements – but he also didn't feel entirely free, always a keen eye somewhere. He certainly hadn't been given a grand tour of the place, or been given a briefing on the inner workings of Jesper's organization.

Time to try and make up for that.

He moved as quietly as he could across the hard carpet. A few sounds drifted over from behind closed doors: snoring, TVs, radios. He made his way downstairs. Voices. From toward the front of the house. Soft voices. Most likely nightwatchmen, bored, chatting but being deliberately quiet so as to not disturb everyone else.

Ryker moved in the opposite direction, past the kitchen, dark and empty, toward the back of the house where he'd yet to fully explore. He passed two plain but big rooms, neither serving any real purpose that Ryker could see, other than for storage. He came to the last room. A closed door. He pulled the handle down and gently pushed the door open. He used the torch on his phone to light up the space. An office. A big office, really. Six desks, three with desktop computers, metal shelves around the sides of the room that were crammed with lever arch files. Papers here, there, and everywhere, though all of it organized, all very... normal. Like an office of a local accountant or lawyer or whatever. But then, even organized crime bosses needed to keep on top of business, their numbers, suppliers, and a lot of the time wealthy criminals like Jesper needed legitimate activities to hide their nefarious ones, to provide additional funds, and to wash their dirty money. All that effort took resource and business know-how, needed accountants and lawyers and others to keep on top of it all.

Ryker glanced over his shoulder. Coast clear, he stepped inside.

He started up one of the desktops. Password protected. He wasn't going to sit and try to break through right now, but of course, he didn't have to. He took out the thumb drive he'd been given by Zhirov. Just hoped that the FSB man could be trusted with the contents. Ryker put the thumb drive into a USB port and the red light blinked twice to say the imaging – taking a direct copy of the hard drive, passwords, encryption and all – had started. Unless Zhirov had lied to him and the software was actually some sort of malware?

He moved to the shelves. Looked over the spines of the files, trying to determine their contents, and if there was anything of interest.

Norway. Three full files all with the same plain title. Now that was of interest, given Jesper's activities in the Scandinavian country that had led Ryker to Jesper's home in the first place.

He took one of the files from the shelves and opened it up. A lot of paperwork. A lot of legal paperwork. Share certificates, property records. Ryker scanned through, trying to take in the key information, trying to figure out if any of it meant anything to him.

A noise outside the closed door. Footsteps.

Ryker pushed the file back in place.

The footsteps got louder. Ryker turned off his phone light and slunk behind the shelves, crouched down. His heart thudded but he slowed his breathing, making each inhale and exhale as silent as he could.

The door opened. A bright torchlight shone inside. Ryker didn't move a muscle. He heard the breaths of the man but could see nothing of the face because of the bright light. One of the watchmen? Reva?

Ryker looked over at the computer, where the login screen remained on display and where his thumb drive remained, little red light still on. Would the man at the door spot it?

The guy took two steps inside. Ryker's mind whirred with his options...

Then the torch went off, the door closed, and Ryker listened, with relief, to the fading footsteps.

He didn't move for a couple minutes more. Then he grabbed the thumb drive, the file from the shelf, and headed out.

Ryker managed no more than another hour's sleep during the night. Partly because of an ever-present wariness, partly because he busied himself scanning through the file he'd taken, trying to figure out what all the information meant, if anything at all, and also trying his best to search the data he'd captured on the thumb drive on the crappy screen of his phone.

He put the lever arch file back at five-thirty. Tried but failed to get some more sleep and by eight-thirty he decided it was time to emerge for some food and refreshment. The house remained strangely quiet when he finally moved out to the corridor, much like it had been during the night. He stood and listened. Didn't like the silence one bit. Had the main crew left on a mission without him?

Perhaps that wasn't the worst thing, everything else considered. Perhaps today was the day for making his move and getting out of town.

He was about to head for the stairs when voices drifted over. Ryker moved toward them. At first, he hadn't been able to place them but as he closed in he realized the voices were a man and a woman. Not a friendly conversation. Eleni. He reached her room. Door closed. A bang and a shout from within. Ryker went for the handle but the door burst open before he could grasp it.

Reva. He looked startled when he spotted Ryker but then stood straight and glared. Beyond him Eleni pulled herself up from the bed, rubbed at her cheek, her hair mussy, her bra – the only clothing on her upper half – askew.

'What?' Reva said.

'Are you okay?' Ryker asked Eleni.

She nodded.

'I told you last night,' Reva said, that horrid grin on his face, 'you're not the first. You won't be the last.'

Reva went to push past. Ryker held his ground.

'If you've hurt her—'

Reva reached out and grabbed Ryker's throat and pushed him up against the door frame.

'Go on, then,' Ryker said. He glared down at his foe. Reva's screwed-up face slowly relaxed and he let go and stepped back.

'You've no time for boning her now,' Reva said. 'You're both wanted downstairs.'

He carried on away. Ryker stepped into the room.

'What did he do?' Ryker asked.

Eleni wouldn't look him in the eye.

'Are you okay?'

'Oh, go to hell, James. I don't need a fucking bodyguard.'

She shot him a look then grabbed a jumper from a chair and stormed past him.

Ryker stood for a moment longer before following.

He found a gaggle of people outside. A crowd of nine in total, circled around Jesper who stood in the middle of the dirt with a walking cane to prop him up. A small number of the men around him were armed. Ryker made his way in among them.

Jesper looked over and nodded.

'We're all here. Two tasks this morning, two groups. Olek is leading the collection to finish what should have been completed yesterday. It wasn't easy but the deal is back on. The rest of you are coming with me.'

And that was it. The groups filtered toward waiting vehicles: Eleni and Jesper and the other unarmed men to one side, Reva and the two other armed men with heavy-duty rifles to the BMW from the previous day. Ryker was left in the middle, unsure which group he belonged to.

'Come on,' Reva shouted over.

Ryker moved to him. Reva slid into the back and beckoned Ryker inside.

Dead man walking? Ryker certainly felt like it. He sat inside, next to Reva, and the next moment they were heading out, while Jesper and the remaining group were still getting themselves organized.

Not long after and Ryker focused on the woods outside his window. To the spot where he knew Henrik's tent was located, somewhere beyond the visible trunks. He really needed to speak to the teenager, particularly in light of what he'd found during the night. Not something he could easily relay over text message or phone call – he needed to gauge the reaction face-to-face. He had to find a way to get out of Jesper's compound and into the woods unseen.

He sighed and glanced over at Reva. Reva, who stared at Ryker, face full of suspicion.

'So what's Jesper's job this morning?' Ryker asked, hoping for a quick deflection.

'Mind your own business,' Reva responded.

'Okay. So what's our job?'

'What do you think?'

'The exchange?'

'Yes.'

'We had a few more guys yesterday.'

'We did. We've had to change it up. Different location, different method.'

Reva went silent. As though his explanation was sufficient.

'And?' Ryker asked.

'And what?'

'What's changed?'

'Nothing to our advantage. The price went up 20 percent. Jesper had to pay in advance. The goods are already waiting for us at a drop location. Or should be. If they're not, it's twelve million down the drain. Because of you.'

Ryker processed the information. Twelve million – euros? – was a hell of a lot of money for a single purchase of weapons. What on earth were they buying?

'So where do we put it all?' Ryker said, glancing behind him at the trunk of the car. An ample space, but certainly not for twelve million's worth.

'We get a truck thrown in,' Reva said, as though it was obvious.

Well, perhaps so if he provided all the information.

But then, something about the whole situation didn't feel right to Ryker at all. Particularly when they detoured off the route they'd taken the previous day and onto a track that was barely a track at all. Within a couple of miles, they were riding across rough, hard ground. A deserted wasteland with nothing in sight all around. Certainly no place for anyone to surveil – perhaps a direct response to the problems of the previous day.

A very good place for burying a body.

Ryker wondered if Petrova and Zhirov – Henrik too? – had some other method for snooping today.

Wait, of course they did. They had Ryker.

He realized Reva was staring again. He looked over and Reva's grin widened. Then Ryker caught the driver's eye in the rearview mirror.

No, he didn't like this at all.

'That's it,' the front passenger called, grabbing everyone's attention. Sure enough, in the distance, perhaps a mile away on the flat, barren ground, Ryker spotted a truck. No sign of anyone, or any other vehicle there.

Perhaps they really were on a simple pick-up mission after all.

'You've had fun with us these past couple of days?' Reva said to Ryker.

Ryker caught his eye. 'Not really.'

'Shame. You seem a good match for Eleni. I can tell she likes you.'

'I can tell she despises you,' Ryker said in return.

Silence. Though the tension in the car ramped up noticeably, and Ryker knew the two up front were eagerly paying attention to the exchange in the back.

'Shame,' Reva said again. 'About Roman, too.'

'Strange, more than anything.'

Reva shrugged. The driver slowed the BMW, then pulled to a stop twenty yards from the truck.

Silence inside. Ryker stared up front, out the windscreen, looking at the truck and all around it. He could see no one there, but were there men inside, ready to ambush?

'Are we ready?' the driver asked as he turned off the engine.

Reva said nothing. His eyes remained firmly fixed on Ryker still.

'I had a call from Crete,' he said. 'From the police there. It's taken a lot longer than it should have done, but we got there in the end.'

Ryker kept his mouth shut, though his heart raced.

'It's taken a while because, even though we were paying some of the police off, some other group from out of town muscled in and got their claws in. With me gone, they've been able to pull strings they shouldn't be pulling. But I've got just enough power there still that I got what I needed, eventually.'

'What's Crete got to do with anything?' Ryker asked.

'Cute. Very cute. They sent me a picture. Of a man they'd arrested out there. A man caught trespassing at Roman's villa. A man asking too many questions about Roman. About Jesper. About a dead teenager.'

Ryker still didn't say a word. The satisfied look on Reva's face grew.

'I know all about you, James Ryker.' Reva reached out and put his hand on Ryker's knee. A strangely tender gesture. 'I know everything.'

44

Ryker expected a sudden attack. He was prepared for it. But no attack came. Reva and the two others opened their doors. Stepped out into the sunshine. Ryker did the same, although as he did so he took out his phone, as discreetly as he could, and sent the simple text message to Henrik.

Get out

He slipped the phone back into his pocket as he shut his door. Looked over the top of the BMW to Reva who glared back.

'Make sure everything's okay,' Reva said, his eyes on Ryker, though the instruction was clearly intended for the two goons. With their rifles at the ready, the two of them moved forward to the truck. Ryker flicked his eyes from them to Reva. He stayed in position at the far side of the BMW, the vehicle protection of sorts from his enemy.

'You have nothing to say to me now?' Reva asked. He took a couple of steps toward the front of the vehicle. Ryker still didn't move. Reva came all the way around the hood until they were face-to-face. 'No?'

'You tell me,' Ryker said. 'What is it you think you know?'

The words sounded weak even to Ryker's ears, though he wasn't bothered about words. He needed to figure out a way to overcome these three and get back to Jesper's. Get back to Henrik. And Eleni?

Inwardly Ryker cursed Petrova and Zhirov. This moment felt inevitable given Ryker's time in Crete which had preceded them scooping him up. It had only been a matter of time before the likes of Reva connected the dots and realized Ryker was the same man who'd been snooping in Crete as who'd come out of jail with Smolov as an ally. Ryker had had little choice but to go along with the plan, but Petrova and Zhirov had always known the risks of the scheme. The risks to Ryker. They just hadn't cared.

'He doesn't know yet, does he?' Ryker said.

'Jesper?' Reva responded.

Ryker nodded. It was the only reason he was still alive. If Jesper had already known of Ryker's betrayal then most likely he'd have been executed on the spot. Or even tied up and tortured to force him to reveal all. The fact he was out here, being taunted by Reva, meant the big man didn't know. This was a power play by Reva. But to what end?

'Why?' Ryker asked.

The two goons wandered back over.

'No problems,' said the taller and broader of the two, who had a big, flat face like a shovel.

'Did you check for IEDs?' Ryker asked.

A raised eyebrow in response from the smaller guy whose bushy beard made him look like a medieval fighting dwarf from... Ryker couldn't recall which series.

'A bomb,' he said. 'Booby trap. Perhaps the moment the engine starts up, or the wheels roll... Kaboom.'

The beardy guy actually growled at Ryker.

'Check again,' Reva said to them.

'Why doesn't he do it?' Shovelhead said, nodding to Ryker. 'If he's so clever.'

All eyes turned to Ryker.

'Fair enough.'

Ryker stepped forward. Walked to the truck, fully aware that all three remained no more than a yard behind him. The two goons had their hands double-gripped on their weapons, Reva had a pistol in his hand. What was their plan?

More importantly, what was Ryker's?

His head was a mess. In many ways he'd rather Reva had simply made his move already.

Ryker ducked down to his haunches to look under each wheel arch. He stopped at the back of the truck, looked up, beyond the gap in the canvas side covers where he could see various crates and pallets. No particular indication of what lay inside though the Cyrillic identifications gave away that the goods were of Russian origin. Ryker turned around and looked at Reva.

'Have you checked inside?' Ryker asked.

'Of course. So you don't need to.'

Ryker hid his disappointment. He remained seriously curious as to the exact nature of the goods in there. He'd find a way to figure it out, sooner or later. If he stayed alive that long.

He spent a few more minutes inspecting the engine bay, the ignition system, whatever else was on show. No indication of any planted devices, and truth be told Ryker looked harder than necessary, buying as much time as he could.

The four regrouped at the front of the BMW.

'Worthwhile bringing you after all,' Reva said.

'So what now?' Ryker asked.

'Now they'll take the truck back. I'll take the BMW.'

'And me?'

The two goons lifted their weapons. The barrels pointed at Ryker's chest. Two yards from him. Not touching distance, but not so far that Ryker couldn't at least try. Though the odds were against him for sure.

His phone buzzed in his pocket. Ryker didn't move. Had he accidentally knocked it from silent when he texted Henrik?

'Aren't you going to get that?'

Ryker still didn't move for several seconds. Neither did the others. Then Ryker, an ache in his chest building, slowly pulled the phone out. Looked at the screen. A message from Henrik.

Too late

He glanced at Reva whose smile broadened. The phone vibrated in Ryker's hand. A call. Henrik's number. The ache in Ryker's chest, the sickly feeling in his stomach, continued to build. He pulled the phone to his ear and accepted the call. He didn't say a word.

He heard heavy breathing. Heavy, panicked breathing.

'James!'

Not Henrik. Not at first. Eleni.

'Please, no!'

Henrik now. A shriek of panic, or pain, and the call went dead.

Ryker pulled the phone down. And now he understood. Now he knew why he was still alive. Not because Jesper didn't know, but because Reva only wanted to taunt him before delivering the fatal blows.

'Bad move,' Ryker said.

Then he lunged forward.

45

Reva moved too. To save his own ass, by the look of it, given he scuttled back. Ryker went for the big gunman. Kicked dirt up with his front foot. The grit and dust caused both goons to flinch. Ryker ducked to the side. Both of them opened fire. The sound, inches from Ryker's face, was deafening, the flash of fire from the rifle of Shovelhead's gun close enough to singe Ryker's cheek. He grabbed the barrel. Pushed it up. Twisted to put pressure on the guy's wrists. Swiveled and kicked out to take his legs away. The rifle came free as he went down.

Beardy was already righting his barrel. Still squeezing on his trigger. The rifle in Ryker's grip pointed the wrong way. He didn't have time to correct it. Instead, he swiped through the air. Metal connected with metal and the rifle flew from Beardy's grip. Now Ryker righted his hold. Sent a double-tap loose. The bullets splatted into Beardy's chest. He went down. Ryker put another two into Shovelhead's chest – a damn big target, all told.

He spun around. To where Reva had been. No sign of him now. Two gunshots boomed. Not a rifle. A handgun. One of the bullets smacked into the metalwork of the BMW, the other into the dirt by Ryker's feet.

Behind him. From by the truck.

Ryker spun and dove for cover behind the SUV, pulling the rifle to face the truck to return fire.

No point. He couldn't see Reva at all.

Ryker moved onto his feet again, but stayed crouched. His eyes searched, under and to the other side of the BMW, under the truck too. No sign of Reva. Was he hunkered behind a wheel? In the truck?

Next to him, Shovelhead groaned, but he wasn't moving. Perhaps he had enough cushioning to seriously slow the bullets before they annihilated his heart. Still, he was out of the fight. Ryker could put him out of his misery...

He didn't.

Focus on Reva.

The truck engine rumbled to life. A thick plume of black smoke choked out of the exhaust and billowed into the air.

Ryker jumped up and raced forward. He reached the passenger side of the cabin. Flung open the door. Bound up the two steps, rifle at the ready...

He pointed the barrel at thin air, the driver's seat empty.

Ryker looked behind him. No Reva. He scooted across the seat. Turned the engine off again. Jumped out of the driver's seat. A bullet smacked into the ground right by him. Ryker flung himself back. Pulled up against the rubber of the front tire.

Where the hell was Reva?

He listened. Above the sound of his own breaths, and the tick-tick of the truck's engine gently cooling, he heard nothing.

But he wouldn't sit and let Reva dictate this cat-and-mouse chase. Ryker pushed his head close to the dirt, making sure there was no sign of Reva around the truck.

No, there wasn't.

Then, without taking another breath, he rushed along the side of the truck and to the back wheel, sliding to a stop there. He had a half view of the BMW too. Still no sign of Reva anywhere.

Couldn't Ryker just get to the SUV and race out of there? This wasn't about killing Reva now. It was about saving Henrik and Eleni.

Ryker made his mind up. But no sooner had he darted into the open than he sensed the movement behind him. Kind of behind him. More above him, really.

Reva jumped down from the back of the truck. Ryker spun, trying to pull the rifle to attack. No time. Reva clattered into him and they both ended up on the deck. Before Ryker could do anything he'd taken a mouthful of metal as Reva smacked the butt of his handgun against his jaw. Another blow to the side of Ryker's head split the flesh around his eye and his vision blurred crimson.

Reva tossed the gun. Prized the rifle from Ryker's grip and tossed that too. He pushed his fists together and hammered them down onto Ryker's ribcage. Ryker coughed and winced in pain. Reva did it again and Ryker's heart juddered and spasmed and felt like it would explode. His eyes went wide. Reva pushed his hands onto Ryker's throat. Big, meaty hands that squeezed hard. Not just choking, it felt like his whole neck was being crushed.

Reva grimaced with determination. Ryker tried to buck. Clawed at Reva's hands and arms but the man was unfeasibly strong.

'I've wanted to do this... since I first met you... Thank you. Thank you for not dying too quickly.'

His hands inexplicably came away from Ryker's neck. Onto his shoulders. No time for recovery. Reva leaned back then his head flew forward. A crushing headbutt caught Ryker on the bridge of his nose. More blood poured. Reva was covered too.

Then Reva grabbed Ryker's head. Smacked it into the ground, two times, and Ryker was drifting.

'How about those pretty eyes,' Reva said. 'Would Eleni still fuck you without them?'

Reva's hands were on Ryker's face. The heels pushed onto his cheeks, keeping his head pinned. The thumbs... On Ryker's eyeballs. Pushing down hard. Forcing inside.

Reva roared with effort. Ryker screamed in agony and horror.

He couldn't die like this.

He didn't even know how he did it. Nothing but pure survival instinct. Using every ounce of strength in his body, every drop of adrenaline, Ryker was on his feet, Reva suspended in the air. The thumbs came out. Ryker could see next to nothing. He drove forward. Crushed Reva up against the truck. Did it again. Not enough to cause serious damage, but at least enough to halt Ryker's punishment.

Ryker let go. Reva slumped. Ryker fell to his knees, coughing, spluttering, panting.

He saw the rifle right in front of him. Heard Reva moving behind him.

Ryker dove for the rifle. Took a mouthful of dirt when he landed face-first. He picked up the weapon, turned, fired.

A shout of pain from Reva. Ryker could barely even see him, just a blur of movement.

Ryker held the trigger down. A flurry of bullets erupted. At least one more hit home – Ryker could tell by the wet thwack, and the groan of pain.

But before long the magazine was spent. Ryker tossed the weapon. Wiped at his eyes. It helped, but only a little. The handgun. Still there in the dirt.

Reva?

A car engine started up. Ryker raced for the gun. The BMW

raced for him. Ryker somehow swiped the weapon from the floor before diving further forward and out of the way of the onrushing SUV, which slid to a halt right next to him, inches from the back of the truck.

Ryker righted himself. Lifted the gun. Fired, trying as best he could to aim. He let off three rounds, four. The BMW reversed at speed, spun around, kicked up dirt as its wheels skidded, trying to gain traction to take it away.

Ryker took a breath. Re-aimed. Squinted to try to improve his vision. It helped only a little.

He let off every remaining shot he had. Not many. A couple hit home, but it wasn't enough. The BMW raced away into the distance.

Ryker desperately wanted to follow. But he couldn't find the strength. Instead, the gun fell from his loose grip, and he collapsed to the ground.

46

Ryker wasn't unconscious, was simply unable to move. For how long? He couldn't be sure. Thirty seconds. A minute. Long enough that by the time he sat up he saw no sign of the BMW.

He got to his feet, groaning as he did so. He wiped at his face again. His eyes burned, his head throbbed. His vision remained clouded. Permanent damage? He had no clue.

Building up some focus, he rushed – as quickly as he could – to the cabin of the truck. He hauled himself up into the driver's seat. The keys remained in the ignition. He fired on the powerful engine. The beast shook and vibrated. He took a deep inhale then put the gearstick into first and released the parking brake. He put his foot on the gas pedal. A little nervously. As though he was genuinely still worried of a car bomb.

No such thing. Ryker was soon thundering across the open ground, the unwieldy truck bouncing and juddering across the bumpy surface. With the size, weight, momentum of the thing, he could easily run the BMW off the road. Crush the damn car and its occupant.

Except Reva was most likely racing, giving Ryker in the hulking truck no chance of catching up.

Ryker's phone weighed heavy in his pocket. A large part of him wanted to make the call to Henrik. But why? What good would it achieve? All he could do was beg.

No. There wouldn't be any begging from him. He'd be back at Jesper's soon enough.

Not long after and Ryker reached tarmac and the background noise died from a constant horrific rumble to a more gentle hum. More easy to think that way. In the distance he spotted the disused rest stop he'd been to the previous day with Petrova and Zhirov. They'd said if he was ever in trouble that he should go there. He also had twelve million euros' worth of weaponry and ammunition in the truck. What would the Russians do, what would they give to get their hands on all of that and to foil Jesper's plans?

But how would he even contact them? How long would he have to wait for them?

No. He wasn't stopping.

The journey seemed to take an age, but only a few minutes later Ryker traveled back along the track to Jesper's compound. No sign of the BMW. No sign of anyone at all.

The gates came into view. Ryker only had a simple plan. Get inside. Fight.

No guards in sight. No one in the watchtower. The gates were closed. But Ryker was driving a multi-ton beast. He could easily crash through...

No. He had a better idea.

He slowed the truck to a stop with the front end inches from the wood. He shut the engine down and listened.

Silence.

What the hell was going on?

Ryker leaned over and checked the glovebox on the passenger

side. Hoping for a handy weapon. Nothing. Well, a few things, but no weapon. He took the gas lighter though.

He jumped down to the outside. Still no sounds or sign of anyone. He didn't like that at all. Were they inside, waiting for his move? Or had he misread this completely? Had they already moved on knowing they had a traitor in their midst?

Ryker moved to the back of the truck. He climbed inside. Looked over the crates and boxes. He moved into the center and prized one of the lids open. Mortars. In another crate he found rifles. RPG rounds in another.

A diesel canister at one side. Handy.

He picked the canister up and sloshed the liquid about, emptying the container, sickly fumes sticking in his nose and throat. He battled against the growing nausea, moved to the back of the truck. A quick look before he jumped down and moved to the side, into the tree line, where he found a small dried-out branch. He used the lighter to set fire to the tip. He held the flame in place until the end of the branch glowed, fully lit. Then he tossed the wood into the truck.

Within a split second flames licked up around the inside from the diesel. Ryker ran back for the trees. He'd made it fifteen yards when the first explosion rocked the ground beneath him, and the blast wave sent him off his feet. He pulled his body behind a thick trunk before the second, even bigger blast came, shortly followed by a third. With each one he ducked and cowered, the heat immense. The sound of the flames almost all-consuming.

Almost. Because he could hear something else above the roar. He could hear men, screaming and shouting.

Focus. Ryker pulled away from the tree. This whole approach depended on making the most of their confusion. He ran toward the inferno. The gates were gone. So, too, a portion of the wall several yards in each direction. The guard tower had collapsed, its structure ablaze. People rushed about inside, no idea what to do.

Ryker stuck his head down and raced forward, ignoring the choking heat. He set his sights on two guards just beyond where the gates used to be. They didn't spot him until it was too late. Ryker grabbed the handgun from the holster of one. Shot him in the foot. Shot the other one in the thigh. Both went down. He used the butt of one of their rifles to keep them down.

Shouts. Others had spotted him. He dashed away from the house, away from the parked vehicles – largely because he could see the back end of Reva's BMW was ablaze. Vehicles on fire rarely exploded readily like they did in the movies – the engines and fuel tanks were too well-protected – but Ryker would still rather give them a wide berth. Particularly given what he was about to do.

Reva's BMW. So he had come back here after all.

Ryker weaved as he ran. Gunshots rang out above the roar of flames. None of the wayward bullets hit him. He slid behind a brick outbuilding. Peeked back around the corner. Could see no one through the smoke and flames.

He took aim. One, two, three shots.

BOOM.

Okay, so vehicles did still readily explode under the right circumstances. Like shooting at the fuel tank.

The BMW went up. Then another vehicle next to it. Two more soon after, a domino effect. A deep rumble accompanied the last explosion. Part of Jesper's home faltering?

Ryker got up and ran around the back of the outbuilding. Went to take a peek from the far side.

Thwack.

He winced. Reached up instinctively to his neck. Not enough pain for a bullet.

No, it wasn't a bullet.

He pulled the dart out.

Heard the whizz of another. In his shoulder. Another into his thigh.

He pulled them both out, tried to move back for cover.

No use. His legs were already heavy, his head already sloshing. He only made it four steps before he fell to his knees. By the time the feet crowded around him, he was flat on his back.

Seconds later, he was out.

47

What surprised Ryker most when he opened his eyes with a start was that he'd opened his eyes at all. His body shuddered, his heart pounded in his chest, and he took a big, panicked inhale of breath as though he'd been resurrected.

It only took him a couple of seconds to understand his response. A shot of adrenaline. The man with the needle stepped back. Ryker needed a few seconds more to process what he could see. A room. He didn't know which one in Jesper's home, though he felt that's where they were. For one, he could smell smoke, superheated metal, burning fuel.

He tried to move. No. Ankles and wrists secured to a chair. Though the chair wasn't secured to anything.

In front of him a gaggle of people. Henrik, Eleni, in identical positions to Ryker, side by side, facing him, although their hands were behind them – cuffed or tied?

To the right of Eleni stood Reva and Jesper. Reva had hastily placed bandages covering the two bullet wounds Ryker had delivered – one on his upper arm, one on his thigh.

'Sorry about your merchandise,' Ryker said, his words slurred, though the look of annoyance on Jesper's face told him the taunt was understood.

Jesper nodded and from nowhere a baseball bat came crashing down onto Ryker's forearm. He groaned in pain, clenched his teeth. How many men were behind him? He turned his head. At least one each side, though it was dark back there.

'You don't know very much about me,' Jesper said, taking a shaky step forward. Ryker noted the tool in his hand. A hunting knife. He continued to take doddery steps. 'You probably see me as an old man. An old, incapable man.'

He moved right up to Ryker. Beyond Jesper, Henrik quivered in his seat. Tears streamed down Eleni's face, though despite their distress Ryker didn't think either looked injured.

'But everyone gets old eventually,' Jesper said. 'It doesn't erase who we are. What we've done. It doesn't make us any less dangerous.'

He crouched down by Ryker's side, grimacing from the effort.

'You met a friend of ours,' Jesper said. 'When you were in Norway. His name was Konstantin Mashchenko. Do you remember?'

Ryker did. The assassin. The sociopath.

'Do you remember!' Jesper boomed, his face contorting, his teeth bared, his eyes wide and fiery. An incredible transformation that revealed what lay beneath, usually hidden by age and ailment. The monster was gone again in a flash.

'I remember,' Ryker said.

'You killed him.'

'No. A policeman shot him in the head. But if he hadn't, then yes, I would have killed him. I would have pounded his head into the tarmac until there was nothing left but mush.'

Ryker kept eye contact with Jesper as he spoke. Neither man blinked.

'Did you know of Konstantin's specialty?' Jesper asked, speaking proudly, like a father might.

'I can imagine.'

'Can you?' He left the question hanging. 'Konstantin was a rare beast. Robotic-like in his actions. He felt little, but he could do so much. His specialty? He was a butcher. He could carve anything, anyhow. But what he liked best was to skin. Skin people. He'd tear the skin from arms, legs, torsos... faces. If you never saw him do it you wouldn't believe what he could do, all the while keeping those people alive.'

Ryker said nothing now, he simply tried to push the grotesque images from his mind.

'But do you know who first taught him? Who first set him on that path?'

Jesper played with the knife in his hands. He stuck the point onto a fingertip and spun the handle. Then he pushed the edge of the blade onto the little finger of Ryker's right hand. Pushed down just enough to nick the skin.

'Who?' Jesper asked, still calm.

'You,' Ryker said.

'Very good. Do you still want to underestimate me?'

He pushed the knife down further. Blood dribbled along the metal and dropped to the floor.

'No,' Ryker said.

'Do you want me to show you what I taught him?'

'No,' Ryker repeated.

'Okay, then. This is how it'll work. I ask you a question. You give me an answer. If you don't, or if I don't like what you say... I think you understand. So let's get started.'

Jesper stood straight and moved into the middle of the room.

'Why are you here?' he said, not looking at anyone, though the question was obviously directed at Ryker.

'To kill you.'

Jesper turned and glared. 'Olek.'

Reva stepped forward, claw hammer in his hand. He lifted it in the air then crashed it down onto Eleni's right foot. She screamed in pain. Ryker bucked in his seat, ready to try to lift himself up but then took a blow to the back of his head and thick arms wrapped around his shoulders to pin him.

'You piece of shit,' Ryker said through gritted teeth.

'Let's try that again,' Jesper said. 'Why are you here?'

Ryker closed his eyes. Would any answer he gave now suffice? Or would it only lead to more suffering for Eleni, Henrik?

'I'm working with the Russians,' Ryker said. He had no loyalty to them, so why hold it back? 'The FSB. They forced me into this. Either I helped them or I would have rotted in that Gulag with Roman.'

'No,' Jesper said with a simple shake of his head.

Reva lifted the hammer and smashed it down onto Eleni's foot again. Her scream was quieter this time, though her mouth wider, her face more pained, everything about her reaction all the more harrowing.

'It's true!' Ryker shouted. 'Two FSB agents recruited me in Crete. They put me in that Gulag. They wanted me here with you. Think about it. Think about their plan. They knew Roman was getting out. They knew I could get out with him. It was all a setup. So think. How can they pull all those strings? Who else close to you must be working with them already to know what they know?'

Ryker blurted the words, then wished he hadn't. His intention wasn't to implicate Eleni, but was that what he'd just done?

Jesper seemed to take pause, staring into space.

'For all I know they're watching or listening to this right now,' Ryker added.

'You think they'll come and save you?'

'Probably not. I'm nothing to them.'

Jesper shook his head, as though disappointed by Ryker's worthlessness.

'You let us go, I'll take you to them,' Ryker said. 'You can do what you want with them, but let us go.'

'Us?' Jesper said. 'You and your two friends here? But we haven't even started to understand why they are here.'

Ryker looked at Eleni and Henrik now. Both remained petrified. Eleni's face was pale as she struggled to cope with the pain.

'Eleni has nothing to do with this. She's not with the Russians.'

'No?'

Ryker shook his head.

'You're certain about that?'

Ryker nodded.

'Except she's not who she says she is, is she?'

Ryker closed his eyes. 'You don't need to punish them. This is down to me. I betrayed you. I destroyed your weapons, your plans.'

'I don't need to punish them? Except, James, me punishing them *is* punishing you. And that's what I want.'

Jesper turned and nodded to Reva who moved across, past Eleni and to Henrik who began to shake violently in his chair.

Ryker found a burst of strength and tried to wrestle himself free but the hands holding him, the restraints, were too much.

'No!' Ryker shouted.

Reva smacked the hammer down onto Henrik's toes and the shriek of pain tore at Ryker's insides. A tear rolled down his cheek. Jesper smiled at him. A callous, evil smile.

'You want to know who I am?' Henrik screamed.

He had Reva's and Jesper's attention.

'I'm the one who's going to kill you,' Henrik said, glaring at Jesper.

Silence for a moment. Then laughter, from Reva and Jesper, cascading across the room to the men behind Ryker.

Jesper turned around again. 'I like him,' he said to Ryker.

'He's stronger than any teenager I ever met,' Ryker said.

'Shame he's got himself into this mess then.'

'All because the locals in his shitty little hometown wouldn't do as they were told,' Reva said.

Henrik laughed, mocking. 'I wondered what you'd be like,' he said, looking at Jesper. 'I imagined a powerful man. Strong, a leader. But you're... you're pathetic.'

Jesper looked like he really didn't know what to say or think.

'Olek,' he said, indicating for his number two to carry on the torture.

'You'd do this to your own son?' Henrik shouted.

Silence once again.

'I'm your son. Did you even know? Did you even care?'

Jesper looked really confused now. He glared at Reva, then at Ryker.

Was this the turning point? Yet Ryker couldn't keep quiet.

'No,' he said.

'No what?' Jesper responded.

'He's not your son. I think you know that.'

Out of everyone, Henrik looked the most shocked.

'Jesper,' Ryker said. 'It's just a name. A figurehead. Not many people know your real identity. That means you can be whoever you want to be. It means other people can be you too.'

Jesper's eyes narrowed.

'You're not this boy's father. Olek is.'

Ryker looked at Reva now. The henchman's face turned to thunder. Why? At the knowledge that he had a son he didn't know about? At the thought that he'd just tortured that son?

'You can't have children now, can you?' Ryker said to Jesper. He knew that from the medical records he'd uncovered. And he knew this man hadn't been to Norway for more than two decades. Reva had taken his place there, using the moniker of Jesper to inject constant fear. But it was Reva's name that covered all of the legal documents of their activities in the Scandinavian country, once the layers were peeled back. 'You sent your chief minions off around the globe in your name. This is the result. How many more bastards have you got out there?'

The question to Reva caused the red mist to descend. Ryker could tell by the way the man's face twisted and contorted.

He roared and lunged forward, the arms released from around Ryker as though the men behind him could sense what was coming. Reva lifted his foot and drove his heel into Ryker's chest, propelling him and the chair backward.

As the chair toppled, Ryker's gaze drifted from Reva's menacing face to Henrik. The boy was rising up from his chair. How the hell had he done that?

Ryker's chair crashed to the ground. The wood splintered. Ryker yanked at his wrists. Reva lifted the hammer... He swiped it down toward Ryker's skull. He could do nothing but twist his head to the side at the last second. The hammerhead glanced across his ear and to the floor. Ryker kicked out and his right foot came free from the restraints. He pulled his knee to his chest and let loose on Reva's ankle. A decent blow, but not enough to topple him, or even to stop the second swipe of the hammer.

Ryker pulled a wrist free. His forearm blocked the shot, Reva's wrist smacking into Ryker's bone.

Then a surprised yelp from across the room. Jesper. Henrik was on him.

Reva looked over and darted that way. The goons descended on Ryker. Bats and boots rained down. Ryker deflected the first few blows, but there was no point in lying and taking the punishment.

He grabbed a foot, tugged as hard as he could and the man tumbled. He took a swipe of a bat on his upper arm, then uncoiled and drove his fist into the guy's groin.

Ryker bounced to his feet. Bits of chair still dangled from his ankle, from his left wrist. He pulled at the wood, taking off a section of chair arm. He drove forward and the jagged end of wood squelched through the neck of the man in front of him, several inches of chair arm disappearing in an instant. He let go and the man gargled as he collapsed. Ryker ducked when he felt the rush of air behind him. The swinging bat missed. He grabbed another piece of broken timber from the floor. Lifted it and thumped it down. The wood sank into the soft flesh of the man's thigh. He yelped in pain and Ryker burst back up, delivering a ferocious uppercut that nearly took the man's head off.

Down and out.

Ryker was only vaguely aware of the melee in front of him. Jesper, Reva, Henrik...

Eleni? On the floor. Her chair on its side as she tried to wrestle free.

Ryker was about to launch toward Reva... Movement to his side. He ducked, spun, pointed his fingers out and drove his arm forward like a spear. The tips of his fingers connected with the guy's throat. Crushed his windpipe. He was done for.

But Reva wasn't. Ryker raced forward. Henrik was on Jesper's back, clawing at him. Reva reached out and grabbed the boy and tossed him to the ground. Still had the hammer in his hand. He lifted it up...

Ryker clattered into him and they both tumbled. Ryker landed on top. The hammer sprang loose. Ryker balled his fists and smacked Reva's head, as hard and as fast as he could, giving him no chance to respond. His mind took him back to earlier. Reva, choking Ryker. Reva, his thumbs in Ryker's eye sockets...

Ryker wanted to punish this man. Except despite the ferocious beating, Reva wasn't finished. He pulled out a knife, slashed at Ryker's arm. He used the distraction of the blow and hauled Ryker off him. Ryker landed awkwardly and Reva got ready to pounce with the knife...

Whack.

Reva's head wobbled.

Whack.

Eleni hit him again with the hammer. Reva... He should have been down. The blows should have killed him, smashed his skull and mashed his brain. Instead, he roared with rage and looked ready to attack once more.

Ryker dove forward. Grabbed Reva's wrist, twisted, and plunged the knife into his chest. Still, Reva held on. Ryker pushed down harder on the blade and Reva gulped. He looked away from Ryker – at Henrik – as his strength slowly faded. His gaze remained there, on his son, until he slumped, unmoving.

Ryker stood straight. Next to him Jesper was on the floor. Henrik, his face pained, stood over him, knife in his hands. Jesper panted and wheezed. The old man looked scared.

Ryker looked at Eleni. She was out of breath. Clearly in pain.

'Thank you,' he said to her.

She didn't say anything.

'It's over,' Ryker said, turning back to Henrik. Except the boy's face suggested anything but.

'Why didn't you tell me?' he said, looking down at Reva's – his father's – bloodied body.

'I never got a chance. I promise you.'

Henrik said nothing, but he returned his focus to Jesper.

'It's over,' Ryker said once more.

'That man might have been my father, but this is still Jesper.

He's still the one in charge. He's still the one who's responsible for everything.'

'Maybe. But he's down. He's finished. We won. Do you really want to kill him like this?'

Henrik shot Ryker an angry glare.

'You don't know anything about what I want.'

'I think I do. But do you want to take this path? It'll change you. I promise you that.'

'He doesn't deserve our mercy.'

Ryker agreed, but still, the idea of the youngster taking a life in cold blood, taking a life when he didn't have to... Ryker knew how that could affect someone. How it affected him.

'Please,' Ryker said.

Henrik fell to his knees and plunged the knife into Jesper's neck. The old man spluttered, gargled, his body squirmed... then flopped.

Ryker turned away, nothing to say.

48

Ryker felt the handcuffs were unnecessary. So, too, the cell really, where he'd spent the last nearly two days. So, too, everything that had happened since the Russian invasion had gathered him and Eleni and Henrik up half a mile outside Jesper's compound. Too little, too late.

Was that why they were so angry?

Petrova and Zhirov sat across the table from Ryker. He'd spent many hours with them since he'd been here, in this strange place. Not a prison, not an anything, really. Some abandoned building they were making use of.

'You should be thanking me,' Ryker said, agitated now by their circular questioning.

'For what?' Zhirov said. 'Sabotaging an operation we've spent three years working on?'

'Jesper's gone. Along with his crew, his cache of weapons.'

'Yet you never even found out his plans. How do we know there isn't someone else close to him who's now taking over?'

Most likely there would be. What Ryker certainly hadn't done was to single-handedly end the conflict in Ukraine. But then that had never been his aim.

'Is there anything useful you can tell us about Jesper? About his organization?'

'We've been through this. You have the data I took. You have access to everything else that was left in that place. There's nothing else I can help you with.'

Zhirov looked disgusted by that, as though Ryker's actions were a personal slight on him. Petrova only looked disappointed. 'Except there was nothing else,' Zhirov said. 'Everything useful was destroyed in the fires. The fires you caused.'

Did Ryker believe that? He wasn't sure.

'So what now? Back to the Gulag?' Ryker asked. 'I'm guessing you two want to stay here, wherever this is, about as much as I do.'

'If it were up to me, yes,' Zhirov said. 'You'd be back in Russia today. Although I'm not sure you're even worth the wasted resource.'

Ryker shrugged.

'We have no need for you here now,' Petrova said after a dejected sigh.

'What about Henrik and Eleni?' Ryker asked.

'We already let Henrik go. He's just a boy.'

'And Eleni?'

Petrova and Zhirov glanced at one another. Ryker didn't like that at all.

'She's in Russia now,' Petrova said. 'We're treating her well. She's under guard but she's not in a prison.'

'For what purpose.'

'A prisoner exchange,' Zhirov said. 'You know who she works for?'

Ryker didn't.

'She's American,' Petrova said. 'Or at least, that's who was giving her orders.'

'Unlike you, she's very valuable,' Zhirov said, almost a taunt. 'That's why you're still here and she's not. We think we'll get at least ten to one.'

Ten – or more – Russian spies exchanged for Eleni. A political agreement that would likely take place well outside the knowledge of the public or mainstream press, but the type of event that occurred regularly between nations who weren't close allies, but also weren't exactly enemies.

'And me?' Ryker asked.

'Like I said before,' Zhirov said. 'You're not worth anything to us.'

He enjoyed saying that a little too much, though Ryker really couldn't have cared less.

Petrova scooped up the papers on the table.

'Ryker, you're free to go. We just need to finalize a few things first.'

'Good,' he said. 'And make sure that exchange happens. Eleni helped bring this to an end too.'

'An end?' Petrova said. 'This is far from over for us. Have a good life, James Ryker. Preferably one well away from here.'

'I think I can abide by that.'

* * *

Three hours later the doors opened and Ryker stepped out into fresh air. He'd been given nothing to help him move on from there other than the belongings the Russians had first stolen from him weeks ago in Athens, and when he'd been arrested in Crete. That was fine. His freedom was all he needed.

He moved down the steps of the abandoned building and to the quiet street. Smiled when he realized he wasn't alone.

'You're very resourceful,' Ryker said to Henrik. 'Though it's quite unnerving how you just pop up out of nowhere.'

He'd quite like to be taught the youngster's tricks.

Ryker glanced around them. The place looked, and felt, like the same town Ryker had been in the day Zhirov had collected him after the failed exchange. Ryker thought he recognized the buildings and the twisty roads.

'I have my uses,' Henrik said.

'Like unshackling yourself without anyone noticing.'

'I've always been good with knots,' Henrik explained. He lifted his hands. 'Plus I have really narrow wrists. The advantage of being a puny fifteen-year-old.'

He smiled.

'Fifteen?'

'Can you believe it, my birthday was a few days ago.' He sank a little.

'Well, happy birthday.'

'It wasn't really. But maybe next year. This way.'

Ryker raised an eyebrow but then followed. Henrik walked with a noticeable limp; his foot was heavily bandaged. But a couple of broken toes was a pretty decent outcome considering the alternatives.

They came to a motorbike. A dirt bike.

'It's not very big but we can both fit on,' he said. 'We'll go to a proper town. Then decide what next.'

Ryker sighed. Henrik looked at him, pleading.

'Do you know what I think?' Ryker asked.

Henrik didn't answer.

'You're fifteen. I know you're not like other kids, but go home.

Go back to Blodstein, Norway at least. Find people you know. Live the rest of your childhood.'

Henrik's face soured. 'You really think that's possible now?'

This time Ryker stayed silent.

'You said it yourself – I can never go back. Once I killed Jesper, that's it. I'm not the same boy. I'm not a boy at all now.'

Ryker really wished he was wrong about that. Yet with the things Henrik had seen and done, how could he be expected to go back to a normal life now? Sitting around playing computer games with his friends or whatever 'normal' teenagers did.

'Don't look so worried,' Henrik said, a little disheartened. 'I was only offering you a ride to a town. I wasn't saying I wanted to tag along with you forever.'

Ryker didn't say anything as he stared, trying to figure out Henrik's mood.

'I don't need a father figure. And honestly? If I did, I really don't think it would be you. No offense intended.'

'None taken,' Ryker lied.

'So?'

Ryker thought for a few moments, then sighed.

'Okay. Let's go.'

49

FIVE DAYS LATER

The ferry bobbed along the glistening water, the sea churning and frothing behind in the craft's wake. Ryker moved from the railing and back along the side gangway, toward the front where he'd perched for most of the journey. The sun blazed in the deep blue sky. Another hot day. There'd be many more yet in this part of the world before the cooler autumn set in, still many weeks away.

His phone buzzed in his pocket as he walked. He took it out. Unknown number, though he hoped he knew who was calling.

'Ryker, it's me,' Peter Winter said.

Just hearing the voice of Ryker's old boss sent a crash of memories through his mind. Mostly bad memories, even if Winter remained a dependable ally, remained forever connected to the British intelligence services. For that reason, Winter was an ally who Ryker would keep his distance from as far as possible. For both their sakes.

Except he'd felt little choice but to follow through this time. He'd called Winter. Told him everything he could think about the events in Blodstein, Athens, Crete, Russia, Ukraine. Everything he could remember about the key players, dead or alive. Why? An exchange of information. He had to know about Eleni.

'Where are you now?' Winter asked.

'Still on the move,' Ryker said.

Winter would no doubt have a tracer on Ryker's device, but that was fine.

'I have to say, this isn't the normal Ryker rampage at all. Apart from what you told me, I've only heard snippets of what went down in Ukraine through pushing various sources, but not a single word of what you did has made it into the mainstream press, or even really caused a stir amongst my circles.'

Ryker had realized the same thing already. Quite a job really for the Russians – and the Ukrainians, for that matter – to have kept the whole mess under wraps. Though Ryker presumed the cover-up had more to do with saving face than anything else.

'It makes a refreshing change,' Winter added.

'Did you find out what I asked?'

Winter sighed, but Ryker held little interest in small talk, even with a man he'd known – and worked closely with – over many years.

'I did. The exchange took place two days ago.'

'She's out.'

'She is. Your friend swapped for eleven suspected Russian spies held stateside.'

'She's in America now?'

'Not that I'm aware of. The exchange took place in Amsterdam.'

Curious. 'Middle ground, I guess,' Ryker said.

'And probably more convenient for her, anyway. She's not American, even though she clearly does work with them. I didn't manage to get confirmation of her real ID, but what I do know is that she's Greek, has ties to the Greek authorities as well as the CIA.'

Ryker took a deep inhale then sighed.

'You still there?' Winter asked.

'Yeah.'

'Do you need me to—'

'No. There's no need to do anything else. What you've found out is plenty.'

'You know, if you ever—'

'I appreciate it. Goodbye, Winter.'

Ryker ended the call, took one look at the phone, then tossed it over the side and into the water. He watched for a few seconds until the device was out of sight, somewhere under the water. A PA system announcement ended just as he turned back around.

'I mean, that's not normally how people end a phone call,' Henrik said, his tone somewhere between amused and bemused.

Ryker shrugged. 'What was the announcement?'

'We arrive in Athens in twenty minutes.'

We. Ryker said nothing as he looked ahead, to the city coming into view in the distance. When they'd set off on that dirt bike in Ukraine he hadn't expected to still be with Henrik five days later. That had just... happened. How long it'd last, he didn't know. He wouldn't ask. He knew sooner or later they'd part.

He thought back to the brief conversation with Winter.

'You look pleased with yourself,' Henrik said. 'It's a little creepy.'

Ryker smiled. He looked down at Henrik, his young face full of confusion. He took the seat next to the boy.

'It's just nice how things work out sometimes.'

Henrik opened his mouth to say something but then closed it again. He shrugged.

Ryker closed his eyes, sat back, his head tilted to enjoy the sun on his face for the rest of the journey to Greece.

ABOUT THE AUTHOR

Rob Sinclair is the million copy bestseller of over twenty thrillers, including the James Ryker series. Rob previously studied Biochemistry at Nottingham University. He also worked for a global accounting firm for 13 years, specialising in global fraud investigations.

Sign up to Rob Sinclair's mailing list for news, competitions and updates on future books.

Visit Rob Sinclair's Website: https://www.robsinclairauthor.com/

Follow Rob on social media here:

facebook.com/robsinclairauthor
x.com/rsinclairauthor
bookbub.com/authors/rob-sinclair

ALSO BY ROB SINCLAIR

THE *Murder* LIST

THE MURDER LIST IS A NEWSLETTER DEDICATED TO SPINE-CHILLING FICTION AND GRIPPING PAGE-TURNERS!

SIGN UP TO MAKE SURE YOU'RE ON OUR HIT LIST FOR EXCLUSIVE DEALS, AUTHOR CONTENT, AND COMPETITIONS.

SIGN UP TO OUR NEWSLETTER

BIT.LY/THEMURDERLISTNEWS

Boldwood

Boldwood Books is an award-winning fiction publishing company seeking out the best stories from around the world.

Find out more at www.boldwoodbooks.com

Join our reader community for brilliant books, competitions and offers!

Follow us
@BoldwoodBooks
@TheBoldBookClub

Sign up to our weekly deals newsletter

https://bit.ly/BoldwoodBNewsletter

Printed in Great Britain
by Amazon

46595936R00205